The Riddle
of
THE DEPLORABLE

DANDY

PATRICIA VERYAN

The Riddle

of

THE DEPLORABLE

DANDY

ST. MARTIN'S PRESS
NEW YORK

www.stmartins.com

Library of Congress Cataloging-in-Publication Data

Veryan, Patricia.
    The riddle of the deplorable dandy : a novel of Georgian England / Patricia Veryan.—1st ed.
       p. cm.
    ISBN 0-312-29097-7
    1. Great Britain—History—George II, 1727–1760—Fiction. 2. Political prisoners—Fiction. 3. British—France—Fiction. 4. Escapes—Fiction. 5. Dandies—Fiction. I. Title.

PS3572.E766 R534 2002
813'.54—dc21

                               2002068121

First Edition: December 2002

10 9 8 7 6 5 4 3 2 1

For Fred—Ever Faithful

The Riddle
of
THE DEPLORABLE

DANDY

Prologue

～～

March 1749

The cold wave, refusing to roll on, tightened its grip on western Europe and gave no indication of imminent departure. Berlin was icy and depressed, London was frosty and a deeper grey than usual, and even lovely Paris shivered and was wrapped in gloom. As dusk fell the crowds on the boulevards and avenues of Montmartre thinned rapidly, and the rattle of wheels, the cries of street vendors, the hurrying footsteps quieted as Parisians made their way to home and fireside.

By the time it was full dark a certain narrow avenue not far from the river was deserted, only the sporadic whine of a bitter wind disturbing the silence.

A sedan chair turned the corner. The bearers, muffled to the ears, proceeded at a trot along the cobbles to halt before a tall house whose windows showed no gleam of light.

The stout chairman lowered the rear poles, rubbed his cold hands and peered at the house uncertainly. "You are sure of this, my Jules?"

His companion stamped his feet up and down, his breath

visible in pale little clouds as he responded, "Of a certainty I am sure. It is perhaps that our gentleman is late."

"Or dead."

"Now why should he be dead? Have you ever a cheerful thought, Pierre, I vow I will fall down in a fit! Go you, and knock on the door before we turn to ice in this beast of a wind."

Pierre started towards the house, grumbling that since Jules had taken the order, Jules should collect their customer. His sacrificial effort was not needed, however. The door of the house swung open, and although no light shone from within, a man ran lightly down the steps, his cloak billowing in a wind gust. Without a sound the door was closed behind him.

The prospective customer paused to glance swiftly up and down the avenue. One hand resting lightly on the hilt of his small-sword, he asked a low-voiced, "You are to convey Monsieur Vance?"

"That is so, monsieur." Pierre's uneasiness faded. The cultured voice had a faint English accent, the dim glow from a nearby flambeau illuminated a lean, well-featured face, and the flying cloak revealed a coat fashioned by a fine tailor. The gleam of a ruby in the laces at the young gentleman's throat did much to reassure the chairman and he managed a smile as he ushered his customer to the chair.

Monsieur Vance bent to the low door that was held open for him.

"Hold!"

A sudden flurry of movement.

The stamp of boots.

A rush of uniformed figures across the pave.

A dismayed shout from Jules.

Monsieur Vance sprang back and whirled about. The sword emerged in a blurred flash from his scabbard.

Caught in a maelstrom of flying steel, fierce shouts and

demands that the "treacherous spy" surrender, the bewildered Pierre thought a numbed, 'Hussars! Help!'

Jules howled, "Come, you fool! Move!"

Pierre moved faster than he had done for several years. Despite his panic, he retained sufficient of his wits to snatch up the poles. The sedan chair was borne to the corner at the gallop and disappeared into the night.

Meanwhile, the struggle in the avenue grew ever more fierce. The light from the flambeau reflected in half a dozen flying blades, the cold air rang to the clash of steel on steel. A trooper went reeling back, his sabre falling as he clutched a bloodied wrist and muttered, "He knows how to fight, this one!" The reluctant admission was well founded; in view of the hopeless odds it was remarkable that the Englishman was still able to defend himself and there could be no doubt but that he was a splendid swordsman.

As the deadly seconds slipped past, oaths of frustration were snarled and tempers became heated, aware of which the officer in charge of the small troop howled, "On no account is the spy to be slain!"

Even as he spoke the sabre of a powerfully built sergeant struck home. The Englishman staggered and went to his knees. The sergeant, elated, whipped up his weapon for the finishing stroke, then swore as it was beaten aside.

"You are without the ears, perhaps?" roared the Captain, who had deflected his blade.

The spy crumpled to lie inert on the cobblestones.

"One of you men—see to him," the Captain commanded. "And if he is dead, you, Sergeant, will be fortunate to become a private!"

A corporal bent over the motionless victim and announced with a sigh of relief that he was still breathing.

His fiery gaze transfixing the dismayed sergeant, the Captain snapped, "Search him!"

3

Eager to make amends, the sergeant obeyed but ventured to ask for what he was to search.

"A letter, you fool! A letter of great import. And you had best find it!"

Going through the Englishman's pockets swiftly, the sergeant sprang up in triumph to announce that he had found the precious document.

"Good!" The Captain snatched the folded paper only to swear and fling it into the hapless sergeant's face. "Dolt! This is some kind of sailing schedule. Does it look to have been penned by La Pompadour?"

At this point a lieutenant rode up and joined the small group. Dismounting, he called hopefully, "You have it, sir?"

"We do not," growled the Captain.

The sergeant announced miserably that the injured man carried no other paper.

Glaring at him, the Captain failed to see a tall gentleman who came around the corner hurriedly only to jerk to a halt as he took in the scene, then jump back and out of sight.

The sergeant and two men were ordered to go into the house and find something to use for bandages, then search for anything that looked to be a letter. "And if they won't open the door—kick it in," commanded the Captain harshly.

The front door proved to be unlocked and the hussars stamped inside. The front windows were soon aglow with lamplight and a moment later a trooper emerged with some torn strips of linen, and the announcement that the house was deserted.

"As I expected," said the Captain. "Get back to the search. You, Corporal, see what you can do for this fellow."

Watching the crude medical efforts, the Lieutenant stepped back a pace to ask softly why the missing letter was so important.

The Captain glanced around and, lowering his voice,

hissed, "It is from the *Maitresse en titre*. The confounded woman is at her meddling again!"

The Lieutenant frowned. "From—whom, Luc?"

"La Pompadour! The King's mistress, you idiot! One would suppose she could be content to please King Louis and live in pampered luxury. But is she? No! Always she must busy herself with affairs that do not concern her. Sending off letters to the Generals, or to the Comte de Clermont."

"But—why? What does she hope to gain?"

"Power, of course. Though the good Lord knows she has too much of that already! She plots and schemes and connives behind the scenes. It is said she is convinced she will be the means to bring about a greater France. More likely she'll contrive to drive us all to our deaths!"

The Lieutenant shook his head and looked down at the casualty. "And—this one is her accomplice, think you?"

"No. The poor fool is a soldier of fortune merely, who was so unwise as to carry one of her letters."

"Which we have not found."

"Not yet. But he either knows where it is, or knows the contents. Heaven help him!"

"Ah. You mean he will be questioned."

"Of a certainty."

"From the look of him they must needs be careful, else he's like to die before they can make him talk."

The Captain grunted his agreement. "They will wait," he said. "My Minister means to know what webs the ambitious lady is weaving this time. Our foolish spy will not be allowed to die until the Minister he is satisfied." He shook his head and muttered, "A pity that he must die so young. He fought right bravely, but in the wrong cause. Now why must you purse up your mouth in that doubting fashion, Philippe? Is it perhaps that you think our Minister's is the wrong cause? If that is in your mind—"

"No, no!" The Lieutenant said hesitantly, "It is only that

I wonder sometimes if ever a soldier knows what he is really fighting for, and whether history will look back and judge his cause to have been justified."

The Captain stepped closer and rapped him on the chest. Speaking very softly he said, "It is as well we are friends, Philippe, for your words might be misunderstood by others. Such thoughts belong to a lawyer rather than a soldier. It is not for us to question. Or to know. Only to do whatever circumstances and our superiors command. A soldier has need of his sword and his courage. For thoughts, he has no need!"

───❦───

The morning dawned clear and with a pale sunlight that drew many citizens of Paris into the open air. The boulevards were brightened by the colourful gowns of ladies at their shopping, the absence of a breeze allowed hoods to be discarded, and plumes waved over elaborately styled wigs. Sedan chairs bustled about with their aristocratic cargoes. Weighed down with band boxes and packages, lackeys and maids followed their ladies.

In mid-afternoon luxurious carriages rumbled over the cobbles, gallant gentlemen displayed the successes of their tailors, their horsemanship and their fine thoroughbreds, while some there were who chose to walk out with friends, thanks to this welcome change in the weather.

Among the pedestrians Sir Brian Beech strolled beside his son. Of average height, Sir Brian was only in his late forties, but already inclining towards portliness. With the aid of a corset he wore his garments well, and they were of the very latest fashion: the foam of lace at his throat, the bunches of ribbons at his knees, a profusion of jewels in cravat, on plump fingers and the buckles of his high-heeled shoes proclaimed a decided tendency to dandyism. His son, Conrad, was tall with a loose-limbed athletic stride that he was obliged to adjust to his father's mincing amble. Both exuded an air of prosperity, but there was little family resemblance between them. Save for a pair of large, rather soulful brown eyes, Sir Brian's manner was affected but mild and lacking distinction. Conrad was judged handsome with his thickly curling brown hair and eyes of a sparkling hazel shade. Today, they wore powder, and Sir Brian affected a long amber cane which he wielded with a graceful flourish as he urged his son to have patience.

Conrad responded, "I am trying, sir. But—what did you mean when you said it is a sad circumstance? Do you refer to the fact that my cousin became a soldier of fortune?"

"Of course. And more to the point that he fell into La Pompadour's toils with the result—" Sir Brian bowed respectfully and wished an opulent dowager good day. "With the result," he continued, "that his neck is now to meet Madame Guillotine."

"Is it, by Jove! Are you sure of that? I've heard nought of it. How has the Pompadour wrought his doom?"

"Keep your voice down, my boy," cautioned Sir Brian. "There are ears everywhere—as I should know, since I employ many of 'em! To good purpose, else I'd not have learned that my gallant nephew was only last evening cut down and hauled off to be questioned."

"Surely it does not follow that the guillotine is inevitable? He may well recover and return to England."

"For that of course, we must pray. Ah, here is your young friend Monsieur Le Tellier. Smile, my son, and greet him fondly."

Conrad's smile and greeting were exemplary and they resumed their walk only to encounter Madame Louvois exercising her little dog and followed by a magnificent footman. Conrad swore under his breath but joined his sire in admiring Madame's charming walking dress and waving away her apologies when the ageing and ill-tempered "Pom-Pom" snapped at Conrad's caressing hand. "Wretched little cur," he growled when they had left Madame's locality. "I loathe poodles! Father, for heaven's sake, tell me. Why should Vance Clayton be executed?"

"Because, dear boy, that very busy beauty La Pompadour is rumoured to now favour an alliance with Austria."

"Gad! That would be a turn-about!"

"True, and is bitterly opposed by several ministers, but the wretched slut has become powerful and the wise tread carefully around her. I have learnt that your hapless cousin carried one of her letters. Probably to the Comte de Clermont. Or Voltaire, perhaps. Those who oppose her are doubtless hoping that this letter might be the means to bring Madame la Marquise, as she calls herself, tumbling down."

Conrad said thoughtfully, "And my poor cousin with her."

"As you say. Sad, is it not? When you think that poor Vance sold his sword in a noble attempt to save his family from destitution."

"The Claytons are not quite destitute, are they, sir?"

"Well on the road, my son. Well on the road. Poor dear Vance. Such a fine boy."

Conrad sighed. "And only think, he is the heir to a great fortune. Are you quite sure of that, father? From what I've heard of Mama's eldest brother—"

"Ah, he was a wild one, was your Uncle Fulton. Who'd ever have believed that he would have sufficient wit to amass a fortune by importing spices? But so it is, child. Fate is indeed a capricious lady!"

"*D*id you hear that, Godmama?" Listening intently, Elspeth Clayton tilted her head. It was a pretty head: light-brown hair curled softly about delicate features and sent little tendrils to flirt with the small ears; the face was oval in shape, the cheekbones high, the nose straight, and the mouth full-lipped and generous. Too generous perhaps, and combining with a resolute jaw-line to defy the current edict demanding (according to Miss Clayton) that all females must appear witless and helpless. She considered herself to be neither witless nor helpless. But if she could not claim the appellation 'Beauty,' her figure was shapely, her outlook on life was buoyant and cheerful, and although at the perilous age of two and twenty she was still unmarried, she was not without several admirers who pronounced her very lovely indeed.

Madame Martha Elspeth Colbert, reclining on a rose velvet chaise in the cozy parlour of her fashionable London house, and ostensibly reading a history book, had fallen into a gentle doze. Startled, she jerked upright exclaiming, "Eh?

Hear what? There is this wretched wind, of course, but save for that I hear nothing. It is, child, that you are not yet accustomed to London's clatters and clamours. Indeed, 'tis fortunate that when your dear mama allowed you to visit the metropolis you were sent to me. South Audley Street is a relatively peaceful thoroughfare, and this house is, my clever brother assures me, of solid construction, so that if I cannot offer you the peace of your country cottage in Wales, you are more peaceful here than are many of London's inhabitants."

"Yes, indeed, ma'am," agreed Elspeth, hurrying to the window and peering down into the street. "I am most grateful that you invited me to share your beautiful home, and I truly appreciate our location. It is just that I thought I heard the doorbell."

Madame Martha settled back on the chaise and stretched forth a hand to the box of comfits on a small nearby table. A charming if rather too plump lady who retained her good looks although she was past fifty, she had fallen in love with the dashing young Monsieur Maurice Colbert while on a visit to Paris some thirty years since, and married him after a shockingly whirlwind courtship. She had not lost touch with her English friends and family, however, and two years ago had returned to London a wealthy widow. She had been welcomed by many former schoolmates, including her lifelong friend, Dora Clayton, and her daughter, to whom Madame stood as Godmother. Madame Colbert was well liked in London Town, and since she was a comely lady of good-natured and generous disposition, her tendency to foolishness was regarded with tolerant amusement and she was seldom without an invitation to some social function.

Now, nibbling a piece of Turkish Delight, she said rather indistinctly, "With all the bluster and howls this wind is creating I would be surprised indeed if you could have heard

10

the bell. Besides, it is too late for a morning call, and too early for an afternoon visit, so—"

She was interrupted by a footman who entered soft-footed and, announcing that a gentleman had called, proffered a silver salver.

Madame took up the card and frowned at it. "Drew?" she muttered. "I think I have not the acquaintance of anyone named—"

"Nicholas!" exclaimed Elspeth, clapping her hands delightedly. "He is my brother's very best friend, Godmama, and will have news of Vance I am sure, for they went to Paris together! We have known him forever. He is a year older than Vance and Papa used to say he was a good influence because although he is such a young fellow he is a proper sobersides. But he is the nicest boy. May I go down, please?"

Madame Martha refused this request, however, desiring instead that Mr. Drew be shown up to the parlour and that refreshments be served. "It is a most inappropriate hour to pay a call," she grumbled, sitting up and straightening her gown. "But if he is a friend of your family, of course, we must receive him. I take it he is well born?"

"Yes, indeed," said Elspeth. "His papa's country estate is in Buckinghamshire and marched with ours—before we lost it, you know. I believe his family spends much of the year down there. You will like him, I feel sure, ma'am."

When Nicholas Drew was shown into the parlour, however, Madame Martha's first reaction was shock rather than liking. She was faced by a tall man she would have guessed to be on the far side of thirty rather than eight and twenty. He came into the parlour briskly; almost, she thought, as though he marched in, and there was about him an air of urgency that made her nervous. He was on the thin side but his bearing was proud and his head held high, reinforcing her impression that he was, or had once been, a military man. He wore neither wig nor powder, his hair of a dark auburn was tied back neatly, a pair of fine blue eyes were set under rather heavy dark brows, and his features were even and would have been unremarkable save for the scar of a sabre cut that marred his left cheek.

She was staring at that scar wonderingly as he straightened from bowing over her hand after Elspeth's introduction. A whimsical twinkle came into his eyes. He said, "You have found me out, ma'am. Yes, it was a duel."

Madame blushed and stammered, but Elspeth laughed and gave him both her hands, saying he was a rogue to embarrass her dear godmother when she had been trying to convince the lady he was "a very nice boy."

He winced at that description, but pressed a kiss on each of the hands he held and apologized if he had put Madame to the blush. "Though I have to say you blush very charmingly, ma'am."

This kind of light flirtation was more to Madame Martha's taste. She said teasingly that she suspected her goddaughter was correct in having named him a rogue, and as he took the chair she indicated, she added that she would forgive him, since her dear late husband had been more than a little bit of a rogue himself.

The conversation went along easily. The footman and a maid arrived with a tray of hot tea and small cakes. Drew apologized for having called at such an hour. He was obliged, he explained, to leave town for a few days and had been anxious to visit Elspeth before departing.

"I understand you were with Vance Clayton in Paris," said Madame.

"Occasionally, ma'am. We sailed on the same packet, but afterwards went our separate ways, having different tasks to accomplish."

Elspeth asked anxiously, "Do you say you have not seen my brother? I had hoped you might have word of him."

Madame was adding milk to her tea and thus missed the

quick warning glance Drew slanted at the girl.

"Oh, I saw him," he said. "In fact, Vance sends you his love and—"

"And does he also say when he will come home?"

"He cannot say with any certainty, Elspeth. It will depend on his work."

Madame helped herself to another cake and asked, "What might his work be, Mr. Drew?"

Very aware of Elspeth's anxious gaze, he replied smoothly, "Why, at present he is a courier, ma'am. And very much in—er, in demand."

"Really?" Curious, the widow said, "It sounds exciting. For whom does he work?"

He answered apologetically, "I think, ma'am, I am not allowed to say. Save only, he is employed by a person of some fame in a matter that is of—great import."

"La, but how intriguing! It sounds as though young Vance has risen to a position of trust. In government, perhaps, sir?"

Drew smiled and spread his hands with a regretful shrug.

Madame pouted prettily. "More tea, Elspeth? Your mama will be so pleased. But I suppose we must not press Mr. Drew to betray a trust. So instead you must tell us of yourself, sir, and what you were about in La Belle France, or is that a state secret also?"

"Not unless shipping is a state secret, madame. I was there in behalf of my father, who is in the import trade."

Madame Martha recoiled from the word "trade" but she expressed interest. She was growing sleepy as she tended to do after luncheon, and she was relieved when Drew enquired after a proper interval if he might be allowed to take Miss Clayton for a drive. Madame looked at the window and the flying clouds dubiously, but Elspeth pleaded that she would so enjoy a breath of fresh air, and reflecting that her goddaughter's absence would give her the opportunity for a comfortable nap, Madame gave her consent.

Within ten minutes Drew was handing Elspeth into his light coach and directing his groom to follow a leisurely path up to Tyburn Road and thence along Oxford Street and down Drury Lane.

Climbing in beside Elspeth, he said, "Your godmama is a delightful lady, But I had to talk to you in private. I hope I was not too obvious."

"No, no," she said. "You charmed her neatly. Nicholas, I've been beside myself, for I sensed that you have something to tell me. Is Vance in trouble?"

He looked into her sweet face and wished he had not to be the one to break such terrible news. Taking her gloved hand, he said gently, "You know that your brother has been engaged in a risky business of late?"

"Yes, of course, for when he left England he confided to me that he had become what they call a—a soldier of fortune. It was only for our sakes, Nick. Mama's and mine. Since my poor father died we have lost just about everything we had. Vance tried so hard to bring us about. I suppose he must have felt this was his only hope. He has sent funds home, which has been a relief to poor Mama. I worried so at first, but he scolded me for doubting his ability, and indeed, he is such a fine swordsman, I hoped . . ." She searched the grave face beside her and her voice trembled as she uttered the question she dreaded to ask. "My brother is not—is not—dead?"

"I pray not." He saw her face whiten, and tightening his clasp on her hand he said quickly, "He entered the service of La Belle Pompadour. Vance is a good looking fellow and she—" He cut off the remark and added, "You will know how the lady interferes in political matters?"

"Yes. And that she has powerful enemies. Oh, Nicholas! Has she persuaded Vance to do something dreadful?"

Trying to keep his voice calm, he answered, "He was caught with one of her letters."

"Oh, my Lord!" A hand flew to her throat. She exclaimed in a voice that fluttered, "They will execute him for treason!"

"For spying, rather. He is not in the Bastille, at least. Madame Pompadour is powerful and it does not do to cross her without proof. Vance is imprisoned in a private chateau."

"Then all he has to do is give them her beastly letter! What value can it have compared to his life?"

He said gently, "I fancy several lives depend on the contents of the letter remaining secret. Vance gave his word to destroy it if he was caught. I have learned it was not found when he was arrested, but—"

Elspeth gave a stifled sob and closed her eyes briefly. "I think you are trying to tell me he is being—questioned. Then—then he is very likely dead already."

Drew sighed and leaned back against the squabs, still holding her hand. "The only hope I can offer will not be of great comfort, alas. Vance fought for his life, as you may guess. He was wounded, Ellie. Yes, I know that terrifies you, but I learned that the minister who has him is most anxious that he not be questioned till he has to an extent recovered."

Elspeth burst into tears and groped for her handkerchief.

Putting his arm around her and holding her close, Nicholas patted her shoulder and waited out the storm. As he had guessed, it was brief.

Impatient with her weakness, she dried her tears, sat straight and said rather huskily, "Vance would never break his given word unless—unless he were forced. So we may have a little t-time in which to do something, is that what you think?"

Drew thought, 'It is what I hope,' but he said, "Yes."

"Then we must go to Whitehall at once! The Horse Guards will intervene if they know a British subject is being

15

held prisoner in . . . France . . ." Her words trailed off as he shook his head. "Why not?"

"I went to our Embassy in Paris straightaway. I was listened to politely and assured that steps would be taken, but as you know, I'm not a stranger to diplomacy and I refused to be fobbed off. It was a struggle, but eventually I wrung the truth from them. It seems Whitehall is particularly anxious that Versailles not be upset at this particular time."

She protested indignantly, "How should an injured British gentleman upset almighty Versailles?"

"Because your British gentleman is known to be a soldier of fortune, m'dear, and is in the pay of La Marquise de Pompadour, the King's favourite, who is also a much too busy political plotter. A tangled skein at best, which could lead to the kind of involvement Whitehall would move heaven and earth to avoid. I could see I would get nowhere at the embassy, so I came home and went to the Horse Guards and to some, er—individuals of influence whom I chance to know."

Watching his stern face, Elspeth said, "Could they offer no hope at all?"

He met her eyes squarely. "I have been warned very plainly to stay clear of the business."

"But you will not?" Clasping his hand again, she said in desperation, "Nicky! Vance is your best friend. Surely, you will not just stand by and do nothing to help him?"

"Of course not. I will do whatever I may. Firstly, I must hire men and a boat."

Awed, she said breathlessly, "You mean to try a rescue yourself?"

"Since I cannot achieve it legally, I must strive to accomplish it illegally."

Her eyes lit up. She exclaimed, "*Dear* Nicky! How splendid! What can I do to help?"

16

He asked with a smile, "Have you the acquaintance of any gentlemen of power and influence?"

Casting about in her mind for such rare commodities, she said worriedly, "Godmama may, but . . . Wait! Yes, I do! In fact, I was to ride with him in the park this afternoon!" She peered out of the window. "I had intended to send a note to postpone our ride, but I do think the wind is dying down, so I shall be able to go." She turned a radiant face. "He will help us, I know it!"

Amused as always by her swift changes of mood, Drew asked, "Does this reliable paragon chance to be known to me?"

"Oh, I am sure he must be. His uncle is a power in the East India Company. I've known Joel since we were in the nursery."

Drew's smile faded. "You never mean Skye? Lord Hayes's nephew?"

"Yes. Lieutenant Joel Skye. He would do anything I asked! Now why must you look so glum? Do you think Joel is too young to help? He has a quick mind and is as brave as he can stare, and—"

"And has always adored you. I know that, certainly. But Lord Hayes is no longer a power in the East India Company. His health has reduced him to an invalid and forced him to retire."

Elspeth's brow wrinkled. "I did not know," she said uneasily. "I am indeed sorry to hear it. Lord Hayes is such a nice gentleman."

"A nicer gentleman than Joel was granted in his sire," said Drew with uncharacteristic acerbity.

"Good gracious! Does their feud continue after all these years?"

"Colonel Sir Walter Skye is as crusty as ever. I think he will never forgive his brother-in-law for influencing Joel to choose the Navy rather than the Army as he had wished."

"Joel had every right to make his choice, and I am proud of him for sticking to his guns." She added thoughtfully, "I wonder what will become of him now. I mean, whether he will continue to be attached to the East India Company?"

"He'll likely be able to tell you during your ride this afternoon. Jupiter! We've reached Drury Lane already! I'd thought to take you into the Bedford for a cup of chocolate or tea, but perhaps you will want to get ready for your ride."

Elspeth agreed that she had better go home, and Drew called to the coachman to return by way of Piccadilly and the side streets. Closing the window once more, he stressed the need for caution. "If Skye can be of help, you shall have to warn him that we don't want the Horse Guards getting wind of our plans. If they do, we will surely be shut down or clapped up, to say the least of it!"

⚜

At the same moment that Nicholas Drew's coach made the turn onto Piccadilly, Lieutenant Joel Skye stood in his father's study enduring an impassioned assessment of the "opportunities" he had allowed to slip past him. Dark haired, of average height and slim build, Skye fell short of being named handsome, his best features being a pair of brilliant dark eyes and the thin nervous hands that were at present tightly gripped behind him. He bore little resemblance to his sire, and Colonel Sir Walter Skye's large frame appeared even more massive as it towered over him; that very lack of resemblance serving as a constant reminder to the Colonel that his firstborn son had the poor taste to take after his wife's side of the family and the brother-in-law he had always detested.

Brandishing a letter in the air, Sir Walter roared angrily that he hoped "the Lieutenant's" feet had been restored to the ground at last. "I warned you that the Navy would take you nowhere," he reminded. "Had you listened to your father

18

you might have had a promising career in the Army. But the saints forbid you should pay heed to me! I am only a colonel! You preferred to soak up the nonsense your almighty lordship of an uncle whispered in your ear! A great man at the East India Company! A director, no less! With everyone fawning and grovelling before him, and you toad-eating him so that he got you appointed his aide, and promised you Lord knows what in the—"

"That is not so, Father!" interrupted Joel, his pale face lit by a flush of resentment. "Uncle Clifford valued—"

"Do not *dare* interrupt me, you disrespectful serpent's tooth!" thundered the Colonel. "Do you fancy me to have been blind all these years? He liked you best because you favoured him—God help you!—and were scrawny-built like him! While your brother, who is worth ten of you and chances to resemble his father, was passed over and ignored!"

"I believe Henry has no leaning towards a military career, sir."

The Colonel was deeply fond of his younger son, who had inherited his sire's large frame and heavy features, and while having scant affection for Sir Walter, catered to his every whim. "Henry is only two and twenty," growled the Colonel defensively, "and has plenty of time to decide on a career. Whereas you are—what? Eight and twenty?"

Joel said coolly, "I am twenty-six, sir."

"Humph! Then belike there's still time for you to mend your ways! Aye, you may stare, but I'm willing to give you the benefit of the doubt." The Colonel's lip curled contemptuously as he glanced down at the letter he still held. "This vital communique is from your beloved uncle, advising me that poor health has forced him into retirement, but that he will—'bend every effort' is the expression he uses—to see that you are given an appointment worthy of your abilities." Cutting off his son's attempt to comment, he barked, "In

19

other words, Lieutenant, sir, your so admired uncle has been cut down in his prime and you—an inept planner at best—are to be thrown to the wolves! Oh, never argue about it! You've lost your guide and protector and are on your own. And if my judgment of you is correct you will go precisely nowhere! If—*if,* I say, you remain in the Navy!"

Astonished, Joel stared at him. "You want me to—to resign my commission, sir?"

"Never wanted you to take it on in the first place! I have some influence in Whitehall and have you the sense to enter a career worthy of a *man* I may be able to pull a string here and there. You damned well don't deserve I should, but sooner than see you sink into naval obscurity . . ." The Colonel tossed his brother-in-law's letter onto the desk and waited, glowering, for his son's appreciation of this magnificent opportunity.

A moment later, his roar of wrath rattled the windows.

⤝❧⤞

"I am only delighted that you agreed to come!" Joel Skye's dark eyes turned to the lady who rode beside him through this chilly afternoon. The cold air had put roses into Elspeth's cheeks, and the claret-coloured habit and wide-brimmed hat with its curling feather became her admirably, so that he thought her lovelier than ever.

They were approaching Hyde Park Corner. The sun had ventured out timidly, a pale sun offering little warmth save to the heart.

"To say truth, Joel," Elspeth admitted with a smile, "I almost sent our page with a note asking to postpone our ride, but then the wind died down, and—well, there is something I would like to discuss with you, if I may."

"Of course. But if it is too cold for you, I can call up my mother's coach. She is perfectly willing for me to use it, you know."

"I am sure she would offer, she is such a sweet person. How does she go on? I fancy she must be distressed by her brother's illness."

"It is indeed a great worry. They've always been very attached, as you know. The doctors had warned him that if he would just live at a slower pace—" Skye hesitated, then went on, "The problem is that he has little respect for their advice. He is so highly strung and energetic, or he was."

Elspeth watched him and thought that he and his uncle were much alike. They both were clever, ambitious men who drove themselves mercilessly and never knew when to rest. 'If he doesn't wed a lady who will take very good care of him, he'll work himself to a shade, as his poor uncle has done,' she thought regretfully. The faint look of strain in his eyes had not escaped her, and because she was deeply fond of him, she said carefully, "I know Lord Hayes had great plans for you. Will you be able to stay on as an aide to his successor in the East India Company?"

Briefly, Skye seemed not to hear the question, a rare frown lingering. Then he answered rather too hurriedly that he expected to be reassigned shortly, and before she could comment, he said, "Now never mind about me, Miss Clayton, ma'am. What is this matter you wish to discuss?"

He hid his feelings well, but having known him since childhood, Elspeth suspected that something was really disturbing him. He had skirted her enquiry about his mother, whom he loved dearly, and it was quite probable that his father had frightened that frail lady again. Deciding to probe a little before she broached the subject of her own troubles, she asked that they adjourn to a nearby bench where they could talk more comfortably.

Skye lifted her from the saddle and tethered the horses to a shrub, then came to sit beside her. "Very well," he said smilingly. "Now tell me what is worrying you, Ellie?"

"Oh, it is Vance, of course," she answered. "Our relations

are the source of most of our anxieties, are they not?" A sidelong glance showed her that his eyes had become blank. She thought, 'Aha!' and said, "Your mama, for instance?" He looked at her quickly, and she shook her head and added a reproachful "Did you think I would not guess? Is your papa angry with her again?"

He patted her hand. "You know us too well, m'dear. But no. Actually I am the source of my sire's displeasure."

"Because of Lord Hayes's early retirement, I suppose. Will that jeopardise your chances? I cannot see why it should. You were born to be an admiral."

He laughed. "Bless you for that vote of confidence. I only wish Sir Walter shared it. He does not, of course, and in fact . . . He wants me to resign my commission."

"Resign your commission? Good gracious! And become an army officer, no doubt?" He nodded and she said in dismay, "But—Joel, surely that's not what you wish?"

"You may believe I do not, and so I told him." He gave a rueful grimace.

"Oh, my! He was put out?"

"Vastly. And loudly. He warned me that unless I distinguish myself with my next assignment he will disinherit me. Not that I would be excessively grieved, you know, but it frightened poor Mama."

"She heard?"

"The whole street heard, I'd guess. I tried to calm her, but she begged me not to do anything to further antagonize him." He shrugged. "I've no need to tell you how his rages terrify her. So you can apprehend that I must tread carefully! And only see how you have diverted me! Now, madam, no more backing and filling, tell me what it is that bothers you."

Elspeth was silent for a moment. She well knew Sir Walter Skye and his ungovernable temper. It never ceased to amaze her that, failing to value Joel's energy and hardworking determination, the Colonel had always favoured his younger son, who was weak and lazy with neither the wit nor the will to succeed in any field of endeavour. Henry was clever with words, however. He was always ready with some piece of flattery to beguile his father and took care never to upset him. It was amazing, really, that a gentleman with Colonel Skye's experience in handling his junior officers would not see through Henry's toad-eating insincerities and realize the young rascal was a complete care-for-nobody.

As for her hope to enlist Joel's aid, unhappily that was now out of the question. It was very possible that being, as he was, the most loyal of friends, he would defy his father's ultimatum and risk an attempt to help Vance. His help could be of enormous value. But it could also lead to his disgrace and the ruination of his career, for it would be typical of Sir Walter to make good his threat and consider himself well justified. Lady Winifred, on the other hand, would be heartbroken, which would grieve Joel deeply. It was no use; she simply could not ask him to take such a chance.

Therefore, she said slowly, "The thing is that I worry about Vance. He has been sending most of his pay home, which is very good of him. But his way of life is too chancy, and—"

She broke off as a loud dispute broke out nearby. A very angry gentleman on the far side of a tall clump of rhododendron bushes was saying in exasperated accents, "No, I tell you! How many times must I say it?"

"Be reasonable, Gervaise." There was a distinct note of pleading in the gentler voice. "I know you think I could not—not help, but I could. Really I could! Only last w-week you said my fencing was much improved, and—"

"And would to heaven I'd never tried to teach you! I should have had more sense. I'd not have mouthed such fustian had I dreamt 'twould give you such an exaggerated notion of your skill!"

"I have no such no-notions. Lord knows I shall never be

as good as you are, but you cannot possibly carry this off without help, and—"

"And *you* are to be my help?" A jeering laugh rang out. "I wish I may see it! Heaven aid me! I would surely be doomed!"

"Faith!" exclaimed Elspeth indignantly. "What a prodigious, unkind person!"

Her remark had been overheard. Hoofbeats sounded and two young men rode from behind the shrubs. In the lead was a tall, well-built man of about thirty, mounted on a magnificent black horse. His features were so clean-cut that despite his obvious arrogance he could only be judged exceptionally handsome. He was clad in a well-tailored dark-blue riding habit, and a gold-laced tricorne was set at a jaunty angle on his thick, dark-brown hair.

The second horseman, at least a decade younger, was a good-looking youth of sufficiently similar colouring and features to suggest that a relationship existed between them, though his manner was shy and he lacked the air of assurance possessed by his companion.

Skye stood as the two riders reined up and said politely, "Good day, Valerian."

The first man nodded and raised his tricorne. "Servant." A scornful glance from a fine pair of darkly lashed grey eyes was slanted at Elspeth. "I trust our small—disagreement did not disturb your—ah, friend."

His manner clearly implied both that they had been eavesdropping and that they were conducting an improper tryst.

Skye began, "Ma'am, may I present—"

Elspeth interrupted coldly, "As a matter of fact, it did disturb me, sir. We were trying to conduct a civilized conversation and for a moment I feared you—ah, gentlemen were about to come to cuffs."

Her sarcasm caused one of his dark brows to fly up. He

24

bowed and said in a bored drawl, "My profound apologies, ma'am. Are you prone to unwarranted fears? Perhaps you are not accustomed to the City."

Clearly, this nasty creature fancied her to be a country bumpkin! Flushed with resentment, Elspeth prepared to take up the gauntlet and give him a splendid set-down, but the opportunity was denied her.

Valerian laughed suddenly. "Though the lady was not so far wrong, eh, Herbert? Come, we must be on our way lest we cause her to fly into hysterics. Charming to have met you, Skye. Ma'am."

A wave of his tricorne, a glimpse of his friend's scarlet and embarrassed countenance, and they were gone.

"We-ell!" gasped Elspeth. "Who was that revolting rudesby?"

Amused, Skye answered, "His name is Gervaise Valerian, and he's not known for tact and diplomacy, though I'll admit I've never heard of his insulting a lady."

"He evidently thought we were listening to his quarrel, as though one could avoid it when he shouted so. How sorry I am for his friend. Mr. Valerian spoke to him as though he were beneath contempt when it was perfectly obvious the poor young man was merely offering his help!"

"I have not his acquaintance, though I've seen him now and then about Town. As I recall, his name is Turner, and they're related in some way, though they're not much alike, do you think?"

"Certainly not! Mr. Turner is a gentleman. Valerian is nothing more than a conceited Dandy!"

With a grin for her vehemence, Skye said, "A very popular Dandy, m'dear. Half of London's ladies are said to pine for him, and you have to admit he's a handsome fellow."

"If one admires the type, I suppose. But if there are two traits I despise they are arrogance and dandyism, and since he possesses both you may be sure I shall join the ranks of the ladies who do *not* pine for the unkind creature!"

"Then I can but be glad of it. Now tell me what Vance has been about that has you in the boughs."

Elspeth dismissed Gervaise Valerian from her mind, and very soon she had convinced Skye that her worries were no more than the understandable apprehensions of a doting sister.

2

When they returned to the house on South Audley Street, Elspeth said her farewells to Joel Skye and parted from him in the entrance hall. Her mind was beset by the need to formulate some plan to help her brother, and now that her hopes to enlist Skye's aid must be abandoned, she climbed the stairs while mentally compiling a list of gentlemen who might offer their help—if properly approached. She was so engrossed in her list, which was sadly short, that she failed to hear her godmother calling to her and was startled by a loud rapping on the wall. Turning, she saw Madame Martha waving to her from the foot of the stairs.

"Your pardon, ma'am," she said, hurrying down to join the lady. "I fear I was wool-gathering."

"Indeed you were," said Madame indulgently. "Thinking of that handsome young officer, I do not doubt! I hope your ride was enjoyable. You have just missed some relations who came to call. Never look so betwattled, child. You certainly have relations. Most people do. I suppose if truth be told, everybody does, for just being born gives one parents, at least."

"I do have relations, of course, Godmama, but none living in London at present. Unless—Oh! Has my Aunt Hortense come up to Town, then? I had thought she was to stay in Wales with Mama."

"As she is doing, of course, for it is her home. Though why your mama would choose to go so far away to live with Hortense after your poor father went to his reward quite baffles me. Now what was I saying? Oh, yes. Your Uncle, Sir Brian Beech, and his son, Conrad, came to call on you. Such a distinguished pair, though I was surprised, as I had quite forgot your mama had a brother. Half-brother he is, actually, is that not so? But of most insinuating address, for all that."

Astonished, Elspeth said, "Small wonder you were surprised. We've heard nothing of them for years. I remember Conrad as a spiteful—that is to say as a mischievous boy who used to tease Vance and enjoyed to pull my hair. I fancy he must be—oh, about five and twenty by now. Mama had thought they might come to my father's funeral, but we heard they were living abroad. Did they leave word for me, Godmama?"

"Yes indeed, and spoke of you most highly. They are eager to see you again. Happily, they are both invited to the Bottesdale party tonight so—Good gracious! Never say you had forgot? My brother is to be our escort and you know how starchy Sir Mortimer is about punctuality. He never used to be, I recall. It seemed to come with the title . . . Never mind. Do hurry and change your dress, my love. We don't want to start off the evening with a fuss. I fancy the dowager will attend. You will like to meet her. Lady Elmira is a shocking tease and speaks her mind when she had better not, but a kinder individual you could never wish to meet, and 'tis good for you to widen your acquaintance with people of Quality."

Elspeth responded appropriately, while thinking that the people she wished to meet were fighting men rather than aristocrats. In her room she listened absently to her maid's chatter and paid little attention to her appearance, noting that her hair was swept up and powdered and an evening gown of pale-green sarsenet trimmed with silver ribbon was fastened over her wide hoops. She selected emerald drop earrings and an emerald pendant, took up her fan and gloves and went downstairs worrying over how her beloved brother was being treated at this moment, and whether Nicholas had managed to hire a boat.

Madame Colbert clapped her hands and declared that her godchild looked delicious and would win hearts tonight. Her brother, Sir Mortimer Hallbridge, arrived in a splendid coach and four. He was a big, raw-boned man who grumbled that although he was willing enough to escort two lovely ladies, he was always more comfortable at his country seat than in Town. As taciturn as his sister was garrulous, he contributed little to the conversation. Madame was not at all offended by his demeanour. She chattered merrily during the carriage drive, attributing Elspeth's rather subdued responses to excitement at the prospect of the evening's entertainment.

About twenty couples had been invited to a dinner party with more guests to arrive later for dancing and cards. The mansion was large and luxurious. The hostess, Lady Ruby Bottesdale, slender, poised, and gracious, was clad in an exquisitely embroidered silver blue gown, the skirts spread over the wide flattened French panniers that were becoming so popular. She held her head regally; perhaps necessarily, Madame Martha later whispered, "Because the elaborate styling of all those hair pieces must have kept her in the powder closet with her hairdresser for hours!"

Lord Bottesdale, whom Elspeth guessed to be at least a decade his wife's senior, was tall and slightly stooped, and so sleepy-looking that she thought it would be remarkable if he stayed awake through dinner. He had charming manners, however, and before bearing Sir Mortimer off to meet a friend, he exclaimed over the beauty of Miss Clayton, who was, he declared kindly, a delightful addition to the *ton* and would become a toast in no time.

The guests were assembled in a beige-and-gold saloon brilliantly lit by a large central chandelier and many candelabra. Madame Colbert shepherded her goddaughter among richly gowned ladies and dashing gentlemen. Some were already known to Elspeth but many she had not met, and although the gentlemen were uniformly admiring, a few of the ladies were so proud that she felt properly snubbed.

She was watching her godmother chat animatedly with a thin matron who said not a word in response and whose face seemed frozen into a perpetual sneer, when a male voice exclaimed, "Can I believe it? Surely, dear lady, you cannot possibly be my little niece?"

Elspeth turned to face two gentlemen whom she would scarcely have recognized but who smiled at her warmly. Sir Brian Beech's coat and waistcoat were works of art but could not conceal the fact that he had become rather stout during the fourteen years since last she had seen him. His round face was thickly painted and rouged, a pearl glowed in one ear, a lacy handkerchief fluttered from one hand, a snuff-box was held in the other, and he minced along in jewelled shoes with high red heels. Elspeth thought an instinctive, 'Faith! We've a Dandy in the family!' His son Conrad, whom she remembered as a fat and untidy boy who delighted in practical jokes, had metamorphosed into a tall, slim gentleman, his good looks enhanced by garments of excellent cut and the latest fashion. Tonight they both wore powdered wigs and jewels sparkled in Conrad's pleated stock and the foaming laces of his father's cravat. Besides the heavily scented handkerchief that Sir Brian wafted about, they exuded an air

30

of polite affluence and nothing marred their grace as they bowed over Elspeth's hand.

Sir Brian was overjoyed by their meeting, and as Madame Colbert joined them, he lost no time in begging permission to call on her the following day. "Since 'twould be most improper for me to monopolize my dear niece this evening," he said, adding lightly that he was very sure all the unattached gentlemen in the room were eager to make the acquaintance of so lovely a young lady.

Conrad said in a deep, well-modulated voice that perhaps they were speaking out of turn. "My cousin may be well acquainted with the company, sir." One eyebrow lifted enquiringly and he went on, "And is likely already betrothed."

"Not possible, my son," argued Sir Brian firmly. "A gentleman who won so fair a flower would be foolish in the extreme did he allow her to go into society without he was by her side."

Madame gave a ripple of laughter, and Elspeth, amused by such flattery, admitted that her uncle was correct in that she was not betrothed. Confirming that fact, Madame invited Sir Brian and his son to take tea with them the following day, and she swept Elspeth off to be presented to the rest of the company.

The Dowager Lady Elmira Bottesdale was indeed present. She was a stout little lady, wearing a magnificent diamond tiara atop her powdered wig, and having a pair of snapping dark eyes and little resemblance to her sleepy son. She was gracious to Elspeth but startled her by asking suddenly if she was well acquainted with Sir Brian and Conrad Beech.

"Sir Brian is my mother's half-brother, ma'am," evaded Elspeth.

The dowager nodded and said with a smile, "Which does not answer my question, does it, child? But then I understand he has been living in Europe for some years and returned to these shores only recently. One cannot but wonder what has brought him back . . . And indeed what led him to abandon England in the first place. Were I you, my dear, I would be *consumed* with curiosity."

At this point Lady Elmira's attention was claimed by her daughter-in-law and four new arrivals. Moving on with her godmother, Elspeth murmured behind her fan, "What a very remarkable old lady!"

"Just so," answered Madame Martha. "With a shrewd mind and, if rumour speaks true, more intrigues than can be attributed to that French baggage who rules the Court of Versailles."

Reminded of her beloved brother, Elspeth suffered a pang and sent up a silent prayer for his survival.

At dinner she was seated between an elderly and rather boring diplomatist who was subject to sudden sneezing attacks, and a pompous naval commodore who spoke of the East India Company as though it were his personal property. He allowed Elspeth little chance for comment, but when she mentioned that she was acquainted with Lieutenant Joel Skye, he uttered a short bark of laughter and said contemptuously, "His sun has set! Small doubt of that! Attached himself to the wrong coat-tail!"

Annoyed, Elspeth stiffened, but before she could comment the diplomatist leant forward and enquired in his high-pitched voice, "And how does *your* son prosper, Commodore? I understand he has ambitions to replace young Skye. Has he found an appropriate, ah—coat-tail?"

The Commodore reddened and blustered, and Elspeth, smiling upon the sneezer, met an amused wink and decided that he was not at all boring.

The dinner was excellent and not so heavy as to deplete the energy of those wishing to dance. Very soon after Lady Bottesdale led the ladies to a beautifully appointed withdrawing room the gentlemen joined them. More guests were arriving and the company began to drift towards either the card room where several tables had been set up, or to a large music room which had been cleared to provide plenty of space for dancing.

Sir Brian Beech and his son gravitated to Elspeth's side, as did her diplomatist dinner partner and two eager young gentlemen who had shown a marked interest when they were presented to her before dinner. A quartet of musicians began to tune their instruments. Elspeth was laughingly attempting to choose a partner for a country dance when she caught sight of a familiar head above the throng and her heart leapt.

Nicholas Drew was impressive tonight, his thick hair powdered and neatly tied back, his evening dress impeccable, and the sabre cut on his cheek piqueing feminine interest. He made his way towards Elspeth and she disappointed her admirers by declaring that she had promised the first dance to an old family friend.

Her uncle and cousin wandered off at once, but the remaining admirers were made of sterner stuff. Drew came up to bow over her hand, and with a nice blend of humour and expertise he succeeded in detaching her from the ardent little male group without incurring too much animosity. Leading her to a quiet corner near a large potted plant, he said, low-voiced, "How glad I am to find you, Ellie. Were you able to enlist Skye's support?"

"Alas, no. Pray do not think me foolish, but—I could not bring myself to ask him."

He looked at her curiously, and she gave him a brief account of the situation and of her decision not to involve a faithful friend in so precarious a venture. Drew was silent, his expression grave, and she said anxiously, "You likely think I should put my brother's life ahead of any other, and that I am involving *you*, regardless. But—I could not, Nicky! I—I simply could *not* ask him. I am very sure he would have

33

agreed to do whatever he might, but he scarcely knows Vance, and his papa is so . . ."

He took up her hand and patted it comfortingly. "I know. Colonel Skye is a proper tartar and I doubt would hesitate to take out his anger on his wife, which understandably would distress her son."

"That's it exactly. Joel adores his mama and she is so frail, poor lady. But in the meanwhile—I am nigh distracted! My dear brother is hurt and so far away; time passes and I am doing *nothing* to help him!"

"Never fret, m'dear. I suspect we've several days before they'll dare question Vance, and I have—" He paused, eyeing her uncertainly. "What is it?"

In her agitation Elspeth had faced him, her back to the big room. On the wall beside them a great gilded mirror reflected a colourful picture of the guests and the dance that was now ending. Across the room Sir Brian Beech and his son were deep in converse. Even as she saw them, Conrad turned his head and looked towards them. He turned away almost instantly and said something to his father. Sir Brian's gaze flashed to them. A gentleman and his partner left the dance floor and blocked Elspeth's view. When they had passed by, Sir Brian and his son were no longer to be seen.

Drew scanned the room and demanded, "What has disturbed you? Has someone been annoying you?"

"No, no," said Elspeth. "My uncle and cousin were here and I'd hoped to introduce you, but I think they have had to leave and—Oh, dear! Here comes Godmama to fetch me. Now tell me quickly, if you please. I failed. Were you more successful?"

"To an extent—yes. I know of a wealthy peer who has been most influential in helping Jacobite fugitives escape our shores. I went to see him and he promised to find me a boat and perhaps one or two men. We have to be extreme cautious in our dealings, for Lord Geoff—the gentleman is suspected of Jacobite sympathies. He warned me not to come to him again but promised to send instructions to you when he has found a way to help us."

Overjoyed, she exclaimed, "*When* he can help? He did not say *if*? Oh, but that's wonderful, Nicky!"

Bowing to Madame Colbert, Drew said, "I give you good even, ma'am. You are looking very lovely tonight."

Madame smiled and said she was glad to see him again. "I thought you were with your uncle, Elspeth. He was anxious to speak with you, and your cousin hoped for the favour of a dance."

"I believe they just left," said Elspeth, glancing again around the room.

Drew suggested that perhaps they had gone into the card room and offered to find the gentlemen. He returned shortly, having been unable to locate them, and soon was saying his farewells, apologizing that he had an engagement this evening that must be kept. "You know where I live, Miss Clayton," he said, meeting Elspeth's eyes steadily. "I would be most grateful if you would let me know when you receive word from Vance."

She agreed to this and watched fondly as his tall figure blended into the crowd.

Madame said, "Such a charming young man. Come now, child. I wish to make Sir Brian and Conrad known to my brother. They must be here somewhere, and Mortimer will scarce believe they are come, after all this while."

Her wish was not granted, however. Neither Sir Brian nor his son were to be found, and upon applying to their hostess, Madame was told that they had slipped away quietly since Sir Brian had been slightly indisposed during the voyage from France and tired easily.

Encouraged as she had been by Drew's progress, Elspeth could not dismiss her anxieties and had to work hard to appear light-hearted through the hours that followed. Fortunately, Sir Mortimer was not what he termed a "break of day fellow," and very shortly after midnight he gathered his ladies together and carried them home.

It had been an eventful day and Elspeth was very weary. She knelt to offer up earnest prayers for Vance's recovery and begged heavenly assistance in their rescue attempt. Climbing gratefully into bed she found that as is so often the case, once her head touched the pillow her mind began to whirl. Her main concern was for her brother. She could no longer count on Joel's help, but Nicholas, bless his heart, had said they had about a week in which to act, and he had also given her new reason for hope. Somewhat of an unknown quantity was Mr. Nicholas Drew, in that, aside from the fact that he had fought in the Low Countries, she really did not know how he occupied his time nowadays, or if he still cherished ambitions towards a military or diplomatic career. Whatever the case, she was perfectly sure that he would do everything in his power to free Vance, and not just because of their friendship; woman-like, she had known for some time that he was extreme fond of her.

Not until she was at last drifting off to sleep did she recall her long-lost relatives. There was really no reason why the reflection she had glimpsed in the Bottesdales' mirror had disturbed her. It was illogical to have imagined that Conrad had stared at Nicholas with pronounced disfavour. Unless . . . could it be that he suspected Nicky of trying to fix his interest and judged him an unworthy candidate for her hand? She frowned into the darkness. Despite their relationship she scarcely knew her cousin. What right had he to criticize her friends? Which he might not have done at all . . . She yawned. More likely, she was being silly because she was worried and upset and her fertile imagination was making a mountain out of a molehill as it tended to do . . . Vance would have laughed and teased that her "mental charades" were active again . . .

She had made many new acquaintances this evening . . . aristocrats of charm or beauty or high position . . . Yet the one who stood out most vividly in her memory was that funny little dowager . . . though she did not seem old enough to be termed such . . . Elspeth's last awareness was of Lady Elmira Bottesdale and the bright dark eyes that had seemed determined to penetrate every corner of her mind . . .

The morning dawned bright and sunny, although, once again, there was a characteristic March wind. In the breakfast parlour, Geroux, Madame's butler, a tall and stately Frenchman of indeterminate age, immaculate appearance and a good command of the English language, kept an eagle eye on the maid who waited on Elspeth. There was the breeze, he imparted, meeting the maid's eye and nodding towards the coffee pot. "But the air she is not so cold as on the yesterday."

Inadvertently, he disappointed Elspeth when he answered her carefully off-hand question by saying that no messages had been received this morning, aside from a large bouquet of flowers that Sir Brian Beech had sent to Madame.

Elspeth told herself that she was being foolishly impatient. The mysterious "Lord Geoff" gentleman who had promised his help was himself under suspicion, so Nicholas had said. He probably had to proceed with great caution; she must not expect an immediate response. Knowing this, she was unable to dismiss her anxieties and having taken a light breakfast wandered about the house restlessly. Her godmother had said she would sleep late this morning and breakfast in bed. It was only ten o'clock. Sir Brian and Conrad were to take tea with them this afternoon. Elspeth told herself sternly that she must keep busy during the intervening hours and not allow her mind to dwell upon terrible possibilities.

She'd scarcely reached that decision than the doorbell and an outburst of barking announced the arrival of a caller. Elspeth's heart jumped into her throat, but so far as she was aware Nicholas had brought none of his dogs to Town. She went into the morning room, wondering if this might possibly be the delivery of the message she so anxiously awaited, but her hopes were dashed when Geroux announced, "Lieutenant Skye," and Joel hurried into the room.

Bright-eyed and windblown he said, "I know it's a trifle blustery outside. But my mother's puppy needs exercising and since I'm free until noon I've come to persuade you into accompanying us."

Elspeth was more than willing and was soon walking beside him along Tyburn Lane, her hands tucked into a warm muff and her hood gathered close against the wind.

Mrs. Skye's puppy was named Busy. He was a little past the puppy stage and seemed to Elspeth to be all ears and long legs that flew about rather haphazardly. His name suited him, for he was an energetic animal. Skye could not name the breed and said with a twinkle that his family tree hinted at the hound clan, "among others." Clearly delighted to be out, Busy's tail wagged constantly and he had a way of turning his head and looking up with what the Lieutenant said could only be a grateful grin.

Elspeth was amused by him and by Joel's comments on his antics and the Colonel's reaction to "the blasted mongrel," but her thoughts kept returning to Vance and the knowledge that this was the second day since Nicholas had broken the dread news of his peril. Two days, and what had she accomplished save to run up against a brick wall? Perhaps in leaving the house she had been unwise . . . Perhaps the message she so anxiously awaited would arrive during her absence . . .

Skye began to look at her uneasily, and when they had crossed into Hyde Park he took a ball from his pocket and invited her to throw it for the puppy, who had become wildly excited at the sight of it. "He won't jump up," he promised.

Elspeth saw the concern in his face. She made an effort to be more cheerful for the sake of this dear friend and said laughingly that she would hold him to his word.

Brightening, Skye apologized for the lateness of the hour. "Had we only been here at six or seven o'clock," he said blithely, "you might have been treated to a real spectacle." He leant closer and said in a dramatically low-pitched voice, "There are often duels fought here, you know."

"Good gracious!" she exclaimed. "How came you to be so remiss, Joel? If there is one thing I have ever yearned to see, 'tis a duel!"

Knowing her aversion to such violence, he chuckled and a moment later gave a gasp of dismay as Busy, who had waited with little patience for the next toss of the ball, began to jump up and down, his muddy paws leaving their mark on Elspeth's cloak.

"Oh, you naughty little beast," she scolded, and involuntarily dropped the ball. Busy plunged for it, but Skye was faster. He retrieved the ball and tossed it back to Elspeth, who caught it before either of them realized it was now covered with mud.

"Ugh!" she exclaimed, and attempting to avoid the prancing dog who clearly did not believe he was in the least naughty, she threw the ball with all her strength towards a nearby clump of trees.

Ears flapping, Busy tore after it.

"I'm sorry, Ellie," began Skye repentantly.

"Hell and the devil *confound* you, sir!" roared the tall exquisite who had caught the ball squarely in the eye as he emerged from the trees.

Skye moaned faintly.

Elspeth's shocked gasp died away as she recognized the extremely irate gentleman whose tricorne now resided in the mud and who was wiping more mud from his face. "Dear me," she exclaimed. " 'Tis the same nasty creature who was being so unkind to his servant yesterday!"

Skye hurried to take up the tricorne and offer it to its fuming owner. "My apologies, Valerian," he said, failing to look at all remorseful.

The Dandy snatched his hat and slammed it upon his head. "So it's you again," he snarled, dabbing a handkerchief at one eye while the other flickered over Elspeth. "One might suppose you and Madam Disaster live in the park!"

The tall young clergyman who accompanied him today murmured, "Just an accident, Gervaise. I'm sure Skye did not intend—"

Busy interrupted this well-meant remark by barking shrilly while bouncing up and down on Valerian's shoes and sending splashes of mud onto his once spotless hose.

"Get away, damn you!" shouted the Dandy, the handkerchief held to his streaming eye.

"Control your temper," snapped Skye. "There is a lady present."

"Control your blasted mongrel," snarled Valerian, taking an abortive swipe at the exuberant Busy.

"Do not hurt the poor puppy," cried Elspeth in alarm.

"He's taken a liking to you, is all," said the cleric soothingly.

"It ain't mutual," snorted the much-tried Dandy.

"And it ain't true," said Skye. "He merely wants you to give back his ball."

"I *haven't got* his bl—his stupid ball," declared Valerian.

"Yes you have," argued Elspeth. "It's in your hat."

Glowering at her, he wrenched off his tricorne. The muddy ball rolled down his forehead and fell from the end of his nose.

Momentarily speechless, he blinked down at Busy, who snatched up his prize and pranced off in triumph.

Skye's ready sense of humour could not be stifled and he gave a shout of laughter.

Viewing the unlovely trail the ball had left down the slim nose of this much-admired Dandy, and his almost pathetic bewilderment, Elspeth could not restrain herself and joined in.

Regaining his voice, Valerian howled, "You'll pay for this, Skye! Curse you, only look at my new tricorne! And my stockings! Thought it amusing to hurl that filthy ball in my eye, did you? Well, devil take it, you'll not be laughing when I've done with you!"

"Oh, for goodness sake stop fussing so," said Elspeth, losing patience with him. "Lieutenant Skye didn't throw the ball. I did. I'm sorry if your eye smarts, but—"

"Smarts!" he cried indignantly, still mopping his hand-kerchief at the damaged article. "You'll be sorrier if I am blinded, madam, I promise you!"

"Come now, Gervaise," put in the clergyman soothingly. "It don't look that bad to me. I'll take you to my rooms and—"

"Oh, no you don't," exclaimed his ungrateful friend. "I'll not have your duchess maudling over me!" Starting away, still holding his eye, he turned back. "As for you, Skye. You've not heard the last of this!"

Watching the fiery individual and his friend march towards Tyburn Lane, Elspeth said uncertainly, "He would not really call you out over so trifling a thing, would he, Joel? Is he dangerous?"

"I've heard he's a fellow to be reckoned with. Of late his temper's a bit more hasty than usual, but I think his bark's worse than his bite."

"Like Busy," said Elspeth with a giggle. "Oh, Joel! Did

ever you see a man so astonished as when that ball rolled down his nose?"

"Fairly conflummerated, wasn't he?" Laughing, Skye said, "I doubt Valerian is well acquainted with mud!"

"His clergyman friend is apparently acquainted with a duchess. Or is he wed to the lady? He seemed a likeable enough gentleman."

"Oh, yes. I'm sorry I had no chance to present him to you. His name is FitzWilliam Boudreaux. He is related to Lord Boudreaux and he's Chaplain to the Duchess of Waterbury. Salt of the earth is old Fitz."

"Perhaps he'll manage to calm his volcanic friend." She asked with a smile, "Do you think I should have offered to replace his tricorne?"

"We certainly didn't improve it, did we?"

"Or his nose," she said, hilarious. "Did you see that glob of mud that hung off the end?"

They were still chuckling over the incident when they returned to South Audley Street. Skye pleaded the call of duty and, refusing an offer of refreshment, allowed Busy to propel him homeward.

From the morning room windows Elspeth watched his erratic progress, smiling fondly as he turned to wave and was jerked away. Such a good man was Joel Skye. It was always a pleasure to be in his company, even if she had been unable to ask his help this time. She allowed the footman to take her cloak before she climbed the stairs to the withdrawing room. The walk in the fresh air and the episode with the muddy Dandy had lightened her spirits. There would surely be a message from Drew today, she thought. Thank heaven she still had his strength to lean on!

Her godmother was not in the big room but came hurrying in as Elspeth prepared to return to her own bedchamber. "There are roses in your cheeks, child," she said fondly.

"And mud on my shoes," said Elspeth ruefully. "We took Lady Skye's puppy for a walk in the park, and..." She paused, noting that Madame was wringing her hands, a sure sign of agitation. "Are you displeased, Godmama? The mud will come off, I'm sure."

"I am displeased because I have news that must grieve you, dear child." Madame took Elspeth's hand and led her to a sofa. "Sit here beside me for a moment."

A dread premonition was chilling Elspeth. She said falteringly, "Is it—my brother? Have you had word of him?"

"No, no. Thank goodness this is not to do with Vance. 'Tis his good friend, dearest. Mr. Drew."

Elspeth gave a gasp of fright.

Madame took her hand and held it. "He was set upon late last evening. His man brought a note round whilst you was out. I'm afraid he is quite badly hurt, poor fellow. These dreadful Mohocks, I suppose. Here is the note—'tis addressed to you, my love."

Pale and trembling, Elspeth read the words inscribed in a neat hand that bore no resemblance to Nicky's untidy scrawl.

Ellie—

Baxter is writing this for me and will have told
you of my misfortune. Pray do not worry about
me. I'll recover, never fear, but the doctor insists I
must keep to my bed for a week or two. Some
maggot-witted idiots mistook me for a rich man, evidently.

I cannot tell you how sorry I am that I must
disappoint you and won't be able to take you for
the boat ride, as I'd promised. When you hear from
the Boatman perhaps you should give Skye the op-

43

portunity of taking my place, after all. With the
very deepest regret, I am,

Yours, as ever,
Nicholas

3

*I*was indeed impressed by Mr. Drew," declared Madame
Colbert, eyeing herself critically in her dressing table
mirror. "And that ringlet is too far forward, Hansen. Yes, I
know you like it, but I do not. It looks like a sickly sausage
hanging over my ear in that abandoned way! Pray retract it."

Hansen, Madame's large, angular and opinionated abigail, pursed her lips and with a long-suffering glance at Elspeth attacked the offending ringlet.

"And certainly we can drive to King Street to visit the
poor fellow," Madame continued. "But not today, my love.
His man told me the doctor said—No! Not *that* far back,
Hansen! It is *with* me, not following along behind! Don't be
so tiresome! The doctor said he was to have no visitors for
the balance of the week, and 'twould be extreme thoughtless
to weary him with company so soon after the attack. Is there
anything more vexing, when one is ill, than to have a constant stream of visitors when all one longs to do is rest?
Never look so tragic, dear child! Mr. Drew is tall and strong
and will survive, I am assured. After all, he survived that

dreadful sabre cut on his cheek, did he not? Which would have put a period to me, I am very sure. Now run along and write him a nice comforting note, and we'll send it round to his rooms directly. Very well, Hansen, that will do nicely."

Elspeth did not "run along." Her steps were slow and her heart heavy as lead as she went down to the escritoire in the morning room. How dreadful that poor dear Nicholas should have fallen victim to murderous thieves! There must have been several of the rogues, for Vance, who was a fine swordsman, had been envious of his friend's skill with the sword and had once remarked laughingly that he pitied any hopeful Mohock who was so unwise as to select Nick for a victim. "Better the fool should throw himself in the Thames, and have done with it," he'd said.

Sitting at the little desk, Elspeth took up a pen. Typical of Geroux, the point was neatly trimmed, with ink ready in the Standish. Nicholas had written guardedly, but there could be no doubt of his meaning. Striving to be as cautious, she expressed her shock and sympathy and promised to come and see him as soon as his doctor permitted. As for the "boat trip," she had not heard from the "Boatman" as yet, but would advise him of her decision when the time came. Meanwhile, he would be in her prayers, and he was to concentrate only upon getting better.

She used the wax jack to seal her note and went into the front hall just as Geroux emerged from the corridor that led to the tradesmen's entrance carrying a bandbox which had, he said, just arrived for her.

"Are you sure?" she asked, taking the box and inspecting it curiously. "I have ordered nothing from Modeste Muguet."

He pointed out that the label bore her name and direction and said with a twinkle, "Might it perhaps be a gift from one of Mademoiselle's admirers?"

With belated perception and a nervous jump of the heart, Elspeth thought it might more possibly be the message she had so longed to receive. With a smile she requested that her note be delivered at once to Mr. Drew's flat in King Street, and she carried the gaily decorated bandbox upstairs.

Freda was gathering garments for the laundress but was at once agog to see what the bandbox contained. She was clearly disappointed when Elspeth told her to please take her cloak downstairs and attempt to remove the mud stains. "Aren't you going to open it, miss?" she asked.

"Yes." Elspeth answered quietly, but with a lift of her brows and a steady look that sent the abigail in a flustered scamper for the door.

Left alone, Elspeth removed the lid with hands that trembled. Inside was a charming mother-of-pearl hair-band, and underneath a note written in a fine copperplate.

Dear Miss Clayton,

I trust I have followed our mutual friend's instructions in selecting this small gift for you. I expect you will be in touch with him. Would you be so good as to tell him I have contacted the owner of a vehicle such as he desires. He can investigate this at The High Tide, Fleetwell Village, near Worthing. He must not delay, as the owner of the vehicle will wait no longer than the 7th inst. Tell our friend that my clerical nephew's name will identify him.

I shall look forward to meeting you very soon, Miss Clayton.

Very truly yrs.

G.

Stunned, Elspeth whispered, "The seventh! Today is the fourth! Who is 'G'? And what is his clerical nephew's name? Heaven aid me! Whatever am I to do?"

47

"Alas, mine is a very ordinary brain." Adjusting the emerald pin that gleamed in his cravat, Sir Brian Beech looked from his hostess to the sofa, where his son chatted with Elspeth. "I think I am not too dense, however," he went on, "to be aware that my pretty niece is nervous and upset. I wish I could make her see that, whatever the difficulty, Conrad and I are only too willing to help in any way we can."

"It is more than good of you to be so concerned." Madame Colbert re-filled his teacup and handed it to him. "But I promise you, if dear Elspeth were troubled I would be the first to know. She is happy living here with me and is already creating quite a stir among gentlemen of the *ton*. Only last evening Lord Bottesdale remarked on her beauty and opined that she will become a toast in no time at all. I quite agree, do not you, sir?"

"Oh, indeed, indeed." Sir Brian dropped four lumps of sugar into his cup and stirred, his little finger extended daintily. "But just as we arrived, Elspeth was sending off your footman with a letter. I distinctly heard her tell him it was a matter of great urgency, and I could not fail to remark that she looked pale and anxious."

"Ah, well, that will be in the matter of poor Mr. Nicholas Drew. Perhaps you are acquainted?"

"I do not recall the name. A relative of yours, ma'am?"

"No. A lifelong friend of the Claytons. His family estate marches with—or marched with—theirs. In Buckinghamshire, you know. So lovely a spot it was. The Claytons', I mean." She proceeded to shock her guest with the news of the injury suffered by Mr. Drew and concluded by saying that she knew Elspeth had intended to send a note to her friend. "I'd thought she had already done so," she said vaguely. "I shall have to ask her about it."

By the time her guests were taking their leave, however,

Madame had forgotten the note and it was Sir Brian who drew Elspeth aside in the entry hall and commiserated with her about Mr. Drew's injuries. "I have no acquaintance with the gentleman," he said kindly. "But I've sensed that something was cutting up your peace." Elspeth thanked him and wondered what he would think if he guessed just how worried she was, and why.

The footman experienced some difficulty in arranging Sir Brian's cloak about his shoulders, the gentleman demanding a precise set to the garment, which took some time to achieve. By the time he was satisfied the footman was flushed with mortification. On the threshold, Sir Brian turned back and again took his niece's hand. "Do not forget, dear child," he murmured throbbingly, "that I am your mama's brother. I know we have been far away from you in the past, and that Vance is not here to come to your aid. But you are no longer without a male relation to turn to in any quandary. If you are troubled about something—*anything*, Conrad and I are here to support you however we may. I beg you, do not deny us the right to do so."

Flustered, Elspeth thanked him again and promised that she would call upon him should the need arise.

He pressed her hand and gazed into her eyes so soulfully that she felt oddly embarrassed and was glad when he had gone with his mincing steps to join Conrad.

They did not set out extra covers for guests this evening; a very light supper was served and Madame Colbert chattered gaily about the play they were to attend and the delights her godchild was to experience. Elspeth responded appropriately, while her mind struggled to find an answer to her problems.

How simple it would be if she just accepted her long-lost uncle's offer of assistance. And how willing he had seemed. Yet she could not dismiss the memory of how Papa had disliked him, and how even Mama had seemed to find it difficult to defend her brother on several occasions. Elspeth had never known exactly how her uncle had offended, but she had overheard some sharp quarrels and had later seen the very grim expression that so seldom darkened her father's face. She had not dared to ask questions, but that the offence was so serious as to be past forgiving had been quite clear, even to someone of her tender years. Yet Sir Brian *was* family. And if she turned her back on his offer, who else was there? Joel, to whom she would normally appeal without hesitation, could no longer be approached; at least, not in good conscience. Nicholas, on whose strength she had counted, was now hurt and would be incapacitated for at least a week. She felt crushed and despairing, her beleaguered mind searching in vain for an answer.

"... the owner of the vehicle will wait no longer than the 7th inst...."

She thought wretchedly, 'Three days only! Each time I try to help my poor brother I fail, and I *cannot* fail the dear soul! He would risk everything were I in difficulties! Lord above, show me what I must do, please guide me to—'

"And I dare swear you've heard not a single word I said!" Madame was leaning forward and watching her searchingly. "Elspeth! Wake up, child! Where are your wits gone a'begging?"

"I ask your pardon, Godmama," said Elspeth agitatedly. "I—I fear I have the headache."

"Poor creature." Madame, who had often remarked that she could not understand people who complained of such afflictions, declared, "I am sure I have never suffered a headache in my life. Indeed, I would likely not recognize one if it should descend upon me. But I have to admit you are pale, my love. I hope you will feel able to join us at the theatre this evening. The Wisters are to take us up at a quarter to eight o'clock. You'll remember them from the Bottesdale party. Such lovely people, and spoke of you most highly."

"I do indeed remember them," replied Elspeth, with more tact than truthfulness. "Although I have to own, God-mama, that my memory for faces does not always serve me well. For instance, only yesterday when I was walking in the park with Lieutenant Skye he was telling me of a friend of his, a clergyman whom he judges to be a most worthy young gentleman. You very likely would know him if I could tell you his name, but all I can recall is that he is tall and has an uncle who is a famous peer. Lord . . . um—now whatever was the name . . . ? It began with a 'G,' I think. I feel so stupid when I forget someone's name!"

"Lord 'G,' " murmured Madame, toying with her cheese puff. "I love puzzles! Now let me think . . . a famous peer with a tall clerical nephew. So many younger sons enter the clergy . . . Hmm . . . There is Garland, you know—his nephew is a vicar somewhere—oh, but he is short and stout, as I recall, and Thomas Garland is a baronet, not a peer." After several more abortive attempts, she said with a sigh that she could only call to mind Lord Geoffrey Boudreaux. "He has a young relative who is chaplain to somebody or other, but he is Geoffrey Boudreaux's grandnephew, not—"

"That sounds right," said Elspeth eagerly. "Do you know what is the clergyman's name, ma'am?"

"He's a Fitz, I believe . . . FitzMorley or—no! FitzWilliam! And, my goodness, yes! A tall, and very shy young man. Can that be the one?"

"It is! Oh, it is!" Elspeth clapped her hands, and feeling very devious she trilled, "How clever you are, my dearest godmama! The Reverend Mr. FitzWilliam Boudreaux. I should have wracked my brains forever and never called it to mind!" And, astonished, she thought, 'And now I even know what he looks like, for he must be the very bashful individual who was with that horrid Dandy in the park! What a coincidence that I have already been introduced to the gen-tleman!'

"You are looking much better," said Madame smilingly. "I am so glad, for I've heard the play is delightful and the Pirate is handsome as can be, so you will surely enjoy it."

As she went up to bed later that evening, however, it would have been difficult for Elspeth to call to mind either the actors or the plot of *The Pirate and the Princess*. She had managed to respond appropriately to the flattering kindness shown her by Mr. and Mrs. Wister as they drove to the theatre together, but throughout the performance her concentration had been upon the problem of how she was to get to the tavern in Fleetwell Village.

Madame scanned her rather anxiously as she took up her candle at the foot of the stairs. "I think the Wisters were charmed, my love," she said. "You were very quiet, which they thought was a becoming shyness. But I suspected your headache had returned. Does it still distress you? Or is it that you are anxious for Mr. Drew?"

Elspeth, having formed a daring plan, said with a smile that she did have a touch of the headache still, probably because she had been for so long away from the noise and bustle of life in the great City. And with Madame's fond assurances that a good night's sleep would put things to rights, she climbed to her bedchamber.

Her nightdress and wrapper were laid ready on the bed and Freda was nodding in the fireside chair. Elspeth crept over to the dainty escritoire and, having verified that stationery, ink and a quill pen were available, woke her maid and was readied for the night. She did not get into bed, however, but sent Freda off, saying that she was "much too excited" by the events of the evening to be able to sleep and would instead sit by the fire and read for a little while.

The moment the door closed behind the yawning abigail, Elspeth hurried to the escritoire and took up the pen. Having spent most of the evening mentally composing this letter, there was no need for several efforts, the biggest obstacle being to disguise her own neat handwriting. She accomplished this by resorting to a rather flourishing printing and within half an hour had finished and sealed her letter. The direction presented a larger challenge, but by the time she had applied and blurred a "frank" and then creased the vital letter, she was quite pleased with her first attempt at forgery. An afterthought, calling for the application of the sole of her shoe, produced a grubby look that inspired a squeak of triumph, and having hidden her effort under the other stationery in the escritoire she was able to climb into bed with the satisfaction, however guilty, of a job well done.

Freda found that her young mistress looked rather wan the next morning, and on learning that last night's headache persisted, and that Miss Elspeth felt "a little stuffy," she concluded that she had caught a nasty cold. Several sneezes and deep sighs confirmed this, and Elspeth went down to breakfast confident that the awareness of her "nasty cold" would be shared by every member of the staff before the meal ended.

Madame Colbert had not yet come downstairs, but the postman had made his first delivery of the day and a small pile of correspondence lay beside her plate. Elspeth told the butler that she would wait a little while for Madame, and if he would just pour her coffee she might wander over to the buffet in a few minutes and serve herself. Geroux eyed her uneasily, but she sneezed, then gave him a brave smile, and he took his elegant self off, clearly thinking that poor Miss Elspeth was indeed a trifle down-pin this morning.

The concerned gentleman would have been astonished had he witnessed the remarkable speed with which "poor Miss Elspeth" sprang up and raced around the table. The all-important forgery was slipped in amongst the other letters awaiting Madame's attention and Elspeth retraced her steps at even greater speed as she heard her godmother approaching.

She had barely sat down before the footman came in to stand behind Madame's chair. Shocked to realize how narrowly she had succeeded in this first step of her plan, Elspeth stood once more, with a mental "Phew!"

Madame accepted her good-morning kiss but, as she took her seat, remarked that her godchild seemed "a little flushed" and asked if she was still feeling poorly.

It would not do to feel too "poorly," so Elspeth declared that she was sure she would feel better after breakfast, and that at worst she might have contracted a slight cold. "The change of air, perhaps, ma'am," she said, planting another seed.

Madame looked relieved and entered at once into a rather one-sided discussion of *The Pirate and the Princess* while she enjoyed an egg on toast and two slices of cold ham. Elspeth settled for some haddock and bread and butter, and she strove to contain her impatience, but her godmother had listed her plans for the day and was drinking her third cup of tea before she excused herself. "Just for a moment, love, while I glance through all these silly letters." She sorted through the pile and exclaimed, "Oh, here is one for you, Ellie. 'Tis franked by Lord somebody or other, I cannot read this dreadful scrawl." She passed the letter to her godchild, saying with a guilty twinkle that perhaps she should not do so. "For it may very well be a love letter, in which case I must desire that you allow me to read it, dear."

Elspeth took the letter eagerly, immensely relieved that no trickery had as yet been detected, and with a mental plea for heavenly forgiveness she exclaimed, "Oh, Godmama! It is from my dearest friend Millicent Crossland! Her family used to spend the summers at their country seat, which was near to ours, as you know, and we swore eternal friendship."

"How nice, dear," murmured Madame, engrossed in her own letter. "What has she to say?"

"That she is betrothed, and longs to see me, and—oh,

gracious! I am invited down to Worthing where they are spending several weeks! How lovely! Only—oh, dear! This letter must have been delayed! I was to have driven down yesterday, and Millicent begs that I be allowed to stay for several days. And tonight there is to be a betrothal party which she especially wishes me to attend! Oh—*Godmama!* What a disappointment!"

Glancing up and meeting tragic blue eyes, Madame was touched, and since her own letter contained an enticing invitation which did not include her protégé, she asked to see the letter. Having struggled through it, she said kindly, "My poor sweet! It is a pretty letter, but Miss Crossland should have given us more time, and I should really have first corresponded with her mama."

"Yes," said Elspeth, with a forlorn little sniff. "But you will remember my father always held that Lady Crossland was something of a widgeon, however well bred."

Madame could not even remember Lady Crossland, but since the late Mr. Clayton had frequently advised her that she herself was similarly afflicted, she felt an affinity with the lady and said, "True. But—never look so sad, love. You do seem to have taken a little cold, and it might be as well for you to escape the city air for a space."

Elspeth gazed at her hopefully. "Do you say I may go, ma'am? Is there time?"

" 'Tis rather a scrambling business, and I doubt your dear mama would approve . . . Still, with your cold . . . Let me see. Miss Crossland says that if our coachman could bring you as far as this posting house in Fleetwell Village one of their ostlers would guide you to the estate her papa has hired. I wonder why on earth he would hire an estate in Worthing with the London Season hovering on the horizon."

Improvising desperately, Elspeth declared that *Millicent* had always loved the seaside, and that the young lady was extremely pretty and very petted and indulged by her doting parents.

"So they allowed that she have her betrothal ball in Worthing ... Hmm. They are eccentric, to say the least. But—then, who isn't? Well, where are we? It is early yet and I have reason to be proud of my bay team. If you were to leave within the hour, Abraham Coachman could drive you down in the new coach and tomorrow bring back word of when you will return. You will take your woman, of course, if she can get you packed up quickly ..."

There was no doubt, declared Elspeth joyously, that Freda would be as quick as winking!

Forty minutes later, Abraham Hines, Madame Colbert's coachman, was less joyous as he loaded Miss Elspeth's portmanteau into the boot of the coach. "If ever I heard of such a scramblement," he grumbled to Freda. "With less'n a hour's warning I'm to go galloping fer a posting house as I never heard tell on and get the young lady there afore dark! I grant yer madame's bays is sixteen mile a hour tits, but I'll have to change teams twice at least, seeing as Madame don't keep changes along any post roads, so no one can't blame me if we end up with two slugs what won't move fer figs!"

"As if you'd be took in by slugs," said Freda. "If ever a coachman knows his horses, it's Mr. Abraham Hines!"

Only slightly mollified, he grumbled, "It ain't decent, it ain't. Does the missus *know* these here Crosslands, even?"

Freda smiled into his narrow, glum countenance and allowed as how the missus wouldn't never do nothing she thought was havey-cavey. Handing him her own valise, she added, "Fairly dotes on my young lady, she do, and likely thinks the sea air will do her good, since she's come down with this nasty cold."

"More likely since Colonel Ritchie's come back from France," observed Coachman Hines with a cynical sniff.

56

"Ooh!" Freda squealed, and dug him in the ribs. "You *are* naughty!"

"*I* ain't," he argued. "But I wouldn't put it past the missus to kick up her heels with the Colonel whilst the coast is clear!"

Shocked, Freda pursed her lips and said righteously, "It not being my place to criticize me betters, I will say nought."

The coachman grunted and scowled after her as she hurried back into the house. "Say nought, indeed," he grumbled. "She'll have plenty to say if I can't find the blasted place!" He glanced up at the pale sky. Not sunny, exactly, but at least there was no sign of ugly weather. It would be a drive of at least six hours, and by the time he got Miss Elspeth to her friend's house it would likely be dusk. Not much doubt but that he'd be given dinner and a bed, of course. With luck, this here Lord Crossland would have a good cook and on the way back to the City tomorrow there'd be no call to race his cattle.

Securing the boot, he brightened. This scrambling journey might not turn out too bad after all.

4

Vance Clayton had once boasted to have driven his light coach from London to Worthing in only five hours, but although Madame's horses were spirited beasts and Abraham Coachman knew his trade, by mid-afternoon they were still a long way from the coast. Elspeth and Freda had enjoyed the drive at first, but the constant pounding of hooves and jolting of the coach had become tedious, and as the hours passed Freda began to be convinced that they could not reach their destination until morning. She had said as much to her young mistress forty minutes ago, but Miss Elspeth was lost in thought and had made no response.

The weather, at least, had continued fair. They'd stopped twice to change horses and once to take an indifferent meal at a large and noisy inn. They had been leaving the yard of that establishment when a splendid blue carriage and four beautifully matched black horses had arrived at a reckless rate of speed and almost collided with them. Abraham Coachman had howled his indignation. The occupant of the blue carriage had given them a scornful glance, revealing a haughty and darkly handsome countenance, and Elspeth, who'd been so quiet all day, had roused to look out of the window and exclaim heatedly, "Oh! It's him again!"

Intrigued, Freda had remarked, "Such a fine gentleman! Who is he, miss?"

"The most intolerable creature in London. At least, I hope there is no other like him! He seems to make a habit of annoying people."

Freda had attempted to continue the conversation, but Elspeth had lapsed into her anxieties once more. She'd decided that once they reached the High Tide tavern she would somehow slip away from Freda and Abraham Coachman and find some likely person of whom to enquire for the Reverend Mr. FitzWilliam Boudreaux. If all went well, that gentleman would be able to hire men willing to attempt the rescue of her beloved brother; he might, in fact, already have done so. She acknowledged with a sinking heart that she did not know where Vance was held, or how to reach him, much less how to win his freedom, and she could only trust that Lord Boudreaux did have this knowledge. Faith, but it all sounded frighteningly vague and a far from well-conceived plan! Her fervent prayer was that the clergyman would be able to advise her. How she was to explain her actions to Godmama was another problem, but that could be worked out on the return journey to London . . . somehow . . .

The coach jolted, and she awoke, surprised to realize that despite all the distractions and worries of this endless journey she had fallen into a doze. "Good gracious!" she exclaimed. "The sun is going down already! Do you know where we are, Freda?"

The abigail imparted plaintively that she knew they had passed Shoreham. "And tired I am of all this rocking and jolting about! It's almost dark, and Abraham Coachman says—"

Elspeth was never to know what her coachman had to

say. There arose sudden shouts, the shrill neighing of frightened horses, and a splintering crash. Elspeth was tossed to one side and Freda screamed as the coach rocked wildly, then lurched to a halt.

Outside, Abraham Coachman was in full cry, and an impassioned voice was accusing him of being a stupid dolt and a blockhead.

Struggling to sit up straight, Elspeth pushed back the hood that had fallen over her eyes and asked anxiously, "Are you all right, Freda?"

"No, I bean't all right, miss," wailed Freda, picking herself up from the floor and rubbing her hip. "Scared witless, I do be, and that's a fact! Whatever happened is what I should like to know?"

"As would I!" Elspeth reached for the door, only to have it swung open.

She was less than astonished to be confronted by Gervaise Valerian's flashing grey eyes. "Nobody seriously damaged, I trust," he snapped brusquely.

Wondering if he ever was amiable, she replied, "Not that you would give a button if we were! I might have known that you were the cause of the collision!"

"Nonsense. And it's more than a collision, ma'am. A full-fledged disaster, more like!"

Abraham Coachman peered over the shoulder of the Dandy's peerlessly tailored driving coat. "The gentleman's coach were trying to pass, Miss Clayton. There weren't room, as I tried to tell—"

"Water under the bridge," interrupted Valerian impatiently. "And I've no time to waste. Be so good as to alight, ma'am."

Elspeth stared at him. "Get out? Why? Is our coach out of commission, Abraham?"

"No," said Valerian. "But mine is. I must borrow yours. I'll send another carriage for you as soon as I—"

Outraged, she argued, "No such thing! Faith, but you bear off the palm for arrogance, sir! I am already late for an appointment, and since this accident was your doing—" She drew back with a little squeal of alarm as his gauntletted hand made a grab for her arm.

Freda shrieked.

Valerian snapped, "Have done! Regardless of where the fault lies, my coach wheel is smashed. The lady who was to have—" He paused, then went on, "My friend has, I fear, sprained her ankle and is quite unable to walk. I must convey her to a physician at once." He frowned and muttered, "Lord knows how I am to find someone to take her place!"

'The wretched libertine can scarce wait to provide himself with a substitute for the poor jade,' thought Elspeth, and offered scornfully, "By all means bring the unfortunate woman here. We will take her as far as the village at least, and since you are so desperate to find a replacement, there may be—"

"Here," he interrupted, his narrowed gaze searching her face. "What village? Where are you bound, ma'am?"

"That is no concern of yours. But I am in a hurry and it's getting dark. Carry your—er, friend over here, and we will be on our way."

Freda emitted another shriek as Valerian instead sprang up the step.

Abraham Coachman, brandishing a large horse-pistol, shouted, "Now, then, sir! You can't go frightening of my ladies like this. I must ask you to get out of there."

"Ask whatever you like, and I'll ask you to stop waving that damned pistol about," retorted the Dandy. "You can't fire it with the women in here, you fool. Put it up at once!" Turning his back on the coachman, he went on harshly, "Your destination is assuredly my concern, madam, since you will carry my friend with you, and there are a number of villages in the vicinity."

61

"Oh." Bowing to the logic of this, Elspeth said, "We go to Fleetwell Village."

Obviously taken aback, he exclaimed, "Good God! Whatever for?"

"For my own personal reasons," she said angrily. "Which are most decidedly none of your affair, Mr. Valerian. Be so good as to remove yourself from my coach at once. I can delay no longer!"

"Nor I." Turning to the wide-eyed Freda, he commanded, "You. Out!"

"Ow! Miss!" wailed the abigail.

"Do not move, Freda!" Her heart beginning to beat very fast, Elspeth called, "Abraham!"

The coachman, who had drawn back during this argument, came up again, his pistol ready. "I can't nowise stand by and let you kidnap my ladies, sir," he growled.

"If I thought 'twould serve, by Jupiter, I would. As it is—" Valerian whipped around and his fist flew out in what Elspeth recognized as a sizzling right jab.

Abraham Coachman howled and reeled back, dropping his pistol and clapping a hand to his nose.

"Oh! You wicked *brute*!" cried Elspeth. "You have hurt him!"

Valerian looked at Freda and jerked his head. "Don't make me say it again!"

"Not without me lady," sobbed the maid, clinging to Elspeth's hand.

"Exactly so," he agreed, and without ceremony pulled Elspeth from the coach, Freda scrambling after her.

Infuriated, Elspeth raged, "You are no gentleman! Faith, but you're no better than a highwayman! A common criminal! I shall lay an information 'gainst you for—"

"Very likely." He shouted, "Hey! Herbert! Stir your stumps, man!"

Elspeth saw that his coach stood beside the road, leaning

at a crazy angle, one wheel buckled. The coachman was beside the vehicle, talking with someone inside who now hurried to join Valerian. She recognized him for the same young man who had been with the Dandy when she and Joel Skye had encountered them in the park. With a troubled glance he raised his tricorne to her respectfully, then asked, "What's to do, coz?"

"I'm borrowing this coach," said Valerian. "Fetch Mistress Hoylake."

"If you do so," advised Elspeth angrily, "you will be aiding in a kidnapping, and just as guilty as this insufferable creature."

The new arrival gave a gasp. "Gervaise? You cannot—"

"Oh, for Lord's sake! *Will* you move? Pay no attention to Milady Huff-n-Puff here. I'll send a coach for her and the rest of these people as soon as we reach the village. Come *on*, Herbert! He'll not wait!"

Herbert gave Elspeth an apologetic glance, then ran back to the other coach.

"It makes no never mind to you, Mr. Valerian, that the world does not revolve around you!" cried Elspeth. "Or that my own case is desperate, and I am far more pressed for time than you are. 'Tis a matter of life and death that—"

"She won't let me carry her, coz," called Herbert.

"Women!" snarled Valerian, taking the leader's bridle and walking the team over to his own coach.

Elspeth exclaimed, "My reticule! I dropped it when that villain dragged me from the coach. Run and get it, Freda. Quickly!"

Her eyes wide with fright, the abigail whimpered, "I dassen't! Oh, miss, I just dassen't go near that gentleman! Clear to see, he's mad as a mangle!"

"Oh, for heaven's sake, girl!" Starting forward, Elspeth said, "Then I'll go."

Freda caught at her arm. "Do not, miss. I beg you! No telling what violence he will visit upon you!"

Wrenching free, Elspeth said, "The wretch is stealing our coach, but he'll not steal my reticule! It contains all my funds. Stay with Abraham."

Valerian and the young man called Herbert, who was his cousin apparently, were busied with the other vehicle. Picking up her skirts, Elspeth ran to her carriage and climbed the steps. The reticule was not to be seen on the seats, and the fading light made it difficult to get a clear view of the floor. Bending to feel about, she heard the door slam behind her.

Valerian shouted, "Poor Bertha's ankle may be broke and I think we had best not move her. I'll drive. I've told the Clayton woman's coachman to wait here till I can send an apothecary to them! Jupiter! Listen to that silly chit screech. Move, you pretty brutes!"

The crack of a whip was augmented by Freda's hysterical outcries.

Appalled by the realization that Valerian must not know she was inside, Elspeth cried, "Oh, no!" She clambered up but was flung down, falling between the seats as the coach jolted and started off, the Deplorable Dandy urging the team on so that they came almost at once to a headlong gallop.

Having grown up with a healthy older brother who delighted in athletic and often risky pursuits, Elspeth was not unfamiliar with coaches driven at reckless speeds, but never had she been subjected to such a wild ride as this. She had scarcely got to her feet than she was tossed to the side as Valerian took a bend in the road on what she was sure were only the two left wheels, and her outraged demand that he stop was choked off before it was properly uttered. She managed to reach the opposite seat and pounded frantically on the panelled wall, but her efforts were drowned by pounding hooves, creaking harness, and the grind and rumble of the flying wheels.

Over the uproar she could hear the two men shouting to each other and was revolted by Valerian's howled: ". . . must have a woman, I tell you! I *must*! And tonight!"

Herbert's barely intelligible response, "Doubt . . . can find one . . . suitable . . . tonight," won a ragefully shouted, "*Must* be tonight! Dammitall, I *cannot* wait till tomorrow!"

"Disgusting *lecher!*" gasped Elspeth, clinging to the side strap. "Your greedy lust will likely overturn us all!" No sooner had she voiced this unhappy prediction than she shrieked as the wheels encountered some obstacle and the coach leapt into the air. She was hurled to the far side, bounced off the seat, and down she went onto the floor once more. Her hood flew over her face, she clawed at the squabs, convinced that she was sadly bruised in several unfortunate areas—which did not much matter, since it appeared she would be slain at any second.

Struggling to get back onto the seat, she was not surprised to find that her hair had come down and was an untidy tangle over her eyes. Pushing it back, she embarked on an impassioned assessment of Mr. Gervaise Valerian's libertine propensities and was not nearly finished with her denunciation when it dawned on her that the coach was slowing. She was still alive! Light flashed past the window. Peering out eagerly, she caught a fleeting glimpse of sails and a large vessel riding at achor. Then they had swept past and were pulling into an inn yard. Now! Now, she would confront the obnoxious Dandy and give him a piece of her mind, though what he really rated was at the least a strong box on the ear, and if Vance were only—

She gave a gasp and her vengeful rage faded into disbelief. An ostler was running up, brandishing a flaming torch. The glow illuminated a sign that swung on the wind; not a large or pretentious sign, and the painting rather am-

65

ateurish, but the scene it depicted was quite recognizably a foaming wave breaking on a rocky shore. Above this work of art the name, printed in bold black letters, proclaimed, THE HIGH TIDE.

Stunned, she sat motionless for a minute. So that rake, Valerian, had come to the very same inn to which she had been bound! Infamous as was his abduction of her, at least it had served some purpose. She must confront him at once. The knowledge that she could accuse him of kidnapping a lady of Quality must terrify even so hardened a rake, and he would lose no time in restoring her maid and coachman to her side. She reached for the door, then drew her hand back as another carriage pulled into the yard. A gentleman alighted and assisted a lady down the steps. Mercy, but she could not face respectable people with her hair hanging over her face and her skirts all anyhow. She could hear the young Herbert giving crisp instructions to the ostler and demanding the whereabouts of an apothecary. She must hasten or Valerian would manage to hide his wicked self while instituting his frenzied search for "a woman"!

Not delaying to retrieve the small comb and mirror from her reticule, she scraped her hair into a semblance of tidiness, restored her hood and straightened her skirts. Then, ready to do battle, she climbed from the coach.

Aready the team was being led away. There was no sign of Valerian or his cousin. The ostler turned and gave a yelp of surprise as he saw her. "Apologies, marm," he gasped, touching his forelock respectfully. "Me helper's gone orf to fetch a poor lady from a wrecked coach, else I'd've see ye 'fore this, but I didn't know as you was still inside."

"That's quite all right," said Elspeth, smiling on him. "My—brother told me to follow him, but quite forgot to tell me where he was going."

The faint look of disapproval faded from his weathered countenance. Elspeth could guess what he had been assuming, logically enough if the Deplorable Dandy was a frequent visitor to the High Tide! She added another item to her inventory of Valerian's misdeeds.

"The gent went into the house, marm," said the ostler. "In a rare hurry, he wuz, though he shouldn't oughter have left a lady like you waiting out here. Mr. Langley will show you where he be. Mr. Langley being the propri'ter, marm."

Elspeth thanked him and hurried across the cobbled yard. The air was more chill now that the sun had gone down, but the cloudy skies were lit by the brief late winter twilight. Opening the back door, she entered a warm and welcoming parlour enriched by the pleasant aromas of burning logs and dinner preparations. The lady and gentleman who had just arrived were talking with a jolly-looking little man at the desk, but there was no sign of Valerian. She was torn between the need to confront him with his villainy and the even more pressing need to find the Reverend Mr. Boudreaux.

The little man at the desk, presumably Langley, the host, rang a handbell and his customers were led away by a maidservant. Elspeth moved forward, saw curiosity come into his eyes and said hurriedly, "I am here to meet a clergyman, Mr. Langley." She kept her voice low, adding, "The Reverend Mr. FitzWilliam Boudreaux."

"Ah. Well, the gentleman be upstairs, miss." Langley's gaze moved past her, obviously seeking.

"I am accompanying my—brother," Elspeth lied. "He came in just now, but I do not seem to see him anywhere."

The host looked relieved. "You'll be meaning Mr. Newell." He rang his little bell once more. "We've two nice rooms available for tonight, miss, should your brother desire to stay." The maid descended the short flight of stairs and was told by the host to guide "Miss Newell" to Room 4.

The girl scanned Elspeth with a shrewd female eye that immediately detected an untidiness at odds with garments bearing the unmistakable stamp of an expensive modiste. She bobbed a curtsy and led the way to the stairs. "Will ye be a overnight guest, ma'am?" she enquired.

"My brother will doubtless make suitable arrangements," evaded Elspeth as they reached the top of the flight. "No, pray do not knock." She smiled and said in woman-to-woman fashion, "The Reverend is an old family friend and I mean to surprise him."

The maid looked puzzled but then grinned conspiratorially and hurried to the stairs again.

Elspeth could hear the murmur of male voices inside. She had hoped to find Mr. Boudreaux alone, but determined not to be thwarted, she lifted the latch with caution and eased the door open. The explanation for the housemaid's perplexity was at once apparent. "Miss Newell" would have little chance of surprising the "old family friend" since her "brother" was even now conversing with him.

'Valerian!' she thought indignantly. The wretched rake was yet again ruining her plans! The two men were seated beside the hearth, the clergyman raking at the glowing coals while Valerian leaned forward in his chair and made his desires known in so irate a voice that the new arrival was not noted by either.

"No, I cannot wait," he rasped. "I need a wench *tonight*! You're acquainted hereabouts, Fitz. You likely know a score of women who would jump at the fee I offer!"

"Oh!" gasped Elspeth, outraged that the Dandy would involve a man of the cloth in his lecherous quest.

" 'Tis such short notice," the clergyman demurred hesitantly. "I don't know if I can in good conscience—"

"The devil fly away with your conscience," raged Valerian. "I'd not ask you save that poor Bertha's ankle is severely sprained and, however willing, she cannot serve me."

Through her teeth, Elspeth hissed, "Foulness! Roué!"

The roué declared hotly, "I am desperate for someone—

tonight, I tell you! And you must find me a woman capable of meeting my needs. No, don't sit there looking righteous, Fitz! It's your mission in life to be of assistance to your fellow man, and I need assistance in the worst—"

"You *evil libertine!*" cried Elspeth, advancing into the room, afire with righteous zeal.

Both men sprang to their feet and turned to her, consternation clearly written on their paling faces.

"I knew you were a selfish care-for-nobody," she accused, flourishing her reticule at Valerian. "But that you would *dare* tempt a man of God into assisting your salacious debaucheries—"

The Dandy was perfectly white. He gasped out feebly, "L-libertine ... debaucheries ... ? What a'plague ails you, ma'am?"

The Reverend Mr. Boudreaux stammered, "I—I think I have not the pleasure, Miss ... ?"

"Miss Elspeth Clayton! And 'tis no pleasure to me, sir, that I find you listening to the—the heathen blandishments of this disgraceful creature!"

The clergyman's jaw dropped.

Glassy-eyed, Valerian declared, "The woman's daft, Fitz! Never heed her babblings!"

"I collect I am daft because you ran us off the road," snapped Elspeth, her own eyes flashing with anger. "I suppose you will deny that you stole my coach and kidnapped me away from my servants and—"

"Gervaise!" exclaimed Boudreaux, much shocked. "You never did?"

"I *borrowed* her coach, merely," argued Valerian stormily. "As for kidnapping you, ma'am, fustian! Even were you my type of lady—which I assure you is not the case—I've not yet found it necessary to kidnap any woman, much less one who is clearly short of a sheet!"

"I distinctly heard you bullying this poor gentleman to

obtain you a—a woman because your unfortunate Bertha could not—er, serve you," said Elspeth, feeling her cheeks become heated.

A gleam of laughter danced into Valerian's grey eyes. He said, "Jupiter! The light begins to dawn! Fitz, spare my blushes, but I think this witless beauty takes you for my procurer!"

Boudreaux's eyes opened very wide. He said faintly, "Miss *Clayton*! Why on earth would you suppose me capable of such a dreadful thing?"

"Because she's far and away too hot-at-hand," interjected Valerian. "Just like her brother! And she was incensed because I dared borrow her coach after her idiot coachman had wrecked mine. She followed me here to call me to account." He bowed mockingly. "Swords or pistols, ma'am?"

"In the first place," said Elspeth, breathing hard and yearning to scratch his mocking face, "after you stole my reticule—"

"Innocent," cried Valerian, raising one hand as if under oath.

"It was in my coach when you commandeered it," Elspeth went on. "And since it contained all my funds, I ran to retrieve it. You slammed the door and drove away, paying no heed to my pleas to be released and driving as if the devil himself sat on your shoulder! Furthermore, I have urgent business of my own with Mr. Boudreaux. You shall have to find your—'woman'—yourself, Mr. Valerian. And now, pray be so good as to go about it and leave us. At once."

Valerian clapped his hands. "Jolly well done, Queen Elspeth! I acknowledge I may have been—just a trifle—impetuous, so I will pay the price of your supper. Now, be a good girl and go down to the dining room. As soon as my cousin returns—"

Elspeth sat in the nearest chair. "My business with the Reverend Mr. Boudreaux is of an extreme vital nature—"

The amusement faded from Valerian's eyes. He said grimly, "And mine is a matter of life and death!" He strode to fling open the door. "Good day, ma'am!"

"You shall have to carry me out," she declared. And as he smiled without mirth and advanced on her chair, she added shrilly, "Screaming at the top of my lungs!"

"Heaven forfend," cried the clergyman, paling. " 'Twould be the undoing of us all, Gervaise!"

"Then we'll gag the wench, and—"

"And toss me in the sea?" said Elspeth, judging him perfectly capable of such infamous conduct.

Valerian slammed the door and strode to face her, his eyes deadly and his fists clenched. He said in a soft voice that chilled her blood, "Do you think for one instant, Fitz, that I've fought and struggled and spat in Death's face for nigh three years, only to be defeated by this cloth-headed chit?"

Very frightened, Elspeth managed, "Do you think for an instant, you immoral ruffian, that a British clergyman would stand by and condone the murder of a lady of Quality?"

There was a moment of breathless silence, and trying to keep her voice from shaking, she added, "My servants are nearby, don't forget! And I told the host I came here with you!"

Glaring down at her through narrowed eyes, Valerian swore deliberately.

Elspeth's heart was hammering and she began to feel sick.

Boudreaux said, "No need for that, Gervaise. With no little justification the lady holds her cause to be every bit as desperate as your own."

Valerian looked at him sharply, "She really does seek your aid? Aha! I begin to see! 'Tis that firebrand of a brother, I'll warrant. What kind of morass has he got himself into this time?"

The clergyman said slowly, "There just may be a way out of this, you know."

Hope resurging, Elspeth searched his face. "How, sir?"

Valerian snapped, "Well, don't just stand there looking judgmental, Fitz! Unscramble your teeth!"

Boudreaux said mildly, "I wonder it ain't occurred to either of you. The simple fact is that Miss Clayton needs—a man! And you, Gervaise—need a female."

Elspeth screamed.

5

Setting down her glass of ratafia, Elspeth said disdainfully, "I thought you were merely a Deplorable Dandy, but what it is, you are a Demented Dandy! Monstrous mad, in fact! You cannot seriously believe that I—or any other lady of Quality—would lend herself to what appears to be an improper if not downright shocking scheme!"

An hour had passed since the clergyman had uttered his inflammatory remark. A crowded hour during which Freda and Abraham Coachman had arrived at the inn to be reunited with their mistress; Valerian's young cousin, the shy and unassuming Mr. Herbert Turner, had found an apothecary; and Mrs. Bertha Hoylake had been gently conveyed to a bedchamber at the inn where the unfortunate lady's sprained ankle was now being tended by the apothecary and the local midwife. Valerian had remained with the victim until convinced that her injury was not of a serious nature and had then rejoined Elspeth and Boudreaux. The clergyman, however, with an uneasy eye on Elspeth's stormy countenance, had refused to outline his plan until they had dined.

The servants had been sent down to take their supper in the coffee room and a private parlour had been hired wherein a surprisingly good meal had been served to Elspeth and the three gentlemen.

The plan the clergyman had then sketched out was greeted by Elspeth with horror, by Herbert Turner with obvious, if speechless, dismay, and by Valerian with delight. "By Jove, Fitz, but you're a genius," he'd proclaimed exuberantly. "Take after his lordship, be da—dashed if you don't! I'd never have thought you'd the wits to concoct so neat a scheme!"

"Nor I have suspected that a man of God could propose such an appalling venture," said Elspeth tartly.

"Aye, 'twill be chancy, that's certain," Valerian acknowledged. "But if we arrange it right and tight, we may just do the thing." He slanted a glance at Elspeth's scornful face and added, "Of course, you must decide whether your brother's life is worth the risk to yourself, ma'am. If it's too much for your sense of propriety, I'll find myself a lady with more backbone."

Elspeth flushed, and Herbert Turner said in his diffident way, "You're asking Miss Clayton to risk ruining herself, Gervaise. If such an escapade should be discovered—"

"If it should be discovered, we'll all be in very hot water," admitted Valerian. "I have no hesitation in running the risk, but if Miss Clayton sets her reputation above her brother's life, I shall have to find a less timid female."

Elspeth did her best to vanquish him with a frigid glare, but perceiving his sneering grin to be unshaken, she said coldly, "Since I am judged a 'timid female,' let me see if I have sufficient wit to perfectly understand Mr. Boudreaux's plan. 'Twould seem that one of Valerian's 'friends'—" She paused and said ironically, "A lady friend, no doubt?"

Valerian waved a languid hand. "But of course." Laughter

danced into those darkly lashed grey eyes. He added in a provocative whisper, "A widow, in fact!"

With a curl of the lip, Elspeth murmured, "I wonder why that should not surprise me. This—friend—had expected to come into a considerable inheritance, is that the case?"

He nodded. "Her late husband's home and fortune. Instead, she learned that everything was to pass to a distant male relative whereupon she would be dispossessed with no more than a pittance."

"It seems excessive harsh," she said, eyeing him dubiously. "Surely her husband must have made some provision for her?"

"I dislike to speak ill of the dead," he declared. "But to say truth, her husband was a nip-cheese. In fairness I own that he was carried off very suddenly, and being in generally good health and on the light side of fifty, he had seen no urgency in drawing up a will. The courts decided that the house and property—the whole estate, even to the bulk of the widow's jewels, must pass to some fellow living in— South America, I believe. Poor Geraldine would be rendered quite penniless. One can scarce blame her for fighting for what she considers to be her own."

"By which you mean she has decided to skip across to France with as many of her valuables as she can convey," said Elspeth dryly.

"A justifiable course of action that the authorities, being a lot of fumble-wits, would deem to be theft." Valerian glanced at his clerical friend, who appeared to have been struck dumb by this summation, and asked, "Right, Fitz?"

"Oh," gulped the clergyman.

"You see?" interposed Elspeth, alarmed by the stunned expression on Mr. Boudreaux's face. "Your friend is a godly man, and he knows that the lady is in the wrong of it."

"Stuff!" exclaimed Valerian rudely. "Fitz has gone off into one of his wide-awake snoozes is all." He reached over and

75

shook Boudreaux's shoulder. "Wake up! You know Geraldine has right on her side!"

"Who?" mumbled the clergyman.

"Merciful mackerels! *Geraldine*—you pious great lamebrain! My *lady friend*!"

"Ah!" Boudreaux blinked owlishly. "Geraldine. Just so!" He drew a deep breath, smiled brightly at Elspeth, and remarked, "That's the barber!"

Valerian turned his head and murmured in a confiding manner, "A jolly good fellow, but wits to let at times. Fell out of a tree when he was six." And in a more normal tone, "So you understand now, do you, ma'am?"

Elspeth forced her attention from the clergyman's vacuous grin and said tartly, "What I understand, sir, is that this lady, Mrs. Geraldine . . . ?"

"Nugent," supplied Turner. "Mrs. Geraldine Nugent."

"Newell!" said Valerian sharply. "She dare not use her own name for this journey so we decided to name her Newell! You've not forgot already, I trust? For Lord's sake keep your wits about you, Herbert!"

Herbert flushed scarlet and stammered an apology.

Valerian glared at him and growled, "You'd a question I believe, ma'am?"

"I hope you'll correct me if I've the wrong impression," said Elspeth coldly. "I gather the lady, whatever her name may be, is using a Bath chair so as to smuggle her jewels and valuables out of the country, which is unlawful. And that I am to become a fellow conspirator by pretending to be her nurse. Though for the life of me I cannot see how that is to help my poor brother, nor what a black cat has to do with the scheme! And since we are rapidly running out of time, I wish you will make it clear to me."

Valerian appeared to grind his teeth. "Had you been listening when Fitz spelled it all out—"

"I was in a state of shock. Understandably."

"The cat is the clue to the thing, don't you see? Geraldine has this revolting black kitten—"

"What is revolting about a kitten? Are you one of those nasty men who dislike cats?"

"But of course! Ascribe every villainy to me if 'twill set your mind at ease. The Deplorable Dandy loathes cats! Which has nothing to say to the fact that my Geraldine loves the little yowlers. When we enter France she will be cuddling Pixie (its name is Pixie) in her lap—"

"In the Bath chair."

"In the Bath chair."

"While sitting on all her worldly and illicit gains."

He snarled softly. "Do you want me to hasten or are you going to enter a caveat to everything I say?"

Elspeth sighed and was silent.

The Reverend Mr. Boudreaux said soothingly, "The thing is that when we arrive in France, you will be guiding the chair, Miss Clayton, with the—lady and the—er, little black kitty, do you see? And when we have conveyed Georgiana—"

"Geraldine!" corrected Valerian, with a long-suffering look at Elspeth.

"Righto!" resumed the clergyman, uttering an embarrassed laugh. "Once the lady is safe—"

"We will proceed to untangle your brother from whatever foolish scrape he has fallen into," interjected Valerian impatiently, "and whisk him to the coast. You, Madam Nurse, will guide the *same* chair, complete with *lady* and *black kitten.* Therefore, should we be recognized by the authorities, no one will suspect we have switched 'ladies' for the return journey."

Her eyes very wide, Elspeth said an awed, "You mean to disguise Vance as—as a *lady?* You're mad! My brother is tall and—and muscular, and—"

"If he's been in the hands of the French military for very

long, he might not be so muscular as you remember," said Valerian bluntly. "But pray tell if you've a better scheme, ma'am."

Elspeth whitened and closed her eyes.

Turning to the quiet clergyman, Valerian asked, "What's the fellow done, Fitz? I take it your uncle is aware?"

"He is aware because Nicholas Drew was with Clayton at the time of his arrest. It was Drew who asked for my great-uncle's aid in the business."

"Drew . . . Hmm . . . Why didn't he appeal to the Horse Guards?"

"Couldn't in this matter, Ger. Vance Clayton served as courier for La Pompadour. Got himself fairly caught."

"By?"

Boudreaux shrugged. "No telling who's at the root of it. The woman is ambitious. She has made enemies in high places and there are those who fear she now means to encourage an alliance with Austria."

Valerian whistled softly. "Which would not please many messieurs in—as you say, Fitz—'high places.' So our British gentlemen in their own high places ain't likely to step in to save Clayton's hide, I take it?"

"Whitehall don't fancy that kind of sticky wicket at this particular time, dear boy."

"So my brother, who sought only to provide for Mama and me, is to be abandoned to Madame Guillotine." Elspeth turned suddenly tear-wet eyes on Valerian. "Vance is wounded and at their mercy, sir. Mr. Drew said they would wait only for him to recover sufficiently to be—to be . . ." Her voice a thread, she whispered, ". . . questioned."

She had, noted Valerian inconsequently, quite lovely eyes. He said thoughtfully, "Is Drew planning to take a hand in this business, Fitz?"

"If he were, he would be handling all this for me," said Elspeth, dabbing a tiny handkerchief at her eyes. "Two nights since he was attacked by Mohocks and badly injured."

"You surprise me," drawled Valerian, frowning. "I should have supposed a fellow like Drew well able to take care of himself. You're—ah, sure it was Mohocks attacked him?"

She stared at him. "How can I be sure who . . . ? Oh! My goodness! You think it was the people who hold Vance prisoner?"

"I've no least idea, save that it seems the greatest coincidence that your brother's closest friend should have been incapacitated just at this particular time. Still, we do no good by theorizing. Fitz—can you tell me where Clayton is being held?"

The clergyman nodded. "Give you a map. A very secluded chateau not far west of Rouen. Likely heavily guarded. Is your—" He glanced at Elspeth and his guileless face reddened. "Is Geraldine prepared to leave?"

'He was going to say "your bird of Paradise," ' thought Elspeth, but her cynicism was forgotten when Valerian answered briskly, "Packed and ready to sail at a moment's notice."

Shocked, she exclaimed, "You do not mean—You cannot mean—not *tonight?*"

"But of course not." One of Valerian's dark brows arched upward as he fixed her with a sardonic stare. "Would a week from Wednesday afford you sufficient time to make up your mind, ma'am? You must pardon me if I had thought you judged your brother's days to be numbered!"

"You are a horrid man," she said through her teeth. "You know very well I am eager to send help to him, but—"

"But you'd no intent to risk your own skin—is that the case?"

"Oooh! How dare you—I would be—"

The clergyman interpolated gently, "Don't tease the lady, Gervaise. You ask a great deal of a gently bred-up girl. There must be other, more worldly-wise people we could hire to—"

"Aye," snapped Valerian. "An actress with courage and capable of carrying off the imposture—had we a week or two! We have not! Every minute we waste is as full of danger for Georgiana as for Vance—"

"You mean 'Geraldine,' " corrected Elspeth sweetly.

"What? Oh—" Valerian gave an impatient gesture. "Small wonder my wits are adrift with all this backing and filling! If dear Bertha Hoylake had not been so badly hurt—thanks to Miss Clayton's inept coachman—we would be already aboard. Bertha knows the situation and the risks and is ready and willing to undertake the voyage. To ask a stranger to run such a gauntlet for someone she doesn't even know—" He broke off, scowling at Elspeth. "But Miss Clayton has as much at stake as have I, so the sacrifice is less."

Elspeth drew a deep breath. What this callous Dandy said was true enough. Suddenly she was very cold and had the feeling that all the colour had left her face. Striving not to tremble, she said, "You are perfectly correct, Mr. Valerian. Fortunately, my maid packed sufficient of my wardrobe for a stay of several days, so—"

"Then you may leave it," he interrupted peremptorily. "No nurse would own the elegant gowns you affect, ma'am." He met the clergyman's eye and said with defiance, "She'll have to wear Bertha's things."

Boudreaux stammered, "But—but they're not at all *similar*. I mean, Miss Clayton's—er, figure is—"

"Less well endowed?" jeered Valerian, his gaze flickering over Elspeth in a way she thought deliberately insulting.

"I mean—she is—is taller, for one thing," persisted the clergyman, his colour deepening as he avoided Elspeth's eyes.

Valerian chuckled. "Yes, well, you'd best not list the other things, Fitz. The lady is ready to box your ears!"

Judging another pair of ears far more deserving of being boxed, Elspeth contained her mortification and said coolly,

"I am sure I shall manage, gentlemen. Though what I am to tell my servants is beyond me."

"It ain't beyond Fitz," declared Valerian, and ignoring his friend's panicked expression, he added, "Now you'd best meet Mrs. Geraldine, ma'am. And after that, Fitz, we'll have a look at your map and try to come at a way to get Vance Clayton out of his pickle barrel."

"A visitor to see you, Geraldine, my love!" With that softly uttered call, Valerian opened the door and ushered Elspeth into a small bedroom dimly lit by two candles and the flickering flames of the fire.

The only occupant was a lady seated in an invalid chair, her back to the door as she gazed pensively at the hearth.

Elspeth's nerves tightened, but she had prepared herself to meet Valerian's mistress, who would certainly be a beauty, and (whatever else) must be well bred (however abandoned).

The Bath chair turned, and Elspeth all but reeled with shock.

The lady was far from young; indeed, the first impression gained was that she must be several years older than the Dandy's mama. She was not unhandsome, but the features were strong rather than delicate and showed haggard despite a liberal application of paint. The eyes, deep-set and a fine grey, reflected weariness but were her best feature, for the nose and chin, although well cut, were too pronounced to be judged dainty. She was clad in a travelling gown of blue wool buttoned high to the throat. Her figure was thin, but even seated it was evident that she was a tall lady. A shawl was about her shoulders, and as if to emphasize the fact that she was no longer young, a lace-trimmed cap was tied over a modest but charmingly curled wig.

Speechless with astonishment, Elspeth blinked at the Dandy.

His narrowed gaze was intent on her. He said, "Make your curtsy, ma'am, to Mrs. Geraldine Newell." Mirth blazed suddenly in his eyes. He added: "My aunt."

"Oh," said Elspeth feebly, as she dropped a curtsy and yearned to scratch him.

"Miss Clayton meant to say how do you do, Aunt Gerry," he explained. "But she is quite off-stride. You see, ma'am, her nature is suspicious and she fancied you to be my—er, *chere amie.*"

Elspeth's cheeks flamed, but before she could speak, Mrs. Newell uttered a throaty chuckle and said in a soft, deep voice, "A fancy I am very sure you encouraged, rascal!" A thin, long-fingered hand was extended. "He is wicked but I hope you will not take his mischief too much to heart. How do you do, my dear?"

Holding the frail fingers briefly, Elspeth managed a disjointed response. Valerian grinned and drew up a chair for her, then sat on the bed beside a sleek black kitten. The little animal rolled over, stretched and yawned enormously, then took possession of his lap.

Mrs. Newell said, "Gervaise tells me your brother is in some difficulty and that you have between you contrived a plan to smuggle me out of England and on your way home to smuggle Mr. Clayton out of France. Your courage is admirable, but you are a well-born young lady. Have you really faced the fact that both your safety and your reputation will be terribly at risk?"

"Heaven aid me!" Valerian looked up from scratching behind the kitten's ears and exclaimed irritably, "I'd not have asked it of Miss Clayton, had not her gapeseed of a coachman forced us off the road and ruined poor Bertha's ankle! It has taken me forever to persuade her! For mercy's sake do not undo what—"

Mrs. Newell's hand raised only slightly, but to Elspeth's surprise Valerian was at once silenced, although he watched his aunt tight-lipped and frowning.

"It will not do, Gervaise," the lady said with quiet gravity. "I do not know what Canterbury tales you've told her, and I quite comprehend why my name was changed, but Miss Clayton must not attempt this venture without a full understanding of the facts."

"Your nephew has explained your circumstances, ma'am," said Elspeth. "And I am willing to risk danger to help my dear brother. It is true that I didn't know you were his aunt, nor that you have been ill, but—"

"But any further explanations will only confuse the lady," interrupted Valerian, "besides which, Aunt, you are looking very tired and should be resting in preparation for the voyage. We sail with the tide."

"Nonsense!" snapped Mrs. Newell, a note of steel coming into her husky voice. "Miss Clayton must have a chaperon, I insist upon it!"

"*You* will be her chaperon, ma'am," said Valerian, his own voice stern. "Who ever heard of a nurse having a—"

Mrs. Newell shook her head. "I know how hard you have worked to arrange this, dear lad. But I will not have a young lady of Quality ruined only for my sake!"

Valerian flushed and his eyes seemed to Elspeth to dart sparks. She interposed hurriedly, "I think perhaps you forget, ma'am, that this 'venture,' as you call it, is as much a rescue for my brother. He is very dear to me, and his life is at dreadful risk. Besides—" She broke off as the door opened and Freda Beck ran in unceremoniously, closely followed by the Reverend Mr. Boudreaux.

The abigail darted a glance from Valerian to Mrs. Newell, then rushed to seize Elspeth's arm, crying frantically, "You cannot do it, miss! This parson gentleman tried to pull the wool over my eyes, saying you was sailing along of a old friend, but I weren't born yesterday! If you ever met this lady, I never heard aught of it. I suspicion the true facts is that you never was meeting your friends here for no wedding, but you meant to give Abraham and me the slip all along!"

"If ever I heard such impertinence," exploded Valerian wrathfully. "How dare you come bursting in here with all this nonsense! Take your babblement off at once, my good girl! Your mistress is under my protection and—"

"And there is a poor choice of words, sir," exclaimed Elspeth, eyeing him with indignation.

"Well, I don't believe him, miss, begging his pardon, I'm sure," swept on Freda, fired with crusading zeal. "Mr. Valerian might be a top o' the trees around London Town, but I know you never liked him above half, and wouldn't run off with him so as to help a stranger, however good and kind your heart is! It's Mr. Vance is in another of his bumble-broths, I'll be bound! It's him as you're going to find, and well I knows it! But you're not setting foot on no packet and sailing off to mingle with them naughty Frenchies without me by your side! Whatever your dear mama would have to say to me I dare not think! No, miss! I knows me duty and I won't leave you!" Turning with her back to Elspeth and both arms flung out as though to shield her from the other occupants of the room, she fixed Valerian with an impassioned glare and said shrilly, "Not though they cut me into gobbets and feed me to them nasty frogs what they eats!"

"Oh, my saints, listen to it," moaned Valerian, running an exasperated hand through his hair. "The silly creature takes us for white slavers!"

Touched by her maid's devotion, Elspeth stepped aside and said, "How can you expect her to understand what is going on? Mrs. Newell, I do apologize, but Beck has been my abigail for years and is—"

"Is loyal and devoted, that is plain to see," put in Mrs. Newell, watching her nephew's stormy countenance. "The woman has every right to fear for her mistress, Gervaise. Besides, this is as well. Beck can serve as the chaperon Miss Clayton should have by her. And do not protest again that I can be her chaperon, for anyone can see I am in no case to chaperon anyone."

Valerian groaned again. "So we are to add another to our desperate sortie! If this keeps up we shall need the hire of an entire packet to transport us! One can but trust that the martyred Mistress Beck will survive the vagaries of the English Channel!"

Freda paled and muttered uneasily, "What's vague-rees. Miss Elspeth?"

"You will find out all too soon," jeered Valerian. "From the look of the sky, we're unlikely to enjoy a smooth crossing."

"Then how fortunate we are to have the escort of an experienced sailor, such as yourself, sir, who is well able to take care of us," said Elspeth coldly.

A twinkle brightened Mrs. Newell's tired eyes.

Valerian's chin lifted. "Exactly so," he said.

With a twinge of apprehension, Elspeth saw that the Reverend Mr. Boudreaux was grinning broadly.

———

There was nothing really remarkable about this individual, thought Joel Skye. The Army Major seated at the table before him was sturdy rather than athletic, his features were good but not striking; the hair, now powdered, showed no sign of thinning despite the fact that he looked to be on the far side of forty, but, to judge from the heavy brows, it was an undistinguished brown. Ordinary, if not nondescript, was how one might have described him. Yet rumours were whispered about Joshua Swift; rumours of extraordinary successes in the field of Military Intelligence; of outstanding achievements in apprehending spies and enemies of the

Crown; of a relentless persistence that, once engaged, never gave up, much to the grief of those he pursued. An awesome record that had made him a power to be reckoned with at Bow Street or in Whitehall. What the Intelligence officer was about in this unpretentious inn outside the quiet village of Little Hampton, and why he himself had been sent down here at such breakneck speed, was a puzzle.

Swift looked up from the papers he was reading and scanned the younger man thoughtfully. First impressions had not inspired much confidence. That Lieutenant Joel Skye was intelligent was unquestionable; on the other hand, most of his commendations had come while he served as aide to Lord Hayes of the East India Company, who also chanced to be his uncle. Family prejudice there, to some extent, no doubt. A good-looking young fellow, the intense kind, and those brilliant dark eyes certainly spoke of energy. But there was nervousness too, as betrayed by the slim, restless hands. All in all, the lad was too thin—too finely drawn. For himself, he preferred the strong and steady type; the plodders who succeeded through dogged determination rather than flashes of inspiration or an application of that too often flawed science: logic. Why in the world Skye had been tossed into his dish was baffling. Someone must think highly of him. Unless it was a case of testing the fellow's mettle now that he was no longer protected by his once prestigious uncle. 'Blast!' thought Swift, and threw the papers onto the table between them.

"How much of it d'you know?" he asked shortly.

Responding instinctively to the note of command, Joel sat straighter in his chair. "I know you've been on the trail of a socially prominent gentleman for several years, sir, and that I'm to be attached to you on temporary duty—'on loan' from the Navy, as it were—to render whatever assistance I may."

"Correct. Do you know who I'm after? And why?"

"No, sir. Only that you believe him to be a traitor."

"I damned well *know* him to be a traitor, but after three years I haven't one blasted grain of proof! You have doubtless heard that I loathe and abominate the breed, above all others. I do!" Swift picked up the papers again and held them out. "It's all here. Run your eyes over these."

Skye leant forward and took the papers. He glanced at the first page briefly and exclaimed, "Jupiter!"

"Know him, do you?" said Swift dryly. "Thought you might. How well?"

"Not well. Enough to be astonished. Are you sure, sir? I'd never have thought—"

"That's why you were sent down to assist me, instead of vice versa. One of the first things we learn in Intelligence, Skye, is never to judge by appearances. That fine gentleman is sufficiently slippery to have eluded me these three years. It galls me to count the number of times I've almost had him! Now he's on the move, and you're going after him. Take those pages with you and commit as much as you can to memory, then burn 'em. I have other copies."

Skye blinked. "Tonight, sir? But it's—"

"I am able to tell the time, Lieutenant. Are you?"

"Your pardon, sir?"

"Your parent is a bosom-bow of my superior. I am advised that Colonel Skye is displeased with your career choices. You'd be a bigger fool than I take you for were you to doubt that your past successes have put some noses out of joint at the Admiralty and in Whitehall." A gleam of humour came into the Intelligence officer's eyes. "You follow me, Skye?"

Joel grinned and said wryly, "A last chance to avoid sinking into obscurity on some sea-going barge, sir?"

"Exactly so. You leave at once. If you ride hard you can reach the inn with time to spare before they sail. I say 'they' because our quarry will doubtless be surrounded by loyal idiots willing to risk their own silly heads in the name of friendship or love, or whatever! I'd give my ears to make the arrest myself, but I'm known to 'em. Oh, I know they're not strangers to you either, but I doubt they'll suspect you're presently assigned to the case, whereas one glimpse of me and they'd scatter like rabbits and we'd lose them again."

"Am I to apprehend them at the inn, sir?"

"Lord—no! Not until they're aboard. I want the whole parcel of the traitorous swine. The fact they're sneaking out of England is proof of their treachery."

"I'll take how many men with me?"

"You'll take yourself. The sudden arrival of a military patrol would give the game away. You can commandeer aid in the King's name if you find yourself at stand. But going in— no uniforms, Lieutenant. This has become a matter of diplomacy. We can nab them in France if need be, but you'll be up against some very dangerous opponents on both sides of the Channel. Guard yourself. I fancy you know enough of this type of work to be aware that if you find it necessary to violate any French laws or citizens and are rumbled, you'll be thrown to the wolves and we'll deny all knowledge of you?"

Joel sighed. "Yes, sir. Thank you, sir."

"Good luck," said Joshua Swift, standing for the handshake. "My reputation rides on your shoulders." And as the door closed behind the young naval officer, he muttered in a disgruntled tone, "And they're not very broad, dammitall!"

6

*O*w!" Freda Beck recoiled, and staring at the slender
young lady reflected in the cheval-glass wailed, "Miss!
You don't never mean to put *that* ugly thing on your sweet
person?"

Elspeth surveyed herself and adjusted the neckline of
the woollen grey round gown. "It could be worse," she murmured critically. "It is at least very clean and nicely pressed."

"But—but it's two sizes too big," moaned Freda, tugging
and pulling. "And only look at the pretty dress you've took
off! I can see why he wants you to use another name, so as
to shield your reputation. But why on earth would Mr. Valerian want you to wear that ugly dress?"

"He feels, and rightly so, that were I to wear my own
gowns the authorities would guess I am not a nurse."

"What authorities?" grumbled Freda, tightening the sash
around the grey gown. "I didn't see no Navy officers nor no
Bow Street Runners watching of the guests what stay in this
here inn. Nor there isn't no law as says a respectable English

lady can't travel to France—if she's so addle-witted as to want to go there!"

"I told you," said Elspeth with a trace of impatience. "Mrs. Newell's family is opposed to this journey and would prevent her did they know of it. It all has to do with her inheritance, and she is obliged to travel in haste despite her indifferent health. Also, Freda, do try to remember you are not to fuss over me when we go to the ship. I am Mrs. Newell's nurse and you are *her* abigail—not mine. Nurses, I fancy, do not as a general rule have personal maids to take care of them."

Freda mumbled something under her breath having to do with "humble ordinary folk" but, seeing her mistress's frown, added hurriedly that she only hoped the old lady was a good sailor. "For she looks fairly foundered before we even step onto the boat, Miss Elspeth, and if she should be took sick I wouldn't know what to do, no more would you."

A knock sounded at the door, and Beck ran to admit the Reverend Mr. Boudreaux. He said diffidently that if the ladies were ready, the coach was waiting, and then jumped back as if fearing to receive a blow.

Elspeth's heart began to bounce about at quite a rate. Freda had already packed the gowns that would hopefully be utilized for the return voyage and she gathered the belongings Elspeth would need while assuming her new identity. Shy Herbert Turner came to blushfully take the valises and they followed him downstairs.

Valerian, beside his aunt's Bath chair, awaited them at the front door. He was bending over to stroke the small black cat on the lady's lap, and as he straightened, Elspeth had a momentary impression that he looked tired. It was not, she thought, to be wondered at. From what he'd said, Mrs. Newell's relations would be enraged to learn of this venture, and it now appeared that he himself was part of that very same family. Even if he were truly estranged from his father, Sir

Simon Valerian must wield considerable power as head of the family, and by aiding his aunt, Valerian was almost certainly risking his sire's wrath.

He glanced up and saw her and at once his dark brows lowered into a scowl. Stepping back, he gestured to her to guide the chair and said irritably, "Past time you put in an appearance! Make haste do—Cotton! Your mistress is anxious to board the packet and get settled in."

The pause had been very brief, but Elspeth thought an indignant 'Cotton?' Gripping the back of the chair, she was preparing to protest this alias when she saw a tall man watching them from the side hall that led to the dining room. He had a dark, stern face, a black tricorne was pulled low over a pair of narrow dark eyes and the long black cloak he wore seemed to emphasize his decidedly sinister aspect. Her protest was forgotten and her heart skipped a beat as he came towards them.

Valerian gave no sign of having noticed his approach, but he gave a quick and concealed warning tug at Elspeth's skirts. "What the deuce is all this?" he demanded, glowering at the two valises Herbert carried. "We do but convey Mrs. Newell to a physician. She is not like to remain in France for more than two days!"

Elspeth tore her gaze from the sinister stranger and said, "Your aunt will require a change of garments even so, Mr. Newell, as will her abigail and I."

"Your pardon, sir," put in an authoritative voice, "do I address Mr. Newell?"

Valerian turned and, putting up his quizzing glass, scanned the dark gentleman with cool disinterest. "You may know me, sir," he drawled. "But I think I have not your acquaintance. Your pardon, but we are in a hurry to—"

"To board the *Sea Lassie*? So I understand. I apologize for the inconvenience, Mr. Newell, but—" A card was offered and his cloak was flung back on one shoulder to reveal a neat blue uniform coat with gold buttons and white facings, worn over white breeches. "Lieutenant Horace Raines, at your service," he announced, adding solemnly, "Duty is duty, sir."

Valerian glanced at the card. "So I am told," he said with barely concealed contempt. "A preventive officer, are you? Perhaps you will condescend to advise me as to how we have incurred your displeasure. However, before you deposit your foot inextricably into your mouth, allow me to point out that the only cargo I transport is my ailing aunt, her abigail and nurse. I cannot think these less than murderous females pose a threat to you. If you mean to inspect our belongings, I suppose I cannot refuse. I trust I am a reasonable man," his voice hardened, "but should the packet sail without us I shall most certainly lodge a complaint with my friend Admiral Lord Branscombe at the Navy Board. To which end I shall keep your card, Lieutenant Raines."

He had dropped a powerful name and the Riding Officer was clearly shaken, but Elspeth's heart pounded wildly. If this nasty official should call what she was sure was a bluff and insist upon inspecting their luggage, there would be no great harm done. But if he should be so thorough as to investigate Mrs. Newell's chair, he was bound to discover the valuables so illegally concealed there, in which case they would all be tossed into prison and her chance to help Vance would be lost!

Freda began to whimper. She never had been searched by no male gent, she sobbed, and if that was what this male gent was intending, she would "fall down in a fit" did he lay so much as a hand on her.

The Lieutenant looked even more alarmed and declared he had no intention of searching anyone. "I see you're thinking along the lines of contraband, sir," he explained, "But it's not some*thing* we seek, but some*one!*"

Valerian swung his quizzing glass and looked amused.

"And you think I am your valued 'someone,' is that the case?"

Lieutenant Raines scanned him narrowly and shook his head. "I had thought at first there was a resemblance to the description I was given," he answered. "But while a gentleman may make himself appear older, sir, I never yet found one what could go back t'other way, as 'twere."

"Then why on earth must you detain me? Unless—" Valerian grinned. "I have it! You suspect Nurse Cotton of being your—what is he? Thief? Murderer?" His grin broadened. " 'Twould be a fine disguise indeed, but I can assure you she is—er, all woman! You have"—he winked conspiratorially— "my word on it!"

The implication was clear and Elspeth's cheeks flamed. "Ooh!" she gasped. "Of all the—"

The Preventive Officer intervened hurriedly, "We seek a gentleman believed to be attempting to escape to France. A traitorous Jacobite sympathizer."

"Do you, by Gad?" exclaimed Valerian, sobering. "In that case you've my full cooperation, Lieutenant. Can't abide the breed myself!"

"I'm glad to hear it, sir. As you doubtless are aware, anyone found to be shielding such a person is condemned to share his fate. And a traitor's death, Mr. Newell, is a very terrible fate."

Once again, Elspeth's anger was wiped away by a surge of fear. Her grip on the handles of the Bath chair tightened and the chair jerked slightly. "Mrs. Newell" uttered a muffled exclamation and Valerian bent to her at once.

"It's quite all right, love," he said, patting her shoulder soothingly. "My aunt is tired, Lieutenant. If there's nothing else . . . ?"

"Nothing, save to ask if you've laid eyes on such a person, Mr. Newell? He's fifty-ish, dark colouring, though likely wearing a wig; not above average height and may appear frail, as he was badly wounded some time back while aiding fugitives. An unusually fine pair of grey eyes, so the description says. Goes like a gentleman, which he is, being a baronet, and will likely be in disguise, but he's said to be, or to have been at one time, a handsome fellow."

"Hmm," muttered Valerian thoughtfully. "And have you a name for this comely traitor, Lieutenant?"

The Riding Officer hesitated. "Not one as we can bandy about, sir. Charges not having been laid as yet, for want of substantial evidence." He glanced around and, lowering his voice, said, "He's got powerful friends, d'ye see? But the initials is S. V."

"And were they A. B. C. would be as much of a conundrum." Valerian shook his head regretfully. "Alas, I cannot help you, Mr. Raines. I'll own myself puzzled, however, that you came seeking me. A case of mistaken identity, was it? Or malicious mischief, perhaps?"

The Lieutenant said with a slow smile, "The latter, more likely. Do you know of anyone eager to do you a mischief, sir?"

"Jove, but I do!" Valerian laughed. "What fellow doesn't?"

"Very true. But might you be more specific?"

"I might. But I won't. I'll own I can call to mind a few husbands who've some cause to harbour grudges. But none I'd accuse of informing 'gainst me in a matter of treason. Not the way of a gentleman, do you think? And it was—I presume—an informant, eh, Mr. Raines?"

"Now, I did not say that, sir."

"Ah, and you're a downy bird, all right, so I'll give up trying to outwit you. By your leave, Lieutenant, I'll see my ladies to the packet, yonder."

"By all means, Mr. Newell." The Riding Officer looked down at the invalid. "Though I shall be obliged to relieve you of one member of your party."

Valerian's smile did not falter in the slightest, but Elspeth saw his left hand drop unobtrusively to the hilt of his sword and her heart stood still. "Your pardon?" he murmured.

Lieutenant Raines stooped to stroke the black kitten that purred on Mrs. Newell's lap. "We cannot have you making off with the High Tide's kitchen cat. Mrs. Langley is inordinately fond of Whiskers." He prepared to lift the cat. "Come, you lazy little rascal."

Mrs. Newell squealed, "No you don't!" Her reticule swung at the startled Riding Officer's hand. "Leave Pixie be, you nasty man!"

"And here we have a true case of mistaken identity," chuckled Valerian. " 'Tis my aunt's pet, I promise you. By name of Pixie, not Whiskers. Pray do not ask me to remove her from my aunt. 'Twould take a better man than I to 're-lieve' her of the creature."

"Egad, but I believe you!" Raines rubbed his hand rue-fully. "My apologies for the mistake, ma'am. But whatever do you carry in your reticule?"

"None of your business, young man," shrilled the invalid.

Again, Elspeth's heart was thundering.

Amused, Valerian said, "After dealing Mr. Raines such a punishing whack, m'dear, I think you might at least be hon-est with the poor fellow. My aunt's reticule is crammed with contraband, of course, sir. Diamonds, pearls, rubies—quite the family fortune, in point of fact."

Elspeth's knees were like blancmange. She thought daz-edly, 'Why must this idiot take such dreadful risks?' Another moment and she would fall at the officer's feet in a dead faint, and Valerian would have no one but himself to blame!

Through an instant of tense stillness, mocking eyes of grey met irked dark ones. Then Mrs. Newell said tartly, "You left out my emeralds, boy. So long as you're talking stuff and nonsense, throw in the whole lot!"

The Lieutenant smiled stiffly. "Never fear, ma'am. I'll not dance to his tune and require you to show me your 'family fortune.' " He touched his hat and with a slight bow added, "A pleasant voyage to you."

After such a nerve-racking beginning Elspeth could not envision "a pleasant voyage," but she had seldom been more relieved than when Valerian and his cousin had lifted Mrs. Newell into the big coach and she and Freda were seated opposite the invalid.

Freda leant forward to adjust a rug about the older lady's knees and Elspeth said kindly, "You must be excessive weary, ma'am. We'll be aboard in no time and you can—"

"Herbert and I will ride on the box," snapped Valerian, preparing to swing the door shut. "Be so good as to leave my aunt in peace so that she can sleep."

"I was only—" began Elspeth, indignant.

"Chattering at her," he interposed. "Close your eyes, Geraldine, and pray the *Sea Lassie* has waited for us!"

"That's another thing," said Elspeth hastily. "Why do we sail on a regular packet? If they are so suspicious of everyone, surely we'd have been better advised to make the crossing with—with a—"

"A free trader, perhaps?" he snapped. "Aye. Don't think we hadn't considered that route. But the authorities are doubtless watching known smugglers closely. Besides which, the Le Havre Estuary is treacherous, and I'd a lot sooner be guided through by an experienced steersman or sailing master than by a rag-tag amateur. Now," he glared at her, "if you've exhausted your endless caveats, ma'am, with your most gracious permission we'll be on our way!"

The door slammed and the coach lurched as the two men mounted to the box.

Elspeth said through her teeth, "Gervaise Valerian is beyond all doubting the rudest individual I have ever met! I'm sorry, ma'am, but your nephew—" She broke off.

Mrs. Newell's eyes were closed; she had evidently followed Valerian's advice and was already asleep.

It was as well, thought Elspeth, seething, else she might have said something decidedly impolite about the Deplorable Dandy.

The coach left the inn yard and rumbled its way into the deeper darkness of the lane. It was cold, and now and then a gusting wind caused the vehicle to sway. Freda began to moan that a storm was blowing up, which would mean a rough crossing. Elspeth tried to calm her fears but inwardly she suspected the abigail was correct; if this wind held, the seas would not be calm.

By the time they reached the dock, lights were bobbing on the several vessels riding at anchor, and to judge by the welter of shouts and the scrambling activity on the *Sea Lassie*, the vessel was being prepared for imminent departure.

Valerian wrenched the carriage door open and Elspeth and Freda were handed out before he and Herbert lifted his sleepy aunt to the Bath chair.

Several port flags were whipping about, cracking like gunshots, and powerful wind gusts set close-reefed sails to flapping and halyards and chains to rattle and clang. Elspeth eyed the gangplank apprehensively. It looked very narrow; below it the sea was black and surging, and the packet was plunging about like a fractious horse. She said to Valerian, "You cannot wheel the chair across, surely?"

"Never intended to. Do you fancy me incapable of maintaining my balance whilst I carry the dear soul over such an unstable surface? You may be right. However..." He glanced up as a crane sent a large bale swinging through the air. "That should do the trick, eh, Aunty?"

Mrs. Newell uttered a muffled protest.

"Very amusing," said Elspeth huffily. "What next will you propose, I wonder?"

"Several things occur to me...," he murmured, scanning her provocatively.

Her eyes searched his face and he raised his brows and

blinked at her, the picture of innocence. "Ah, but I collect you refer to my aunt's transfer to the packet? Nothing could be simpler. Herbert will go aboard and wait at the rail and I'll heave her over to him."

Elspeth's lower lip sagged. "H-heave . . . her?"

"Just so."

"From . . . here?"

"Well, I told you I'm not capable of—"

Recovering her aplomb, she interrupted severely, "I wish you will not talk nonsense, Mr. Valerian!"

He chuckled, then turned away as a sailor crossed the deck to the gangplank and bellowed at them, "We'm casting off direct-like, sir. Cap'n says be pleased to come aboard."

Valerian bent over his aunt and detached Pixie from her lap. Thrusting the little cat at Elspeth, he said, "Don't drop this, if you—" He straightened and jerked around as a horse galloped across the cobbles towards them. The rider was tall, and as he sprang from the saddle Elspeth's heart did its now familiar leap into her throat.

Valerian called irately, "Fitz! You shouldn't be seen here, you idiot. If that Riding Officer is still lurking about—"

"He ain't." The clergyman dragged a sheaf of papers from the pocket of his riding coat. "Forgot to give you the documents I promised."

"You gave 'em to me, you block."

"Those are for your—er, aunt. These are what we've been able to learn of Miss Elspeth's brother. You'll have to commit them to memory in case you're questioned on the other side."

An urgent shout from the packet spurred Valerian to action. He shoved the papers at Herbert, saying a terse, "Thanks, Fitz. Now go!"

"I'll help you carry her. You can't—"

"Devil I can't! Go!"

Boudreaux tightened his lips, glanced at Elspeth, then met Valerian's eyes in a steady stare.

Valerian slid one arm under his aunt's knees. She said in rather an odd voice, "I'm no lightweight, you know, Gervaise. Are you sure you—"

He swung her into his arms and called a breathless, "Take the ladies first, Herbert, and do try not to drop the Bath chair over the side!"

Obediently, Herbert, carrying the Bath chair, led the way. Elspeth and Freda followed, gingerly clutching the rope that formed a crude handrail alongside.

Valerian said tersely, "All right, Fitz. What is it?"

"That fellow in the park who heaved the muddy ball at your nose," muttered Boudreaux. "Navy, ain't he?"

"Who did—what? Oh! You mean Skye. Yes, he's Navy. And what a'Beelzebub d'ye find so fascinating about the dolt that you must keep me balancing on this confounded plank swing whilst you babble—"

"Why would he follow you down here?"

Valerian tensed. "You're sure he has?"

"Came into the High Tide just after you left. Told the host he was a friend of yours and asked if you'd hired rooms."

Reeling as the gangplank swung violently, Valerian said, "Skye has a *tendre* for Miss Clayton. The silly clod probably fancies I'm abducting the chit, is all."

"He don't know Miss Clayton is here. And he's not after you at this moment because I set a couple of my fellows to— ah, delay him. Poor chap. I'm afraid it's more likely that he's working with Joshua Swift and the Intelligence lot."

Mrs. Newell said huskily, "Put me down, Gervaise. I can manage."

Breathless but determined, Valerian snapped, "Certainly not. If that miserable hound Joshua Swift's after us, I'm obliged to you, Fitz, for delaying Skye. Adieu, m'friend. We'll be under way in a few minutes and—"

"And Skye will be hard after you in the first frigate he can commandeer!"

"Perhaps. But you've done your best. Now—get ye gone, man!"

Elspeth, meanwhile, holding the alarmed Pixie tightly, was making her difficult way down to the ship. She was almost across when the gangplank lurched sickeningly beneath her. The little cat uttered a yowl and dug in her claws. Whispering a prayer, Elspeth tightened her grip on the rope, felt Freda clutching at her cloak and between wind gusts heard the maid's moaned lamentations. The ship loomed close at last, heaving but offering a far more steady surface than the erratically gyrating gangplank. Herbert was waiting to take her arm, assist Freda and give her the box of earth which had been provided by the obliging landlord for Pixie's use.

Elspeth turned anxiously. The Reverend Mr. Boudreaux, his cloak flying in the wind, was walking backwards up the bank, watching Valerian's less than rapid progress. Her eyes glued on that same progress, it seemed to Elspeth that with Mrs. Newell in his arms he was taking two steps back for every one step forwards, and she gave a gasp of fright as an inrushing wave caused the packet to yaw dangerously.

A seaman rushed up, howling something about making the gangplank secure. Before Elspeth's horrified eyes the flimsy structure sagged to the left. The chain which secured that side to the deck snapped. The seaman reacted without hesitation, catching the chain and hanging on for dear life as another sailor ran to help. Suddenly icy-cold, Elspeth heard Freda scream and her heart seemed to stop beating. She paid no heed to the frigid blast of wind that sent her skirts flying, her entire concentration was on that slim figure swaying on the rocking gangplank. It was all too evident that

Valerian could no longer keep his balance and retain his hold on his aunt, but if he set the poor lady down she would surely fall—

Imbued with the strength of desperation, Valerian hurled himself across the last few feet and reached the deck even as the chain was torn from the sailor's hands and the gangplank plunged down towards the black and icy water.

Herbert took Mrs. Newell, and Valerian sank to his knees, panting heavily.

"Jolly good, Gervaise," said Herbert, assisting the invalid into the Bath chair.

"Thank heaven you're both safely aboard," said Elspeth, able to breathe again. "That last gust was hair-raising."

"But worth it!" Valerian was very pale as he knelt there looking up at her, but he managed an unsteady laugh. "Since it raised a few other charming things besides!"

His eyes quizzed her and she felt her cheeks grow hot. "Oh! You are disgraceful," she exclaimed, holding down her flying skirts.

"I'm alive," he retorted, and getting to his feet bent over his aunt, and added: "No thanks to you, m'dear. You weigh a ton!"

In view of the lady's frailty, Elspeth thought his remark an unkind exaggeration, but the memory of that teetering gangplank gave her gooseflesh and she made no comment. Mrs. Newell reached up for her pet and Elspeth dropped the little cat into her lap, then took the chair's handles and remarked shiveringly that the wind was bitter. "We must get you inside, ma'am."

She had spoken soothingly, for she would not have been surprised had Mrs. Newell lapsed into hysterics after such a terrifying ordeal, but the invalid was made of sterner stuff and showed no sign of tears or agitation. A deckhand came up and shouted an offer to show them to their cabin. He and Herbert had to lift the chair over the raised threshold, but when Elspeth made to follow, Valerian put his arm across the doorway. "You're worn to a shade, ma'am," he said with rare kindness. "Herbert will conduct you and Beck to your own cabin so you may rest."

Astonished, she protested, "No such thing! I agreed to take care of your aunt. She must be—"

"Accustomed to her needs being attended to by me. Run along now. Herbert will arrange for tea or whatever you may—" His words were cut off as the packet dropped like a stone and then rocked wildly with much creaking of woodwork, augmented by the howl of the wind and crashings of fallen objects.

Herbert was taken off-balance and went flying across the cabin to land sprawling on a bunk. Valerian swore and made a wild lunge for the Bath chair but it collided with the washstand and spun before toppling. Elspeth was clinging to the door handle, and her horror was supplanted by surprise as Mrs. Newell sprang from the chair in the nick of time while managing to retain her hold on Pixie.

Valerian threw an arm about her shoulders. "Well done, m'dear," he said with obvious pride.

"Well done, indeed," said Elspeth, staring at the older lady in no little astonishment.

Valerian glanced at her. "Yes. Well, I think we may take it that we're under way." He assisted his now wilting aunt onto a bunk. "Come, Miss Elspeth. I'll escort you and Beck to your cabin."

"Thank you, no. The sailors will conduct us and you'd best stay with Mrs. Newell. She must be very shaken. In fact I really think I should—"

"I'm sure you do, but it's not necessary, I promise you. Besides, I must find those fellows who hung onto the gangplank. Had it not been for their extraordinary presence of mind, Geraldine and I would likely have had our notice to quit!"

Herbert tottered over to the invalid and Valerian opened the cabin door and ushered the two women into the windy darkness.

The motion of the ship confirmed his surmise that they were under way and made progress along the lurching deck no easy feat. Valerian opened the door to a small cabin. There were two bunks, and the light from a lamp attached to the wall revealed neat surroundings, and cleaner bedding than Elspeth had dared to hope for.

Valerian promised that hot tea and a supper would be delivered to them as soon as possible and bade them an optimistic good night.

Elspeth laid a detaining hand on his arm and asked how long the voyage was likely to take.

He shrugged. "Hard to say in this wind, ma'am. Perhaps six hours, perhaps sixty. You have my word that I'll advise you in plenty of time before we disembark."

Sixty hours! Her thoughts flew to her beloved brother and her heart sank. She managed to say, "Thank you. Meanwhile, if your aunt needs me, pray do not hesitate to let me know. I cannot feel I am living up to my part of our bargain by abandoning her in this fashion."

Searching her face, he saw that she was really troubled. He said, "You've done more than you know, Miss Elspeth. Now rest easy. We'll get to your brother in time, I promise you, despite this exuberant vessel!"

A flashing grin with a lack of cynicism that made him look unexpectedly boyish, and he was gone.

Oddly confused, Elspeth gazed at the closing door.

Beck said, "Now there's a gent as leaves me all at sixes and sevens. One minute a sharp word as fair skewers a body, and the next he's got his arm round me, keeping me from falling on that slippery deck."

"As any gentleman should do, Freda."

"Aye. For the likes o' you, miss. But there's a many as

wouldn't bother to aid the likes o' a humble servant girl."

"Then such a creature could in no way be named a gentleman!"

Taking her lady's cloak, Freda murmured blandly, "Nor Mr. Valerian quite so deplorable as you thunk, eh, miss?"

For a moment Elspeth did not reply, then she said lightly, "I'll reserve judgment till he's fetched us our tea, though he has likely quite forgot about it."

In this, however, she was mistaken. Valerian fought his way along to the ship's galley and ordered the nimbly swaying cook to have tea sent to both "Nurse Cotton" and his own cabin. Having accomplished this, he and the cook helped each other to regain their feet.

"A bit of a blow, sir," said the cook, his weathered features wreathed in a grin.

"Is that what you call it? I'd judge it a sizeable hurricane! Shall you be able to send the tea before we're on the bottom?"

Assured that the tea would arrive "in two shakes of a lamb's tail," Valerian slipped a tip into a ready hand and struggled back to join Herbert and Mrs. Newell.

It was a headlong journey. The wind battered at him and an icy rain sent stinging drops at his face so that he bowed his head against it. Opening the cabin door gratefully, he entered with an unrehearsed rush, threw back the hood of his cloak and said laughingly, "Well, the first step is done, praise—"

He stopped abruptly and stood very still.

A long duelling pistol was aiming steadily at his heart and a pair of dark eyes watched him with icy inflexibility.

"Skye!" he half-whispered, frustrated and furious.

Joel Skye said coolly, "You surely didn't fancy you'd get away with it, did you, Valerian?"

7

Between a series of involuntary sprints from one side of the cabin to the other, Freda Beck moaned, "Whatever Madame . . . will have to say . . . I dare'st not think." Returning at speed to the valise she was in the process of unpacking, she clung to the side of the bunk and detached a dressing gown and nightdress. "Here miss. You'll like to put on your night-rail—oops!—I fancy. Though never did I dream . . . as I'd be getting you ready for bed in a horrid boat 'stead of . . . stead of your friend's house, as you'd planned."

"Nor I." Elspeth sat on the bunk and hung on for dear life as she took off her wet shoes. She said wearily, "But I'll shed no more than my gown tonight, Freda. With luck we'll reach land by morning in spite of this dreadful gale. Besides, I want to be ready to help with Mrs. Newell should she need me."

Assisting her young mistress with buttons, Freda sniffed, then snatched for the side of the bunk as the cabin lunged upwards, then dropped alarmingly. Her voice shook when she gulped, "I suppose we can swim as well in our petticoats as in our night-rail."

"I pray it won't come to that." Elspeth forced a smile. "My brother holds that I'm something lacking in sporting accomplishments. Can you swim, Freda?"

Balancing precariously while extracting a brush and comb and hand mirror from the valise, Beck was shocked. "Swim? Lor', but I surely can't, miss! Me pa holds as folks what jump about in the water, even if no more'n a lake or a river, is tempting Providence. And as for sea-water, 'tis full of germs and ugly wriggling things, he says, and nine times out of ten them what flaunts about in it is struck down by a fateful disease sooner or later! And now—only look at us! I got splashed all over with sea-water on that horrid deck outside, and you did as well!" Having succeeded in frightening herself, she recovered a small box of tooth powder and a toothbrush and, clutching them to her bosom, turned to Elspeth and cried tearfully, "Oh, miss! *Whatever* is we doing here? With Mr. Valerian (what is if I dare remark it, naughty—for all he's as handsome as he can stare!)—What with him calling everyone by the wrong names, and his lady aunt what is so very strange, and Mr. Herbert who I declare looked so green as grass just now!" She frowned, having lost her train of thought, then said, "I know you're trying to help dear Mr. Vance out've some trouble, but—oh, miss! If you had just spoke to your fine uncle about whatever 'tis, 'stead of running off like this! Sir Brian is a proper gentleman and would've been glad to help Mr. Vance. And Mr. Conrad Beech too, I 'spect."

"So they said." Elspeth sighed. To have been able to allow a male member of her family to shoulder the responsibility for rescuing Vance would have been such a tremendous relief. Heaven knows she was doing her very best for the brother she adored, but she was all too aware that she was a woman in a man's world, a world that seemed to delight in throwing formidable obstacles in her path. The truth was that she should probably have jumped at her uncle's offer of help the instant he made it. Looking back, she wondered why she had not done so. Except—Sir Brian was so very fastidious and fashionable and rather languid-seeming . . . In fact, another of the obnoxious Dandy set! She thought guiltily, 'But very kind, I'm sure!' And although Cousin Conrad had grown to be elegant and charming and it would be the height of folly to hold long-ago childish pranks against him, he hadn't impressed her as being a man of action.

She frowned. So only look to whom foolishness and hesitancy had led her! Gervaise Valerian was not in the least languid, and with a reputation for duelling he very likely courted danger. He was also insolent, sarcastic, abrupt, hasty-tempered and another Dandy. And yet . . . she sensed a restrained power about the man; the occasional glint in his grey eyes . . . very beautiful grey eyes they were, deep-set, darkly lashed, so much like those of his aunt . . . She pulled herself up hurriedly. Whatever was she rambling on about? Oh, yes—resolution, that was it. She had glimpsed resolution in Mr. Valerian's eyes, and that strong chin argued stubbornness, which led her to believe he would not be turned aside from his chosen path, whatever obstacles were thrown in his way.

She looked up. Beck had said something and was staring at her. "I'm sorry, Freda. I was wool-gathering. What did you say?"

"You said as Sir Brian had offered to help, miss."

"Yes, he did. But you see, I scarcely know him. I've not so much as seen him for years and years. It seemed such a lot to ask. Besides, when I did decide to accept his offer he and my cousin had left Town. Goodness knows how long they will be gone and I dare not wait. Mr. Vance is in terrible danger. I need help right away and Mr. Valerian is willing to—"

She broke off as someone pounded at the door. Beck staggered to respond, and Elspeth gathered her dressing gown about her as the wind sent sheets of rain inside and Beck conducted a brief and howled conversation with a sailor. He went off, having imparted the cheering news that just about everyone aboard was "so sick as any dawgs" and that "this here blow" might delay them a hour "or several" but that "pretty li'l Mistress Beck and her lady" wasn't to be in a taking because the skipper knowed his business and would bring 'em all safe into harbour. Beck informed him that he was too saucy for his own good and slammed the door. She carried in the deep covered tray he had brought and remarked indignantly that all sailors were terrible flirtatious, but since her cheeks were quite rosy and her eyes very bright, Elspeth doubted her maid's sensibilities had been greatly offended.

The tray contained a pot of tea, a covered milk jug, a sugar bowl, two mugs and some biscuits. Elspeth enjoyed the small supper but Beck was looking a little pale, and, after taking only half a mug of tea she retreated to her bunk and turned her face to the wall. Curling up under the blankets, Elspeth composed herself to rest, although she had little hope of sleeping through such a tumultuous uproar. Towards dawn, however, the violence of the storm abated somewhat and she was surprised to awaken to daylight and the realization that she had slept for several hours. Beck was at the door accepting a ewer of hot water. The chill breath of the wind swept into the cabin, rattling the garments on their hangers and carrying the clean and invigorating smell of the sea.

In response to Elspeth's call the cabin boy who'd brought the hot water stepped inside. She had fastened her dressing gown, but he averted his eyes as he shyly relayed the information that they'd come within sight of land at first light but the seas were running too high for the "Cap'n" to dare put in to the estuary.

Elspeth said anxiously, "But the wind has dropped, surely?"

"Aye, ma'am. Not enough, though, and the *Sea Lassie* be heavy loaded and too low in the water to risk it. P'raps by noon, ma'am." He threw a quick glance at her. He judged her an uncommon beautiful lady and, noting her troubled expression, said bracingly, "There'll be a breakfast served in what the Cap'n calls the Coffee Cabin at half-past eight o'clock, though not many passengers be in any state to want it. You're a good sailor, Miss Cotton, and Miss Beck, too. Take heart! You'll be in France s'afternoon, never worrit."

Elspeth was worried indeed, but she thanked him and told him to wait while Beck found her reticule. Handing him a shilling, she smiled at his round-eyed delight and asked if Mrs. Nu—Newell had passed a restful night.

The boy grinned broadly and said that from what he'd heard it had been anything but restful. "Turble fuss there was, miss. My mate said as he'd a thunk there were a right war goin' on in there. Shoutin' an' yellin' and sounded like the lady were throwin' things. Cap'n were minded to go and bang on the door hisself but he were too busy an' then they quieted down." He shook his head and closed the door behind him, saying an amused, "The Quality, eh, miss?"

"Good gracious!" Exchanging a startled glance with Beck, Elspeth declared, "I must go down there at once! Poor Mrs. Newell! She must still be worried lest she be arrested!"

Beck poured water into the washbowl and said she doubted the lady had anything to fear now that she was safely out of England. "She can't be took in charge in France, can she?"

"Not by French law officers—or their military. But I believe British authorities can arrest British subjects even in another country if there is sufficient cause, and I fancy Mrs. Newell's relations are powerful."

Elspeth washed and dressed hurriedly and dragged a comb through her tumbled curls. Beck, however, was so upset by this scrambling procedure that Elspeth submitted to being sat down before the mirror while her hair was "dressed as become a lady of Quality."

When she stepped outside, her warm cloak was whipped by the wind that still blew strongly. The dark waves were crowned with foam and the decks of the *Sea Lassie* tilted as she slipped into a trough. Elspeth clutched her hood with one hand and held tightly to the rail with the other. Low-hanging grey clouds scudded across the sky and the misted air reduced visibility, so that although she strained her eyes, she could see no trace of the French coastline. For the moment, at least, the rain had ceased nor was the air as bitterly cold as it had been last evening. A few passengers were huddled on the deck looking miserably ill, and several crewmen were busied with the sails and coils of rope.

Reaching Valerian's cabin door, Elspeth knocked without result. Suddenly she could see again the mischievous grin she'd glimpsed on the Reverend Mr. Boudreaux's face shortly before they'd sailed. At that moment Valerian had been taunting Beck with the warning that they were unlikely to enjoy a smooth crossing. She'd been annoyed by his insensitivity and had commented tartly that they were fortunate to have "such an experienced sailor as Mr. Valerian" to guide them. Mrs. Newell's lips had twitched and the clergyman had definitely looked amused. Very likely the truth was that the Deplorable Dandy was a poor sailor and now lay prostrate in his bunk quite unable to care for his invalid aunt. Irked, she pounded at the door in a sustained and determined assault until it was wrenched open.

"What in Hades—" snarled Valerian, then paused. "Oh. It's you. Well, ma'am? If you must pound on my door at this ungodly hour you should not expect perfection!"

"Per-perfection?" gasped Elspeth. "My goodness, sir! Whatever happened to you? Let me in at once!"

"No! I mean—you can't come in. Just at present."

"But your poor face is bruised and your mouth cut and you look positively—"

"A moment, if you will please to stand clear."

The door was slammed in her face. Elspeth had to jump back to avoid being struck on the nose. Outraged by such rudeness, she raised her fist to knock again, but the door swung open so suddenly that she barely missed adding another bruise to his face. She caught a brief glimpse of Mrs. Newell bending over a bunk, then Valerian had whipped himself outside and pulled the door shut. His cloak swirled about him. He proffered his arm and, ignoring her indignant protests, said blandly, "If you will refrain from striking me, I shall escort you to what is referred to as the Coffee Cabin, ma'am, since I suspect 'tis where you were bound."

"Well it is not," she argued. "And I had no intention to strike you. I simply wanted to—"

"Don't dawdle about." Starting off purposefully, he tugged at her arm. "I cannot—" The words ended in a strangled squawk. He paled and halted abruptly.

"Cannot—what?" she asked, scanning him anxiously.

"Breathe," he gasped, grabbing at his throat. "Gad! I—I never thought . . . that little . . . bastard had . . ."

Elspeth said icily, "Your language is insupportable, sir. And your cloak is caught in the door, merely."

"Oh." Flushed with chagrin, he stepped back and reached for the door.

Elspeth darted forward. "Allow me," she said, and snatched for the latch.

Fingers of steel fastened on her wrist. "Not unless you're so smitten with my cousin that you yearn to see him in his undergarments," he leered, and blocked her view as he

111

opened the door just sufficiently to free his cloak, then slammed it again.

"If *ever* I heard such a whisker!" she exclaimed. "It looked to me as if your poor aunt was tending to Herbert, and what's more—"

"What naughty terms you do use, Nurse Cotton! Your brother's influence, I've no doubt."

Anxiety came into her face at this mention of Vance, seeing which Valerian added quickly, "And if you paid more attention to what should concern you and less to what don't, you'd be aware that the wind is chill, this wretched ship is leaping about like a demented gazelle again and you stand here arguing nonsense though you're likely as hungry as am I. Kindly exercise your feet, madam, and give your tongue a rest."

His hand was resistless. Borne along willy-nilly, she said pantingly, "You seek to turn my thoughts with your filthy language and your—your vulgar insinuations! But I am more than seven, Mr. Valerian! The sailors heard sounds of violence coming from your cabin last night, and you have clearly been indulging in fisticuffs or some such male savagery. If poor Herbert is hurt—"

"Well, he ain't, ma'am." He wrenched open the door to the Coffee Cabin and murmured ominously as he bowed her inside, "He provoked me once too often is all!"

The Coffee Cabin was rather dim and not very large, but there were two long tables and several benches. At one end of the room a counter held a rack containing mugs, tankards and plates, which were protected from falling by means of a guardrail. The only occupant was a morose-looking man who sat holding a steaming mug and surveying them glumly. He said "G'day" in a failing voice.

Valerian replied, "Good day to you, sir," and led Elspeth to the end of the other table. "Sit down and try to control your spleen," he said softly, smiling at her in a besotted, if lopsided way.

"I will not sit down," she said angrily, "until you tell me what you have done to poor Herbert!"

The morose-looking man turned his head and peered at them.

"I murdered him, of course," hissed Valerian, narrowing his eyes in a sinister fashion. "And long overdue."

It was nonsense, of course. But Herbert had certainly been stretched out on a bunk, and aware of the Dandy's ungovernable rages, Elspeth stared at him.

He said reproachfully, "Now only see what you've done! Creating an uproar in front of all these people!"

"There is only one—"

"That's not true, because here comes a trusty tar to discover our wishes." He bent lower and warned, "If you do not want to be thrown bodily onto this bench, madam, lower—your—derriere!"

"Oh!" gasped Elspeth. "You—are insuppor—" But meeting his eyes, she sat down rather hurriedly.

"Mornin,' sir and ma'am." A huskily built seaman with very bushy eyebrows and whiskers touched his forelock respectfully as he approached. His welcoming grin revealed the loss of three front teeth, then disappeared as he exclaimed with a slight lisp, "Crumbs! Come a cropper, did ye, milor'? Seas was roughish last night. Ye ain't the only one with bruises t'show fer it, milor'. Cap'n can't rightly be blamed, though there's them as is blaming him."

"Your *Sea Lassie* took me off-balance and tossed me 'gainst the wash-stand," said Valerian, bestowing a friendly grin on the sailor. "But unless your Captain goes by the name of Neptune, I won't hold him accountable."

"Thankee, I'm sure, sir." The sailor beamed, obviously relieved. "And never worrit 'bout his name what is not Neptoon or naught foreign-like, but plain and simple English.

Ramsbottom, 'e do be. Cap'n Rinalldo Ramsbottom."

"Poor fellow," murmured Valerian, preserving his countenance with an effort.

"Ar," said the sailor, fixing him with a hard stare. "I'll own as 'Rinalldo' be a bit unordin'ry, but he's a man as knows his trade, which a cap'n needs in these waters if he's to manage without the help of a river pilot, and in behoof o' Cap'n Ramsbottom I says again—thankee."

"And nicely said," remarked Valerian, avoiding Elspeth's eyes. "Now what can you offer us this morning?"

"A fine spread, sir, weather considered. We've freshcooked porridge, or a kipper, or eggs boiled or fried, cold roast beef, and crusty French bread and butter. Ale or coffee to wash it down. What's it t'be, milor'?"

Valerian ordered soft-boiled eggs, roast beef slices and the French bread and butter, with ale for himself and coffee "for the lady."

Turning to Elspeth as the big man went off, Valerian said an amused, "Note that rolling gait, Nurse Cotton. 'Tis the mark of all true sons of the sea. Help! Why that terrifying glare?"

"Now that you've finished making mock of the poor soul I—"

"Who made mock?" He argued defensively, "Did I not tell him 'twas nicely said?"

"Yes. And sniggered at him up your sleeve."

"I never snigger. I may have stretched a point, but not far if you stop to think that he was probably born in some malodorous alley but has fought his way into a respectable employment and an impressive vocabulary. D'ye realize, Miss Cotton, how few of our gallant sailor-men would know what 'behoof' means, much less—"

"Oh, how you jabber, sir, and to no purpose for I will not be turned aside! I am waiting to hear what you've done to poor Herbert! And pray do not squander that wistful smile

114

on me! I've noted how you use it to get what you want from gullible folk!"

"No, is it still endearing?" He touched his mouth tentatively. "I feared it might be less effective with a cut lip."

His grey eyes twinkled at her in a way that was very effective indeed, but Elspeth clung to common sense and hissed, "Either answer me at once, Mr. Valerian, or I will ask that honest sailor-man to escort me to your cabin and see for myself whether poor Herbert has been manhandled!"

"What it is, you want for gratitude, Nurse Cotton. I've noted it before." He sighed. "And after I've generously ordered a sustaining meal for you!"

"Without having had the simple courtesy to first ask what I would like," she snapped, momentarily forgetting "poor Herbert."

"Gad, what a turnip-brain!" He clutched his brow. "Our valiant Cap'n Rinalldo will order me keel-hauled for such stupidity! I should have guessed that like all ladies with an eye to keeping their lovely shapeliness, you would prefer no more than tea and a crust of bread!" He pushed back his bench. "Hey! Christopher Columbus!"

"What are you doing?" demanded Elspeth in alarm.

"Why, changing our order, of course. Bad enough that you and I should be seen eating breakfast together, ma'am, let alone that I must undermine your dietary reso—"

"Have done!" she cried, so imperiously that the morose passenger who was half asleep started up and almost dropped his mug. Flushing hotly and lowering her voice, Elspeth pointed out, "The sailor is coming back. I shall ask him to escort—"

"Poor Herbert is merely a victim of mal-de-mer," said Valerian quickly, then asked the Honest Sailorman to see that trays be conveyed to Mrs. Newell and his cousin and to his aunt's maid, who was sharing Nurse Cotton's cabin.

The sailor nodded and went away again.

115

Elspeth eyed Valerian with suspicion. "I do not see how a simple fall would have bruised your face on one side and cut your lip on the other. I think it more likely that you lost your temper with poor Herbert and did away with him, just as you claimed to have done."

" 'Twas a foolish whim to have said such a thing," he admitted. "But you look charmingly when your eyes get so round and I couldn't resist temptation. Besides, I really was ah, taken off-balance, just as I said. There, now, I have done as you asked and here comes our breakfast. I apologize for my presumption in having ordered such a gargantuan meal for you. Do not feel obliged to eat it all, for I quite understand that you are wise to guard against putting on more flesh and—*Now* what have I said? Mercy, but you're hot at hand, Nurse Cotton! Pray be so good as to control your emotions. I believe you have already quite overset our fellow diner."

Elspeth ignored him and smiled upon the Honest Sailorman, who managed to serve them without spilling too much of Valerian's ale. Conversation lagged during the meal. Elspeth was hungrier than she had realised; perhaps the sea air had whetted her appetite, but whatever the cause she found the food delicious and her resolve to eat sparingly was forgotten. Noting belatedly the emptiness of her plate, she threw a guilty glance at the Dandy. He was leaning back against the bench, holding his tankard in one hand and watching her with his sly grin. She felt her face get hot and lowered her eyes.

He asked innocently, "Did you enjoy your breakfast, Nurse Cotton?"

It would be foolish to deny that she had enjoyed it. Flustered, she said, "Yes, I thank you, though—What happened to your hand?"

He shifted the tankard to his left hand at once but she had seen the skinned knuckles, and, triumphant, she said, "You *were* in a turn-up!"

His brows lifted ironically.

"As my brother would say," she added hurriedly. "And—"

"And now"—he rose and pulled back her bench—"now you shall come and visit Poor Herbert and see that there is not a mark on him."

The waves looked even darker and more mountainous as they made their way back to the cabin, their progress slowed by the wind and the gyrations of the vessel. Holding Elspeth's arm securely, Valerian shouted something in her ear.

She asked, "No—what?"

"No seagulls. They go inland during a storm, you know."

"I wish we could do the same. I worry so about Vance. Every hour that passes . . ."

He tightened his hold on her arm and said comfortingly, "I looked over the papers Fitz gave me. His uncle has managed to arrange help for us. And so soon as we have my aunt safely disposed I shall keep my part of our bargain, unless . . ."

He didn't finish the sentence, and peering up at him, Elspeth thought he looked unusually stern. She felt a pang of apprehension but found herself reluctant to ask what disturbed him.

He pounded on the cabin door before entering. "So as not to catch my aunt *en deshabille*," he said.

Herbert let them in. Mrs. Newell, fully dressed, was sitting in the lower bunk, reading a newspaper. Elspeth's concern for Herbert appeared to have been well founded, though in not quite the way she'd supposed. As Valerian had claimed, the young man showed no sign of a violent encounter, but his face had a greenish tinge, and after a mumbled attempt at civility, he retired to another bunk, apologizing faintly as he lay down.

Valerian said with his twisted grin, "There, you see what ails him, m'dear."

"What did you call me?" she demanded suspiciously.

"Gervaise—really," scolded Mrs. Newell.

"A slip of the tongue merely," he declared, and as a faint moan was heard he warned, "Unless you're ready to hold the basin, Nurse Cotton, I would earnestly recommend that you leave us. At once."

Elspeth hesitated. "Ma'am, I am here to care for you. Is there nothing I may do to make you more comfortable?"

"I am comfortable, dear child," said Mrs. Newell. "Comparatively. And my nephew is quite right, you know. If I were you—"

Herbert moaned loudly.

Valerian took Elspeth's elbow. "Abandon your noble heroics, Miss Cotton," he advised, urging her towards the door.

Even as she ceased to resist there came another sound as of someone knocking, only it seemed to her that the sound did not emanate from the outer door. She paused, glancing curiously at the single wardrobe cupboard against the wall. "What on earth . . . ?" she muttered.

"Someone outside," said Valerian, swinging the cabin door open and sticking his head outside. "Very well," he called, then turned back to say, " 'Twas the cabin boy to say we're putting in to port at last. Come along now, ma'am. You should be packing your frills and furbelows so as to—"

"But it was not from outside," argued Elspeth, drawing back. "I feel sure it came from in here."

"That is because we have the haunted cabin," he said, tugging at her arm. "Did I not tell you?"

"Really, Gervaise," scolded his aunt. " 'Twas but poor Herbert, my dear. He is so wretched, and—"

With a crash the wardrobe door burst open. A dishevelled figure leapt out and sprang towards Valerian, who at once pushed Elspeth away from him.

"Murderous traitor!" shouted the newcomer, drawing back his fist.

Herbert jumped from the bunk and reeled forward and the blow intended for Valerian sent him sprawling.

"Joel!" cried Elspeth, recovering from her momentary stupefaction.

Equally astonished, Skye halted as if turned to stone. "Elspeth," he gasped. "What—on earth . . . ?"

Valerian's powerful left jab caught him under the ear and he went down as if shot.

"Oh! You horrid, horrid brute!" exclaimed Elspeth, and snatching up Mrs. Newell's reticule from the wash-stand, she swung it with all her strength at the head of the Dandy. It occurred to her even as she did so that the reticule was much heavier than she had anticipated and there came a brief half-formed thought that perhaps it did contain the jewels Valerian had listed. Whatever the case, the impact brought a smothered cry from him. He went to his knees, then sagged and lay inert on the floor.

8

*F*or an instant the cabin was very still. Elspeth stood staring numbly at the three young men spread out at her feet, fully expecting that Valerian, whom she had begun to believe was indestructible, would get up at any second. He made no move, however. She thought, horrified, 'God forgive me! I've killed him!'

The murder weapon fell from her nerveless hand and landed with a heavy thud.

As if restored by the sound, Mrs. Newell left the bunk and ran to kneel beside Valerian, whispering his name in a distraught fashion that struck Elspeth to the heart. She half-sobbed, "Oh! I didn't think—I didn't mean—I am so sorry!"

Valerian moaned faintly and moved his head.

Elspeth drew a steadying breath and said defiantly, "No, I'm not! He deserved it!" She bent over Skye, who was still motionless. "Joel, dear, please wake up!"

Mrs. Newell commanded authoritatively, "Get some water and a rag, Miss Clayton! Quickly!"

Elspeth went at once to the wash-stand. She soaked a

towel in the water jug, took up the jug and, turning back, saw that Herbert was stirring. She poured a little water on his face and, as he spluttered and coughed, proceeded to pour a much larger amount of water over the Dandy.

Valerian jerked up, swore and clutched his head.

Elspeth knelt at Skye's side and bathed his pale face gently with the dripping towel. "My poor dear," she said sympathetically. "Are you feeling better?"

He blinked up at her and muttered, "I must be . . . dreaming . . ."

"How are you, Herbert?" asked Mrs. Newell. Her voice sounded odd. Glancing at her, Elspeth gained an impression of unladylike abandonment. But even as she wondered that her mind could hold such a prim and nonsensical thought at so tense a moment, she compounded the felony by a vague awareness that the lady had rather big feet.

Herbert said a muddled, "Very—good . . . thank you, sir."

"You little—wretch!" On one elbow and with his aunt's arm still about his shoulders, Valerian was holding the reticule that had struck him down. He sounded faintly admiring rather than enraged, but there was a streak of blood on his temple and he was very white. "Never had so many men at your feet at one time, I'll warrant," he said ironically.

Elspeth felt a pang of remorse, but said a defiant, "I'm sorry if I hit you harder than I'd meant, but you had no business to knock down Lieutenant Skye so viciously!"

"Oh, had I not!" Coming to his feet with the assistance of his aunt, he swayed slightly, then drew a long pistol from the reticule.

Taken aback to discover that so gentle a creature as Mrs. Newell should bravely carry a weapon that she almost certainly would not know how to fire, Elspeth exclaimed, "Good gracious!"

Valerian rasped, "Stand away from him!"

"No! I will not! Are you gone mad, sir? Lieutenant Skye

121

has very kindly come to help me, and there is no—"

"Nonsense! He hadn't the vaguest notion you were here, nor has he come to help your foolish brother, if that's the melodrama you're concocting!" His eyes were narrowed painfully, and he allowed his aunt to guide him to sit on a bunk, but kept the pistol trained on Skye as he called, "How do you go on, Herbert?"

"Better, I thank you." Herbert's voice was still shaken, but he was on his feet and clinging to a bunk. "What're we going to do, Gervaise?"

Skye struggled to sit up and Elspeth helped him lean back against the wall. Bewildered, she said, "Joel, I don't understand. Does Mr. Valerian mean that you've been sent to arrest his poor aunt?"

Valerian uttered a snort of mirthless laughter, then ducked his head, wincing.

Glancing at Mrs. Newell, Skye said coldly, "No, m'dear. I am assigned to arrest an enemy of the Crown we've been chasing these three years! And what in heaven's name you are doing on this packet, and with this unholy trio, is what I cannot fathom! Unless—are you perchance travelling under the protection of Sir Conrad Beech?"

"By no chance! The lady travels under *my* protection," declared Valerian with deliberate double entendre.

"You—lie!" Skye dragged himself to his feet. "You filthy-mouthed swine! Miss Clayton wouldn't cross—cross the street with you! Elspeth, if he has involved you—"

"I'm afraid that is not the way of it," faltered Elspeth miserably. "The truth is—"

"You've no need to explain anything to him," snapped Valerian.

"You prefer to 'explain matters' to my Commanding Officer," Skye flung at him.

Herbert said wearily, "He's right about one thing, Ger-

122

vaise. We have involved the lady. She will likely be judged an accomplice."

"For Mrs. Newell to claim her own jewellery is scarcely treasonable," said Elspeth.

Skye frowned and asked a perplexed, "What jewellery? Elspeth, what jiggery-pokery Canterbury tale have they hoaxed you with? You surely must be aware that this person is not Mrs. Newell?"

Elspeth said uncertainly, "Perhaps the lady had to use a false name whilst we were still in England, but—"

"Enough!" The firm command came from Mrs. Newell, though the voice was harsher than her usual soft tones. Standing, she declared, "I think our charade is done!"

Valerian argued, "Not necessarily. We shall have to be rid of Skye is all. He knows—"

Horrified, Elspeth interposed, "What do you mean—'be *rid* of' him?"

"He means I'm to be thrown overboard," said Skye grimly. "Or murdered and my corpse stowed away somewhere."

Valerian sneered, "Jolly good thinking!"

"How can you be so wicked?" cried Elspeth. "I know that I promised to help you, ma'am, but no jewels ever bought are worth the sacrifice of a human life!"

Skye demanded tersely, "Why would you have made such a promise, Elspeth? Never say you are betrothed to this villain?"

"Of course I am not," declared Elspeth.

Valerian grinned and muttered something *sotto voce.*

Ignoring him and the sensation that, stupidly, her face was red, Elspeth went on: "Mr. Valerian has agreed to help me get Vance home safely, Joel. He has been arrested for acting as courier for Madame de Pompadour. He is wounded and imprisoned somewhere near Rouen, and I am—I am so terribly afraid he will be sent to the guillotine before we can rescue him!"

Skye growled angrily, "And you turned to this traitor for assistance instead of to me?"

"How could I ask you to help me again, when I knew your father would be enraged if you agreed? And poor Nicholas cannot help, because he is recovering from being attacked by Mohocks. Mr. Valerian needed a lady to assist his aunt on a—a matter of personal business, and I needed a gentleman to help poor Vance, so we—we reached an understanding. I know you cannot like it, dear Joel, and that my reputation is very likely ruined, but—truly, Mr. Valerian is neither a villain nor a traitor!"

"Anyone who gives aid to an enemy of the King is a traitor," said Skye inexorably.

"I am not an enemy of the King," declared Elspeth, incensed, "no more is Vance!"

"But I am!" The individual Elspeth knew as Mrs. Newell stood and took off her elegant wig to reveal close-cropped greying hair. With an imperious gesture she commanded in a cultured but decidedly masculine voice, "Be still, Gervaise! I shall make my own apologies, if you please!"

Valerian, who had come to his feet also and attempted to intervene, gave a resigned shrug and was silent.

Gazing from one to the other, bewildered, Elspeth stammered, "*You*—are a traitor, ma'am—er, sir?"

"I am also Sir Simon Valerian." With a weary sigh, the erstwhile 'Mrs. Newell' sat down again.

"Who harbours a fondness for Jacobites," grunted Skye.

Valerian snarled, "Who has a generous heart and a willingness to risk his own life so as to help anyone hunted to a cruel death!"

"They took arms 'gainst their country!" said Skye hotly.

The little cat, which had taken refuge somewhere, now jumped onto the bunk again and made itself comfortable on

Sir Simon's lap. Stroking it fondly, he argued, "They fought bravely for a cause they believed best for England, and when they were defeated they had a right to be treated as honourable men, instead of which they were persecuted and slaughtered like animals!"

Valerian said, "My sire's heinous crime was that he sought nothing more evil than to help them, and—"

"And was so foolish as to get in the way of a musket ball," interposed Sir Simon with a wry smile. "As a result of which my very faithful and gallant son has struggled for three years to keep me hidden, win me back to health and bring me safely to France."

Trying to take it all in, Elspeth said, "But—but everyone believes you and Mr. Valerian are hopelessly estranged."

"A clever ruse," muttered Skye. "Concocted to screen Gervaise Valerian's efforts to protect his father."

Her eyes glowing, Elspeth said, "Oh, my! Well, I think it splendid! So there were no jewels at all, Sir Simon?"

"No jewels, child," he admitted. "My son has a ready imagination. And he strives to see me reunited with his mother, who awaits us in Italy. I'm sorry we had to lie to you, but Gervaise thought that for your own sake the less you knew the better."

Elspeth nodded. "I quite understand, and I am so glad he has stood by you. I'll keep my word and help in any way possible, but—"

"Devil you will!" interrupted Skye angrily. "D'you not realize that by taking part in this crazy scheme you may well be putting your pretty head on the block alongside theirs?"

It was a fearsome truth and Elspeth was suddenly very cold. Her voice trembled slightly when she said, "Mr. Valerian has promised to help free Vance. The least I can do in return is to keep my word to them." Turning to Sir Simon, she added, "But you must not kill Joel, sir."

Valerian said impatiently, "It's his life or ours, and your

125

precious brother's, to boot! Have some sense, do!"

Elspeth smiled into Skye's strained and bruised face. "You will not betray us, will you, my dear friend?"

Skye knew that resolute tilt to her chin and his heart sank, but he did not answer.

Herbert, who had said very little during this intense discussion, now pointed out quietly, "He is a serving officer, Miss Elspeth. He has no choice."

Elspeth looked searchingly at the unhappy Skye. "Joel . . . ? I beg you. Surely, you could just look the other way? Does your Commanding Officer know you suspect us?"

Valerian interposed, "Who is your CO, by the way?"

"A friend of yours, I believe. Joshua Swift."

Father and son exchanged grim glances.

"Well, that throws the fox in with the hens," muttered Sir Simon.

Gervaise said slowly, "Swift is Military Intelligence. You're Navy. Temporary assignment?"

Skye nodded.

"With your future resting on success, I'll wager," said Sir Simon.

"And your father watching you like a hawk." Elspeth sighed. "Poor Joel. Herbert's right—you have no choice. But if we—you gentlemen—were to tie him up and lock him in— in the hold or somewhere, he could not be blamed."

"Were he under my command I'd blame him," grunted Valerian. "Besides, he'd break free and be after us again! We're far from safe yet, Miss Elspeth."

Herbert said, "Perhaps the Lieutenant can offer a solution."

For a moment while they all watched him, Skye was silent, looking down, his lips set into a thin, uncompromising line. He raised his eyes then and gazed at Elspeth. How anxious she was, poor girl, how dear and desirable and foolish. He loved her so very much and he knew how she adored

126

her brother . . . With a sigh that was something of a groan, he said, "If you will allow me to take you back to England, I'll give my word to say nought to the authorities that would jeopardize Sir Simon, or hinder his son's attempt to help Vance. That's the best I can offer, Elspeth."

"And it's not good enough," grated Valerian.

Deeply moved, Elspeth said, " 'Twould mean the ruin of your career, Joel."

"And the breaking of your oath to serve your country," murmured Sir Simon.

Skye reached out and took Elspeth's hand. "My dearest girl—you know how I feel where you are concerned. How I have always felt. You love Vance, but he's a grown man, and must have understood the chances he took when he worked for La Pompadour. He'd not thank me if I allowed you to run yourself into danger. You've taken too many chances already in this forlorn venture. You've tried, Ella. Be done now, and come home with me, I beg you!"

Tears dimmed Elspeth's eyes. She knew how hard he had fought to rise in his chosen career and how much it meant to him. She said huskily, "It is so very dear of you to make such an offer, but—I cannot, Joel. Mr. Valerian really needs me to go with them. Besides, I gave my word!"

"No!" Skye pulled Elspeth aside and faced Valerian, demanding fiercely, "Do you want her to die? Release her of her promise, you conscienceless care-for-nobody!"

Valerian drawled, "Of course I don't want Miss Clayton to die. To the contrary, I shall do all in my power to prevent such a disaster. But *I* care for my father, the *lady* cares for her brother, and forlorn or not, we are partners in this endeavour. 'Twould appear you are the one who puts us all in jeopardy."

Sir Simon said gravely, "Even so, Gervaise, the Lieutenant is correct. Miss Clayton has taken great risks to assist us and should not be held to a promise that will further endanger her."

With the pistol still steadily aimed, Valerian argued, "Without her help it will be more risky to smuggle you ashore, sir. Or smuggle her silly brother out of France! If she chooses to break her given word, however, I'll accept that, and we'll manage somehow. If not—Skye must be dealt with. Make up your mind, ma'am."

Elspeth wrung her hands distractedly. "What a dreadful choice you give me! My beloved brother—or my dear friend!" She reached out to Sir Simon. "Sir—please! I cannot abandon Vance to a cruel death! I cannot! If Mr. Valerian will but promise not to murder Joel—"

Sir Simon looked at his son steadily.

Valerian's eyes fell. "Oh, very well," he growled. "I hope we may not all pay a bitter price! Herbert, find something to tie and gag this military opportunist, and we'll stow him away somewhere!"

After a brief and subdued consultation, Herbert and Sir Simon began to tear a sheet into strips.

Dabbing a handkerchief at her eyes, Elspeth said a choked, "Thank you, Mr. Valerian! I swear I'll do all in my power to help. Joel, dear—forgive me, but—"

Very white, Skye said harshly, "How can I forgive? Not that your friends threaten me, but that your dear life is endangered by their probably ill-conceived schemes. Valerian— at least tell me you *do* have a plan to rescue Vance Clayton."

Valerian said, "We know where he's being held and we've been promised help along the way. To what extent I cannot say."

Skye groaned, "Is that all? My dear God! You'll walk into a hornet's nest and drag this precious lady with you!"

Sir Simon, who was looking increasingly troubled, said, "Gervaise, I am so very grateful for all your care of me, but—"

Valerian intervened, "I know, sir. But 'tis the lady's brother. The decision must be her own."

Skye drew a despairing hand across his eyes, then drew his shoulders back, took a deep breath and said, "Never mind about your blasted makeshift rope. I can't leave Miss Clayton in such careless hands. I shall have to go with you."

They all stared at him speechlessly.

Then, "You'll—what?" said Valerian.

"I mean what I say. I'm coming with you, if only to protect Miss Clayton."

Valerian smiled cynically. "And to report us to the authorities as soon as we land, no doubt! A real feather in your cap that would be, eh, Skye?"

"Joel never would do such a thing!" said Elspeth firmly. "I've known him most of my life. His word is his bond."

Sir Simon observed, "I think we do not have the Lieutenant's word as yet, Gervaise."

"Then you have it now," said Skye resolutely. "I will help in whatever way I am able. I'll not betray any of you. I swear it."

Elspeth gave a smothered sob and threw her arms around his neck.

Skye hugged her tight and over her curls his steady gaze challenged Valerian's scowl.

"Very well," said Sir Simon. "I accept, unless you object, dear boy."

Gervaise grunted and lowered the pistol. "I do object. But I believe he'll honour his word." With a wry grin he added, "Whatever else, it saves us the bother of doing away with the curst nuisance."

"But I am sure 'twas Sir Brian," said Elspeth, peering eagerly at the crowded quay below them.

Valerian muttered, "Do try to restrain your exuberance,

Nurse Cotton. We have no desire to attract attention and if you don't attend to where you're going you'll wheel your patient into the sea!"

"Yes. I'm sorry." Elspeth straightened the Bath chair and sent a guilty glance at "Mrs. Newell."

The wind had eased at last, but the entrance to the estuary was clearly a difficult one. Skye and Valerian had exchanged low-voiced remarks about pilots and unusual tides and "basins" and then been so cheerful that Elspeth guessed they were trying not to alarm her. Despite their obvious concern, however, and as a result of what Valerian had said was some very skilled navigation, the *Sea Lassie* had been manoeuvred safely into port at half-past three o'clock. Elspeth was surprised by the number of vessels riding at anchor or tied up at the quay. Clearly, Le Havre was a much busier port than she'd anticipated. Confirming this, there had ensued an immediate and increasingly confused welter of howled orders, darting sailors, passengers hurrying to and fro and making their way to join those waiting at the rail for the gangplank to be lowered. On the quay people who had come to meet disembarking family members or friends mingled with stevedores and hopeful vendors of pastries, apples, sweets and assorted items few people were likely to need, all shouting their wares at the tops of their lungs. It was among this bevy of humanity that Elspeth had thought to catch sight of her uncle.

They made their way slowly along the deck, Skye in the lead as if travelling alone. Behind him, Herbert carried two valises. Freda, a bandbox in one hand and a dressing case in the other, walked close beside the Bath chair in which "Mrs. Newell" was settled under a warm rug with Pixie curled up on her lap. Elspeth pushed the chair, and Valerian brought up the rear followed by a husky cabin boy laden with the rest of their luggage.

As they neared the gangplank Skye dropped back. Without appearing to address Valerian, he said softly, "More than a customary collection of military down there, have you noticed?"

"I have. Ours."

"And theirs, besides the occasional *garde-cote.*"

Elspeth's heart gave its familiar leap into her throat. She gasped, "Oh, my heavens! Coast Guard?"

Valerian nodded. "I'm glad you speak French, Nurse. You'll need it. They appear to be looking for someone. Have a care, Aunt Geraldine."

Elspeth's nerves tightened.

Sir Simon raised an acknowledging hand.

"Oh, I *knew* we should have sailed with free traders," moaned Elspeth.

Valerian growled, "In which case we'd likely have been apprehended long since!"

Edging forward once more Skye drew level with Elspeth and urged, "It's not too late for you to change your mind, dear soul. I can arrange—"

"You are very good," she said with a dismissing gesture, "but—I cannot. Joel, I saw Sir Brian down there on the quay just now. I'm sure of it!"

"Your uncle? Did you, by Jove! Was he on the packet, then? Or might he have come to meet you?"

"He didn't know I was sailing. Nobody did. But he and Conrad lived abroad for years. Perhaps he had to return to France on some matter of business. If you should see him, do please tell me."

Skye said hesitantly. "I cannot think he would approve of this escapade. He might try to put a stop to it. Likely he could, you know."

Without turning, Elspeth pictured the jut of Valerian's chin and smiled faintly. "In London I think my uncle guessed that Vance is in difficulties. He seemed to sense that I was worrying and urged me to let him help."

Skye said sharply, "Then why did you not? This is man's business and he is a close relation. He has the right—"

"I know he has, and I decided to accept his offer, but when I sent a message to him he and Conrad had suddenly left Town."

Their steps had slowed. Valerian saw the cabin boy eyeing Elspeth and the Lieutenant curiously. Irked, he stamped to them and snapped, "Tend to your business, Nurse! And you, sir, be so good as to stop pestering my servants!"

Skye glared at him, then raised his tricorne politely to Elspeth and strode off towards the group waiting at the rail.

Elspeth said, "He meant no harm and was only trying to—"

"I know what he was 'trying to,' and if you don't *try to* remember your present station in life, my girl, you'll have small chance of seeing your brother again!"

His brows were pulled into a daunting frown and his eyes seemed to shoot sparks at her, but what he said was all too true, aware of which, Elspeth quailed and murmured, "I'm sorry. Sir."

"Well there's no call to fall into a despondency," he said in a kinder tone. "But the next few minutes will be chancy enough without our inviting unwelcome attention."

When they at last reached the rail Valerian removed Pixie from his father's lap and handed her to Elspeth. "I'll take the chair down the gangplank. You take this. And for heaven's sake don't lose it!"

Despite his brusque manner Elspeth noticed that he handled the little cat very gently and that she showed no sign of fear.

Valerian shouted, "Herbert! Where the deuce are you? Come and help the ladies!" Belatedly he saw that Herbert was already on the quay. He cursed under his breath and ordered the cabin boy to assist Nurse Cotton and his aunt's maid if they needed help. The cabin boy, juggling luggage, muttered an indignant response which it was as well the Dandy did not hear.

Sir Simon took possession of the dressing case, allowing Freda to cling nervously to Elspeth's cloak as they stepped onto the gangplank, but her fears were unwarranted; the wind had dropped, the packet rocked gently to the pull of the tide and their disembarking was easy by comparison with the perils of their boarding.

Dry land felt strangely unsteady under Elspeth's shoes, but she could only be grateful that they were safely ashore. Her gratitude was tempered, however, when they were directed to a roped-off enclosure where several passengers were being questioned by uniformed officials.

Valerian leaned to her ear and muttered, "Do try not to look so alarmed."

"But—Joel said those men are Coast Guard officers! Will we be stopped, do you think?"

"Very likely." He took Pixie and deposited the little cat in Mrs. Newell's lap once more. His eyes very stern, he said, "Take the chair again, Nurse, and bear in mind that those fellows are not nearly so much to be feared—at this stage of the game—as the British Intelligence people with whom your dear friend is so merrily chatting!"

Dismayed, Elspeth craned her neck and over his shoulder saw that Skye was indeed in deep discussion with two soberly clad men who at once seemed to her to be ineffably menacing. Handing the dressing case to Freda, she reiterated, "Joel will not betray you, never fear."

"If he does," said Valerian grimly, " 'twill be the last time he betrays anyone! Mistress Beck! Don't stare at people!"

Freda protested, "If ever I heard so many folks jabbering Frenchy-talk!"

Exasperated, Valerian exclaimed, "You're in France, you silly creature! What would you expect?"

"Why I'd think they could talk sensible-like, sir, but only

133

listen to 'em! Nineteen to the dozen, and at that rate they couldn't never understand one single word of it!"

"Lord give me strength!" moaned Valerian.

Sir Simon called softly, "Gervaise . . ."

One of the men who'd been chatting with Skye was approaching. A tall, thin individual, his face was scarred by smallpox and his pallor was accentuated by the fact that he had no visible brows or lashes. He raised his tricorne politely to Mrs. Newell, drew a small notebook from the deep pocket of his coat and said in English, "My apologies, ma'am, that you are delayed."

Valerian demanded autocratically, "Your name, sir?"

A pair of pale shrewd eyes flickered over him. "My name is Ballard. I am here on detached service from Britain's Coast Guard." Consulting his notebook, he murmured, "You, I take it, sir, are a Mr.—er. Dear me! There appears to be some confusion." He smiled and said mildly, "Your cousin gave your name as Nugent, but you are on the passenger list as Mr. Newell . . ."

9

*E*lspeth was sure that her heartbeat was so loud as to drown out all other sounds, and she was faintly surprised when she heard Sir Simon declare in his soft "Mrs. Newell" voice: "Did I not tell you to correct that idiotic error, Gervaise?"

Ballard had bent lower over the Bath chair so as to hear the remark, and slanting a frightened glance at Valerian, Elspeth saw the brief and murderous glare he directed at his cousin. It was gone at once and he replied coolly, "So you did, Aunt. I fear, Mr. Ballard, that I tend to be short of tolerance for stupidity. My unfortunate cousin is besotted over Miss Gertrude Nugent and his few wits are so fixed upon the lady that he gave her name to the ship's purser. I corrected the mistake when we boarded, of course, but I doubt the thimble-wit who confirmed our booking could spell his own name—much less mine. I lacked the patience to do his spelling for him."

"You are arrogant as usual," scolded his "aunt." "And now see the trouble you've caused!"

With a wry smile he admitted, "Mea culpa. And you are right as usual, m'dear. I trust you can prevail upon this zealous officer to spare me from being guillotined out of hand."

"No fear of that, sir," said Ballard. "Especially since Lieutenant Skye vouches for you."

Elspeth felt numb. Wracked with guilt, she didn't hear Valerian's response and dared not glance towards Joel.

Again consulting his notebook, Ballard said, "It is my understanding that you convey your aunt to a physician in Paris. Shall you be returning shortly?"

Valerian answered that he expected to be in Paris for only a few days and, if all went well, would leave as soon as his aunt had consulted with the Specialist. His voice hardening, he said, "By your leave, Ballard, we'll be on our way now. Mrs. Newell is very tired."

"Afraid you shall have to deal with the French authorities first," said the Coast Guard officer. "And I'd clear up the misunderstanding over your name, were I you."

Valerian nodded and directed "Nurse Cotton" to "move along."

Relieved, Elspeth guided the Bath chair forward, thinking, 'Another danger overcome, thank goodness!'

A large hand closed over her own, halting the chair.

Ballard said, "One moment, Nurse! I'll have a closer look at your patient if you don't mind!"

Freda uttered an audible yelp.

Valerian snapped irascibly, "The devil! Now what?"

Elspeth froze and, perfectly sure that she had lost all her colour, gazed blankly at the small flowers that were sewn in amongst the lace fringing Mrs. Newell's cap.

"How," demanded the Coast Guard officer, "do you account for this, sir?"

Time seemed to stand still. What it was, thought Elspeth, was one long series of nightmares. If this horrid creature had discovered Sir Simon's imposture, they were all doomed . . .

She would never be able to help her so loved brother . . . She and Valerian and Herbert and Sir Simon would be tried for treason and executed, as would dear Joel, who had risked so much to try and help them . . . even poor Freda might be accused . . . 'Oh, Lord,' she prayed desperately, 'help us! Please—help us!'

Mr. Ballard leaned down to "Mrs. Newell" and reached out.

From the corner of her eye Elspeth saw Valerian stiffen, then crouch slightly. She recognised that deadly posture and nerved herself to see him whip out his sword. How he could hope to prevail against such odds she couldn't imagine, but she was quite sure he would try to fight his way through if they were threatened with arrest. Tense with fear, she stifled a gasp as he said mockingly, "Jove, but you fellows are all alike! It belongs to my aunt. A wretched object, I grant you, but scarcely grounds for criminal charges!"

Ballard straightened. "What have you to say for yourself, ma'am?" he demanded, holding up the "wretched object."

Dizzied with relief, Elspeth breathed, "Pixie!"

Valerian said with a chuckle, "You won't get much out of her. A preventive tried to appropriate her just before we sailed and got his ears boxed for his pains. My aunt is very fond of Miss Pixie and takes her wherever we go."

"Miss Pixie, is it?" Ballard stroked the little animal and remarked that he appreciated cats. "Much more clever than most folks realise," he said, restoring Pixie to her owner's lap. "D'you mean to take her back with you?"

"Most definitely," said Mrs. Newell sharply.

Ballard grinned. "Then you'd best keep her close, ma'am. Some of the folks here have 'em for supper!"

Mrs. Newell emitted a shocked cry. The Coast Guard officer lifted his tricorne politely, and they moved on.

Freda moaned softly, "Happen I don't faint 'twill be a miracle, Miss Elspeth! What a nasty man!"

"Nonsense," said Valerian. "He was just doing what he's paid to do. Nor did he appear to reduce you to blancmange, Nurse."

"I suppose I may live through this," said Elspeth, her knees feeling very wobbly. "We seem to attract attention wherever we go, which is the last thing we want."

"To the contrary," he argued, "It may stand us in good stead when we come back. I warrant they'll remember the invalid lady with the black cat. Though"—his tone hardened—"I shall likely strangle my blockhead of a cousin!"

"It was a natural enough mistake," argued Elspeth. "You had originally chosen the name Nugent, after all, and in the stress of the moment I suppose your cousin became confused."

"A confusion that could have resulted in your unnatural death! And what's more—"

The sentence was abandoned as they were summoned by the French Port Authorities. These minions of the law were self-important and much less amiable. Questions were thrown at Valerian in rapid succession. A dashing young fellow clad in a splendid uniform demanded to know what was the English monsieur's business in France? For how long did he intend to remain? Where would his party be staying? What was the name of the physician he intended to consult?

Valerian answered in impeccable French and with a cool hauteur that awed Elspeth and seemed to impress the officials. Breaking off in the midst of naming a physician who probably, she thought, did not exist, he raised his quizzing glass, scanned the Frenchman from head to toe and demanded irately, "And what a 'God's name have my affairs to do with you, sir? I've visited your beautiful capital many times and never been subjected to such an inquisition! I've a mind to register a complaint with Charles Fouquet, be damned if I—"

The dashing young officer lost considerable of his dash.

His jaw dropping, he stammered, "Monsieur is—is perhaps acquainted with the Duc de Belle-Isle?"

"There is no perhaps about it," said Valerian with perfect if oblique honesty. "Be so good as to furnish me with your name and unit, and—"

"Ah, but there is not the need, monsieur." All but gabbling in his eagerness to make amends, the dashing gentleman declared, "It is that we are warned to be on the alert. Some dangerous spies they will seek to enter France. Only there is believed to be a beautiful young lady of Quality in their party, whereas you are accompanied only by your servants, who can scarce be described in such terms! You will please not be offended, monsieur, and as you see, you are delayed not one further instant! Your carriage awaits, no doubt? Then by all means, monsieur, convey your so charming aunt and her delightful little cat—is of a blackness that one, no? And Pierre, do but remark the so pretty little whiteness on the tail!—Do proceed, Monsieur Newell, without the further embarrassments! Au revoir, monsieur! A pleasant journey to you!"

They were clear at last! Elspeth guided the Bath chair in shaken silence.

Sir Simon murmured, "Gervaise, you rogue! I'd not known you were acquainted with Charles Fouquet?"

"No more had I, sir. No, never name me rogue. Did I actually make such a claim? If the silly fellow chose to misinterpret my remark . . ." Valerian shrugged.

Sir Simon chuckled and said low-voiced, "And that slippery play on words won our freedom, did it not! Well done, my dear boy. But is there really a coach?"

"Aye, together with a pair of reliable mounts and a suite reserved at a comfortable nearby pension, so Boudreaux advised."

"Bless old Geoffrey's generous heart for all the lives he has saved! Here comes our Herbert. Only see how remorseful he looks. Never glower at him so, Gervaise, you'll frighten him into a spasm."

"I ought to strangle the thimble-wit," growled Valerian. "Much good his remorse would serve had we all been arrested and put to the question! At the very least he'll get a flea in his ear from me! We can't have his careless tongue placing us all at risk! Don't forget, we're responsible for the safety of the ladies, sir."

Herbert came up, looking pale and distressed, to advise that the carriage was waiting to convey them all to the pension. "I am so sorry, sir," he murmured to Sir Simon. "I knew as soon as I said it that I'd used the wrong name!"

"What a very great pity that you didn't know it *before* you said it," growled Valerian. "Try to bear in mind that you carry all our lives in your empty brainbox and make an effort to keep your few wits about you! What ever possessed me to allow you to come with us is past understanding!" He continued to grumble as they made their way to the carriage, Herbert quailing under the lash of his words, and the others maintaining an uncomfortable silence.

Leading a likely looking bay hack, Joel Skye came up with them as they reached the waiting carriage and declared that he would ride escort.

With a stern glance at his cousin, Valerian said pithily, "You risk more than you know, Skye."

"We owe you our thanks for interceding for us with that Coast Guard officer," said Sir Simon. "I only hope you may not pay a high price for your kindness, Lieutenant."

With his ardent gaze on Elspeth's lovely face, Skye answered, "I'm only grateful that I could be of some help, sir. Ballard is an old friend and a good fellow. Still, we were lucky to squeak past, I think."

"This time," grunted Valerian, regarding him without delight.

"Pay no attention to my grouch of a son," advised Sir

Simon laughingly. "He'll not rest easy 'til I am safe in Italy. Do you go to the pension with us?"

"And all the rest of the way," said Skye. "For *I'll* not rest easy 'til Miss Elspeth is safely back in England!"

He handed Elspeth and Freda into the carriage while Valerian engaged in a brief conversation with the coachman.

Herbert loaded their luggage into the boot, then hurried forward to help Sir Simon inside, but Valerian motioned him aside and himself aided his father.

Pausing on the step, his arm across his son's shoulders, Sir Simon asked shrewdly, "What maggot is plaguing your mind now, Gervaise? After all this time you have succeeded in bringing me safely to France, so the first half of your task is almost completed, is it not?"

"It is indeed, sir," said Valerian with rather too hearty optimism.

"Then 'tis the rescue of young Clayton that concerns you. But you said a rescue attempt would be unexpected and easy of accomplishment."

"Aye, and so I think—at least if your friend Lord Boudreaux is to be believed. There are details I must discuss with the coachman, so I'll ride on the box. Now, in with you, sir. And no more fretting. If I have concerns they are to do with my silly chub of a cousin, and the so sickeningly smitten Lieutenant Skye! Gad, what a revolting demonstration of Cupid's archery!"

Sir Simon, who had his own thoughts about Cupid's skills, smiled and climbed into the carriage.

Valerian ordered Herbert to ride with Skye, then slammed the door and swung up onto the box. The coachman cracked his whip, the four sturdy horses leaned into their collars, and the big coach lumbered and creaked on its way with Herbert and Skye riding alongside.

They were surprised to find a small forest in the very heart of the port city and they were intrigued by the abun-

141

dant bird life. Geese, wild ducks and herons were everywhere, only diminishing when the flat land gave way to fields
and occasional low hills, framed always by the bright gleam
of the river.

When they were clear of the town and bowling along
country roads that were in even worse repair than those in
England, Valerian entered into an involved discussion with
the coachman regarding their further plans. Once the details
were known to him, he lapsed into a thoughtful silence.

The miles slipped past, the short winter afternoon began
to fade to dusk and still Valerian said nothing. The coachman
glanced curiously at the stern face and wondered if this elegant young man was daunted by the role he was to play in
the rescue of Monsieur Clayton.

In point of fact, Valerian had not been entirely truthful
with his sire. There was indeed a "maggot" plaguing his
mind. The words of the *garde-cote* officer who had detained
them on the quay still echoed in his ears: "We are warned
to be on the alert. Some dangerous spies they will seek to
enter France. There is a beautiful young lady of Quality in
their party . . ."

The silly clod had been blind to Elspeth's beauty, noting
only that she was a servant. But he had said, "We are warned."
If the fool had a brain in his head their adventure would have
been brought to a tragic end. "We are warned . . ." Who had
warned them? Not the British authorities, surely, for even if
they knew of his attempt to smuggle his father out of England,
they'd be unaware of Elspeth's part in this venture. Skye had
very obviously been stunned by her participation. Unless . . .
was it possible that the relentless Intelligence officer, Joshua
Swift, determined to finalize his long hunt for Sir Simon, had
ordered Skye to pursue them without revealing his awareness
of the part Elspeth was to play? But—no, that was not possible. Not until last evening had any of them known of her in-

voluntary involvement; so how had the authorities learned of it so soon?

He frowned, worrying at it.

Clearly, someone wanted them caught. That someone might very well be an enemy of Jacobites in general or Sir Simon in particular. Conversely, he could be a French diplomat, working behind the scenes for the overthrow of the powerful and dangerous Marquise de Pompadour.

Either way, thought Valerian, their opponents presented a formidable challenge that must be met with the utmost caution. Regardless of who they were, they'd been incredibly fast in relaying the word that Elspeth was with "Mrs. Newell's" little party. From here on there could be no more slips with names—or anything else! They must be ever alert and on guard, for even at this stage of the game it was all too possible that his father could be apprehended and returned to England for trial—and execution!

———※———

Peering from the window as the coach lurched to a stop, Elspeth exclaimed, "What a pretty little house! How lovely it will be to sit at a table that does not leap up and down!"

Skye had already dismounted and now swung open the carriage door and let down the step. "It's almost dark, Valerian," he pointed out. "D'you think your cousin will be able to find the blacksmith?"

"I think Herbert couldn't find the end of his nose without guidance," grunted Valerian, who was very tired.

"And I wish you could find it in your heart to be kinder to the poor boy," chided Elspeth.

" 'If wishes were horses beggars might ride,' " he quoted dryly.

Sir Simon murmured, "Herbert is in unfamiliar country and did not force his mount to lose a shoe. Nor was he obliged to risk his life so as to help in this perilous enterprise."

"True, and clearly I am judged a great villain," sighed Valerian. "But let's make sure we're in the right place before we send out a search party." He jumped down the step, and after a few words with the coachman, he strode up the path to the front door of the cottage.

Sir Simon patted Elspeth's hand. "Try not to judge him too harshly, m'dear. He's had very little sleep and worries too much about me. And to be fair he sets a much higher standard for himself than for others. Poor Herbert cannot always meet it. But in truth Gervaise is more fond of the boy than he admits."

Skye said, "Put up your hood, Elspeth. It's coming on to rain."

Valerian hurried back to them. "This is the right place, thank heaven, but curse this damp! We'd best get you inside, ladies. 'Fraid you'll have to remain Mrs. Newell for another day or so, Father."

Elspeth scanned the lane as he handed her down the step. Logically enough, everything looked strange and unfamiliar. She'd already discovered that Herbert's command of the French tongue was limited and she again wondered uneasily if he would be able to find his way here from the smithy.

Valerian said in her ear, "Stop looking so betwattled. I'll go back for the lame—for my dear cousin."

"Not alone!" she said sharply. "Your papa told me you've had hardly any sleep, and don't forget those two riders we thought followed us from the quay."

"The more reason to fish Herbert out of his predicament. Now hurry into the pension, and try worrying for yourself instead of for everybody else. We'll bring home the lost sheep, if he really is lost."

At that instant Herbert was feeling very much the lost

sheep. He had been quite proud of himself when he'd found the smithy in the failing light, and despite his far from fluent command of the language he had managed to convey his requirements to the sooty blacksmith. The smithy was little more than a cluttered yard and an overgrown shed with large and ill-fitting doors now standing wide. An elegant coach, poles up, waited in the cobbled yard while one of the horses received a new shoe. The procedure seemed to Herbert to take an inordinate length of time, but when at last it was completed it became evident that what the blacksmith lacked in speed he made up in salesmanship, and he convinced the coachman that one of the coach wheels was in need of attention.

The darkening sky caused Herbert's apprehensions to increase, but his attempts to have his own mount shod before the smith worked on the coach wheel were brushed aside. The smith muttered something to the coachman about *les milor Anglais*, and they both looked at Herbert from the corners of their eyes and sniggered.

Fuming, he struggled to come up with a sharp demand for immediate service and, trying to speak as authoritatively as his cousin would do, stammered, *"Aussi vite que je peux!"* which caused them both to roar with laughter. Clearly, his command had not been received as he'd intended. The smith waved a placating hand at him and said something he interpreted to be a suggestion that he be at ease, and a promise that his horse would be shod very soon. This seemed doubtful; the smith's movements were leisurely and he paused often in his work to chat with the coachman. Herbert realised that he stood little chance of leaving the smithy before the light was completely gone. Unhappily aware that Valerian would judge him a proper gudgeon if he became lost and delayed them, he stamped out into the lane.

It was already almost dark and there was no sign of a moon, besides which it was starting to rain. He peered about hoping to fix some familiar landmark in his mind so that at least he'd know which way to turn once he started off. There was a tavern of sorts a short distance from the smithy; perhaps he could enquire there for directions to the pension. If he could recollect the name of the place . . . ! With a smothered groan at his own stupidity, he turned back into the smithy, only to recoil with a shocked exclamation as a yelp sounded directly behind him.

"Do please take care, sir!" cried a childish and very English voice. "You stamped all over him!"

Jerking around, Herbert faced a boy of about seven who clutched a small dog in his arms. Both boy and dog regarded him resentfully.

"My apologies," he said. "I didn't see you. You're English, aren't you?"

"I am half English. My mama is French. You may stroke my Tueur if you want to make up with him. He may forgive you, though he is very fierce."

Undaunted, Herbert availed himself of the offer; the small ears went back, the dog wriggled ecstatically and licked his hand. "Tueur," he repeated uncertainly. "He doesn't seem very terrible to me, but I think I am forgiven."

"Course. Animals are better forgivers than people are." The boy giggled and added mischievously: "You don't speak French, do you sir?"

"Very little, I fear. Didn't I pronounce it properly?"

"Oh, yes, only *tueur* doesn't mean 'terrible.' It means 'killer'! I named him that 'cause my papa calls him a nondog, and Tueur's feelings get hurt. I could tell you didn't speak much French when you made the blacksmith laugh. My papa says the fellow is of an impert'nence."

Herbert felt his face get hot. "There was nothing to laugh at," he said defensively. "I simply told him to shoe my horse as quickly as he can."

The boy giggled again.

With a rueful grin Herbert asked, "Didn't I?"

"No, sir. You told him—you told him to ... to do it as quickly as *you* can!"

They both laughed heartily and the small *tueur* barked with excitement.

A lantern was raised, sending a beam directly into Herbert's eyes. Dazzled, he heard a male voice exclaim in English, "By Jove, sir, but you've a charming smile! Small wonder you've captivated my son."

A large hand was extended. Blinking, Herbert took it and introduced himself. The shadowy stranger, who was materializing into a tall, stout gentleman, responded with the information that he was Sir Harold Walters, conveying his son, Luke, to Paris to visit his maternal grandparents. They exchanged a few commonplaces, Sir Harold confiding that the blacksmith was a curst lazy fellow who worked with the speed of an intoxicated snail. He was excessively bored and invited his fellow traveller to join him in a game of dice while they waited.

Herbert hesitated. Sir Harold had a rather odd way of leaning very close and scanning his face penetratingly. Ruddy-complected, he had a ready smile that revealed yellowing and uneven teeth, but despite rather harsh features he seemed an amiable gentleman. Herbert, very aware that he was not quick-witted, found it a pleasant change to be so immediately approved of and accepted as an equal. The end of it was that they adjourned to the coach, Sir Harold's coachman lit the lamps, dice and a board were brought out, these soon augmented by a flask of wine. The two players were fairly well matched at the game and enjoyed a discussion on French customs and cooking. Sir Harold called to his son to come in with his "non-dog." The boy and his pet climbed into the coach and proceeded to fall asleep, and time slipped away pleasantly enough until the carriage door was wrenched open and an irate voice cried, "So here you are!"

"Oh, egad!" gasped Herbert, confronted by a handsome but enraged countenance.

Tueur woke up and yapped half-heartedly.

"You were not asked to speak!" Valerian informed the small animal.

Recognizing the voice of authority, Tueur sat down and wriggled hopefully.

"Nor were you asked to sh-shcold our non-dog," observed Sir Harold, who had not stinted himself with the wine.

Valerian ran a scornful glance over him, then demanded, "What the deuce are you about, cousin?"

Herbert stammered, "It is—I was j-just getting my horse shod, Gervaise!"

"Ish this cross-grained fellow your coushin, then?" enquired Sir Harold.

"One might think you'd had every horse in Le Havre shod," snorted Valerian, rendering Tueur ecstatic by scratching behind his ears. "I've had to abandon my—the ladies in that dismal pension while I wasted *hours* searching for you in the confounded rain! And what do I find? Here you lounge, cosy and warm, well on the way to being lushy and having a jolly time gaming with this—person!"

"I shay now," protested Sir Harold, blinking at him. "Y'got no right t'call me a p-pershon! Have a droppa wine. Make y'feel better!"

"No, really, Gervaise," said Herbert. "Not *hours*, surely? I can see why you're put out, and I apologise. But the smith was so slow, you see, and—Jupiter! I'm forgetting my manners! This is Sir Harold Walters—Mr. Gervaise Va—Newell."

Valerian groaned and shot him a dagger glance and Herbert bit his lip in mortification.

"How de do, Mr. VaNewell," mumbled Sir Harold affably. "Y'r coushin's right 'bout the smith. Slow's three shnails."

"Well, he's long finished and waiting to be paid. And since I've much to do, you'll excuse if I drag my cousin away.

Good evening, sir. Try if you can stir your stumps, Herbert!"

Flushed with embarrassment, Herbert shook hands with his new friend, murmured an apology and said his farewells.

Sir Harold leaned closer and although his eyes were reddened, once again his gaze was fixed on Herbert's face as he murmured with a grin, "Hot at hand f'la, ain't he! Never mind 'bout hish hoity-toity mannersh. I'd like another word or two with you, but—" He glanced at Valerian from the corner of his eye and amended hurriedly, " 'Nother time, p'raps. Well met, Bert. Jolly fine shmile. Said it 'fore. Shay it 'gain. Charmin'."

Outside the air was chill and a drizzling rain veiled the lights from scattered cottages. Valerian rode out at speed but was obliged to slow so as to find his way. Herbert spurred to come up with him and said humbly, "I'm truly glad you found me, Gervaise. I doubt I'd have remembered how to get back to the pension."

"Since you again failed to remember that I travel under the name *Newell*, not *Nugent*, I doubt it also."

They rode on side by side in silence until Valerian demanded abruptly, "Disguised, are you, coz? *He* was, surely!"

"The deuce! I'm no such thing! Sir Harold allowed me to share his wine is all, and I took very little."

"Why? I mean, why did he share his bounty with you? Had you his prior acquaintance?"

"Not previously, no. I chanced to meet his little son and his dog, and then Sir Harold and I got to chatting. I know it may not have been quite the thing since we'd not been introduced, but—well, he—took a fancy to me, I think." There was no comment and he added shyly, "He—he said he liked my smile."

"Did he, by Gad! To judge from the way he gawked at you one might think he was eager to adopt you!"

Irritated, Herbert said with rare hauteur, "Is that so? I

collect you'd think it more likely for him to have taken me in aversion. Not *everybody* does, you know!"

"True. Don't fly into a pucker. Have you a pistol handy?"

"In my pocket. Why? Trouble?"

"Just keep your eyes open. It's damnably dark—which may be as well. After I left the pension those two varmints we saw earlier followed me for a short while. I gave 'em the slip. Likely they were after my purse. I hope that's what they were after."

"You think they were thieves?"

"Perhaps."

"You're not convinced. Jove! You never fancy they were after Sir Simon? Lord forbid he should be taken at this stage of the game!"

"They weren't military. I'd swear to that. At least Skye's there. They could be after Miss Clayton. Though why? . . . and how anyone could know who she is . . ."

"True. And Lieutenant Skye's a good man. As you said, they were probably thieves, and—Hi! Hold up! Gervaise! Not at the gallop on this road, you madman! Slow down! Do you want to break your neck?"

His cousin's alarmed shouts faded as Valerian, narrowed eyes peering into the darkness, urged his horse to greater speed. In a remote fashion he knew that Herbert was right. It was reckless to ride at such a rate on a dark and unfamiliar road. But the unease that had gibbered at him since he'd left the pension had tightened its grip. His suspicions of the men who'd seemed to be following him had been lulled by the fact that they'd been well mounted. Now the thought kept recurring that they'd been too well mounted to be a couple of common thieves! What a fool not to have realised that fact before! In the event of real trouble Joel Skye and Sir Simon would acquit themselves well, of that he was sure. But—if they should be taken by surprise . . . his father was still weak . . . and Elspeth was much too beautiful! If she should be harmed . . .

He swore and snarled through gritted teeth, "I'll have their rotten hearts out! I swear it!"

10

*H*ow very nice you look, Miss Clayton." "Mrs. Newell" smiled as Elspeth came back into the cosy parlour of the pension, having, as she said, "tidied" herself. Sir Simon had a kind heart, and being sensitive to the feelings of others, he was very aware of the worry that lurked at the back of this young woman's beautiful eyes. "It never ceases to amaze me," he said, "that after the most trying ordeal you ladies contrive to look refreshed and immaculate in the wink of an eye, whereas we hapless males continue to be rumpled and dishevelled for hours! Come and sit beside me, child. You must be tired."

"And hungry," she admitted, returning his smile but crossing to peer out of the front bow window. "But you look neither rumpled nor dishevelled—*ma'am*." He groaned, and she added with a chuckle, "Quite the lady of fashion, in fact."

"How you can endure all these frills and furbelows I shall never know." His voice lowered and he said with earnest intensity, "Nor shall I ever be able to thank you for so bravely helping us in this chancy endeavour."

Elspeth came to sit on the sofa near his Bath chair and he reached out to pat her hand. "Never look so troubled, my dear. Gervaise is a man of his word. And with Herbert and that fine young naval officer to help, why they'll win your brother free in jig time. Speaking of Mr. Skye, where is he?"

"In the stable, tending the horses. Joel is very particular about his cattle. And you're right; I know they'll do all they can to help Vance." She was gripping her hands tightly and, seeing that he watched her, said apologetically, "I don't mean to fret, but—but surely your son must have come up with Herbert by now?"

"Perhaps Herbert missed his road, or they were delayed at the smithy. Whatever the case, Gervaise seldom fails at what he sets his hand to, I promise you. And you're worrying at something else, no?"

Stifling a sigh, she nodded. "My godmama, Madame Colbert, you know, has been only good to me and I ran off leaving her with a pack of lies!"

"You must have given her some explanation or she'd not have let you go. Will she have missed you already?"

"I pray not, else she'll be worried to death!"

He said kindly, "I feel sure the lady will understand you were desperate to help your brother."

"If she knows that, yes. But—well, I thought I could arrange things and hire men to rescue Vance. I mean, this has been exciting, but I'd no intent to—to—"

"You mean you'd not anticipated being well-nigh kidnapped by my errant son and inveigled into helping me."

"I don't begrudge that, sir. I just wish I could have got word to her, but I dared not send back a message with my coachman for fear of alarming Godmama perhaps needlessly, besides implicating Lieutenant Skye, and I clung to the hope I would be safe home again before she realised I'd not told her the truth. Do you think I am making mountains out of molehills? I don't mean to be silly, 'tis only that—the time is flying past and—and I dread to think what my poor Vance may be enduring."

"From what I've heard of him, your brother is a high-couraged young fellow. If he's anything like his lovely sister, he must be! Now take that scared look from your pretty eyes, and have faith in my son. I know he must appear a foppish Dandy to you, but—"

"No, indeed!" she said with a vehemence that delighted him. "Mr. Valerian is not at all what he seems! I'll own that at first I thought him—well, I didn't much like him, but . . ."

He prompted gently, "But—you've changed your mind, I think."

"Oh, yes. He pretends to be cynical and a care-for-nobody, but he's not really like that at all. I've seen him be very kind and considerate."

"He has been so to me, certainly."

"Of course. You are his papa and 'tis clear to see he idolizes you."

Sir Simon smiled but was silent.

After a moment Elspeth murmured half to herself, "When he thinks no one is by there is quite a different light in his eyes. I only wish—" She broke off, embarrassed to realise she was saying more than she'd intended. Pixie came scampering in from the kitchen, and to hide her confusion Elspeth bent to stroke the little cat. "Here is a case in point: your son affects to dislike your pet, but he plays with her and I believe is quite fond of her."

" 'Twas Gervaise brought her to keep me company. And you're perfectly right, Miss Clayton. You're aware that for years he played a part so as to conceal the truth from the world?"

"The truth being that he was striving to bring you safely out of England, which the authorities would never suspect, since everyone believed you to be hopelessly estranged."

"Almost everyone." Sir Simon tightened his lips and murmured, "There is one very zealous officer in London . . ."

"Joshua Swift?"

He nodded. "A dangerous man."

Troubled, Elspeth said, "Who is now Joel's superior officer, temporarily, at least."

"So I understand." Sir Simon shook his head. "Your young naval friend is taking a most desperate chance for your sake. Swift is relentless and has hunted me for so long that I think it has become a sort of obsession with him."

With ready sympathy, Elspeth said, "It must have been a dreadful time for you—and for Mr. Valerian."

"I'll own it has been a long and difficult struggle, with many setbacks. Sometimes we came so close to success only to be balked at the last minute. My son has railed so furiously 'gainst what he calls 'our archaic laws and Pitiful Parliamentarians' that at times I've really feared for his safety. I also fear he has become rather hard and embittered. I can only pray that a real love will come into his life and warm his heart."

Her cheeks rather pink, Elspeth avoided his eyes.

Pixie, who had been stalking an unwary twig, sprang onto his lap, and he said with a twinkle, "This little lady has quite won my own heart, but 'tis past time for Gervaise to make me a grandpapa, you know."

"And past time for supper, ma'am," said Freda, bustling into the room and bringing a welcome aroma of cooking with her. "The French lady and her cook can talk more'n any two ladies I ever heard, not that I understand a word of it. But she's a fine cook for all that, and—"

A piercing scream in the corridor cut her words short.

Sir Simon whipped his chair around and Pixie jumped to the floor and disappeared behind the sofa.

Elspeth sprang to her feet.

Joel Skye staggered into the room, obviously barely conscious, blood trickling down his face, while a burly individual with cold eyes and a mirthless grin held his right arm twisted up behind him.

"Oh, *lor'!*" wailed Freda, her eyes all but starting from her head.

The intruder gestured with the pistol he grasped in his free hand. In French he snarled, "No screeches. We want no more of the screeches! You do as we say, no one will be damaged."

A second man with a scrawny wig and a red, confident face swaggered in. "Madame, she is bound and will be quiet, and the two servants are locked in a cupboard." He looked at Elspeth curiously. "This is the one? You're sure of it? She is a servant, merely. She waits on the old woman." He glanced at Freda. "These both are servants. It is my thought that we are led astray, Pepe."

"If you have come for money," said Sir Simon, his Mrs. Newell voice faint and trembling, "you risk your heads for very little."

The large "Pepe" released his victim's arm and gave Skye a shove towards the sofa. Skye, who had appeared scarcely able to stand, spun around, his fist shot out and Pepe howled and reeled back, the pistol falling from his hand.

Skye lunged for the pistol but he was slowed and a third rogue ran from the kitchen to kick the pistol clear and flourish a wicked-looking knife under Skye's nose. A wiry fellow with a narrow ferrety face and savage eyes, he invited mockingly, "Well, come on, hero! You wouldn't let a few inches of steel postpone your gallantries?"

Skye had to jerk back to avoid the blade. Pepe picked up his pistol, eyed Skye murderously and started for him. "I do not like to be struck," he growled.

Sir Simon quavered, "There is not the need for violence. Tell us what you want."

"This," said Pepe, and with a swipe of his pistol sent Skye to his knees.

Elspeth cried out and ran to him as he crumpled against the sofa.

Pepe pushed her away and drew back his boot.

Freda screamed shrilly.

"Stop, you horrid creature!" cried Elspeth.

The latest arrival said laughingly, "Have done, Pepe. We waste time and you frighten the women."

"Yours is not the tooth that is now loose," grumbled Pepe.

"But Georges he is right," said the red-faced bully. "That one"—he pointed at Elspeth—"speaks like the Quality and she has with it the English way. Let us take her and go before the others they come."

Elspeth shrank back, and although unaware of what had been said, Freda was further alarmed and ran to cling to her.

Sir Simon wheeled his chair forward. "Now you just listen to me—"

The ferrety Georges who was evidently the leader of this unlovely trio said contemptuously, "Keep your mouth closed, hag!"

Pepe jerked the Bath chair aside roughly. "Out of the way, Grandma!" he brayed. His jaw dropped then, and he stared in stupefaction as "Grandma" sprang from the chair and whirled about, skirts flying. A well-aimed fist whizzed at him, his sagging jaw was closed with efficiency if not kindness and he measured his length on the floor.

The red-faced man stared in disbelief at this militant "old lady."

Georges, made of sterner stuff, swung up his knife.

Elspeth seized the Bath chair and with all her strength sent it hurtling at Georges, who skipped aside to avoid it.

Recovering his wits, the red-faced man snatched up Pepe's pistol and held it steadily on Sir Simon. "This one, I think, is not what she seems," he remarked.

"But can be dealt with," said Georges. There was no

157

trace of amusement in his face now. He added curtly, "Give the pistol to me. Now—get that fat idiot on his feet. As for you, madame"—he stared at Sir Simon who had returned to the Bath chair—"or is it monsieur? There is a story here, and one that I feel is in my best interests to know. You will of a certainty be willing to share it with us."

"I perceive that you are a considerable optimist," drawled Sir Simon.

Georges said sharply, "Armand!" and tossed his knife to the red-faced man. "I think a little persuasion with this, and the so strange 'lady' will confess his sins to—No—not him, you fool!" He jerked his head towards Freda. "The little servant is a good screamer, as we have heard."

"My Gawd!" wailed Freda, as Armand, leering menacingly, started towards her, knife in hand.

Wrapping her arms about the terrified girl, Elspeth cried, "We have nothing you can want. Why—"

Armand seized Freda's arm.

Elspeth promptly boxed his ears.

He cursed and slapped her hard even as the front door flew open.

Entering, Valerian's eyes widened. "Be *damned!*" he gasped.

Several things happened very fast. It seemed to Elspeth that he crossed the room in a blur and a glitter of steel. Holding her stinging cheek, scarcely daring to breathe, she heard the man who had struck her howl louder than Freda had done and saw him stagger towards the kitchen, hugging his middle.

She screamed a warning as Georges swung up his pistol and fired at Valerian, who ducked swiftly.

Sir Simon sprang at Georges from the Bath chair. It was a valiant effort, but the sick man was no match for this healthy rogue and Valerian leapt to his defence.

The big Pepe snatched up a chair and whipped it at Valerian's back.

Skye, dragging himself up onto the sofa, stuck out his foot and Pepe went down with a crash that rocked the room and flattened the chair.

Snarling like the ferret he so resembled, Georges wrenched Sir Simon into a shield in front of him, one arm hooked around his throat. "If you do not wish to watch me break the neck of whatever this is, you will surrender," he shouted.

Valerian hesitated.

Sir Simon kicked back. "Mrs. Newell's" high Spanish heel ground into Georges's shin, and as his grip slackened Sir Simon flung himself clear.

Sword levelled, Valerian sprang to the attack.

The front door burst open again, slamming against Valerian and sending the sword spinning from his hand.

Stamping inside, Herbert stared around that violent room and stammered a bewildered "What—the deuce . . . ?"

Georges decided that enough was enough. With an incoherent shout to his accomplices, he raced for the kitchen.

Leaping to retrieve his sword, Valerian collided with Pepe, who had struggled to his feet. The big man struck out in panic, and caught off-balance, Valerian reeled.

Belatedly comprehending, Herbert ran to steady him. "Hey!" he exclaimed, stepping on the fallen sword.

"Oh, get *away!*" snarled Valerian, tugging at his sword with one hand and exasperatedly pushing his disastrous cousin aside with the other.

There came the sound of pounding hooves in the lane.

Sir Simon panted, "They're off, lad. Just as well."

"Like *hell!*" Valerian spun to face Elspeth, his eyes frantic. "Are you all right? That bastard—my apologies, but he is!— struck you!"

159

"I'm all right," she assured him, managing a shaken smile. "And you were splendid—as usual."

"Splendid," agreed Sir Simon. "But not quite 'as usual,' eh, lad?"

His gaze still fixed on Elspeth, Valerian shrugged. "Nought to matter, sir."

Herbert said contritely, "I'm dashed sorry. I didn't mean to rush in and spoil everything."

"We know that," said Sir Simon. "You'd best go and see to our proprietor, and her servants, they're likely overset by this uproar. And perhaps Mistress Freda can find water and some linen, since my son persists in bleeding all over her rug!"

Freda moaned but went with Herbert to the kitchen regions at once.

Whitening, Elspeth cried, "Heavens! You're hurt! Where?" Scanning Valerian anxiously, she saw the tear in his sleeve and commanded, "Take off your coat!"

Joel Skye helped him remove the coat and Elspeth gasped to see that the ruffle of his left shirt-sleeve was wet and crimson. "Oh my! We must get you to bed!"

"Stuff. It's a scrape, merely." He sat on the arm of the sofa and glanced at his father. "I didn't jump far enough, I'm afraid. Or perhaps that wart with the pistol had such poor aim I'd have been wiser not to have dodged at all!"

Skye said, "Let me do that, Elspeth." He ripped the torn ruffle and, examining the wound, said, "A deep graze, no worse, fortunately."

Sir Simon had left his chair so as to inspect the injury. He said calmly, "I think you're right, Lieutenant. But I am unfortunately acquainted with bullet wounds. It must be properly dealt with."

Freda came back carrying a tray with a bowl of water and medical supplies, and Herbert escorted the pension's hostess to join them. A tall woman of late middle age, Madame Bossuet had kept her figure; she was neatly gowned and wore a fashionable wig which just now was rather lopsided on her head. Catching sight of Valerian's bloodied sleeve, she threw up her arms, wailing tearfully that never had such violence been perpetrated in her pension; that her cook had nigh suffered a spasm, and her maid would probably desert her! Her voice rose to near hysteria.

Herbert drew back in alarm.

Valerian said soothingly, "They were thieves, madame, but they have fled and I promise you they won't come back now they know we are armed and ready for them. I am only sorry you have suffered such a distressing experience. As for me, have no fear, this trifling hurt will not even require the attention of an apothecary."

She dabbed a handkerchief at her eyes and smiled at him uncertainly. "Mrs. Newell" leaned forward to take her hand and pat it while talking to her with warm sympathy.

Valerian turned to his cousin and said in English, "Don't stand there taking root, Herbert! Help the poor lady back to the kitchen and give her some wine."

"Your sire is taking better care of her than I could," Herbert protested. "I tried to calm her down, but you know very well my French ain't fluent."

"I also know that my father is tired. She won't mind your incoherencies. Just hold her hand and smile kindly and the poor creature will accept you as a native son."

His cousin looked dubious but was glad enough to do something to redeem himself and led their hostess back into the kitchen. Pixie emerged from behind the sofa and with tail held high darted after them in pursuit of the enticing smells of cooking.

Skye had cut away Valerian's torn shirt-sleeve and Elspeth began to bathe the gash.

Valerian flinched a little. She lifted anxious eyes to his face and he said lightly, "You're doing very nicely, ma'am.

Had some experience with that hare-brained brother of yours, eh?"

She smiled, but she was still very pale and the sight of the darkening bruise on her cheekbone infuriated him.

Frowning, he said, "You must think me a poor champion. I should have cut that filthy swine's heart out! I'd meant to, you know."

"From the way you looked," said Skye with a grin, "I believe you!"

With his gaze steady on Elspeth, Valerian growled, "When I think that he dared—he *dared* to strike you! By God! I hope he comes my way again!"

Suddenly shy, she met his eyes squarely and saw the fury in their grey depths soften into an expression that took her breath away. It was a brief awareness, then she bent to her task again.

The room was hushed. Neither of the two men who witnessed that revealing exchange spoke, and their reactions were very different. Sir Simon was faintly smiling, but it seemed to Joel Skye that time was frozen and he watched the little tableau as from a great distance, a smile very far from his eyes and his lips set into a thin, tight line.

Elspeth finished her bandage as Herbert came to announce that Madame Bossuet urged them to prepare for dinner. They were all tired; Elspeth longed for her bed and had to force herself not to snap at Freda, who gabbled on incessantly about their "drefful ordeals," and that she "dursn't think" what dear Mrs. Clayton would say if any of it reached her ears.

Elspeth's thoughts had taken a different turn. She judged Valerian to be near exhaustion, but her recommendation that he lie down upon his bed, where a tray could be carried to him, was flatly rejected. She protested indignantly that she'd done her best for him but he must face the fact that he had taken a nasty cut and she could only do so much to help. Her efforts, he acknowledged gratefully, were very much appreciated but there were still plans to be made, and speedily. Persisting, she turned to Joel and pleaded that he add his "always sensible" opinion to her own, only to be shocked when he replied with unusual acerbity that Valerian was a grown man who must be aware of his limitations. Sir Simon promised he would see to it that his son retire directly after they dined, with which she had to be content, and Valerian bowed and thanked "Nurse," then went off to find another shirt.

It was a weary and subdued group who gathered in the dining room shortly afterwards. Valerian came downstairs, his elegance restored, bringing with him a cheerful attitude, reminding them of their successes to this point and urging that they not put on the airs of a funeral party.

The stout and rosy-cheeked maid who carried in a large tureen of leek soup looked pleasurably excited rather than distraught. Madame Bossuet seemed less nervous as she filled serving bowls and explained to "Madame Newell" that Cook had done her best to ensure that the guests would enjoy a splendid dinner. Cook fulfilled this promise, following the excellent soup with a steamed fish stuffed with crabmeat, creamed mushrooms, tiny potatoes tossed with butter, and fragrant freshly baked rolls; the second remove consisted of chicken wrapped in flaky pastry, green beans with pearl onions, and thinly sliced beef stewed in red wine, which latter dish was provided, declared Madame Bossuet proudly, especially for the English palates around her table.

Sir Simon and Herbert did justice to this excellent repast, but Elspeth noted that Valerian ate sparingly and took no wine, which his father murmured was "very wise." She was rather ashamed to discover that in spite of the ordeals of this hectic day she was ravenous, and she even indulged herself with a small portion of the caramel creme that was served with sugar wafers and tarts as dessert.

Conversation was guarded while Madame Bossuet or the maid were in the room. When the meal ended and the ladies adjourned to the front parlour, Valerian, Skye and Herbert lost no time in joining them.

"Now we must decide our route," Valerian began, then stopped as his father lifted a delaying hand.

"A moment, Gervaise," said Sir Simon, stroking the little cat which had again taken possession of his lap. "Do you know what our unwelcome visitors wanted with you, Miss Elspeth?"

Valerian had leaned back wearily in his chair but at this he jerked upright, flinched involuntarily but demanded, "What's this?"

The fierce struggle and her impromptu attempt at nursing had driven the memory from Elspeth's mind, but she now felt a pang of apprehension and exclaimed, "Good gracious, that's right! I'd quite forgot! And indeed, I've no least notion, sir."

"About what? Tell me!" demanded Valerian.

Skye said, "As far as I recall, one of them, the ringleader, I think, said that Miss Clayton is of the Quality, and English, and that they should take her away at once!"

"My dear God!" gasped Valerian. "Did they think to hold an English lady for ransom? Is that why they followed us?"

Sir Simon pursed his lips, then said slowly, "I rather doubt it. They were definitely looking for someone. In fact— this was while you were down, Lieutenant—one of them said that Miss Elspeth was dressed like a servant, and he thought they had been . . . ah, 'misled' was the word, as I recall. I was surprised, as I'd assumed they'd come for me!"

Valerian lifted a hand to his temple and muttered dazedly, "As had I. Jupiter! I'm properly bowled out!"

"But since they apparently didn't want you, sir," said Herbert, "why would they have tried to abduct Miss Clayton, unless it was for the white-slave traffic?"

Valerian said, "Or perhaps they planned to use her to force her brother to tell what was in the letter he carried and what has become of it."

Skye saw that Elspeth was looking frightened and he said gently, "Never fret, ma'am. They didn't succeed and you may be sure we'll guard you from now on."

"But how could they know who I am, or why I am in France?" argued Elspeth, bewildered. "Nobody knew. Even my poor godmama doesn't know! 'Twas such a scrambling last-minute arrangement."

"What other reason could there be?" said Herbert. "If it were just a matter of kidnapping an English lady for ransom, heaven knows there are plenty of them in France. Not only did they go to the trouble of following us here, but they appear to have been intent on you and you alone, ma'am. No, to my . . . mind . . ." He glanced at his cousin and the glare in the grey eyes caused him to falter, "Not that I want to—to alarm you, Miss Elspeth."

"How glad I am to know that," snarled Valerian.

"I think 'tis a puzzle we're not like to solve tonight," interposed Sir Simon. "Gervaise, you should be in your bed, and I'm very sure Miss Clayton is weary. Let us retire now and—"

"Before we do, and by your leave, sir," said Valerian sharply, "I must tell you that a coach will come early in the morning to convey you to meet Mama."

Sir Simon's eyes blazed and a flush warmed his haggard cheek. "You believe we are safe, then?"

"Unless our naval gentleman has a surprise for us," answered his son, his sardonic gaze turning to Skye.

"Did I intend to spring that surprise, I'd have arrested Sir Simon at the port, where I'd have had plenty of help," said Skye with cool deliberation. "As it is, I go wherever Miss Clayton goes."

"Which is—where, lad?" asked Sir Simon anxiously.

Valerian glanced to the closed door, then leaned forward and said softly, "To a chateau on the Seine near Rouen."

Herbert asked, "Do we ride, or hire a boat?"

"You and the Lieutenant ride," answered Valerian. "Miss Clayton and her maid will travel in the coach Lord Boudreaux has so kindly provided us."

Elspeth's heart had sunk at the prospect of another water journey, but at this she said, "How very helpful he has been. Shall we be driven by the same coachman? The little man who drove us today?"

"Just so. He is called Marcel and I gather has worked for Lord Boudreaux on several occasions."

"You are sure he's trustworthy?" asked Herbert uneasily. "If you've doubts about the fellow, I can drive us. I can handle a four-in-hand, you know."

"Heaven forfend," said Valerian. "The last time you drove for me—"

Flushing darkly, Herbert interrupted, "That's not fair. You said yourself it was the fault of Miss Clayton's coachman."

Elspeth opened her mouth to argue this point, but meeting Herbert's unhappy glance closed it again.

"True," said Valerian, adding with a teasing grin, "I apologize, cousin."

"Now I know you are not well," said Elspeth. "Sir Simon, cannot the rest of it wait till tomorrow morning?"

"It can, and shall," he said, Pixie in his arms as he rose from the Bath chair. "By Jupiter but I shall be free of these con—er, these confining garments at last!"

Ushered to the stairs where their candles waited, Elspeth heard him say to his son, "Thanks to you I'm free, and very soon I shall see my dear wife again! I can scarce believe it!"

Joel handed Elspeth her candle and wished her good night. She smiled at him, but her thoughts turned to Vance. How wonderful it would be if within another day or so she would see him and, somehow, they would succeed in freeing him from those who held him prisoner in the Rouen chateau.

11

*E*lspeth came downstairs early the following morning drawn by the fragrance of freshly baked bread. A weak sun slanted its pale beams through the windows of the dining parlour where Sir Simon, clad in his own garments, had arrived before her. He was bright-eyed and cheerful and wished her a good day. Joel Skye sprang up from the table to pull out her chair, from which Pixie then had to be evicted. The table was laden with various cheeses, little pots of preserves, slices of cold veal and ham, warm bread, rich fresh butter and bowls of apples and pears. The maid came bustling in to pour Elspeth's coffee and gather her selections. The coffee was excellent and Elspeth was spreading butter on a slice of bread when Valerian came from the stables grumbling because the coach that was to carry his father to Italy should have arrived by this time. He greeted Elspeth with rather forced courtesy and responded to her enquiry with a brusque assurance that he felt very well this morning. Herbert, he announced, was "earning his keep" having ridden out to conduct a reconnaissance of the neighbourhood.

With a stern glance at Elspeth he added, "In case more of Miss Clayton's admirers are lurking about."

She had learned by now that he disliked being, as he put it, "maudled over," so she retaliated by commenting sweetly that despite his alleged "recovery" he looked pale and she was sure Madame Bossuet's cook would gladly prepare him some gruel. Sir Simon looked amused but nodded in agreement. Valerian growled under his breath and, having already helped himself from several of the platters on the table, proceeded to convey an additional slice of cheese to his plate while eyeing Elspeth defiantly.

She said with a sigh, "Why must men be such naughty little boys?"

He grinned at that, but before he could comment Herbert ran in to announce cheerfully that he'd seen no sign of their former antagonists, so they could breakfast in peace.

His optimism proved justified and the meal was almost over when the rumble of wheels outside announced the arrival of a coach. Sir Simon sprang to his feet, but Valerian, hurrying to the window, said a frowning, "Wait, sir!" and his father sat down again. A moment later Valerian reported that both the expected coaches were here.

Through a sudden silence Valerian and Sir Simon gazed at each other and scarcely noticed when the others quietly left them alone.

———————

Soon afterwards, they gathered to bid Sir Simon farewell. He thanked them profusely for their help, but clearly he was reluctant to part from his son and he lingered, worrying for his injury until Valerian laughed at him and said he knew very well his father would forget all about him the moment he saw his beloved wife again. He gave Sir Simon a letter he'd written to his mother, the two men embraced, and having caressed Pixie and made Valerian promise to restore her to him at the earliest opportunity, Sir Simon walked hurriedly down the steps to the yard, where a servant and two outriders waited beside a fine carriage.

They all waved as the team leaned into their collars, and Valerian stood watching until the coach was quite out of sight. Pulling back his shoulders then, he said brightly that a great weight had been removed from him now that Sir Simon was at last safely delivered into the hands of his mother's people.

Elspeth was not deceived. Father and son were deeply attached and that their parting had been wrenching she knew very well. She hurried upstairs to help Freda gather their belongings while Valerian and Skye went out to confer with Coachman Marcel and the guard Lord Boudreaux had hired to transport them to the unknown chateau near Rouen. Valerian had muttered something to Herbert, who'd been about to accompany them but had at once glanced at Elspeth and stationed himself at the foot of the stairs.

She'd said teasingly, "Does your cousin fancy I mean to run away, Herbert?" And he'd answered, "He wants you guarded, ma'am, lest more of those varmints come after you!"

It was a chilling reminder and she had to concentrate on the belief that she had been chosen to be abducted at random and not for some evil purpose connected with her brother's captivity. She was relieved when Valerian came back as she was descending the stairs. He waved a folded paper at her which he said contained instructions as to the fighting men who'd been hired to assist Elspeth's rescue attempt, as well as a map to the chateau where they would find Vance.

"Do we have a plan to free my brother?" she asked eagerly.

He shrugged. "We'll have to play the cards as they are dealt."

"But we do know he's still alive?"

"We know he was when this map was drawn."

Impatient, she said, "When was that? Do you know? Where are we to meet these men who will help us? What are you not telling me? Is there—"

He clutched his hurt wrist, bowed his head and groaned loudly.

At once all concern, she lifted his chin gently and scanned his face. The twinkle in his eyes gave him away.

"Oh!" she exclaimed. "You're teasing! How can you when you know how worried I am!"

He protested indignantly, "I am a severely wounded man and entitled to freedom from persecution, so—"

"And so is my poor brother!" she flared. "Tell me, I beg you!"

Sobering, he answered, "When there is something worth sharing, ma'am, I'll tell you. Meanwhile, you'd do well to check your room again for the things you've neglected to pack. You women always forget something!"

"As you know from your vast experience," she said with a curl of the lip.

"But of course." He bowed. "Freda, run to the kitchen and be sure Pixie's food and water bowls and her—ah, personal commode are put in the coach. Oh, egad! And did I make you blush, Nurse Cotton?"

Elspeth ignored him and went, she trusted with dignity, upstairs, where she found to her chagrin that she had indeed overlooked her reticule that had been accidentally covered by the eiderdown. When she went downstairs again Valerian was no longer at the foot of the stairs and she was spared the ironic lift of his dark brow, which she'd feared would await her.

At last their valises and trunks were packed into the boot, Herbert and Skye mounted up, the carriage door was slammed, the guard climbed to the box, Coachman Marcel cracked his whip, chirruped to his horses and the coach rumbled out of the yard and into the lane.

Pixie wandered restlessly from lap to lap and stood on her hind legs to peer out of the window. Clearly distressed, she began to wail and the attempts of Elspeth and Freda to console her were unavailing.

Valerian was morose and silent. Suspecting that he and the cat shared a similar grief, Elspeth tried to amuse Pixie with a piece of ribbon and eventually the little animal curled up on her lap and went to sleep.

In a few minutes Valerian apologized for being "poor company" and pointed out the numerous ocean-going barges and quite large vessels that were making their way to and from the estuary. He drew their attention also to the chalk cliffs and the numerous churches with which he told them Normandy abounded. Elspeth and Freda were intrigued by the differing architecture of the structures they passed, their comments amusing Valerian until the coach turned onto a lane lined with poplars. Valerian stiffened, and Elspeth watched him uneasily. He let the window down, and as Skye rode alongside, called, "Why do we turn off? More varmints?"

"Not that we've seen. The coachman wants to change teams and knows of a fine inn about half a league ahead." Skye bent his head and peered in at Elspeth. "How do you go on, Ellie? This is tiresome for you."

"Nonsense," snapped Valerian. "Miss Elspeth's concern is for her brother and with luck, we'll free him before nightfall!"

Skye gave him a hard look.

Elspeth called, "But—thank you, Jo—!" The name was cut short as Valerian jerked the window closed again.

"Joe," he muttered, "Is that how you call him?"

"You know perfectly well what I call him. And you hurt yourself when you so rudely slammed the window in his face. Which serves you right."

"He's supposed to be keeping watch for rank riders, highwaymen, Mohocks, or their ilk—not slobbering over you. Disgusting!"

" 'Tis odd," said Elspeth demurely, "but I'd not describe Lieutenant Skye's demeanour toward me as either slobbering or disgusting."

He growled, "You will if fifty Mohocks take us by surprise!"

At this point Pixie woke up and wailed again.

Valerian said, "Can't you keep that brute quiet? She's disturbing poor Beck."

In fact, Freda had dozed off and was snoring softly.

Elspeth picked the kitten up and cuddled her. "She's pining for your father, poor little dear."

Incredulous, he said, "Pining for—If ever I heard such fustian! She's a *cat*, ma'am! A dog may pine. A cat don't give a button! They're aloof creatures, I give 'em credit for that."

"She was devoted to Sir Simon. She misses him."

"Likely because my father pampered her and would persist in having her by him all the time. She amused him."

"Whereas you prefer dogs."

"Infinitely!"

"Then how very kind it was of you to find her for him. Oh, never look so taken aback. Sir Simon told me you brought her to keep him company. In which case, you must take some responsibility for the little girl."

"Little *girl*?"

"Well, she's not a boy cat, is she?"

Before he could protest, Elspeth put the kitten in his lap and beamed into his startled eyes. "There. Only see how she is settling down."

"She is kneading me!"

"I told you she needs you. Ah, look, she's curling up happily. Perhaps she thinks you are Sir Simon. Truly, you are a kind gentleman, sir."

He said gruffly, "If you spread that rumour around London my reputation will be ruined!"

Freda woke up and, glancing to the windows, exclaimed,

"Oh, my! The sun has gone away already! Wherever are we, Miss Elspeth?"

"In the middle of nowhere," she answered. "And it's starting to rain."

"This area is famous for rain," muttered Valerian.

"Is that what you are watching so closely?"

"I am hoping that our gallant outriders are keeping their eyes open even while they chatter like a pair of magpies."

It seemed to Elspeth that his gaze scanned the adjacent fields and clumps of trees rather than dwelling upon Herbert and Skye, who had indeed joined forces and were riding side by side.

The light rain became heavier, and Elspeth said, "Oh, my. The poor creatures will be soaked!"

"They're hardy men and not like to be washed away like two dainty schoolroom misses," sneered Valerian, adding, "And here is the coachman's 'fine inn.' My God!" He peered at the faded sign that swung from a post and depicted a very stiff animal with a proudly arched neck and one front leg held high. "Now what in the world are you supposed to be, I wonder? A lion or a camelopard?"

Elspeth pointed out, "The sign says *Le cheval de Trois.*"

"Trojan Horse, indeed! It looks to be more of a thieves' den! But at least you ladies will be able to stretch your—er, limbs, if you'll forgive me the crude expression."

"Why?" asked Elspeth, raising her brows at him. "We do have them, you know."

"Crude expressions? Miss Clayton! I am shocked!"

Freda giggled.

Elspeth sighed with exaggerated patience. "I suppose you are so crusty because your wound troubles you. I am very sorry for it, sir. Is there aught I may do to make you more comfortable?"

"Many things," he said, leering at her suggestively. "But

for the moment put up your hoods, ladies, else your prettily powdered locks will be turned into glue!"

The carriage rattled its way into the yard of a small and rather forlorn-looking inn set back from the road under a fine old beech tree. The many-gabled building was sadly in need of paint; a few hens scratched about, seemingly undaunted by the rain, and a solitary coach waited.

Herbert dismounted and swung the carriage door open. "You will want to alight, Miss Elspeth," he said with his ingenuous smile.

"Why should you suppose she would wish to get wet?" asked Valerian, all innocence.

The youth's face flushed darkly. He stammered, "I—er, I only meant—Well, it's a long drive, and—and—"

"Be so good as to give me your hand, Herbert," said Elspeth kindly. "Your cousin tells me I need to stretch my— er, limbs and I try to obey his commands."

"And that properly drives me to the ropes," murmured Valerian. "But I suggest you wait in the coach for a minute or two, ma'am."

"Well done, Ellie!" said Skye, leaving his mount in the care of an ostler and walking over to them, grinning broadly.

"For what?" she asked.

"For whatever you said to drive our mighty leader to the ropes! Allow me to take you inside."

"After you've first inspected the premises," said Valerian.

Skye asked sharply, "What do you expect to find? Possible marauders?"

"Or anything that strikes you as suspicious." He added caustically, "And the sooner you accomplish it, the sooner Miss Clayton can go in."

Skye gritted his teeth but hurried after Herbert, who was already entering the arched door to the inn, and Valerian went off, saying he wished to have a word with Coachman Marcel.

Freda moaned, "Oh, miss! I thought we was safe now!"

Elspeth sat back against the squabs and tried to stifle her own unease. "I think we are, Freda. We are well protected with Mr. Valerian and the Lieutenant and—"

A loud gunshot cut off her words. Freda screamed and flung herself down between the seats. Elspeth made a dive for the window and struggled unsuccessfully to lower it.

Horses squealed and stamped, and the coach rocked.

There came a flurry of shots, sharp and ear-splitting.

Valerian ran to the window. Smoke curled up from the horse pistol in his hand, and he shouted angrily, "Get down, woman! For the love of God—*Get down!*"

Her heart pounding, Elspeth drew back.

Several men wearing head masks were running at Valerian who faced them, the pistol in one hand and his sword in the other. Terrified, she thought, 'He can't fight them alone! Why aren't Joel and Herbert helping?'

The thieves, however, ran to the front of the carriage. One of them clambered onto the box, shouting, "Whip 'em up, Coachman, or die here. You may take your choice!"

The coach lurched.

"Not again!" whispered Elspeth. "Oh, please, God! Not again!"

Valerian roared, "Get down from there, you filthy varmint!" and raced forwards.

Two of the thieves turned on him, pistols levelled.

Scarcely daring to look, Elspeth heard Freda sobbing frenziedly. She heard also the thunder of fast-approaching hooves. "Thank the Lord," she cried. "Somebody's coming!"

She shrank as more shots blasted the air.

Two horsemen galloped into the yard. Both were firing pistols. The horses squealed in fright and the coach rocked wildly as Valerian flung himself onto the box. Elspeth heard a shout and saw a body plummet down past the window. Someone howled, "Away! Away!" She caught a glimpse of

175

flashing steel, then came more shouts, running footsteps, and hoofbeats rapidly diminishing.

"Freda," she cried, "for heaven's sake, get up! I think Mr. Valerian fell and—I can't get this wretched door open!"

"Don't never, miss!" wailed Freda. "It's likely them same wicked men! You'll be stole, surely!"

"Oh, you stupid girl! *Get up!*"

Freda knelt and, weeping, dragged herself onto the seat.

Tearing at the door, Elspeth broke a nail as it was flung open. Valerian, looking frantic and dishevelled, sword in hand, stared up at her and demanded hoarsely, "You're all right, then?"

"Yes. And you?"

"I'm well, but they've put our extra guard out of commission. The poor fellow managed to get to the house." He handed her out and Pixie darted down the steps and tore towards the inn. "Blast!" he exclaimed breathlessly. "You'd best wait here while I find out what's become of Herbert and Skye."

She paused but called after him, "Where are the gentlemen who came to help?"

Over his shoulder he shouted, "They went haring off after those rank riders." He was gone then, running through the inn doorway.

Suddenly weak in the knees, Elspeth sat down inelegantly on the carriage step, heedless of the rain.

Hooves sounded on the cobblestones and two men rode into the yard.

Sighing, Elspeth blinked up at them gratefully.

The older of the pair demanded curtly, "Where is your mistress, girl?"

Speechless, she stared at a gentleman of middle age, richly clad, with large dark eyes in a painted and somewhat puffy face.

Behind her, Freda squeaked an astonished "Sir Brian! Oh, thank Gawd!"

Conrad Beech, coming up beside his father, exclaimed in English, "Beck? What in the name of—"

Elspeth found her voice. "Sir! This is incredible! You cannot know how glad I am to see you!"

"Elspeth?" His eyes fairly goggling, Sir Brian gasped, "How on *earth* come you to be here? And in that—that dreadful gown, and your hair all anyhow—Is Madame Colbert with you? I'd not known you planned to journey to France."

Valerian came out of the inn, unfolding an umbrella. "Those varmints held Skye and Herbert at gunpoint," he began, then paused.

"You!" gasped Conrad.

"Elspeth," said his father, very stiff and stern. "Do you travel in this gentleman's company?"

"Among others," drawled Valerian. "And we are deeply indebted to you, sir, for your very timely assistance with those murderous—"

"Never mind about that," said Conrad, glaring. "What the devil d'you mean—'among others'?"

'Oh dear,' thought Elspeth.

Sir Brian dismounted awkwardly and carefully straightened his tricorne and adjusted the lace at his wrists. "I think I must demand an explanation, Mr. Valerian. This lady is my niece!"

"I'm aware, sir." Valerian glanced at the coachman, who stood at the heads of the horses. "I've sent a man off for an apothecary, Marcel. He'll take care of the guard. Have the team changed as soon as may be. We must get on our way."

"Not so!" snapped Sir Brian, "An explanation, if you please!"

"Yes, of course," said Valerian rather wearily. "But I suggest we talk inside."

'Whatever,' thought Elspeth, 'are we to tell him?'

"God bless my soul!" Half an hour later, seated in a faded wing chair in the shabby parlour that had been reserved for them at *Le cheval de Trois*, Sir Brian fanned himself with a beautifully embroidered handkerchief, his large brown eyes holding a glazed look. "I find it past comprehension, Elspeth," he said feebly, "that you are journeying, unchaperoned, with not one but *three* bachelor gentlemen!"

Valerian had gone out with the apothecary to attend to the injured guard, but he returned to the parlour in time to hear this remark and his dark brows drew into a frown. "Would you find it more convenable, sir, had Miss Clayton been travelling with only one bachelor gentleman? Myself, for instance?"

"Under these circumstances your levity is out of place, sir!" said Conrad, his chin jutting as he moved his chair closer to Elspeth.

"Most decidedly out of place," agreed his father. "Miss Clayton is my niece! I appreciate the fact that she is anxious for her brother—though it is wounding to think that my own offer of assistance was rejected—but how it comes about that Madame Colbert permitted her to embark on a venture that will leave her with not a shred of reputation—not one *shred*!—is quite beyond me! I cannot believe that her dear mama would countenance that she snap her fingers in the face of convention. Indeed, I suspect the poor lady would swoon away did she learn of her daughter's reckless folly! Madame Colbert has much explaining to do!"

Watching Valerian, Elspeth asked, "What of the guard, Mr. Valerian? Will he recover?"

"Oh, I think so," he answered, sitting on the arm of the sofa beside her. "But he won't be able to go on with us."

"Go *on*? Where?" demanded Sir Brian, pausing in the act of adjusting the pearl that shone in one ear.

"Your pardon, Uncle," Elspeth interposed determinedly. "Can the poor man stay here, Gervaise? What is to become of him?"

"All arranged, never fear," he answered, smiling at her. "He'll be cared for at the apothecary's clinic until his employer sends for him, so do not be—"

"I see, cousin, that you are on a first-name basis with your abductor," interrupted Conrad.

Startled, Elspeth felt her cheeks burn. "Oh, my! Did I use such an address? I must have been wool-gathering!"

With a gesture of impatience, Valerian said, "Oh, have done! I told you the way of it, sir. Miss Clayton is willing to endanger her own life to help her brother. I call that courage, not folly."

"Nor did Mr. Valerian abduct me, Uncle," said Elspeth.

"He evidently persuaded you that your participation was needed in a rescue attempt that should be attempted only by your male relatives," said Sir Brian. "I am appalled, sir, that anyone held to be a gentleman—"

"Oh, but I'm not held to be a gentleman! I am rather described as a Dandy." Valerian slanted a mischievous glance at Elspeth. "In some quarters, alas, a Deplorable Dandy!"

Flushed and angry, Conrad leant forward in his chair.

Before he could voice the response that Elspeth guessed would not be conciliating, she said, "My abigail is with me, sir. And Lieutenant Skye and Mr. Herbert Turner have most gallantly escorted us."

"From here on my son and I will escort you, poor misguided child," declared Sir Brian. "Back to England, where we can only pray this most improper escapade will not become public knowledge."

Valerian said thoughtfully, "Are you then anxious to see Vance Clayton go to his death, gentlemen?"

The response was explosive. Sir Brian sprang to his feet

and his son jumped up so suddenly that his chair went over with a crash.

"How *dare* you, Valerian?" shouted Sir Brian, his countenance purpling alarmingly.

"You'll answer to me for that insult!" roared Conrad, as pale suddenly as his father was flushed.

Herbert and Skye, who had prudently absented themselves from this discussion, burst into the room.

Looking from Elspeth's distressed face to the fury of the Beeches and the bored disdain on Valerian's handsome features, Skye demanded, "What's to do, gentlemen?"

"You three—*fellows*," sputtered Sir Brian, "have compromised my niece, is what's to do! The poor child is ruined!"

"My uncle wants to take me back to England," said Elspeth miserably.

"And Valerian had the damned gall to imply that we wish my cousin Vance dead!" raged Conrad.

"As he assuredly will be do we waste much more time," said Skye.

Valerian gave him an appreciative grin.

Wringing her hands, Elspeth said, "That is all too true. Uncle Brian, Conrad, I am so very grateful—we all are grateful—that you came to our aid. But Ger—Mr. Valerian explained my brother's terrible danger. We dare not delay. He *must* be won to freedom—before they take his dear life!"

"A task for men," growled Conrad, still glaring fiercely at Valerian. "And not for you, my dear Elspeth."

"Ah," murmured Valerian. "Then you are willing to join us? Very good! With two more in our rescue party, the odds improve. Especially two such intrepid fighting men."

Dismayed, Elspeth searched his face, and although it was solemn, she knew him well enough by this time to recognize the dance of wicked laughter in his eyes.

Conrad snapped, "We will gladly assist in attempting a rescue."

"After we have escorted my niece home," qualified Sir Brian firmly.

"No!" exclaimed Elspeth. " 'Tis more than kind, sir. But I gave my word of honour to help Mr. Valerian! And he has a plan—"

"The promise he obtained was not an honourable one," said Conrad icily. "And your best hope—perhaps your *only* hope—of preserving your good name is that we convey you back to London before any of the *ton* hear of this disgraceful episode."

"Certainly, to take my niece into Paris would be disastrous," put in Sir Brian. "There are many English there, as usual. She would be sure to be recognized."

"Not where we are going," said Valerian.

"Which is—where, exactly?" demanded Conrad.

Valerian stood. "We do not have the exact location. Friends are arranging matters for us. Miss Clayton spoke truly, however. Time is of the essence. If you can leave now, gentlemen, we'd best get mounted." The Beeches exchanged troubled glances. He went on blandly, "You *did* say you were willing to help?"

"Of course we will help," said Sir Brian. "But we also have a task we're sworn to complete. A desperate task, though not one that would endanger my niece. The moment that is done, we'll be at your disposal."

Valerian bowed. "You are all conciliation, sir," he drawled mockingly. "Alas, but we have already waited over-long. Miss Clayton, if you're ready to proceed . . ."

Pale with fury, Conrad shouted, "She is *not* ready to go she knows not where, on a hare-brained scheme that has little chance of succeeding! Elspeth, I know how dearly you love Vance, but you *must* see the folly of going with these—these thrill-seekers! Come. We'll see you safe home to your god-mama and then, I swear it, we'll rush back to help Valerian!"

"Which will be much too late." Reaching her hands to

her uncle and cousin, she said resolutely, "I am more grateful than I can say for your concern. But I am a grown woman, and I'll not change my mind."

Sir Brian groaned and swept her into a hug. Conrad took up her hand and kissed it gently. "God aid you, my poor foolish little cousin."

Snatching up his hat and cloak, Sir Brian stamped to the door, then turned back to scowl at the three young men who watched him expressionlessly. "And may God forgive you all," he cried. "If anything happens to my niece I shall hold you personally to blame!" His gaze shifted. "You in particular, Valerian! I know you're behind this dastardly plot!" He swung his cloak about his shoulders and adjusted the great cuffs of his coat fastidiously, saying a condemning "I hope you're proud of yourself, sir! Rather, you should hang your head in shame!"

Valerian offered another deep and flourishing bow.

Elspeth hurried to the door to say her good-byes.

Valerian started to follow but checked as Herbert tugged at his sleeve, murmuring, "A word, coz."

Watching Skye follow Elspeth, Valerian said irritably, "What now?"

Herbert half-whispered, "I saw it again, Ger!"

"Saw—what? Oh, your phantom coach? Are, you sure?"

"Quite sure. It ain't a phantom coach. 'Tis a blue coach. And I'm curst sure it follows!"

"This is a well-travelled road. Likely someone chances to be taking the same route is all. Did Skye see it?"

"He says not, but *I* did!"

"Yes. Well, next time you spot the dastardly villains, be sure to tell me and we'll call them to account and split their gizzards!" Valerian stamped outside.

Watching him resentfully, Herbert called, "You may laugh, but—"

"Thank you," responded Valerian.

12

They delayed long enough to take a light luncheon at *Le cheval de Trois*. The food was surprisingly good but Valerian shocked the host, a dowdy little man with a mournful face, by ordering coffee and ale rather than wine. When Skye said he would enjoy a glass of wine, Valerian murmured that he'd as soon the Lieutenant didn't fall asleep after lunch, and taking the hint, Skye settled for ale. Pixie was pleased by the offer of finely cut-up chicken giblets and a bowl of fresh water.

By the time their hasty meal was over the rain had drifted away, although the skies were gloomy and overcast. Valerian went out to inspect the team and confer with Coachman Marcel. He had delegated Herbert to see to it that the kitten's "commode" was replenished with fresh earth, while Skye, watchful and alert, escorted Elspeth and Pixie on a stroll through the gardens and for a short distance along the lane and back. The little animal paced along in a more or less orderly fashion on her lead, until she paused to declare war on a torn piece of newspaper that fluttered in a shrub and, having won that battle, regarded with exaggerated suspicion an old broken boot abandoned in a ditch.

"I'm so glad she's getting a little exercise," said Elspeth. "She has to spend so much time cooped up, poor mite."

Skye patted the hand that rested in his arm. "Perhaps she has sense enough to appreciate that she is fed and cared for. Do you suppose Valerian will return her to his father when this business is done?"

"He promised Sir Simon he would do so, though I think that will have to be after we're safely on a packet bound for England." Looking up into his ardent dark eyes, she said anxiously, "We will be in time, won't we, Joel? Valerian will find Vance in time?"

"He certainly seems determined to keep his promise to you. I'll own that surprises me."

"Why? Do you judge him to be lacking in honour?"

"Say rather that I've always thought him a frippery sort of fellow, more interested in the whims of fashion and society than in a serious undertaking of this nature."

She said with a smile, "He played a part these past three years, and played it well. Did you know him before that?"

"No. I was too busily occupied with my duties to cultivate new friends among the *haut ton*." He paused, then, watching her, said slowly, "You like him, don't you, Ellie?"

"Yes. I never dreamt I would, for I thoroughly despised him when first we met, if you recall."

He said, as Sir Simon had observed earlier, "But you've changed your mind." He pressed her hand. "Be careful, my dear. He has the reputation of being a dangerous man—in more ways than one. Don't let him throw dust in your lovely eyes."

"Good gracious, Joel!" With a little ripple of laughter, she said, "I cannot suppose he has the least intention of doing so. In fact, I think he finds me annoying rather than intriguing. Oh, look! What a fine team! Who'd ever have guessed we'd be able to hire such horses in this funny little place! Do you suppose Lord Boudreaux owns them?"

The Lieutenant stifled a sigh. He had tried, at least. "Probably. And if they move as well as they look, we should make good time. The question is—to where?"

The team was poled up and the horses stamping impatiently when they returned to the inn.

Swinging into the saddle, Skye asked, "Is our destination this side of Rouen, Valerian? Or are we to go through the city?"

"As I understand it our destination is a chateau between La Bouille and Rouen. More than that I know only that it has a fine view." Valerian stooped to lift Pixie and hand her to Beck, who was already in the coach. "On a hill, no doubt," he added.

"There are probably dozens of such chateaux," said Skye indignantly. "How the deuce are we to know which one? Does our coachman know?"

Marcel looked down from his lofty perch and said in halting English, "These will you learn at the hour . . ." He hesitated, then finished triumphantly, "at the hour of establishments!"

Herbert grunted, "Which tells us nothing."

"Except perhaps," said Valerian, "to ask no questions." He handed Elspeth up the carriage step. "Meanwhile, gentlemen, we draw near and, whatever our plan, we should have our weapons primed and ready. I trust you've seen to that important detail."

They assured him the detail had been attended to. He warned them to stay alert, then waved to the coachman and climbed inside.

"Before you start," he said as Elspeth opened her mouth to speak, "I don't know what the fellow meant, but I'm sure he has worked for his lordship before and is perfectly reliable."

"I was merely going to ask how much longer this will take," she said. "No, I don't mean to pinch at you. I know you are doing all you can, and I am more than grateful, but I'm so afraid we won't get there in time."

"I know." He took her hand and she did not protest as he held it strongly. " 'Tis natural that you'd be worried. Take heart, ma'am. You've been splendid through all our trials and setbacks. Most ladies would have had the vapours at the first sign of the attack we suffered today, but you go on, courageous as ever. I wonder—Ow!" He had been stroking her fingers gently and the kitten had pounced without warning. "Vicious brute," he grumbled, rubbing his hand.

Undaunted, Pixie stood on her back feet and waved both front arms at him, then tumbled as the carriage lurched.

Elspeth laughed and retrieved the little animal. "I think 'twould have been kinder to let Sir Simon take her with him than to drag her about like this."

"Kinder to her, but riskier for your brother."

"We could certainly have found another black kitten, heaven knows there are plenty of the poor little things abandoned and starving."

"True. But you are forgetting the admiration she attracted en route. That dashing lieutenant when we were leaving England—what was his name? Raines, I think—was most taken with her. As was the British Coast Guard officer at Le Havre—to say nothing of that irritating young French official I had to set down. Now *he* particularly noticed the white spot on Pixie's tail, remember?"

"Yes, indeed. But we could quite safely have left her at the pension with Madame Bossuet, or even at the Trojan Horse, and collected her on our way back."

"And would have been lucky to find her still there! At either hostelry they'd likely have let her wander off and she might have tried to find my father again! No, m'dear. Too risky by half!"

The conversation languished. Elspeth watched villages and pastures and farms appear and disappear, her mind's eye conjuring up her beloved brother's laughing, handsome face. Valerian's thoughts alternated between his parents and their joyous reunion, and the girl sitting beside him. Watching her, he prayed he'd not have to disappoint her.

Freda murmured drowsily, "Some poor soul is in difficulty, sir."

Looking out of the window, Valerian said, "The coachman is slowing. Be curst if it's not a troupe of rascally gypsies! Why would the numbskull stop? This could be another ambush!" He swung the door open as the coach slowed, snapped, "Stay inside!" and jumped down the step.

The short winter afternoon was already fading, but the clouds had drifted away and the skies were clear. Off to the side of the road stood a gaily coloured gypsy caravan, ahead of which a fine berlin was drawn up, an outrider waiting beside it.

Joel Skye walked his mount to join Valerian, who demanded, "Why a'plague are we stopping?"

Skye said, "Our coachman seemed to think the berlin was in difficulties. It's a magnificent coach. Your cousin has gone over to see if they need assistance. It would appear that a lady of rank is consulting the gypsy—a fortune-teller, likely."

"One might suppose a lady of rank would travel with more than one outrider," said Valerian, irritated. "Confound my cousin! I wish to hell he wouldn't continually get himself into these—Well, never mind that. Stay with the coach if you please. I'll see what's to do."

He stalked across the muddy road and came up with his cousin, who had dismounted and stood holding his reins and watching the gypsy coach.

Herbert saw his frown and said quickly, "No cause to

glower at me. The lady tripped in the mud, so I came across to help."

"And was most gallant," said a musical voice.

A lady emerged from the caravan. A little above average height and exquisitely robed, she wore an ermine-trimmed hood, one hand resided in a deep ermine muff, in the other she held up a mask which concealed most of what Valerian guessed to be a very pretty face; certainly the eyes were unusually brilliant. He experienced a brief sense of familiarity, but before he could speak she turned to Herbert.

"I am indebted to you, monsieur," she said earnestly.

"No—I er, I mean—not at all," he stammered.

"But—yes. I could have been injured, and see—the mud is all gone. The old gypsy woman was able to brush it out of my cloak."

Watching her intently, Valerian said, "Your pardon, madame, but I think we have—"

The outrider had ridden closer and interrupted harshly, "You will stand away from my lady!"

She made a graceful restraining gesture and said, "There is no cause for alarm, Frederic. This gentleman is with Monsieur Turner. But at all events, I must go. Good day to you, messeurs."

A warm smile for Herbert, a friendly nod to Valerian and she was gone, walking quickly to the berlin, where a liveried footman held the door open and handed her up the steps.

A moment later the beautifully matched white team had drawn the vehicle away.

Valerian looked after the departing coach thoughtfully. "No crest on the panel," he muttered. "I wonder who she is. A beauty, and I've the feeling we've met somewhere. Did she give you her name?"

"No, and I didn't dare to ask." With a wistful sigh Herbert said, "Have you ever seen such eyes? Such a soft green."

"Were they? I'd thought they looked blue, rather." Glancing to the caravan Valerian saw that a small, plump and elderly gypsy woman stood in the open door watching them. "Give you good day, ma'am," he said, raising his tricorne politely. "The lady who just left—could you tell me her name?"

"I could, but I won't," she replied in English.

Surprised by both the words and the cultured voice, he said with a smile, "An English gypsy, I see. But a gypsy nonetheless." He took out his purse. "Were I to cross your palm with silver . . ."

"Do try not to be so ridiculous, Valerian," she snapped, and, surprising him even more, added, "I'd not expected you to be with Marcel. You will have an explanation, I feel sure, but at all events, you're late!" Her small dark eyes went past him to where the coachman was guiding the horses across the road to pull up where the berlin had stood.

Speechless, Valerian hurried to open the door of the coach and assist Elspeth down the step.

She looked at him enquiringly. "Another delay?"

"It appears," he answered, "that we are expected."

"Here?" Elspeth's puzzled gaze turned to the caravan. "But I thought—"

"So did I. Come and meet a remarkable gypsy. You'd best wait here, Beck, and take care of Pixie."

Walking beside him, Elspeth said, "I'm sorry if there is trouble here, but Gervaise—" She flushed at the slip, but the laughter in his eyes reassured her. "Mr. Valerian," she corrected. "I do apologize."

"So I should hope," he teased.

"It is that I cannot fathom why we stop here. The time is going by so fast and—"

"As time tends to do," said the gypsy woman briskly. "Wherefore I suggest that you stop wasting it and step inside!"

Valerian watched appreciatively as Elspeth's lower lip

189

sagged in a way he thought particularly delicious.

Staring in wide-eyed disbelief at this plump little gypsy clad in a head-scarf and shawl, a brilliant red blouse and a voluminous and very creased skirt of blue velvet, Elspeth could all but see the costly evening gown and jewels worn by this same lady at a dinner party in a luxurious London mansion. Astounded, she gasped, "Heavens above! It *is* you! Lady *Elmira Bottesdale*? What on—earth?"

The dowager gave Valerian a conspiratorial grin and bustled into the caravan.

Pausing only to exchange an incredulous glance with him, Elspeth followed. She seemed to enter another world. Bright curtains hung at windows in the front and rear of the caravan; there were numerous cluttered shelves, and an assortment of pots and pans hung from wall hooks. An oil lamp suspended from the ceiling cast a warm glow on the few items of furniture: a narrow bed piled with cushions and blankets, three small chairs, a chest of drawers also small, and a little table that held a round glass ball, some cards and numerous papers.

Waving her guests to chairs, Lady Bottesdale sat down at the table. "I can't invite the others in," she said, her eyes twinkling. "No room. But you'll not be staying long."

Valerian returned her smile but said, "I'll own 'tis beyond me, ma'am, to know why we stay at all. Or how you come to be involved. Though I could hazard a guess, bizarre as it may be."

She nodded. "Hazard away. I've always judged you to be more intelligent than you appear. You may get some of it right."

"Three facts come to mind," he said. "One—you've the reputation of being a strong-willed lady, not averse to acting on your convictions boldly, however unpopular such convictions may be. Two—you are a close friend of Lord Geoffrey Boudreaux, in fact, 'tis said you once were betrothed to him, and you are known to have strong loyalties. Three—the lady who just left here was masked to her very lovely eyes—famous eyes, and belonging I believe to a charming creature who also holds strong convictions, and is sometimes named *La maitresse en titre.*"

"Madame de Pompadour?" exclaimed Elspeth, her eyes wider than ever.

"From all of which," said the dowager, nodding again, "you conclude—what, exactly, Valerian?"

"If I put it together with the fact that you know the name of our coachman and that you were clearly expecting him—if not me—I can only suppose you are here to help Miss Clayton rescue her brother. And jolly brave of you to do so!"

The dowager clapped her white little hands. "Very good! And you have surprised me, young man. It was long ago, and very few people know of my broken engagement to Geoffrey Boudreaux. I expect you had that from your father, and you've kept silent else the whole *ton* would be reminded of one of my more foolish faux pas—for which I thank you. Yes, you've guessed rightly. I am here to render what assistance I may to Miss Clayton's unfortunate brother."

Elspeth said, "Oh, how very good in you, ma'am."

"Pish!" snorted the dowager. "Society gossip and intrigues bore me. I dote on excitement. Boudreaux knows this, and I've worked with him from time to time when he asked it. I only wish I had better news for you."

Paling, Elspeth cried, "Dear God! Never say we are too late and my dear Vance is killed?"

"Be at ease, child. Your brother yet lives—though not for long, I fear. Fortunately, we were warned of a possible ambush, which is why we decided to move our rendezvous point."

Valerian asked, "Since your man Marcel was unaware of this, am I right in assuming that is why the Pompadour was here? To warn you?"

"To warn me. But not of the ambush. I should explain that Reinette—as we used to call her in her youth—had a very lovely mama, poor Madame Poisson, who was judged very bad *ton*. I must own she was rather naughty—but even so I was most fond of her and I've known Reinette since she was a small and very sickly child. She has come a long way, little Mademoiselle Poisson, but even today, although she is the King's favourite and despite her wealth and power, she is looked down upon as a bourgeoise by many of the aristocracy. On the other hand there are plenty of folk who adore her, for she has a very kind heart and is always willing to lend a helping hand where she can. Unfortunately, she is also ambitious and much interested in politics, and she will persist in meddling, which has got her into trouble several times. She was greatly distressed to learn of your brother's plight, Miss Clayton. She trusts him implicitly and is anxious to know what became of a letter he was carrying. She arranged in secret to send some of her servants to attempt his release. One of these was the guard who rode on Marcel's coach, another was waylaid en route to meet you and guide you here. Meanwhile, those who oppose Reinette have let it be known—very subtly, you understand, but with deep malice—that they are close to finding proof of her involvement in a certain international intrigue, and once they have it Louis himself will be told of her scheming. At the very least it would lead to a scandal and the King very much dislikes scandal. At worst, he might be put in such a difficult position that he'd be forced to sever their relationship. He adores her, and she is madly in love with him. You comprehend? To be separated forever would destroy her. So . . ." She shrugged.

Elspeth said, "And you believe the proof her enemies seek is in the letter my brother carried?"

"I do."

Valerian said gravely, "So—*en effet* we are on our own."

"Not completely, but I'm relieved to see you have two

192

strapping young fellows to assist you. Skye I know slightly. The other . . . ?"

"My cousin, ma'am. And a fine fighting man—at need. What do we have in opposition?"

Her ladyship pursed her lips before answering, "A deal more than I'd expected. But you have not told me the whole, I think."

"True. We were attacked soon after we landed. But that rascality had nothing to do with our attempt to free Clayton. Their aim was to steal his sister—to be sold to some eastern potentate, probably."

"Hmm. No other criminal incidents?"

"Yes, indeed!" declared Elspeth. "My friend Nicholas Drew had intended to help, but he was badly wounded in London."

"Word of that reached me only two days since," muttered her ladyship. "I understood it was the work of Mohocks. I'd been sure he would be the one to come and help your brother. I certainly didn't expect you, Miss Clayton—nor that you'd be in company with this rascal. I think there is a story there. You'd best paint me the complete picture. From the beginning."

Between them, they related the violence that had marred their journey. Lady Bottesdale looked glum when Elspeth told her of Skye's part in all this, and she muttered "Joshua Swift! That is bad! Your naval friend baits a tiger, Miss Clayton, and it does not do to twist the tail of a tiger!"

She made no further comment until she had the full account, and then said thoughtfully, "I think you are mistaken, Valerian, in supposing those intruders at Le Havre were not connected with this mission of yours. There is too much here for it to be a coincidence. It is all part of a pattern, though there would seem to be oddly conflicting efforts."

Valerian asked curiously, "How so, ma'am? Do you know of the Le Havre bullies?"

193

"I know the methods of the rogues who hold Vance Clayton prisoner. The men who give the orders are shrewd and those who carry out their orders are professionals and would never attempt so crude a ploy as you describe. I'm afraid that there are other fingers in this pie, which will complicate matters."

"In which case," he said, "we'd best proceed as quickly as may be. What can you tell us of this chateau we must storm, ma'am?"

"It lies half a league from here. You may have caught a glimpse of it atop its hill. It is a large and formidable place, and well guarded. The ancestral home of the Comtes d'Ebroin.

"The deuce!" exclaimed Valerian.

Elspeth asked anxiously, "You know the gentleman?"

"I know of him. He has—" he paused. "He has a reputation for being ambitious."

"An understatement," said her ladyship dryly. "The man is power-mad and hates La Pompadour with a passion. My original plan was to create a diversion which would give you a chance to get to Mr. Clayton. A fire is often effective, but without the men I'd counted on . . ."

Elspeth said, "We will need a different diversion, perhaps?"

Lady Bottesdale smiled slowly. "I think we may have one, my dear. Depending on the extent of your pride."

"Oh, my," said Elspeth hollowly.

Twenty minutes later Freda Beck adjusted the scarf tied about her mistress's head, then tightened her own brightly coloured sash. "Who'd ever have thought we'd dare do anything so wicked, miss," she said. "Big skirts what shows our *ankles*! And sandals and *no stockings* at all! Dreadful!"

Despite the words, her eyes were sparkling and Elspeth was not deceived. Freda looked very pretty in the bright gypsy clothes Lady Elmira had provided, and she knew it.

Surveying her image in the mirror that hung on the caravan wall, she shook her head, setting her golden earrings to swinging. She said with a giggle, "Whatever would Abraham Coachman say if he could see me now, I wonder?"

"I don't think he'd recognise either of us," said Elspeth. "When we are safely home, Freda, we must never breathe a word of this! I only pray Lady Bottesdale's plan works."

"A prayer I second," said her ladyship, hurrying into the caravan. "How pretty you both look in your shocking disguises! Well, Lieutenant Skye, Valerian and his cousin are off to take up positions where they can watch the chateau and be ready to attack so soon as we've succeeded with our 'diversion.' "

"Have they taken Pixie with them, ma'am?" asked Elspeth.

"No. The kitten is asleep in your coach, still. Now tell me, you play the spinet, I'm very sure, Miss Clayton. Any other musical talents?"

"I can manage the harp, a little. But poorly, I fear."

"In that case take this tambourine. You can shake it to accompany me, and you may have to sing."

"Oh dear," said Elspeth ruefully. "I can carry a tune, but my voice is far from exceptional."

"It probably won't matter a button. You have other attributes that are sure to please a group of bored males. What about you, Beck?"

"I can play the mandola, milady."

"Good! I've a lute, which is similar. And whatever you do—don't call me 'milady.' Once we leave here I become Madame Granada! One 'milady' and we're undone!"

She searched through the shelves without success and at last found the instruments in a large trunk half-concealed by the bedding. "Excelsior!" she exclaimed, brandishing the tambourine merrily. She opened the door and shouted, "All right, Marcel? Ah, I see you've got Fandango poled up, poor

195

old fellow. You get along to the gentlemen and good luck, my friend!" She climbed through the small front door to the seat and took up the reins. "Giddap, Fandango! Hoist your hooves, lad!"

The caravan rocked and started to jolt along the lane. Lady Elmira called, "Try not to be anxious, Miss Clayton. We'll have your brother in your arms quick as winking. We must make another change, however. Elspeth won't do— don't sound right for the part. You shall be 'Tina.' Beck can remain as Freda, and I'm Madame Granada, don't forget."

Steadying herself as she peered through the open door, Elspeth asked, "But what is our plan, La—Madame? What are we to do?"

"We're to do our best to draw as many of the guards outside as we can. The rest we leave to your friends—plus I've a fellow on watch who knows exactly where your brother is held and will join them the instant he spots Marcel. Once we have your brother clear, you'll make a dash for the coast and I shall disappear into the countryside, as I know very well how to do." Watching Elspeth's troubled face, she slapped the reins on the horse's broad back and said kindly, "I fancy you think it not much of a plan, but sometimes, you know, 'tis the plans most loosely drawn that prove the most effective."

Elspeth thought, 'God grant this is one of them!'

13

The higher they climbed, the larger loomed the chateau. The setting sun nudged stray beams of amber light through the clouds to gleam fitfully on high Norman chimneys and reflect from mullioned window panes. Grey, tall and austere, its walls embellished with numerous stone gryphons and toothless grinning gnomes, it rose from tumbled boulders and sloping treeless lawns, the lack of softening flower beds adding to an impression of impregnable might.

Gazing at it, Elspeth murmured. " 'Tis formidable, my— Madame."

"And with formidable gates," said her ladyship. "Which are, as you see, closed."

"Oh, lawks," exclaimed Freda. "If we can't get inside, your plan can't work, ma'am!"

The dowager grumbled, "Why is it, I wonder, that things never go quite as one expects? I'd fancied they would have opened the gates by now. Well, we shall just have to—" Interrupted by a harsh male voice, she smiled broadly. "Aha!"

A clatter of hooves and a heavy waggon was vying for the right of way.

The same voice bellowed, "Out of the way, worthless one!"

The caravan jerked and jolted its way off the road and came to a halt on the grassy verge. "A bully sans manners," said the dowager softly, and smiled ingratiatingly at the large and scowling individual who sat his horse exuding hostility.

"There is a difficulty, perhaps, monsieur?" she called. "We were given permission to come and—"

"By whom?" demanded the man, who seemed unable to speak below a roar.

Madame waited until the large waggon had scraped past. Two more horsemen who'd ridden behind it now joined their companion beside the caravan. Uniformly muscular types, they were attired after the fashion of superior servants. The youngest among them, who appeared to be less than twenty years old, wore a scratch wig and affected an air of bravado; the second, a grim-looking individual with a scarred face and icy black eyes, had powdered his hair. The shouter's massive shoulders strained at the seams of his well-cut brown coat, and his crinkly black locks, which looked as if many months had elapsed since last they'd been washed, were pulled back and tied behind his head.

"I asked you a question," he boomed. "Answer me, woman! Who gave you permission? As if anyone would do so stupid a thing as to invite thieving gypsies onto his lands!"

"Monsieur le Comte summoned me a sennight since," said her ladyship blandly. "I am to tell his fortune and—"

"Monsieur le Comte is gone to Paris. So you may turn your lying face around and return to whichever gutter you crept from."

Behind her back, "Madame Granada" gestured urgently.

Elspeth and Freda moved forward and peeped over her shoulder.

"What a pity," sighed Madame. "I am loath to disappoint you when you young fellows would likely have been glad of a little music and song—eh?"

At the sight of the two girls, three sneering faces became wreathed in smiles.

"The old one is right, Dag," declared the younger of them.

"I'm of a mind with Edmond," urged the scarred rogue with the powdered hair. " 'Twould be a real tragedy were these two lovesome creatures sent away."

The shouter, whose name appeared to be Dag, chuckled and with reduced volume agreed that for once his comrades were perfectly correct. All but licking his lips, he commanded, "Go forwards then, woman. We'll hold the gates for you." His eyes lingered on Elspeth and his grin widened.

"Madame Granada" guided the caravan back onto the narrow road, escorted by the three guards who were so intrigued with its occupants that they failed to see a brief flash from a rocky formation at the brow of the hill.

Madame saw, however, and murmured, "Our companions have seen us and will be ready. We must play our parts well. Freda, since your French is execrable, if you are challenged I think you'd best hail from Spain."

Freda said uneasily, "I didn't like the way that big brute looked at my lady."

"Nor did I," said Elspeth. "I felt positively unclad when his eyes slithered over me."

"We shall have to exercise great care," warned the dowager. "These, they are animals and will surely demand a good deal more than singing and dancing. If we can hoodwink them for a little while, we'll have them. Now, under that chair you will see a crate. Pull it more into the open, if you please, ladies."

The crate was heavy and Elspeth said, "So many bottles, Madame. Do you mean to offer the wine as a bribe?"

"I don't mean to offer it at all." Her ladyship said with a wink, "Were I to offer it they'd likely be suspicious. So I am relying on their greed to work for me. We must all pray not one of them has a conscience."

Elspeth asked in a half-whisper, "Is it poisoned, ma'am?"

"Acquit me of murder," the old lady replied. "If they consume enough they will become very slow and silly and then drift into dreamland. By the time they awaken, with God's help we'll have your brother and our lads safe away!"

The caravan rattled through the now wide-open gates and bounced over a cobbled courtyard to halt at the foot of wide stone steps that led up to a terrace.

Dag wrenched the back door open. "Here we are, my pretties," he boomed. "Come, I'll help you out."

"And I also!" declared the scarred man, meeting Dag's challenging glare with defiance.

"Are we to go inside?" asked Madame Granada. " 'Tis chilly out here."

It was indeed colder atop the hill than it had seemed on lower ground.

With a leering grin he apparently judged beguiling but that would have beguiled many gentle ladies into a dead swoon, Dag said, "We'll build a fire for you. Moret—go and summon a couple of those lazy lackeys to bring wood to us. Don't look death at me, you great stupid. The sooner we've a fire and everything made comfortable, the sooner we can— enjoy these ladies."

For a moment Moret stood motionless, slightly stooped, his jet eyes lit by a savage glow. Then he murmured, "Very well. But—one of these days my so dear Dag . . . ! One of these days . . ."

Watching him walk to the house with a supple swinging stride, Madame shivered. "He did not like that, Monsieur Dag. It is well you know how to handle him."

Elspeth said, "He gives me a cold chill!"

Dag eyed her young loveliness, his eyes glinting hungrily. "I think you will find we know how to—keep you warm, mademoiselle," he declared.

Elspeth felt gooseflesh start on her skin that was, she knew, not induced by the lowered temperature.

Freda said boldly, "You're a naughty rascal!"

Dag stiffened. "What kind of accent is that? Where do you hail from, little girl?"

"She is from Spain," interposed Madame Granada swiftly, "and has very little French. We'll need some assistance in getting our instruments out, if you please."

"But we'll be *glad* to assist," said the young Edmond, springing past Dag and into the caravan.

"What d'you wish carried?" boomed Dag, elbowing his colleague out of the way and glancing curiously around the interior. "A cosy little nest you've made here, eh?"

"It serves," said Madame, unobtrusively drawing a blanket across the crate of wine. "If one of you can carry this lute, and we'll need cushions if you're not allowed to bring chairs out of the chateau."

"We'll have no need of chairs," he said, taking up the blanket she had dragged over the crate. "A blanket or two will serve—Hey! Only look at this, Edmond! Small wonder she tried to hide it. Wine! A fine wine and enough for us all! A gift from the gods, no less!"

"A good omen," agreed Edmond with enthusiasm.

"But no!" wailed Madame Granada. "The wine is paid for by Monsieur Bernais in Duclair! I am to deliver it to him tomorrow! You cannot—"

He pushed her aside roughly and, lifting the crate, said, "You will be surprised, madame, at what I can do! Here, Edmond, take this, and if you drop it I'll break your neck! Madame, I think our meeting you was a piece of great good fortune. Now, give me your musical instruments and we'll have some of the entertainment you promised. If you're a good gypsy dame I may even cross your palm with silver and let you read *my* fortune!" Laughing heartily at this witticism, he carried the lute and tambourine and Madame's fiddle case outside and set them down beside the crate of wine.

Lady Elmira, Elspeth and Freda drew warm shawls about their shoulders and followed.

Freda whispered, "What horrid yobboes they is, miss! We'll need our guardian angels tonight, surely."

"Do you understand what he is saying?" asked Elspeth softly, as Dag roared a command for Moret to move his "lazy stumps."

"It don't take much understanding to know what that lump of evil has in mind," answered Freda. "Mr. Valerian had best be quick, that's all I got to say! Very quick!"

At that same instant, crouching beside the south wall of the chateau and watching the courtyard far below, Valerian was murmuring, "Once inside we'll have to move fast. Marcel knows where Clayton is held. That is so, Marcel?"

The sturdy little Frenchman had made haste to join them and was out of breath. "In the north tower, monsieur," he panted. One reaches it by a narrow servants' staircase and— and thence up some spiral steps. It will, I fear, be well guarded."

"I doubt that," argued Valerian. "Of what need to guard a badly wounded man who has likely been weakened by torture and is locked inside a damned great fortress like this monstrosity? We'll place our trust in that whatever guards are inside will hurry out when our brave ladies start their music."

"They are a crude set of rabble-rousers," said Marcel dubiously. "But well trained in the art of death and destruction. You'd do well not to underestimate them, my friend."

Skye said grimly, "Valerian may, but I won't, I've run up against that breed before."

"I'll not underestimate them," said Valerian. "But, by heaven, if they harm Miss Clayton . . . !"

"And Freda Beck and her ladyship," put in Herbert quietly.

"Well, of course," grunted Valerian, shooting an exasperated glance at his cousin. "And what the deuce are you peering at so intently? Never say you're still convinced that legendary blue coach has followed us here?"

Herbert flushed. "If we had a glass I could prove it to you."

"Prove it to me now. My eyesight is sufficient that I could see it—if it exists. Point me the right direction, Herbert. Just once I'd like to catch a glimpse of your persistent pursuers!"

Herbert narrowed his eyes, then grumbled, "Well, I can't see it just at the moment, but—"

Valerian grinned.

"You choose to mock me, as usual," his cousin flared in a rare burst of irritation. "But I *have* seen it, I tell you! Ever since we left that miserable pension!"

"You said you *thought* it was the same coach. And even if it is, it must be nothing more than coincidence. Had that lushy fellow—what did you say his name was?"

"Walters. Sir Harold Walters."

"Had this Walters fellow been alone, it might make some sense. But for a stout middle-aged gentleman travelling with a small boy and a non-dog to follow us with such persistence makes no sense at all."

Herbert said defiantly, "Not all of life is governed by sense!"

"*That* I will acknowledge," said Valerian, with a long-suffering look.

"You are too harsh," said Skye, amused. "Marcel, is the name Sir Harold Walters at all familiar? Have you heard of such a person being involved in this business in any way?"

Marcel tugged at his lower lip, then shook his head.

"Alas, no, monsieur. And the English have such exceeding odd names. That one, I am certain I would recollect."

"Look!" exclaimed Herbert, pointing down at the courtyard. "They've started a fire!"

"Aha! Then the word has gone out," said Valerian. "And there go a couple of footmen to join the party!"

"How many more, I wonder?" muttered Skye uneasily. "Damme, but I hope the wine don't run out!"

"From the look of those first cutthroats," said Valerian, "they'll not be generous with it."

Marcel said, "There are not as many as usual in the chateau. Monsieur le Comte ordered most of his staff and all the maids to his home in Paris."

"Wants as few witnesses as possible," grunted Skye. "Time to go, Valerian!"

"In a minute or two. We'll first let the sounds of their revelry reach to the tower and lure away whatever guards are up there."

With his gaze on the leaping flames of the fire and the men who sat or sprawled about it watching the three women and drinking from wine bottles, Marcel said, "Do not wait too long, messieurs—if you value your womenfolk!"

Herbert said urgently, "He's right! Come on, Gervaise!" He sprang up, drew his pistol and ran for the side door, which they'd already found, as Marcel had promised, to be unlocked. He ignored his cousin's hissed "Easy, you fool!" and sprinted impetuously into a long, gloomy hall. A short but powerfully built individual lounging at the foot of a flight of stone steps turned around, startled by the sound of the opening door.

Aided by the element of surprise, Herbert sprang, flailing his pistol at the guard who reeled back and went down without a sound. As Valerian and Skye raced in behind him, Herbert exclaimed triumphantly, "One less to reckon with, cousin! And taken out of commission silently!"

"But unwisely, alas," sighed Marcel, trotting to join them. "This was Hector Basseport, Madame's spy, on whose aid we were counting!"

Herbert's groan was drowned by Valerian's snarled "Fumble-wit!"

"No time for blame," snapped Skye. "Are these the stairs you spoke of, Marcel?"

The coachman dolefully confirming this, Valerian told him to wait and try to warn them if the need arose, then the three young men sprinted up the steps, along another cold and deserted passage to where a spiral staircase lifted into a gloomy darkness.

Valerian drew the others to a halt and whispered a tense "Listen!"

Above them they could hear men's voices and laughter that became louder. "They're coming down!" hissed Skye.

"We'll welcome them," said Valerian. "Under here! Quick!"

They crouched under the staircase, close against the wall, hearing now the faint strains of a violin and what sounded to be a mandolin accompanied by the rhythmic chimes of a tambourine. Heavy boots pounded above their heads, and the glow of candles gleamed through the treads. Valerian tensed, expecting at any instant to hear shouts of alarm and prepared to respond to a challenge.

A voice with an Italian accent shouted gleefully, ". . . and there are women, my good comrades! And wine!"

They came clumping down the stairs, stumbling in their eagerness.

One of them laughed and remarked upon how fortunate it was that Monsieur le Comte was away.

"While the cat's away . . . ," jeered another.

'Three!' thought Valerian. 'Easy odds!'

In that instant Skye's scabbard struck against the wall.

"Hi!" exclaimed the first voice. "I thought I heard—"

"Likely the unfortunate Englishman above-stairs!" said the Italian impatiently. "Who else could it be? And he's helpless, poor stubborn fool. Move! If we don't make haste that great glutton Dag will drink up all the wine!"

"Ah, but there will still be the women!"

"Oh, no there will not!" muttered Valerian between his teeth, holding back Skye and Herbert as they inched forward.

The guards were down then and all but running along the passageway towards the lower staircase, while dwelling so exultantly on the treats in store that they didn't hear the nemesis that followed.

The first man took the steps two at a time, his friends galloping noisily after him.

Valerian cried, "Now!"

The third guard checked, one foot on the second step. Before he could turn, Valerian shoved him between the shoulder blades with all his strength. The guard was hurled forward to land with a howl on the back of his comrade, who in turn caromed into the first man. All three were down then, tumbling and rolling in a wild helter-skelter of arms and legs and breathless yells and curses that ceased abruptly as they crashed onto the lower corridor.

Two lay unmoving. The third rogue dragged himself dazedly to a sitting position, mumbling something in Italian.

Valerian swung up the barrel of his pistol.

Herbert said, "Allow me, cousin."

With a flourishing bow Valerian stepped aside.

Herbert flailed his pistol and the Italian joined his comrades in slumber.

A moment later the door to the tower room burst open. Sword in hand Valerian sprang inside, crouched and ready for action, but the stark little chamber was empty save for a skeletal individual who lay on a cot and watched him in helpless apprehension.

"A new interrogator?" he said, with a feeble attempt at a laugh. "You'd as well . . . kill me, and not . . . not waste more time. I'll never—"

"Good God!" exclaimed Valerian in English, striding to the bed. "Are you Vance Clayton? They've really had a merry time with you, poor fellow!"

Struggling onto one elbow, Clayton gasped, "Who—who the deuce are you? Seen you before . . . I think."

"Then you should certainly remember me." Valerian slid an arm under his shoulders. "Can you walk? Jove! You weigh no more than a pound of feathers!"

His hazel eyes suddenly full of tears, Clayton said chokingly, "Are you Valerian? I can't believe . . . Have—have you come to . . ."

"We've come to remove you from this palatial suite," said Skye, hurrying to him. "Poor devil! We'll have to carry him, Valerian."

"No," gulped Clayton, faint but with new hope dawning in his ravaged, beard-stubbled face. "Stronger than—than they think. How you come to be here I can't . . . imagine. But—can stand . . . with a little help."

Between them, they got him down the stairs to the lower landing, where Herbert was bending over the fallen. Straightening, he said, "You have him! My heavens, but he's a mess! His sister will swoon away if she sees—"

Valerian interrupted hurriedly, "We don't need to hang about here, gentlemen."

Sagging in their supporting arms, Clayton gasped, "What—'bout my sister? Never say—"

"We won't, for there's no time," said Skye briskly. "We must get on, gentlemen!"

Valerian agreed. "By all means. We've finished the verse, let's tend to the chorus. Marcel tells me he and Madame will convey this lad partway, but there's some tidying up to be done here." He adjusted his scabbard, adding: "Which may not be accomplished quite so neatly."

"Oh, I don't know," murmured Herbert. "There are three of them, cousin."

Valerian looked at him sharply. "And three of us? A good thought! And a quick change of costume is indicated!" Taking off his own coat, he rolled one of the guards onto his back, pulled off his waistcoat and shrugged into it with a grimace of distaste. "Ugh! It fits here and there, but that's the best that can be said for the poor thing! Let's have Marcel in now, Herbert. He can take charge of poor Clayton and our own clothes. Be damned if I'll venture out in public wearing these hideous garments!"

"A Dandy," sighed Skye, appropriating a passable tricorne from another of the guards. "Even as I was told!"

Donning an ill-fitting coat, Valerian said with a grin, "A Deplorable Dandy, to be precise!"

Clayton was half-lying on the lower step, still looking as though he could scarcely believe this miraculous rescue. Glancing at him, Skye muttered, "It seems harsh to keep him and his sister apart. I doubt she'll forgive you, Valerian."

"Oh, no. I'll be the complete villain, I've no doubt. But let her once catch sight of the sorry pass he's come to and her every womanly instinct will demand that she stay at his side! And maudle over him all the way back to the port."

"Well, and why not? Poor old Clayton could use some maudling."

"Perhaps, but for a score of reasons it would be unwise. Clearly he's a very sick man. She'd be fussing at every point—we were driving too fast, or we didn't stop often enough to allow her darling to rest, or we must procure him some medicine or nourishment, or some such thing." He knew Skye was staring at him, and he added gruffly, "Besides which, I'd feel safer were she in my—our care than with Madame Granada, however resourceful that grande dame may be."

"Humph," grunted Skye. "Just as I thought!"

With a touch of defiance, Valerian said, "Well, here's Marcel, so you may stop overworking your brain-box and devote your energies to helping us get Clayton to the coach."

Hurrying in after Marcel, Herbert said urgently, "And then we must help the ladies! Those clods are clean raddled!"

"Is that all?" exclaimed Valerian. "Gad, they must have hard heads! I'd fancied they'd be sound asleep by this time! Up with you, Vance, my lad! You are going out driving, and we've to attend a party!"

───※───

"Sing an' . . . d-dance, girlsh," howled Dag, stretched out by the fire, one hand propping his head and the other waving a wine bottle in time with the melody Madame Granada played on her fiddle.

"Louder! Louder," roared the youthful Edmond, his scratch wig sagging to the side of his head, his eyes glazed and his face very red.

"I cannot play louder," moaned Elspeth, rattling her tambourine vigorously. "Oh, why does Valerian not come? Only look how that horrid Dag leers at us!"

"Never mind him, miss," said Freda, strumming fiercely on her lute. "The one to watch is that ugly Moret. He didn't drink hardly any of the wine, and he puts me in mind of— of a crouching wolf!"

"About to spring!" agreed Madame.

No sooner had she spoken than a savage grin dawned on the scarred face and Moret was on his feet and stalking forward.

"None of that!" cried Madame Granada, moving quickly between him and Elspeth. "We're here to play for you. Nothing more!"

"Out of the way, crone," he growled, shoving her aside, his hungry gaze steady on Elspeth. "You're here to play whatever games *we* want. And me, I want . . . her!"

With the word he sprang. Elspeth gave a shriek and jumped away, but his long arm flashed out, he caught her skirt and dragged her to him.

"Not . . . fair!" bellowed Dag, staggering up and seizing Moret's shoulder. "I found 'em, so—so I'm first!"

"What you are—is drunk, you sot," snarled Moret, fending him off. "You can take—Ow!" He released Elspeth hurriedly and clutched at his hand. Glaring at her balefully as she ran back, he snarled, "Scratch me, will you? Well, me, I never did—like cats!" He was after her but tripped on an empty bottle and fell to his knees, cursing.

Dag uttered a roar of laughter and sat down abruptly.

"Sing!" cried Madame Granada urgently. "Sing!"

Freda began to dance about, twirling her long skirts and singing shrilly,

"There was a youth and a well-beloved youth,
And he was a squire's son.
He loved the Bailiff's daughter dear,
That lived in Islington."

Elspeth pounded the tambourine, two footmen joined in and sang the next verse lustily, until one snuggled down and went to sleep.

Rubbing his knee, Moret got to his feet again.

Watching him, praying Valerian would come with Vance, Elspeth caught a glimpse of three more ruffians running from the side of the chateau and her heart sank. "Madame!" she called despairingly. "Only look!"

They all turned to the newcomers, but, more single-minded, Moret lunged at Elspeth and clamped his arms about her. "I'll teach you . . . pretty vixen," he mumbled thickly, nuzzling at her throat. "When Moret wants a wench—"

Struggling frenziedly, she heard a familiar voice enquire, "What exactly have you in mind to teach the lady, Monsieur Crudity?"

Moret thrust Elspeth away and whirled about. Staggering, she saw Valerian, wearing odd-looking clothes and smiling mildly, but with his eyes fixed in a deadly challenge.

"Oh, thank the Lord," she breathed, then gave a squeal of fear as Moret whipped out a horse pistol.

Valerian's sword flashed into his hand and beat the pistol from the ruffian's hand.

With lightning reaction Moret's sword was in his other hand and he circled warily. "Where you have *come* from, I do not know," he said softly. "But it is that where you *go*, I've no doubt." He lunged with savage eagerness.

Valerian parried and thrust in a fierce and immediate response.

Elspeth was vaguely aware that Joel and Herbert were busily subduing the other rogues, but her fearful concentration was on this battle and she could not tear her eyes away. Moret was mouthing obscenities. Valerian was all smiles. Torn between fear and indignation, she thought, 'He is *enjoying* this, the wretched creature!'

Skye came up beside her and put his arm around her shoulders. "Are you all right, my poor girl?"

"Yes, yes," she said, not glancing at him. "Joel, that man is murderous, I know it! Stop this before he kills Gervaise!"

"He's a fine swordsman," said Skye, "and if I interfere he very well *may* kill Valerian."

Elspeth gave a whimper of fear and pressed tightly clasped hands to her lips as Valerian swung lithely to one side, at the last instant avoiding a sizzling thrust. "Oh, my heavens!"

Skye said, "Come. We must leave this charming palace."

Shocked by the awareness that for a moment she had forgotten their reason for being here, she turned to face him and asked eagerly, "My brother?"

"Safely away," he said. "Hurry now. They'll—"

Madame Granada hurried to them and said admiringly, "Only look at that boy fight! A born swordsman if ever I saw one, but Moret's a killing machine and 'tis not wise to toy with such ruffians."

Swinging around to watch the fierce battle once more, Elspeth gave a sob of fear as Valerian eluded by a hair's breadth the glittering blade that shot for his throat. He laughed and sprang to the attack, beating his opponent back, taunting him with every step.

Skye said severely, "He takes too many chances!"

Herbert ran up, shouting, "Come on, Gervaise! Don't play with him, we must go!"

"Don't! Oh, do not distract him!" cried Elspeth, terrified.

Valerian darted a glance at her, ducked under Moret's flying sword, stamped forward and thrust straight and true.

"Finis!" said Skye, admiringly. "Jolly well done!"

His weapon falling, Moret stood staring at Valerian for an instant, then coughed, and his knees buckled.

Valerian swung his sword into the salute. "A good fight, monsieur," he said, only slightly out of breath. "I thank you." He turned to the little group watching and said with a sideways grin, "Why do you all stand there with your mouths at half-cock?" He wiped his sword on the coat he was discarding, then caught Elspeth's hand and gave it a little tug. "Come along, do! I cannot fripper about here all night!"

14

No, I do not understand!" said Elspeth heatedly. "Why am I not allowed to ride with Vance? Why have I not caught so much as a glimpse of him?"

Seated beside her in the rocking coach, Valerian said mildly, "Why are we returning in Marcel's coach instead of riding with Lady Elmira? You forgot that one—among the other things you appear to have forgotten."

"If you mean I forget to thank you for all you've done—of course I do not forget! You have my heartfelt thanks for keeping *your* part of our bargain!"

"Touché," he murmured with a cynical smile. "That will keep me in my place. No, never scowl at me, brave girl, nor feel the need to remind me of how deeply I'm indebted to you for helping save my father. I told you we were able to bring Vance out of the hole where they had him—"

"Yes, but—"

"I told you he is well, but still weak, and therefore we deemed it advisable to spirit him away as quickly as possible."

"I don't see why I could not at least—"

"I know." He took up her hand and planted a swift kiss on it, then seized the opportunity offered by her astonished reaction to this flagrant piece of flirtation to go on hurriedly: "But there was not the time. We'd intended, as you know, to let you both journey to Le Havre with Lady Elmira. For several reasons this became impractical . . ."

She was gazing at him in a startled fashion, her lips slightly parted. Not for the first time he noted that she really had the most adorable little mouth, the lips full and sweetly shaped and so innocent of affectation . . . He gave himself a mental shake and said, "No, close those pretty lips and let me explain. Firstly, Herbert rides with them and will be better able to transform your brother into the new edition of Mrs. Newell without a crowd hampering his efforts. Also—"

"I am scarce a crowd!" protested Elspeth, collecting the wits scattered by the unexpectedly delicious pressure of his warm lips on her hand. "You know how much I'd looked forward to seeing my dear brother, but you tricked me into going to Marcel's coach believing he was there, and then told me he had instead been taken to the caravan! I am very sure he wanted—"

"Yes, but we cannot always have what we want in life, can we? And I'd think you should care more about his safety than satisfying your own wishes. Also, my cousin is convinced we're being followed by—"

"By a brown coach. So I noticed, but—"

He tensed. "You mean a *blue* coach."

"To the contrary, the coach I saw was quite definitely *brown*. It did seem to follow us for a while, but then it turned off, so I fancy 'twas merest coincidence. And since you set so little store by your poor cousin's opinions, I fail to see why you'd take note of anything he claims to have seen."

"I take note of this particular claim," he said slowly, "because I dare not ignore any possibility that we are really being followed."

"And that is why you let Vance travel with Lady Elmira? You think he will be safer in her coach."

He avoided her searching gaze and added a feeble reinforcement: "It will give your brother the chance to become acquainted with Pixie."

For a while there was silence in the coach. As it rumbled along through the early evening, Freda watched Valerian and wondered if her mistress would detect the obvious flaws in his explanation.

Elspeth turned her head and caught Valerian looking swiftly away. She caught his arm and pleaded earnestly, "Gervaise—you're not deceiving me? If Vance is really in very bad case you *would* tell me?"

He patted the small hand on his arm and said with a smile of rare sweetness, "I would—or at least, I think I would. But he is not. I'll own he's thin and has had a nasty time of it. I was uneasy at your seeing him while he looked bearded and unkempt—which Herbert will remedy, I trust. But I suspect your brother has many healthy years ahead of him."

"Faith, but I am not so missish as you paint me," she argued. "I've managed to survive seeing Vance often when he was ill or had taken some hurt! And what you say makes little sense. I suppose you sent Joel Skye with them to be her coachman, but Madame's caravan is small and cumbersome, and her horse far from swift. Surely they will be easily recognised and those evil men will soon overtake them?"

"Not so, m'dear. The caravan will be left at an isolated cottage in the woods, where Lady Elmira's coachman, a fine team and her own horses wait. Lieutenant Skye will then ride ahead to join us, but my cousin will stay with Lady Elmira. If the rogues who kidnapped your brother should come up with them, they'll encounter a luxurious coach carrying two elderly ladies of quality, a courier, and a little black cat. They'll never have the wits to connect them with a fortune-telling gypsy and their injured prisoner."

"Ah," said Elspeth, clapping her hands. "How splendid! And Lady Elmira and Vance will come to us at *Le cheval de Trois?*"

"Just so. I wish I could say we'll overnight there, but I think we must put as much distance as possible between us and that murderous crew from the unpleasant chateau. The men we fought on the rear staircase will likely soon be in pursuit and I don't know for how long Madame's drugged wine retains its potency. I know you must be very tired, but—"

"No such thing! I can only rejoice we're safe away! Freda and I will be able to rest well enough in the coach, I promise you."

"Bravo! Now, I intend to ride on the box for the rest of the way and give you ladies a chance to exchange those—er, colourful—garments for your own." He added with a grin: "But you may be advised to keep the curtains closed in case Herbert's mysterious blue coach comes up with us!"

Elspeth promised to do so, and he called to Marcel to pull up, then climbed from the coach.

It was not easy for Elspeth and Freda to change their garments in the swaying vehicle, but at last it was done and their gypsy garb tied into a bundle.

Settling back against the squabs, Elspeth gave a sigh of relief. "Thank heaven! I feel almost respectable again! Freda, we've triumphed! Sir Simon is on his way to rejoin his wife in Italy, and my dear brother will soon be safely back in England! Is it not marvellous?"

"Mr. Valerian is a marvellous gentleman," said Freda. "Are you still vexed because he didn't let you see Mr. Vance?"

216

Elspeth said slowly, "I suppose he had his reasons, though they seemed to me rather muddled."

With a mischievous twinkle Freda murmured, "Not so much muddled as self-serving, if I may venture a guess, miss."

Indignant, Elspeth demanded, "What on earth can you mean? He risked his life so as to—"

"Pray don't take umbrage, Miss Elspeth! I only meant—well, I think Mr. Valerian wanted to make sure you was safe in—in *his own* care."

Indignation fled. Glad of the deepening shadows that hid cheeks she was sure were very pink, Elspeth said a considerably deflated "Oh."

A short way from *Le cheval de Trois* Valerian ordered Marcel to stop the coach and pull up behind a clump of trees at the side of the road. He swung down from the box and proceeded on foot, keeping to the trees and shrubs and pausing now and then to watch and listen for any signs of an ambush. Not until he had reached the inn and found everything quiet did he wave to Marcel, whereupon the coachman guided his team back onto the road and continued to the inn.

Once inside it seemed to Elspeth as if they had scarcely left. The inn was as shabby, the proprietor as mournful as ever. Yet during their short absence so much had changed. Their ordeal was over. Vance was rescued, and in only a few minutes she would see him! Meanwhile, Valerian had arranged for rooms and ordered an ample meal to be served in half an hour, these orders causing the gloom on the host's face to lighten somewhat.

The room a shy maid led the ladies to was so devoid of any semblance of decoration as to be positively stark, but Freda's suspicious investigation concluded with the verdict that it was quite clean, although she would not trust the sheets to be free from damp. Since they were not to sleep in the bed, Elspeth was satisfied. It was a delight to wash in the hot water that was carried to them, and when Freda had brushed out and arranged her hair in the ringlets she was magically able to coax into a charming style, Elspeth praised her skill and declared that although her gown was creased, she felt sure her brother would not view her with dismay. Pleased, Freda urged her to rest, but Elspeth was too excited by the prospect of Vance's imminent arrival, and she left the maid busily restoring her own appearance and made her way down the narrow stairs.

There was quite a flurry of activity in the lower hallway; two more coaches had arrived and the occupants, three clerical gentlemen and their servants, were arguing with the flustered host as to accommodations for the night. They made no attempt to step aside so that Elspeth could pass and she was hesitating when a crisp voice snapped, "Your *pardon*, gentlemen," and Valerian came to offer his arm. Amid profuse apologies the clergymen drew back. With no more than a curt nod by way of thanks, Valerian led her to the small parlour and seated her beside the fire. Instead of sitting beside her, he took the chair across the hearth and frowned at her.

Too happy to be anything but amused, she asked, "Now what crime have I committed to warrant so forbidding a scowl?"

He said bluntly, "Could not your maid have pressed your gown?"

She blinked, taken aback. "Had there been time. But I was under the impression you wanted to go on as soon as my brother arrives. Oh—I see! Do you think t'was because of my creased gown that the clergymen would not allow me to pass?"

"Indirectly. Because you wear that hideous and rumpled nurse's dress they took you for a servant, whereas any fool with eyes in his head can see you are a lady. I yearned to knock their stupid noses together!"

Shocked but perversely pleased, she exclaimed, "Valerian! Pray keep your voice down. They are priests!"

"They are clods! One might think a man of God would respect a woman were she a scullery maid or a duchess! Pah! Enough of them! Now tell me truly, Elspeth, your lovely eyes are bright as stars, but you've suffered a frightening ordeal. Are you as fully restored as you seem? Or are you very tired?"

Suddenly and unaccustomedly shy, she said, "Thank you. I'll own 'twas an experience I'd not want to go through ever again, but—oh, Valerian! I am so eager to meet my brother! I expect I shall find myself tired later, but at the moment I can only feel joy and gratitude. In especial, gratitude to you for—"

He stood and interrupted loudly, "I think I hear their coach. Come, ma'am."

Surprised, Elspeth looked around and saw that the new arrivals were entering the parlour, all smiles.

The most impressive among them, a tall man, distinguished in his black garb, and wearing a fashionable wig that spoke of an affluent congregation, bowed and said, "I ask your pardon, monsieur. We do not mean to intrude. Pray be seated, and we will withdraw."

Offering his own brief bow, Valerian replied, "You do not intrude, Father. We are meeting friends. The parlour is yours." He held out his hand to Elspeth and she rose and accompanied him.

In the hallway again, she asked eagerly, "Did you really hear a coach?"

He nodded and said low-voiced, "Into the dining room with you. If it is Clayton, hopefully he'll have become Mrs. Newell, don't forget, so you'll have to contain your sisterly exuberance."

A moment later familiar voices could be heard. The front

door was held open by Joel Skye while Herbert manipulated the Bath chair and the "invalid" up the step.

Peeping into the hall, Elspeth could see no sign of the clerical group, and she was emboldened to leave the dining room. Drawing closer, she could scarcely believe that the elderly occupant of the chair was indeed her beloved brother. Truly, Herbert had worked miracles in transforming him into Mrs. Newell. Her eyes dimmed with tears as she saw that he looked so thin and ill that he made an even more believable invalid than had Sir Simon. Her every instinct was to run to him. She started forward involuntarily, only to be restrained by Valerian's iron hand and his whispered "Easy—lest you wreck everything!"

Herbert wheeled the chair across the hall and Vance's eyes lit up as he saw his sister. With a half-gasped "Ellie!" he held out his arms and in another second Elspeth was in his embrace and whispering, "My dearest! Thank God! Oh, thank God!" She heard his husky "And bless you . . . best of sisters!"

Valerian said coolly, "What a touching reunion! You will be glad to have your nurse restored to you, ma'am," and his hand clamped hard on Elspeth's shoulder.

She bowed her head, wiped surreptitiously at her eyes and managed to say, "We've a room reserved where you can rest, Mrs. Newell, and a tray will be carried up to you."

"I thank you, child," said Vance in a voice pitched higher than his normal tones. "However, I rested in the coach and would as soon take my supper down here so that we can resume our journey without further delay."

Herbert and Skye, who had gone outside again, came back in, Herbert carrying Pixie's "commode" and Skye holding the kitten, which he placed on Vance's lap. To Elspeth's relief, having turned around the required number of times, Pixie curled up and settled down quite contentedly. Skye and Herbert found an inconspicuous corner for the box of earth, then hurried upstairs to, as they said, remove their dirt before supper.

Elspeth took the handles of the Bath chair and turned it towards the dining room, but she stopped when the elderly priest intercepted her.

"Aha. So here we have an invalid, I see," he murmured. And smiling down at "Mrs. Newell," he asked benevolently, "Is there any way I can be of service, ma'am?"

Valerian said pithily, "The lady is scarcely in need of the last rites."

Elspeth gave a gasp, and her brother said, "Really, nephew! I thank you for the offer, sir. But as you see, I am well cared for." And as an afterthought, "Your blessing, perhaps?"

"But of course, dear lady." A hand rested on the lace-trimmed cap; the other hand was raised heavenward, and a sonorous voice invoked a lengthy and involved blessing.

Glancing obliquely at Valerian, Elspeth saw his expression at its most cynical as he eyed the clerical hand on "Mrs. Newell's" cap. He drawled, "Thank you, monsieur. With your permission my aunt will take her supper." He muttered *sotto voce,* "Hopefully, before midnight!"

As Elspeth informed him when they were all gathered about a table in the dining room, he would do well to say a prayer of repentance tonight. "To speak so to a priest is insupportable!"

He said enigmatically, "I'm sure you are correct, ma'am. How do you go on, Clayton? Can you endure a long drive tonight?"

Vance said softly, "I could endure it if I had to crawl all the way!"

"Let us hope we won't come to that." Valerian lowered his voice. "But the sooner we leave here the better I shall like it."

Watching him, Skye said, "You're not impressed by our

221

fellow diners, I see. Why? They look harmless enough."

Elspeth glanced up and saw that the clergymen were seated at a nearby table. She said lightly, "He has a guilty conscience, Joel. He was rude to the elder priest."

Herbert grinned. "Don't say an innocent cleric was so reckless as to flirt with you, ma'am?"

She was irritated to feel herself blushing again, but before she could respond, Valerian asked softly, "Why did you not ride ahead and join us as we planned, Skye?"

"I did," answered the Lieutenant. "At least, I started out to do so. But the half-light is deceiving and I took the wrong road. There's no moon up. Not to excuse my faulty sense of direction, and I don't mean to be a gloom merchant, but I doubt you'll be able to travel far tonight."

"Oh dear!" At once anxious, Elspeth reached out to take her brother's ready hand.

"Don't fly into the boughs," said Valerian coolly.

Herbert put in, "I asked Marcel about it, and he assured me he could drive to Le Havre blindfold."

"Don't doubt it in the least," said Valerian. "So we'll let him be the judge of whether we can proceed. Besides, if 'tis too dark for us, it is likely also too dark for pursuit."

"Will Lady Elmira come in?" asked Elspeth. "In the confusion of the moment I didn't thank her properly, and we owe her so much."

"I thanked her," said Vance. "And she told me that you and Freda were exceeding courageous and saved the day with your 'performance.' Be warned, sister mine, I shall require to know more about that episode!"

With a mischievous twinkle Elspeth said, "I think you have never properly appreciated my skill as a musician, dear."

"We certainly appreciated whichever of you was pounding away at that tambourine," said Herbert. "The uproar quite covered any sounds we made!"

"It was well done," acknowledged Skye, with an admiring smile at Elspeth. "And Madame Granada is a courageous lady!"

Valerian nodded. "Very courageous. And too wise to join us, Miss Elspeth. Were she seen in our company, Monsieur le Comte's rogues might well put two and two together, and it could jeopardise her ability to be of help to Lord Boudreaux in future."

The maids hurried in with fragrant and laden trays, and conversation languished while the weary diners enjoyed a plain but satisfying supper. When the meal ended Skye sought out the host to pay their shot, Valerian went in search of Marcel and Freda, who had eaten together in a small parlour reserved for the servants of guests, and Herbert carried Pixie's commode outside to gather fresh earth.

Walking out to the stables with Marcel, Valerian took note of the dark skies and the coachman admitted that unless the moon could break through the clouds their journey would be difficult.

Valerian persisted, "But if the moon were to come out, even dimly, you could follow the river, no?"

"Our beautiful Seine, it wanders through this area like a coiling snake, monsieur," answered Marcel dubiously. "And were we to follow all the twists and turns of it, we would be like to reach the port in time for break—" He checked to a whispered "Hush!" and Valerian's hand clamping onto his arm.

Two of the clergymen were strolling towards them. They murmured polite wishes for a good evening, Marcel removed his hat and bowed, and Valerian nodded in silence as they went to confer with two grooms who were tending their carriage horses.

Looking after them Marcel murmured, "They are but priests, monsieur."

"You know them?"

"No. Never before have I seen them."

"Are you sure? Might they be some of the ruffians from the chateau?"

The coachman's eyes goggled. "But—no, monsieur! They are *priests*!"

"Yes, yes. But suppose those ruffians were to put on clerical garb, might they not also appear to be men of God?"

Marcel shook his head decisively. "Me, I watched the chateau with milady for several days. My eyes they are of an excellence, and I would know any of those rogues in a trice, I promise you! Monsieur is quite mistaken."

"I hope so," muttered Valerian. "Let's have our team poled up, Marcel. We'll get as far as we can."

He no sooner finished the remark than Herbert came running to them, out of breath and clearly agitated. "The blue coach!" he panted. "I s-saw it again, Gervaise!"

"Show me," said Valerian.

"It's gone now. Drove past at—at the gallop while I was refilling Pixie's box!"

Valerian left Marcel to ready the carriage and strode across the yard beside his cousin.

Now that it was fully dark it was possible to see only a short distance, and there was no sign of coach lamps along the tree-lined road.

Herbert said in frustration, "I knew how it would be! You don't believe me!"

"You're quite sure it was the same coach?"

"Yes! Beyond all doubting!"

Valerian said thoughtfully, "If they're innocent travellers they follow a strange route!"

"Yes! You see? I *told* you they've been following us!"

"So you did . . . And if they *are* following us they may be after Vance Clayton. Though 'tis an odd sort of father would take his small son on such a quest."

"Perhaps to lull any suspicions."

"Perhaps. And if they're the ones pursuing us, then I may be wrong about . . . Tell me more of this Sir Henry—Jupiter! What's the fellow's name again?"

"Sir Harold Walters. You met him at the smith's forge, don't you remember?"

Valerian gritted his teeth. "Thank you! I'm aware of that much, but I paid him little heed. My impression was that he was more than a little up in the world, but of a mild disposition. Scarcely the type to engage in political intrigue, though one can be deceived, of course."

"That coach was being driven at reckless speed on night roads."

"True. And if they realise they've overshot us, they may come back! We'll collect Skye and the girls and be on our way!"

Side by side they returned to the inn. The dining room was deserted. A shiver of warning crept down Valerian's spine. He called to a maid who was clearing the tables and she ran to answer his question. A gentleman had called, she said, and the nurse had taken him to see the elderly invalid lady and her little cat.

Valerian, ice joining the shiver between his shoulder blades, demanded, "Taken him—where?"

His tone frightened the maid, who bobbed a curtsy and stammered, "To the p-parlour, milord, b-but I'm sure there was no—"

Not waiting to discover what she was sure of, Valerian sprinted to the parlour, Herbert following.

Flinging the door open, Valerian stood rigid for an instant, petrified by the scene before him.

Elspeth was huddled on her knees beside a sofa. Sir Harold Walters bent over her, and his son was punching Vance Clayton in the back.

15

With an inarticulate snarl of rage Valerian tore across the room, his sword whipping into his hand, his face livid.

"Damn your eyes!" he raged. "Stand away from her!"

The reactions were as immediate as they were unexpected.

Sir Harold Walters spun around, saw doom rushing upon him and, with remarkable agility for so large a man, shot behind a chair, yelping, "Hi! Hi, now!"

Elspeth straightened and exclaimed in a near scream, "Gervaise! *Whatever* are you about?"

The boy left "Mrs. Newell" and ran in front of his father crying, "Let be, you wicked man! Do not *dare* touch my papa!"

Clayton sat wheezing in the Bath chair, holding a handkerchief to his streaming eyes.

Barking shrilly, a small dog raced from behind the sofa and bit Valerian on the ankle.

"Ow!" said Valerian, confused but lowering his sword. "Get away, you brute!"

"Don't *kill* him!" wailed the child, snatching up his pet and retreating with him to a far corner. "Oh, please don't kill my Tueur!"

"It appears," said Valerian, sheathing his sword and looking from one to the other of them in bafflement, "that I labour under a false impression. Perhaps someone will be so good as to tell me what is going on here." He walked over to give a hand to Elspeth and restore her to her feet. "For instance, why were you on your knees, ma'am?"

Eyeing him anxiously, she said, "You're limping! Did he really bite?"

"To the bone," he replied. "That great hound is well named! I will likely perish!"

"Then you should take to your bed at once, sir," said Sir Harold, emerging cautiously from behind the chair. "Certainly, you need to cool your temper! If ever I saw a more hot-at-hand individual!"

"If you had harmed the lady," said Valerian grimly, "you'd really have seen a hot-at-hand individual! No, don't pitch me your gammon, sir. I'll hear it from Nurse—er," unable to recall the name he'd bestowed on Elspeth, he extemporized, "Nurse Muslin." Meeting her startled and amused glance, he realised he had failed to name the correct fabric.

Sir Harold folded his arms and looked affronted.

Crossing to her brother to hide her twitching lips, Elspeth sat near to him and said, "Luke's dog frightened Pixie, sir, and I was trying to coax her from under the sofa. Are you better now, er, ma'am?"

In a strangled voice Clayton gasped that he would be the better for a glass of water, and Sir Harold sent his son in search of one.

"Do you encourage your boy to beat sick old ladies?" asked Valerian.

"No such thing!" declared Sir Harold, firing up. "Mrs. Newell laughed so much when the dog was chasing the cat around the room that she had a choking fit. Luke was patting her on the back—simply trying to help, you know."

"Your son has a heavy hand," said Valerian dryly. "And even if what you say is truth, it does not explain why you've been following us since we left Le Havre. We followed a circuitous route that makes it impossible for you to have taken the same roads by sheer chance. We've seen you on several occasions, so pray do not deny that you *have* followed us."

"I was not following *you*, Van Newell," argued Sir Harold, drawing himself up haughtily.

"Considering the fact that you were well over the oar when we were first introduced," said Valerian, "your memory is good, but your facts are faulty. "My name is Newell. No Van—just plain Newell."

"Well, whatever your name is don't signify. As I said before, I wasn't following *you*. I was following *him!*" Sir Harold indicated Herbert, who started and stepped back in obvious apprehension. "Although," Sir Harold added, "had I known what a firebrand accompanied him, I doubt I'd have made him the lucrative offer I had in mind!"

Sitting on the end of the sofa and dangling one foot lazily, Valerian echoed, "Lucrative—offer?"

Sir Harold nodded, then glanced uneasily at the Bath chair. "It is by way of being a—a personal matter." His colour considerably heightened, he requested gruffly, "Perhaps the ladies would be so good as to leave us."

Uncertain, Elspeth looked at Valerian. He hesitated, then said, "Very well, pray take my aunt in search of that long-lost glass of water, Nurse. Lieutenant Skye's about somewhere. Stay with him and don't wander off. We'll be leaving directly."

Elspeth said a meek "Yes, sir," and took the handles of the Bath chair.

Herbert closed the door behind them, and Valerian said curtly, "Your offer, Walters? Pray be brief, we've been sufficiently delayed by this nonsense."

"It is not at all nonsense!" declared Sir Harold. "Faith, sir, but your manners—" Given pause by the expression on the younger man's face, he amended hastily, "At all events, you may be assured that 'tis a matter of prime importance to me. It concerns my—um . . . ah—my . . . teeth, d'you see?"

Herbert's jaw dropped.

Valerian stared incredulously. "Your . . . *what*? I'd have sworn you said—"

"I said, as you know very well, my *teeth*! Oh, 'tis all well and good for a young fellow like you, still in possession of a fine set, to smirk and think it a trivial matter! It ain't, I promise you! I once had a splendid mouthful. My smile, in fact, was much admired by the fair sex! But—through a series of unhappy events, I lost several, and—"

"Ladies?" interposed Herbert, fascinated.

"*Teeth*, blast your dim wits! I lost several *teeth*!"

"Good God, sir!" exploded Valerian. "If you've followed us halfway across France and back to ask for a recommendation to a good dentist—"

Sir Harold interrupted huffily, "Of course I have not! I *have* a good dentist. At least, he's proud of his skill at pouring hot lead into cavities and tearing one's rotted fangs out with a pair of pincers! But when it comes to replacing 'em—Hah! Another story!"

Battling an urge to laugh, Valerian said, "You surely must have found a competent fellow to make you a—a plate, or whatever they're called."

"Competent, sir! *Competent*? London's full of upstarts who dub themselves *Skilled Craftsmen* in the art. What they are is charlatans, sir! *Charlatans!* To the last man! I've had

229

two sets made—at considerable expense! One set made me look like a goat! And t'other fits well enough but the teeth are *yellow*, sir! Furthermore, they are different *shades* of *yellow*!" He added sadly, "More'n I dare do to crack a smile! Would make me a laughing-stock!"

Beginning to indulge a suspicion, Valerian restrained himself and ventured cautiously, "So you're in France to try again?"

"I spend a good deal of time in Paris. I've been keeping my eyes open, I admit, but most men don't take good care of their teeth, and I've seen none to compare with . . ." He turned an admiring smile upon Herbert, who edged closer to his cousin.

Unable to stifle the bubble of mirth that had been welling up, Valerian shouted with laughter and rocked back and forth on the sofa.

Scarlet with vexation, Sir Harold protested, "I'm able to pay handsomely! Damme, it ain't amusing, Valerian!

"What—what it is," gasped Valerian disjointedly, "is—hilarious! Herbert, n-never look so conflummerated! This fellow—this silly fellow is—is after your teeth!"

His mirth turned to a howl as he discovered that it is unwise to dangle one's foot over the edge of a sofa when a cat is hiding under it.

Ten minutes later, while Joel Skye and Marcel poled up the team, Valerian related the incident to Elspeth and a convulsed Clayton. Wiping tearful eyes and weak with laughter, he said, "At least we know that Herbert's legendary blue coach presented no danger to us. Did you mark the speed Walters came to as he drove out? His face was nigh purple with mortification. Poor simpleton! He must be short of a sheet!"

"Why? Because he admired my teeth?" said Herbert, grinning.

"He admired 'em, all right! So much that he was eager

to draw three! Of course, he did say he'd pay handsomely."

Clayton said laughingly, "Perhaps you should have considered his offer, Mr. Turner."

Herbert shook his head and shuddered.

"Whatever else," said Elspeth, "it brought a smile to our journey. Though I understand you were the victim of another attack, Mr. Valerian?"

"I was indeed," he said aggrievedly. "Which confirms my belief that cats are treacherous creatures. I rescued that vicious little beast! 'Tis purely thanks to my kindness that she was housed and indulged and well fed by my trusting sire, and what do I get in return? Great gouges down my ankle! Had I not been wearing shoes my foot would be in shreds!"

"Faith, but animals would seem to take you in aversion," murmured Elspeth, demure but with dimples peeping. "Even one of your admired dogs bit you!"

Fascinated by the dimples, he said absently, "Tueur is well named, I grant you, but he was under no obligation to me as is Pixie. Nor did he hide and spring from ambush as— Jupiter! What nonsense am I talking when we should be on our way? What has become of Skye?"

Elspeth said, "I'll go out and see what is delaying them."

"Oh, no you won't!" Valerian caught her wrist as she turned to the door. "Wait here!"

He snatched up his cloak and went out to the yard. It was quite dark now, the air was chill and all was quiet save for the muted sounds of crockery rattling in the kitchen and the occasional stamp of a horse in the stables. Fastening his cloak, he peered around the yard but could see nothing untoward. Neither could he hear the sounds from the stables that he should hear: Marcel and Skye talking together, or the ostler at work. His nerves tightened and his earlier suspicions, which had been lulled by the arrival of Sir Harold's blue coach, flared again.

Treading lightly, sword in hand, he sprinted across the

yard. The door to the barn was half-closed and the lantern inside revealed only a narrow view of a coach. There was no sign of groom, ostler, Skye, or Marcel. Pausing in the deep shadows beyond the doors, he watched the coach intently. It stood perfectly still with none of the motion that would be caused by the fresh and impatient horses that should be poled up by this time.

The sensible thing would be to return to the inn for reinforcements, but he had little faith in the fighting spirit of the host. There was no doubt but that Vance Clayton, who was a fine swordsman, would come willingly, but he was struggling to recover from his ordeal and too weakened to be of much aid. Be damned if he'd call Herbert away from Elspeth! If his suspicions were justified at least two of the rogues were in the barn, waiting for them all to come out. Had they been on level ground in daylight he'd have tackled them gladly, but they were inside and probably well armed, whereas he was out here without his pistol, and the instant he went through that door he would present an easy target.

He crept around to the side of the barn and peered at a solitary window, but it appeared not to have been washed in several years and only a blurred glow showed through the grime. A quick scan of the yard revealed nothing that would serve as a weapon, but his eyes brightened when he saw a broken wheelbarrow propped against the wall. He whispered, "Aha!" sheathed his sword and lifted the wheelbarrow. It was heavier than he'd supposed, but he managed to hoist it above his head and, gritting his teeth with the effort, hurled it at the dirty window. Whipping out his sword then, he raced to the barn door as the sound of shattering glass was followed by the roar of twin pistol shots.

He was inside before the would-be murderers had turned from the broken window. His flashing glance around the stables revealed no sign of Marcel or Skye. He had no time for more than that brief scan as he sprang to the attack. He'd guessed rightly; two "priests" flung down their useless pistols and snatched for swords.

The element of surprise and the extra few seconds it took for them to whip back their black robes served Valerian well; he was on them before their weapons were free of the scabbards. One he despatched with a sizzling thrust that sent the man to his knees. But these were seasoned cutthroats and before Valerian could disengage, the second rogue was attacking and he had to jump aside to avoid the steel that whistled past his ear. It was a battle then, the pseudo priest attacked ferociously, probably, thought Valerian, because he realised the shots would have been heard and help would come from the inn. The light in the barn was poor, but after the first flurry of swordplay Valerian knew that he was the more skilled and would overpower this villain without much difficulty. At the back of his mind, however, was the nagging worry that the third "priest" was still inside, and he set a brutal pace, driven by the need to make sure that Elspeth was not threatened.

The air rang with the keening scrape of steel on steel and the stamping of boots in advance and retreat. Outside now were shouts and running footsteps. The impostor's clerical robes flapped wildly as Valerian drove him back.

From the doorway, Herbert shouted, "Skye? Marcel?"

Enraged, Valerian thought, '*Herbert?* Then who the devil is with Elspeth?' His attention diverted, he tripped over the wheelbarrow and went down heavily. Sprawling, he saw the blade that arced down at him. With lightning reaction he whipped up his own sword to deflect the thrust but had to swing his blade aside to avoid impaling his cousin, who leapt valiantly to the rescue.

Valerian swore as white-hot pain lanced through his sword-arm and the weapon fell from his grasp.

Herbert howled triumphantly, "Courage, Gervaise! I have the bastard!"

The attacker, evidently deciding that he was outnumbered, fled.

"I'll 'courage' you!" panted Valerian, clambering to his feet in time to see Skye and Marcel subduing the first assailant, who'd recovered sufficiently to attempt to follow his friend.

Herbert snatched up Valerian's sword, then threw a supporting arm about him. "Jupiter! That fellow winged you, I see! Lean on me, old fellow!"

The host ran up to aim a horse pistol at the assassin, then back away crying a dismayed "The priest! Mon Dieu! This it is a sacrilege!"

Valerian thrust his cousin away and, clutching his arm, reeled towards the yard, shouting wrathfully, "Who's with Elspeth?"

"Her brother," said Herbert, eyeing him with resentment. "And I'd think you might have a word of thanks, rather than—"

But Valerian was already running to the inn.

Two maids peering nervously from the open door jumped aside as he leapt up the steps. One of them caught sight of his bloodied hand and called out an offer of help. He scarcely heard her. Elspeth wasn't there. If all were well, that indomitable lady would have been halfway across the yard by now. With a groan of apprehension he tore open the door to the parlour and his worst fears were realised: white-faced, Elspeth stood by the sofa. Behind her, the elder "priest" had an arm clamped around her throat. The pistol in his free hand was aimed steadily at her head. Clayton was still seated in the Bath chair, watching his sister in horror.

The impostor purred softly, "Close the door, hero."

Valerian stepped back and kicked the door shut. "Your accomplices have been overpowered and can't help you. You're trapped. Give yourself up. You've no way out."

"But of course I've a way out."

The arm about Elspeth's throat was tightened, and she gave a little choked cry.

Valerian stamped forward, only to halt abruptly as the impostor snarled, "Do you want her killed? Then keep back and keep your stupid friends away! She goes with me, if she's sensible and tells me what I want to know. Otherwise," he shrugged and said with a mirthless grin, "she won't be the first woman I've put an end to!"

Looking into his savage eyes, Valerian didn't doubt it. He heard Herbert's voice and then Skye pushed at the door. "Gervaise? Let us in, man!"

Valerian held the door closed. "Keep away! The other pseudo-priest has a pistol pointing at Nurse Muslin!"

The outside voices were abruptly silenced.

The impostor said, "I've nothing against the old woman. But you're wasting my time! Now, mademoiselle who is not a nurse, tell me, and tell me quickly before I break your pretty neck! Where are you to meet your brother?"

Elspeth gasped out something unintelligible.

Edging forward, seething, Valerian snarled, "How can she speak, you great imbecile, when you're strangling the poor girl?"

"Keep back!" cried the pseudo-cleric, but he slightly relaxed his hold around Elspeth's throat.

She sagged, coughing, then crumpled in a swoon.

Unexpectedly supporting her full weight, her captor was taken off-balance, and the pistol jerked in his hand as he instinctively attempted to keep her from falling.

It was all Valerian needed. He sprang forward, so enraged that he forgot his sword and struck hard and true with his fist. The impostor was smashed backwards and Elspeth twisted from his grasp, but in so doing she loosened the pin Freda had used to fasten her bodice. Clutching the sagging bodice, she saw that her captor had contrived to raise the pistol again.

"Horrid beast!" she exclaimed furiously, and retrieving the pin, without an instant's hesitation she drove it hard into the impostor's gun hand. With a howl, he lost his grip on the pistol and simultaneously Valerian seized him by the throat.

Clayton meanwhile had left the Bath chair and he now picked up the pistol, then threw one arm about his sister, asking anxiously, "Are you all right, love?"

"Yes, yes," she answered, her frantic gaze on Valerian. "Stop that wicked priest, Vance! Please! Gervaise is hurt!"

Watching the two men as they struggled and plunged about, Clayton smiled faintly and called without much force, "Let be, Valerian! I have his pistol and if you'll just step clear I'll blow the swine's brains out."

Valerian scarcely heard him. Blinded to everything but his overmastering fury, he tightened his grip on the throat of this scheming murderer who had dared lay brutal hands on a gentle lady. He was vaguely aware that his victim's countenance was distorted and turning blue, the beady dark eyes were starting out, the mouth gaped wide, and the attempts to escape had ceased. Clayton was shouting something. A door opened, then hands were pulling him. He swore at them savagely, demanding that they let be. A faint and delicate scent drifted to him and a beloved voice pleaded, "Gervaise, I'm quite all right, truly. Please stop. You're hurting yourself. Please, Gervaise. Don't kill the horrid creature!"

The words penetrated the red mists that clouded his brain. His fingers were as if frozen and he had to force them open, whereupon his assailant fell to the floor with a thud. He turned his head to find Elspeth beside him, smiling but tearful and with crimson splotches on her gown. Rage seized him again. He snarled, "He *did* injure you!" Bending over his crumpled adversary, he gripped him by the stock and hauled mightily. "Get up, filth, so I can kill you!"

"It's not my blood," cried Elspeth shrilly. "Herbert, for pity's sake, stop him!"

With the combined efforts of his cousin and Skye, Valerian was restrained and at length convinced that Elspeth was unharmed. Breathing hard, he blinked down at her uncertainly. "You're really all right?"

"Yes, I promise you. But you are not."

"Eh?" He peered down at his crimson hand and muttered a bewildered "How was I so clumsy as to do that? Ah!" He raised his head and scowled at his cousin.

"That's better," said Elspeth. "I was beginning to worry, but I see you are your usual amiable self. Now come into the kitchen."

The host plunged into the room, pale and distraught. "Another priest?" he moaned. *"Mon Dieu!* Have you perhaps a loathing for the clergy, monsieur?"

"They're not clergy," said Skye briskly. "You must lock them up, host, and summon your constable. These men are hired assassins come to kidnap the lady!"

Drawing Valerian away from the excitable discussion that followed, Elspeth persisted, "Do you mean to stand here and bleed to death? I won't allow it! We must tend your wound."

"On one condition," he murmured, leaning on her as she slipped an arm about him.

"Nonsense!" She led him into the hall where curiosity got the better of her, and she said, "One condition, indeed! What, for instance?"

A frightened maid came hurrying to help.

Valerian lowered his voice as if faint, and Elspeth turned to him anxiously.

He whispered in her ear, "Promise not to replace that pin you stabbed him with."

"Oh!" exclaimed Elspeth, her cheeks flaming, but a relieved gleam in her eye. "You are outrageous!"

He prompted, "As well as deplorable?"

"As well as deplorable!"

―⟨❧⟩―

"We were completely taken by surprise." Joel Skye poured brandy into a glass and set it on the table in front of Valerian.

Elspeth came into the parlour and sat in the chair Herbert pulled out for her. "The host's lady says she will have your shirt washed and dry before we leave, Gervaise. It's fortunate that you brought another in your valise." Scanning his face she thought he looked haggard and said, "I suppose 'tis useless to ask how you go on, for you'd feel obliged to declare that you are perfectly fit."

"Most of me is just so," he answered with a slightly uncertain smile. "And thanks to your excellent bandaging my arm will heal rapidly. I have to own they were formidable fighting men, our ungentle priests!"

Herbert said stoutly, "They'd have to be to have succeeded in knocking you down, cousin. I'd have said few men could best you in swordplay."

Looking into his earnest face, Valerian gritted his teeth but managed to hold back his indignant response and say an immodest "So would I."

"Likely they caught you by surprise," said Skye excusingly, "even as they surprised us. And who the deuce would have suspected those three pious frauds?

Elspeth said, "Valerian did, I believe from the beginning. Didn't you?"

He was feeling considerably wrung out and the wound which had not been very painful at first was making up for lost time, but he said lightly, "But of course. Their impersonation was not quite perfect."

Herbert selected a biscuit from a bowl on the table and, waving it at his cousin, asked, "In what way?"

"In two ways," said Valerian thoughtfully. "There were

probably more, but I only counted two. Firstly, when their nasty leader gave you his blessing, Clayton, you'll recall he rested his hand on your pretty cap?" Clayton made a face, and Valerian grinned and said, "His fingernails were very dirty. Perhaps there is no ecclesiastical canon that says a man of God must keep clean fingernails, but it struck me as being somewhat incongruous. Secondly, they had no Bibles. Not that I expect a priest to haul one about at all hours of the day and night, but with three of 'em travelling together, you'd think there'd be a Good Book in evidence some-where—especially when they were lounging about in the cof-fee room or the parlour."

Elspeth nodded. "I thought there must be a reason why you were so rude to them."

"If you suspected the bounders, why a'plague could you not have warned the rest of us?" demanded Skye irately.

"Because I was so foolish as to fancy my suspicions un-founded," Valerian admitted. "When Herbert's legendary blue coach hove into view I thought the threat came from that direction and abandoned my impressions of our priestly trio. I should have realized sooner that the unhappy Walters in his covetous pursuit of my cousin's teeth actually had nought to do with the infamous Comte d'Ebroin. I let you down. I'm sorry for it."

Elspeth said, "What fustian you do talk, sir! And small wonder. I'm very sure that arm is exceeding painful. We're safe now and there's time for you to rest as my brother is doing before we go on. To bed with you, Mr. Valerian!"

"Your brother is in far worse case than am I," he argued. "And as lovely as you look, there are shadows under your eyes, Nurse—What the deuce *is* your name? I keep forget-ting."

"Brocade," she said pertly.

They all laughed, Valerian said Herbert would assist him up the stairs in a minute or two, and having extracted his promise to rest for an hour or so, Elspeth, who ached with weariness, allowed Herbert to light her way up the stairs to the room where Freda awaited her.

Hurrying back to the parlour, Herbert interrupted a low-voiced discussion. Closing the door, he sat down again and looked from his cousin to Skye suspiciously. "Very well. What did I miss? You have something more to say, I think, Gervaise?"

Skye said, "He thinks our imitation priests were not from the chateau."

Puzzled, Herbert asked, "Why?"

Valerian said, "For one thing, they were a cut above Monsieur le Comte's bravos."

"More to the point," inserted Skye slowly, "they knew Nurse—ah, 'Brocade's' true identity, which the fellows at the chateau did not know."

"And also," said Valerian wearily, "they wanted to know where Elspeth was *to meet* her brother. The men from the chateau would know she has already met him and guess he was either here with us, or with Lady Bottesdale."

"Egad!" exclaimed Herbert, dismayed. "If the clerical trio did not come from the chateau . . ."

Skye nodded and finished the sentence. "From where else could they have come?"

16

*D*o stop shaking me, Freda! I'm awake." Elspeth
stretched sleepily. "Good gracious! You're up and
dressed already! Whatever is the hour?"

"Nigh seven o'clock, Miss Elspeth."

"It seems we just went to bed!"

"Yes, miss. But Mr. Valerian says as we must press on.
There's hot water ready, Mr. Herbert is changing the bandages on Mr. Valerian's arm, and the Lieutenant is arranging
for breakfast."

"I must see how my brother goes on. He is improved, or
so I think, but still far from well."

"Mr. Herbert means to help him be Mrs. Newell so soon
as he finishes with Mr. Valerian, he said, which means as
Mr. Vance must first be shaved very close. Mr. Herbert says
as he's grateful Mr. Vance is a fair gentleman and not one
with a dark beard as grows fast. They will meet you in the
dining parlour and he's likely done with Mr. Valerian by this
time, so we'd best be quick, miss."

"Very well." Hurrying through the ritual of washing and

dressing, Elspeth said, "I thought there was no great need for haste now. But I expect I'm being thoughtless. Mr. Herbert is anxious for his cousin to be seen by an apothecary, which is very right. Oh, you managed to iron this poor gown! Thank you, Freda! It looks so much better!"

"T'weren't none of my doing, miss. I planned to get up early and press it for you, but Mr. Valerian sent up a housemaid last night just after you fell asleep, with strict orders as she were to iron it for you. I said as I could do it in the morning, but he'd told her I'd had a long day and must get some sleep. Kind, I thought it were. Very kind."

Elspeth agreed warmly that it had been a thoughtful gesture and Freda murmured pertly, "P'raps the gentleman mayn't be quite so deplorable as what you fancied, miss."

Very aware that she had reached the same conclusion, Elspeth smiled and, leaving the maid to gather their belongings together, went downstairs, pondering the enigma that was Gervaise Valerian.

He soon joined her in the dining room. There were dark shadows under his eyes and she thought he looked pale and more haggard than he had the previous evening, but he greeted her cheerfully and in response to her enquiry assured her he was feeling "much more the thing."

"You do not look at all 'the thing,'" she said, scanning him uneasily. "Before we go on we must find an apothecary and have that arm properly tended."

"You are very good." He pulled out a chair awkwardly and sat beside her. "But you know doctors and quacks of that ilk love to warn with ponderous solemnity that you've one foot in the grave when you consult them for no more than a hangnail. Gives 'em a chance to demand a larger fee."

"You do not require care for a hangnail," she argued. "That is a very nasty wound. You could scarce pull out that chair—oh, never deny it, I have sharp eyes, sir!"

"And very lovely they are, Nurse Brocade, but—"

"Never mind the pretty compliments, Mr. Valerian! Better you should keep in mind that you named me Nurse 'Cotton.'"

"Brocade has more of a ring to it."

"Oh, I agree—No! I will pour your coffee, the pot is heavy. Since you are convinced the authorities both here and in England will remember Pixie, they will likely remember my name, so—Now what is the trouble?"

He said meekly but with a glint of laughter in his eyes, "I'm not sure if I can lift this cup. Perhaps you would be so kind as to help me."

"If you will stop being foolish I will help you into carrying your arm in a sling." She made an effort to speak sternly, but her treacherous dimples betrayed her.

He said absently, "How sad for your brother that he was not blessed with such charming dimples, poor fellow."

Ignoring this provocation, she thanked the maid who carried in a platter of eggs and buttered toast but then said, "No, no! This will never do! Mr. Newell and his aunt must have bowls of gruel!"

The maid responded nervously that Lieutenant Skye had ordered gruel, "but Monsieur Newell changed the order, mademoiselle."

"And Monsieur Newell will throw through the window the first bowl of gruel that comes his way," said the culprit, taking up knife and fork. "Begone, fair maid—and no gruel as you value your life!"

Giggling, the maid fled.

Elspeth sighed and helped him to one egg and a slice of toast. "'Tis not yet sun-up," she said, passing him a dish of preserves. "I thought you were going to sleep late. You were still up when I retired, arranging for my gown to be ironed, no doubt, for which I thank you."

"Purely selfish," he said. "I've my reputation to consider

and cannot be seen jauntering about France with a nurse who wears a rumpled gown."

"How could the shocking conduct of 'Mr. Newell' damage the reputation of that famous beau, Gervaise Valerian?"

"You said it yourself, Miss Elspeth Cotton! I *am* famous. At any instant I expect to meet someone who knows me!" She chuckled and he went on: "Besides, we had to wait for the local forces of law and order to arrive and take our prisoners into custody. From the looks of 'em, I've no great confidence those three villains will be confined for long."

"Ah. So that's why you want to hasten."

"To rest on one's laurels can be a chancy business, and— Good morning, Aunt Geraldine! You look better every day!"

"I wish I might say the same for you, nephew," said Clayton, as a red-faced Herbert guided the Bath chair to join them at table. "You look thoroughly pulled, and Herbert says—"

"Now is that kind?" said Valerian aggrievedly.

"What does Herbert say?" asked Elspeth, blowing a kiss to her brother.

"That my cousin's arm is inflamed and he should see a surgeon," said Herbert, mopping his brow. "Those stairs are the devil!"

Clayton said, "Oh, I don't know. I floated down on the aroma of breakfast. Jove, but those eggs look fine! I'll take three if you please, Ellie!"

"You will take *one*," she said, passing his plate. "Which is more than you should! Were I a proper nurse—"

Valerian broke into a loud fit of coughing and behind his napkin slanted a warning glance at her.

The host had wandered into the room and, looking dolefully around the table, imparted the news that Monsieur l'agent, the local policeman, had locked up the vicious criminals securely but desired that Monsieur Newell call upon him at his convenience to fill out a report of the crime.

Valerian glanced at Elspeth, and rising to the occasion,

she said that as a nurse she must urge that Monsieur l'agent be patient. "Monsieur Newell needs rest," she declared. "In fact, his wound is proving so troublesome that I intend to fashion a sling for his arm."

"Perhaps a little later in the day I will be better able to see him," murmured Valerian, drooping in his chair and darting an irked glance at her.

A little later in the day, however, Monsieur l'agent was still waiting for Monsieur Newell to call, and the coach was bowling along the Le Havre road with Monsieur Newell, Elspeth, and Clayton inside. Freda had voiced a desire to ride on the box next to Marcel, so Herbert rode escort with Skye.

A lingering morning mist hung over the Seine, but it was a bright day that offered a hope for some afternoon sunshine. Clayton, who had become fond of Pixie, was dangling a knotted piece of string which she pounced at and pedalled fiercely. Valerian was quiet and irritable, due to the fact, thought Elspeth, that she had outmanoeuvred him in the matter of carrying his arm in a sling.

In this she wronged him, however; his arm throbbed with wearying persistence, and although he complained of looking like a proper figure of fun, he was inwardly glad of the support the sling offered. His irritability stemmed from the fact that Elspeth had clapped her hands when they'd driven away from *Le cheval de Trois* and declared with joyful triumph that they left their troubles behind them and were "Safe, at last!" For her sake, he wished with all his heart that were so, but he knew he would not count them safe until they were back on British soil. Elspeth appeared to have forgotten the brown coach she'd thought was following them. He had taken Skye aside before they left and warned him quietly to be on the alert if such a vehicle should appear, and several times along the way he'd leaned closer to the window, peering at the road behind them.

Clayton asked him shrewdly, "Do you agree that we're safe away?"

Valerian was tempted to voice his inner misgivings, but the sight of Elspeth's happy face prompted him to summon a grin and say lightly, "Your sister will tell you I'm a disagreeable man, Clayton."

Elspeth laughed at him and told him to cheer up and not borrow trouble. "Only look at the countryside this morning. It was dusk when we travelled this road before and now I see that it is much prettier than the Le Havre area, which was so marshy and flat. Here there are little green hills and copses of trees everywhere, and so many boats on the river. Do you see the chalk cliffs, Vance? Just like our Dover!"

The miles slipped away; Pixie and Clayton dozed, and Valerian watched Elspeth, who was still fascinated by the changing scene. He was thinking that they soon must rest the team when the coach slowed and Herbert rode up to the window to announce that they were approaching a village where Marcel knew of a reputable apothecary.

Secretly disturbed when Valerian raised only a token protest, Elspeth said, " 'Tis nicely timed, and if you do not appreciate it, sir, I shall be glad to escape from the coach for a while."

Marcel gave them directions, then turned the team into the yard of a humble little wayside inn. Skye helped Clayton down the step and wheeled him into the building, and Herbert said he would give the kitten a little exercise and led her into the back garden secured to her ribbon.

Elspeth accompanied Valerian to the cottage of the apothecary, which was only a short distance from the inn.

The apothecary was a big man with a scrawny and ineptly powdered wig, a startlingly high-pitched voice and an abrupt manner. There were no other patients in the tiny and immaculate waiting room into which he ushered them. He looked at Elspeth curiously and Valerian explained that "Nurse Cotton" was attending his invalid aunt and had graciously taken him under her wing also. The apothecary grinned and in a low-voiced aside told Valerian that he would be happy to have such a wing at his disposal. The cold stare he received banished his grin, and with a nervous cough he led them into his surgery, remarking in a gruff and business-like manner that Nurse Cotton could assist him.

Apprehensive, Elspeth was releved when her assistance consisted mostly of gathering the tools of his trade with which, thanks to the youthful escapades of her reckless brother, she was familiar. When the existing bandages were cut through, however, Valerian clapped a hand over them and ordered her to wait outside.

"Certainly not," she said, perversely indignant. "I am quite capable—

"You are quite capable of attending an elderly lady," he said in a tone that brooked no interference. "But be dashed if I'll have a female maudling over me! Into the waiting room with you, Nurse. At once!"

She bit her lip to stifle the set-down she would have de-lighted to give him, but since she was supposedly in his em-ploy she had no choice but to do as he said and wait, fuming, in the chilly waiting room.

When the inner door opened at last, Valerian winked at her cheerfully and said that the apothecary had repaired him to the point that he would go on nicely until they reached England. He was very pale, however, with a sheen of per-spiration on his brow and a pinched look about the mouth that frightened her. She threw a searching glance at the apothecary and he shook his head and looked stern.

Dismayed, she asked, "Is that the case, sir?"

"Have I not said it?" snapped Valerian, taking her arm. "Come, we must not keep my aunt waiting."

Elspeth shook off his hand. "As soon as I hear what this gentleman has to say. Your aunt will expect me to have in-structions regarding your care, as you well know."

"My *care*?" he spluttered. "I'm not a small child in nankeens, ma'am!"

"Then do not behave like one," she said firmly. "Pray tell me, sir. Is Mr. Newell well enough to travel?"

"By all means," said the apothecary, smiling at her with new respect.

Resisting Valerian's tug at her elbow, she persisted, "But he is so white as any sheet. Are you sure?"

"Well, it was necessary that I cauterize the wound, which is not pleasant, as you know, Nurse. But he is young and healthy and should go along without complications—provided he stays abed for a week or so."

"Stuff!" exploded Valerian rudely, and went on in English, "Did I not tell you, ma'am? They're all alike, these quacks, whether they call themselves doctor or apothecary! Makes no difference, they'll spout gloom and doom and are likely responsible for many a healthy fellow turning up his toes when had he steered clear of 'em he'd have made a fine recovery! Now I've paid this glummery twice what he warrants, and I've no more time to waste. Come!"

All but dragged to the front door, Elspeth hissed, "What a rudesby you are! Suppose he speaks English?"

"Suppose pigs can fly," he said mockingly.

Hurrying to open the door for them, the apothecary said in perfect English, "You've a stubborn patient, Nurse, and my sympathy. If you will accept the advice of this 'glummery' try to keep him quiet and he may not turn up his toes before his time!"

Scarlet-faced, Elspeth stammered an apology.

For once speechless, Valerian hurried her away.

When they approached the inn a man ran past them at speed, shouting something excitedly and incoherently.

Valerian recovered his voice. "Hello," he muttered. "*Now* what's to do?"

Several people were gathered around the yard, a carriage

248

was drawn up on the far side of the inn, and Marcel was bending over Joel Skye, who sat on a bale of hay, head down. A large lady wearing a voluminous and snowy apron, presumably the wife of the innkeeper, was running about in great consternation, shrilling conflicting orders at an ostler and stable-boy, having to do with an injured gentleman in the house.

Elspeth's heart began to pound with fear. She whispered, "Vance!"

Valerian clasped her hand firmly and pushed his way through the small crowd. "Marcel! What's happened here?"

The coachman turned swiftly. He looked distraught. "Ah, monsieur," he said. "It is that I go inside for a word with Monsieur the Lieutenant, and we call for some wine, then hear a great amount of confusion outside."

Managing to get a clear view of Skye, Elspeth exclaimed, "Joel! You are hurt!" She ran to his side. "Oh, your poor head is cut! Did you fall?"

Skye blinked up at her with a twisted attempt at a smile. "Just a shade—damaged," he admitted jerkily. "Nought for—for you to worry about. My—my own fault."

Valerian demanded, "Continue, Marcel!"

"The Lieutenant, he run out to see," the coachman explained, dabbing a wet cloth at a cut above Skye's temple. "I follow, and I find this one lying with a broken head, and the other poor gentleman prostrate and—"

Elspeth gave a gasp of fright.

"My aunt?" snapped Valerian.

The innkeeper's wife, who had followed this conversation anxiously, burst out, "No, no, monsieur! Madame Newell, she rests in my parlour. It is not a lady who lay prostrate on my husband's cobbles but, as your coachman have say, a gentleman, who has been most viciously attacked and robbed! Here! In the broadest of daylight! Here, in our fine house that is always peaceful and quiet until—"

Marcel cut into this impassioned declaration to announce, "The gentleman is this—er, is—"

Skye interrupted in turn, "It is Sir Brian Beech, Valerian."

Astonished, Elspeth exclaimed, "My *uncle*? What on earth—Is he badly injured? Where is he?"

"Inside," said Skye, holding his head painfully. "And I think he is not seriously hurt. His son is with him now and they've sent—for the apothecary."

With a shocked cry, Elspeth ran into the inn.

Valerian bent over Skye and said in English, "Let me help you up, poor fellow. Now, take it slow and carefully, and tell me before we go inside, what the deuce is all this, and how come the Beeches to be here?"

Skye was obviously dazed, but as he stumbled along with the aid of Valerian's good arm he managed to convey that, as Marcel had said, they'd been taking a glass of wine when they'd heard shouting outside. "I thought 'twas a collision perhaps," he said. "So like a fool I ran out, thinking to help. I had time only to see Beech lying in the dirt, and then a club or a brick or something properly levelled me."

Frowning, Valerian asked, "Did you catch sight of the rogue who hit you?"

"No. He must have been behind the door and caught me fairly as I ran out."

"And nobody saw him—or them?"

"Apparently not. By what I've been able to gather, Sir Brian's son—Conrad—had waited in their coach, while his father went inside to make enquiries. He came running when I was knocked over and a housemaid started screaming, but by that time the thieves were well away and had robbed Sir Brian of his watch and a valuable jewelled pin."

"Was anything of yours taken?"

"I think not. They likely hadn't time."

Valerian grunted and helped him up the steps and into

the rather dim interior, where the host hurried to assist the Lieutenant to a faded and worn but comfortable chair in his own parlour.

Leaving the host and a maid caring for Skye, Valerian went in search of Elspeth. It was not necessary for him to ask where he would find the injured man. He followed the wailing outcries to a bedchamber where Elspeth sat on one side of a bed, holding her uncle's hand, and Conrad stood on the other side, watching Sir Brian anxiously.

"... no safety anywhere, for the innocent traveller!" Fingering his lace-trimmed cravat with trembling fingers, and with a coverlet spread over him, Sir Brian Beech lay propped by many pillows and gazed with varying degrees of tragedy and indignation from one to the other of his relatives. "This is a perilous and lawless land," he declared, and catching sight of Valerian as the door opened, he added, "So you're here are you, sir! And from the look of you another victim of the violence that threatens us all!"

Valerian said with a slight shrug, "We can but play the cards as they are dealt, sir. I go along very well, but I grieve to hear that you've suffered an attack. I suppose you are in this locality seeking us?"

"We were, and glad I am of it, despite what it has cost me, for no sacrifice is too great if it enables us to find dear Elspeth at last! But," he moaned distractedly, "my poor new coat, Valerian! Do you see it on the chair there? Such a rare and exceptional shade of green velvet! And the cut! Perfection! The shoulder is quite ruined! I did but have it from my Parisian tailor in February! And my cravat! Those varmints tore it when they wrenched my very favourite pin away! My emerald pin! A precious family heirloom of great sentimental value in addition to its monetary worth, which is incalculable for it is irreplaceable, and so much admired! Do you see my fine coat there? Only look at such wickedness!"

251

Valerian looked, clicked his tongue, and agreed sympathetically that it was a wicked world.

Conrad intervened at this point to remark that he was very glad they had come up with his cousin at last. "My father is perfectly right, Valerian. 'Tis a wicked world, and France of all places the most wicked! I take it you have been unsuccessful in freeing your poor brother, Elspeth, and will be eager to return home."

Elspeth's face lit up and her lips parted, but Valerian intervened coolly, "Do you, Mr. Beech?"

Elspeth started and turned to him questioningly.

He met her eyes, his own unfathomable.

"What's that?" snapped Sir Brian, starting up from his pillows. "Why should my niece not wish to go home, sir?"

Conrad said, "Do you say that you were successful, Mr. Valerian, and have brought Vance Clayton to safety, and unharmed?"

"Oh, I'd not go so far as to say that," Valerian replied.

Elspeth declared eagerly, "They were simply wonderful, Conrad! Joel Skye and Mr. Valerian and his cousin! You'd never believe—"

"Which reminds me," Valerian interrupted, "Skye has a concussion, I fear, and is asking for you, Miss Elspeth."

"Oh, heavens!" Frightened, she jumped to her feet. "Forgive me, Uncle, but I must go to him at once! He has been so good!"

Sir Brian reached out to her and said faintly, "Pray do not leave me so soon, dear niece." He dabbed a lace-edged handkerchief at his eyes. "I have been cruelly upset and it eases my pain to have your gentle presence at my side while I am—alas, so weak and ill."

Torn, Elspeth hesitated.

Conrad urged, "Stay with my sire, dear cousin. I'll go down and see how Skye goes on."

"You are most kind," said Valerian. "But, do you know,

Mr. Beech, I really think poor Skye would so much more appreciate words of comfort from a lovely lady than from a man—even so noble a gentleman as yourself."

It was mildly said, but Conrad's eyes glinted angrily. Before he could respond, Valerian had swung the door open and led Elspeth into the narrow passage.

"Ellie . . . ," wailed Sir Brian pathetically.

"She will be up again directly, sir," said Valerian, pulling the door shut.

Conrad jerked it open again. "See here, Valerian! I do not care for your high-handed interference in our—"

"Ah, here is the apothecary," said Valerian. "You will find your next patient in this bedchamber, sir!" And in a low-voiced aside to Conrad: "He's a good man, Mr. Beech, and will, I feel sure, want Miss Clayton elsewhere so that he may give your unfortunate father a complete examination. I expect you will elect to stay by your sire. Should you wish me to tell your coachman to pull your vehicle into the barn?"

Conrad stared at him. "How's that?"

"Oh, a relatively simple task, sir." Valerian expounded kindly, "He merely has to guide the hacks into the yard and—"

"I *know* how it's done, confound you!" grated Conrad through his teeth.

Puzzled, Elspeth said, "Gervaise, whatever are you talking about?"

He answered with an apologetic smile, "A matter on which I am mistaken, apparently. You will think me wits to let, Mr. Beech, for I'd fancied the vehicle waiting in the side lane to be yours."

"Oh," said Conrad, relieved. "Is that the case, then? In all the confusion I'll own I had quite forgot, but it can wait. I'll go down and give our coachman his orders in a minute or two. Thank you for reminding me."

"Not at all." Valerian bowed politely. "We will meet again, sir."

"We will indeed," agreed Conrad Beech.

17

Valerian bespoke a light luncheon to be served in the only private parlour the inn offered. Skye insisted he was sufficiently recovered to join them, but when the meal was over and the other two men left the table he lingered with Elspeth. She refilled his coffee cup and murmured worriedly, "I still cannot think who they can have been. Surely those horrid ruffians from the chateau lost us long since?"

"And as surely will know our direction," he pointed out wryly. "Though why they should attack your uncle is beyond me!"

"Exactly my own thought! They could not have known of our relationship. The beasts at the chateau did not even know who I am. Joel, do you not want your coffee? You ate hardly any of the soup and the cheeses and hot bread."

He smiled at her fondly. "Never look so anxious for me, Ellie. 'Tis just the headache and will soon fade." And in an effort to turn her thoughts, he asked, "Where is everyone gone? Valerian is seldom far from your side."

Aware that she was blushing, she poured a mug of coffee

for herself and answered with what she hoped was nonchalance, "Oh, I fancy he is chatting with my cousin in the tap—or what passes for the tap. This is a very small inn, you know."

"True. At home it would be judged no more than a hedge tavern. I'm surprised to hear that Valerian and Mr. Beech are enjoying a convivial talk. I'd somehow gained the impression they were not exactly—er, kindred spirits."

Elspeth sighed, "I wish they could be friends. Mr. Valerian has been splendid, and it is so good of my uncle and Conrad to have come all this way trying to help me."

"Especially since your uncle was very much against your taking such chances to free Vance. But you've done it, Ellie! Just as you so bravely set out to do. It's all over now! We'll be back in England in a day or so and your life will go on as smoothly as it did before you embarked on this adventure." Watching her intently, he saw her smile fade and his heart sank. He asked gently, "That *is* what you want, isn't it, dear girl?"

It had long since occurred to Elspeth that the future he painted was just what she did *not* want, and she suffered the same little pang that so often seemed to pierce her of late. Knowing how anxiously this devoted young man gazed at her, she summoned a smile. "Of course it is," she lied. "But what of you, Joel? Whatever is to become of you when we get home? I couldn't bear it if your career were—"

He reached out to clasp her hand. "Let's worry about that when the time comes. Meanwhile, where has Herbert got to? You know, I like that boy. He idolizes his cousin, and if Valerian could just be a little more patient with him I believe he'd be less apt to—er—"

Elspeth chuckled and said, "To tumble into his little embarrassments? Perhaps. But Sir Simon told me that Valerian is more fond of him than he shows. Herbert has gone out to the stable. Marcel found something wrong with one of the coach wheels, and Herbert went to see if he could be of assistance."

"So that's why we are tied by the heels here! I don't care for these delays. The sooner you are safe home the better I shall like it."

"So shall we all. But at least it gives you and Vance a chance to rest for a while."

"A rest won't hurt Valerian, either. Jupiter! What a sorry rescue party we are come to! The halt and the lame, no less!"

"Say rather the brave and undaunted." Elspeth smiled and stood. "Even so, I think I'll go and see how my brother goes on. Try to sleep for a little while, Joel. I'll let you know in plenty of time when the coach is ready."

Leaving him, she closed the parlour door quietly and made her way to the stairs. The innkeeper's wife hurried to meet her in the entrance hall and point out the door to her private parlour. "It is behind the curtain, beyond the tap," she said, in the nervous flow of words that appeared to be her normal way of speech. "Madame Newell drank some soup and admires my brioche. Mademoiselle Nurse will pardon if I do not accompany her. It is that we have more guests arriving and must now make changes in the rooms, and the maids are in great excitement because of all the trouble. We are not accustomed to trouble in this quiet corner of France. But your patient, Madame Newell, she now sleeps quietly with her little cat. Please to go in, mademoiselle, and send a maid if anything is required."

Elspeth thanked her and hurried along the passageway. She heard laughter as she passed the tap and lifted her eyebrows slightly. 'Twould seem her cousin and Valerian were enjoying a more comfortable cose than she'd envisioned.

Anyone observing the two gentlemen in the tap would have shared Elspeth's opinion. They both lounged on settles, a half-empty bottle of wine on the table between them and their mirth decidedly raucous.

Waving his glass with an abandon that sent the contents splashing, Valerian hiccuped, mumbled, "Y'r pardon,

B-Beech, ol' fella!" and asked a slurred, "S'what ha-happened then? Was th' lady amen-amen—friendly? I've found these French lassies often . . . Hic! Le's have 'nother bottle up! This wine's dev'lish flat! Hey! Wench!" Rising, he weaved unsteadily and half-fell back into his chair again. "Deuce take't . . . ," he exclaimed, laughingly. "*You* get it, Conr'd ol' f'la. M'silly legs melted . . . be damned to 'em! Melted!"

With a faint grin, Beech strolled over to the bar and leaned to the pretty serving maid.

A swift pounce towards a nearby potted plant and Valerian's glass was quite empty and sagging in his hand when Beech returned, his own gait unsteady and a fresh bottle carried with care. "Here we gooo . . . ," he crowed. "Egad! Empty 'gain? You c'n really stow it away, Ger-Germain! Heard you had a hard head, b-but—"

"Vaise," Valerian corrected with another howl of laughter. "Ger-*vaise*, dear boy! Not 'Main.'"

"Thass right! Vaise, b'Jove! Sort've like Vance . . . same number've letters. Vaise 'n Vance. Which 'minds me—jolly good've you to have got him free. M'cousin dotes on him, y'know. Been—been meanin' t'ask you—where'd you hide him, dear boy? Somewhere safe, I tr-trust?"

Valerian waved his glass and put one unsteady finger against his nose. "Extry safe," he said owlishly. "You'd never guess . . . Hic!" His heavy lids drooped and closed, his head sagged and he began to snore softly.

Conrad Beech shook his shoulder. "Wake up! You're drunk, sir! Wake up!"

Valerian started and peered up at him. "Whazzat?"

Beech prompted, "You was 'bout to tell me where you'd hid m'cousin Vance."

"Oh, yes. Was. Lemme tell'ya, Conrad ol' f'la . . . Hic! You'd never guess . . . where . . ." A deep sigh, and his head sagged again.

Conrad swore and glanced up as the door opened and his father joined him.

Taking in the scene at a glance, Sir Brian wandered over to the bar and murmured something to the serving wench. She giggled, held out her hand, then tucked some coins into her bodice and ran out of the tap, closing the door behind her.

Sir Brian joined his son, put up his jewelled quizzing glass and surveyed the sleeping man without delight.

"You must be feeling better, sir," said Conrad dryly.

His father glanced at him, smiled faintly at the ironic tone and shook his head sorrowfully. "Whatever have you done to the poor fellow?" he asked. "It took you long enough, with the result that, deuce take it, you're nigh as far gone as this drunken sot! Shame on you!"

"He has a dev'lish hard head," mumbled Conrad sulkily. "But almost I had him! He was about to tell me when you walked in."

"In that case," Sir Brian poked Valerian with his quizzing glass, "you must wake him up. And as soon as may be!"

Conrad shook Valerian again, less gently this time. "Wake up, damn you!" Repeated attempts were no more successful than the first. Valerian muttered something inaudible and incoherent but did not open his eyes. Frustrated, Conrad growled, "Is useless, sir! You see how it is—he's in a drunken stupor, I can't wake the fool!"

Sir Brian smiled and smoothed a crease from the fine red satin coat he now wore. "I put it to you, my dear boy," he said softly, "that you had *better* wake him! I've not followed my slut of a niece all this way only to be foiled because you allowed this arrogant pest to fall into the bottle! If we do not get our hands on Vance Clayton before the lawyers do, he will inherit and the fortune will be lost to us. I *need* that inheritance, dear son of mine! And be damned if I'm going to allow that wretched girl to outwit—"

With a lithe spring Valerian was out of the chair and

258

confronting them, eyes flashing and a pistol held steadily in his left hand. "So that's it!" he cried, with not the suggestion of a slur to his words. "I *knew* you were up to your ears in this puzzle!"

Sir Brian grated an oath and started for him.

"Stay back!" said Valerian. "And be assured I can shoot as well with either hand! If all I suspect of you two rogues is truth, Elspeth's father had good reason for refusing to acknowledge you! Hand in glove with that murderous schemer who tried to break Vance Clayton at his chateau, no doubt. Only your ignoble motivation was not politics but pure greed! You dogged our trail to make sure we didn't help Clayton escape and go on living! A fortune, you said, I believe, dear sir? One that will go by rights to Vance Clayton, unless you remove him from the line of succession! That's it, no?" Reading confirmation in their enraged faces, he laughed. "Aye, that's the root of it, I'll wager! So to clear your path to riches you plotted the murder of your own kinsman! What a pair of conscienceless scoundrels!" He waved his pistol. "Over there, beside your sire, Mr. Beech! Now keep your hands where I can see—"

Perhaps because his injury had dulled his senses he underestimated the depths to which greed can drive a man. As Conrad moved reluctantly between Valerian's pistol and his father, Sir Brian seized his opportunity and shoved his son with all his strength. Conrad staggered and fell heavily against Valerian.

Slammed backwards, Valerian crashed into a settle. A blinding wave of pain ripped through his injured arm. His bones seemed to melt away and he sagged helplessly. Echoing with distance he heard Conrad's shrill protest: "Damme, sir! You could've got me shot!" and Sir Brian's bland response, "But I didn't, did I, dear boy! Quickly now—we must help Elspeth's knight errant remember where he has hidden my accursed nephew . . . !"

Dimly aware that the pistol was being wrenched from his hand, Valerian heard Sir Brian demand, "Where is he? I know you got him away!"

He said nothing.

A back-handed blow across his mouth.

He managed something uncomplimentary. The price of that defiance made him feel sick.

Sir Brian snarled, "Answer me, damn your eyes!"

He was being shaken agonizingly.

Conrad said, "Do not hope that help will come. We've paid the serving wench handsomely to say the tap is closed. Speak up, you fool! Why put yourself through this misery? My cousin is nothing to you, and we're not unreasonable. A single word and we'll be gone. Where—is—Clayton?"

He gave them a single and very vulgar single word.

One of them struck him brutally.

All too briefly he lost touch with the proceedings.

<hr />

The instant Elspeth opened the door to the host's parlour, she wrinkled her nose. It was very apparent that, as the inn-keeper's lady had remarked, something "was required."

The room was cluttered and overfurnished, but it was warm and quiet. The second Mrs. Newell was fast asleep in a deep chair, a rug thrown over his knees. The wig was slightly askew on his head, but it warmed her heart to see him resting so peacefully. She smiled at him fondly and sent up a small prayer of thanks that he was here and safe. Curled up on his lap, Pixie stretched out her front legs, uttered a welcoming trill and gave a huge yawn, but showed no inclination to leave her comfortable haven.

Elspeth whispered, "Be *a l'aise*, you lazy creature! Much you care if we poor humans are obliged to tidy up after you!"

It crossed her mind to summon Freda to attend to matters, but reminding herself that a nurse did not have her own maid, she took up the kitten's commode and carried it to the door, hoping she would not encounter anyone en route to the yard.

There were sounds of activity from a bedchamber; the host's wife and her maids, no doubt, preparing the room for the expected guests. Elspeth hurried past, but luck was with her and she was downstairs before she saw anyone. A serving maid was dusting a cabinet half-heartedly. Elspeth walked towards the side door to the stables, then checked. For a moment she'd thought to hear her uncle's voice, though at a far from weakened volume. Pausing, she turned to the tap. The maid shot in front of her, bobbing a curtsy, as she announced, "The tap it be closed this afternoon, mam'zelle."

"No it is not," argued Elspeth. "I heard my uncle's voice! Stand aside!"

The authoritative tone caused the maid to hesitate. She looked at the box Elspeth held and backed away.

Pushing the door open, Elspeth took two steps and halted, stunned with shock.

Ashen-faced, his mouth bloodied, his injured arm twisted up behind him, Valerian sagged in the grip of her cousin. Even as she watched numbly, Sir Brian said a harsh "Speak, you stubborn damned idiot! Where is Vance Clayton? You'd best be quick in answering me! We've sent word to the Comte d'Ebroin of your whereabouts and dragoons are at this very moment on their way to arrest you!"

Obviously near collapse, Valerian croaked something incoherent. With a snarl of rage, Sir Brian struck him in the face.

Finding her voice, Elspeth ran forward. "What are you doing? Are you gone mad? Let him go at once!"

Conrad whirled around with a horrified gasp, releasing Valerian, who sank weakly to his knees, clutching his wounded arm.

The expression of maddened rage on Sir Brian's face was

wiped away as he turned, smiling, but Elspeth had seen it.

"My poor child," he purred, strolling towards her and fanning himself daintily with his lacy handkerchief. "This unscrupulous wretch has deceived you, just as I suspected. He holds your poor brother captive somewhere, and refuses—"

"Get away from me!" cried Elspeth, drawing back.

With a great effort Valerian pulled his head up and choked a warning, "Run . . . ! Get—"

Sir Brian's face convulsed with fury and he kicked out, sending Valerian sprawling.

A rage such as she had never before known wiped away all restraints. With a muffled cry, Elspeth resorted to her only weapon, and as her uncle stamped towards her she hurled the contents of the commode directly into his face.

His scream was ear-splitting. Spitting and swearing, tearing frantically at his face, ripping off his wig, running about blindly, he gave every indication of a man gone completely demented.

The door burst open and Herbert rushed in with the host beside him.

Conrad slipped quietly from the room.

Herbert exclaimed, "Gervaise!" and running to drop to one knee beside his cousin, he put an arm about him and lifted him gently. "My God! What on earth has—" He stopped speaking and looked up, appalled, as a panicked Elspeth rushed to his side.

"My dear Lord!" she gulped. "Is he—"

Awed, Herbert whispered, "He's crying!"

"No, he's not." Smiling through tears, Elspeth said brokenly, "He's laughing!"

Their small parlour was quite crowded when they had gathered there. Only Joel Skye was absent as he related a considerably edited account of events to the pompous local agent of the law whom the landlord had summoned.

"How I should love to have seen it," mourned Vance Clayton after yet another burst of merriment. "My dainty dandified uncle, adorned with the—er, contents of Pixie's commode!"

Wiping tearful eyes, Valerian said, "Shall I ever forget it? Truly, you could not have devised a more devastating punishment, my demure little Nurse Cotton!"

"For a moment," said Herbert, sighfully reminiscent, "when I first arrived and saw him dancing about, I really thought he had gone berserk."

"And you may have been correct," agreed Valerian. "Certainly, whatever wits he had were thoroughly scrambled!"

Watching him, Elspeth was relieved to see that the savage interrogation he'd endured had left his spirits undaunted. The cut beside his mouth and the bruises on his jaw and temple she judged to be relatively minor, but she was a little worried by the glitter of his eyes and the faint flush high on his cheekbones. The wound in his arm, she decided, was not so minor. At this point she became aware that Vance was smiling at her, probably expecting her to comment, and she said hurriedly, "Even so, he is a very bad man and should not have been allowed to escape."

Joining them in time to hear her remark, Joel Skye tossed his tricorne onto a credenza and, pouring himself a glass of wine, said, "I rather suspect he and his son will waste no time in leaving the area. It seems they are suspected of involvement in several unsavoury matters and there have been notices sent from Paris instructing the authorities to detain them should they come this way."

Valerian said, "Small wonder we were so beset with disasters throughout our travels. Those supposed Mohocks who attacked Nicholas Drew in Town were undoubtedly hired by Beech, as were the bravos who broke into the pension outside Le Havre. You'll remember, Elspeth, that they knew who you were."

"So they did," she exclaimed. "My goodness! So all the time it was my uncle's hirelings who meant to stop us!"

"And when my uncle and Conrad so gallantly came to our rescue at the Trojan Horse, they had actually arranged the attack themselves," said Vance wonderingly. "What dogged persistence!"

Herbert said, "Then those pseudo-priests were in their pay also! And some of the bravos at at the Chateau d'Ebroin. But I think most of that ugly crew belonged to the fine gentlemen who want to bring down La Pompadour."

"Yes, but somehow the Beeches had learned who was holding Vance," said Valerian. "Just think how well it would have suited their plans had he died at the hands of La Pompadour's enemies. They would have been rid of the threat he posed and could be held blameless for his untimely demise. They were likely happily preparing to shed tears at your funeral, Clayton!"

Skye said thoughtfully, "They took a chance, though. Suppose he'd survived, or told what he knew and been released?"

"I suspect they'd prepared for just such an unlikely development," said Valerian. "They may have paid one of the chateau guards to murder Clayton. Certainly, they had no intention of allowing him to escape alive."

"And how extreme glad I am that you were able to elude my uncle's traps and rescue me from that loathsome hole," said Vance fervently.

Amused, Valerian observed, "Gratitude you possess in abundance, Clayton. But your lack of curiosity amazes me. Have you no least interest in learning about this mysterious inheritance?"

Elspeth said, "Valerian is right, Vance! Who on earth can have made you heir to what would appear to be a large fortune?"

Her brother shook his head. "I've no least notion. Didn't

think anyone in our family had a feather to fly with, but—"

"Oh, my goodness!" cried Elspeth. "Speaking of flying—Gervaise, with all the violence and excitement I quite forgot! What was it my uncle said about dragoons? Remember? When he was threatening you."

They all waited uneasily.

Puzzled, Valerian said, "I've no idea. I don't recall him saying anything of that nature."

She wrung her hands agitatedly. "Likely you were in no condition to hear him. But he did! I know it!"

Skye walked closer to her and said gently, "Try to remember, Ellie. Was this after you emptied Pixie's box over him?"

"No, no! It was when I first walked into that dreadful room! Sir Brian was trying to force Gervaise to tell him where we were hiding Vance." She put a hand to her brow and went on, "I was so horrified that at first I couldn't even move, but I heard him say something about . . . about Gervaise answering quickly because—Oh! Now I recollect! Because, he said, dragoons were on their way to arrest us all!" She reached up to Skye frantically, and he took her hand and held it. "Joel! We must go! At once!"

Frowning, Valerian stood. "Yes, indeed! We cannot fail now! We're almost to Le Havre!"

He sent Herbert running to the stables to find Marcel and have the team poled up and the horses saddled; Skye went to gather their belongings; Elspeth hurried in search of Freda, and he himself sought out the host and paid their bill. Over Elspeth's protests he chose to ride for this last stage of their journey. He claimed that he felt the need for some fresh evening air. The truth was that he was very tired and had a nagging presentiment that he must keep awake in case of more trouble.

Within minutes he had ushered the girls and Vance into the coach, Marcel was on the box, and Skye was climbing up beside him, having loaded the Bath chair into the boot. The ostler brought up their extra horse. Valerian's swing into the saddle was stiff and awkward. His arm was miserably painful, his head pounded and his bruises ached. It was as well, he thought wearily, that he'd insisted on riding. Had he been comfortably installed in the warm, coach, he'd have been asleep in jig time.

Herbert, who had ridden to nearby high ground to get a good view of the road, returned at the gallop, shouting, "Sir Brian didn't lie about this, Gervaise! There's a fair-sized troop coming this way!"

So his apprehensions had been justified! He called, "*En avant,* Marcel!" only to exclaim, "Hi! Stop! Jupiter! Where are my wits flown? Who has our Pixie?"

There was consternation. In the rush to depart they had all forgotten the little cat that was so necessary to their plans. Comparing notes, it was clear that no one had seen her since the confrontation with the Beeches in the tap.

Herbert drew near and called urgently, "Make haste! They're almost here!"

"When did you last see Pixie?" shouted Valerian.

At once dismayed, Herbert answered, "Not since we took Skye inside after he was knocked down. Jove! Is she not in the coach?"

"No, and we must find her!" Dismounting, Valerian called, "Marcel—drive out! And spring 'em! Herbert, you ride escort!"

Leaning from the window as the coach jolted on its way, Elspeth cried, "No! Gervaise, don't—"

"Go on," he ordered harshly, and ran back to the inn.

A frantic search was instituted. Valerian, the host and his lady, the maids and even two of the guests looked everywhere, but there was no sign of Pixie. Realizing that they dare delay no longer, Valerian sprinted into the yard. He encountered his cousin, whom he'd thought was riding beside the now vanished coach, and yelled, "Herbert! What the deuce . . . ! Come on, man! We'll find another black kitten!"

Herbert spun about and ran to the horses. Mounting up and starting across the yard, Valerian saw that the coach had turned back also. Voicing some heart-felt oaths, he galloped towards it, gesturing imperatively, and the team was wheeled and began to move forward again.

From the box Skye shouted, "Did you find her?"

"No," answered Valerian.

Leaning from the open window, Elspeth said, "Oh, Gervaise! Your father will be so disappointed. She's such an affectionate little creature."

He guided his mount close to the coach. "True. But she's only a cat and your brother's life must take precedence! My cousin saw the dragoons almost upon us. We'll have to find another black kitten is all. It's sad, but—" Glancing around, he discovered that Herbert was nowhere in sight. "Now blast that idiot!" he raged. "I told him to give it up! Of all the stupid—Well, he'll just have to take his chances!"

Elspeth said agitatedly, "We cannot just abandon him!"

"I think we have no choice. He's a grown man and has at least a particle of common sense. He'll likely hide and come up with us later. Lord knows, I warned the cloth-head!" His lips tightened into a thin, hard line. He called harshly, "Spring 'em, Marcel!"

Gathering speed, the coach rattled and jolted through the gathering dusk. Riding beside it, fuming, Valerian glanced back frequently. There was no sign of Herbert, but distantly a fugitive ray of sunlight shone on breastplates. "Here they come," he groaned. "Curse you for a ramshackle court-card, Herbert Turner! Do you *never* do anything right?"

The staccato bark of gunshots reached his ears. He swore bitterly and, reining his horse around, tore at a headlong gallop back towards the inn.

18

All too soon Valerian could see the flashes of another burst of gunfire, but strain his eyes as he might he could discern no sign of a rider. Furthermore, the shots seemed to be off to his right instead of straight ahead. He realised then that the dragoons had left the Le Havre road and turned inland. He grinned in appreciation. Herbert was leading them in the wrong direction! "Bravo, coz!" he muttered, and reined around to head them off.

Cutting across country was risky business in the half-light of early evening, and twice he had to gather his mount together so as to make a last-minute leap; once over a fallen tree trunk, and once a barely completed jump across a fast-running stream, culminating in a wild scramble up the far bank. He patted the neck of his hired mare and told her she was "a jolly good girl!"

The dragoons, undoubtedly mounted on heavier steeds than his sleek mare, were riding cautiously, but when he judged them to be less than a mile away he still could not distinguish another rider ahead of him. He leaned forward in the saddle, his eyes straining to pierce the gathering darkness. A solitary farmhouse loomed up, and by the faint candlelight from a downstairs window he glimpsed the silhouette of his cousin at last. Small wonder the dragoons had located their target whereas he had been unable to do so: he'd been looking for a horseman; Herbert was on foot, limping badly and looking to be far spent. He lurched around as Valerian galloped towards him and stood swaying, as though acknowledging that he was trapped.

"Hi!" Valerian reined to a sliding halt. "Why resort to shank's mare, chawbacon?"

"Praise . . . God!" gasped Herbert. "Horse shot out . . . from under me! You shouldn't have come—"

As if to echo his words, another shot rang out and they heard the hum of the musket ball.

"Very true," agreed Valerian, reaching down with his good arm. "And they're getting too close, so I'll retreat posthaste. Can you mount up behind me? For Lord's sake don't stand there chewing your teeth! Placate your conscience with the knowledge that with you at my back if they shoot straight they'll hit you, not me!"

Herbert stuffed something into the capacious pocket of his cloak, took his cousin's hand, put one foot over Valerian's in the stirrup and swung up behind him.

The mare sidled nervously but took the added weight and steadied herself.

Touching his spurs to the mare's side, Valerian heard a muffled groan. "Winged you, did they?" he shouted.

"Just—my leg," replied Herbert, gasping as the animal plunged forward.

"Hang on tight, lad! Our mount is a prime little lady. I'm going to pop into that copse ahead and then, with luck, we'll leave these clods to search the trees while we get back to the road."

Once they were in amongst the trees it was very dark,

but luck was with them. Valerian turned the mare in the direction of the road and let her choose her own path, and she picked her way unerringly through the roots and underbrush. Behind them arose crashings, tramplings and grumbling curses that fortunately drowned the sounds of their own progress. Very soon they left the dragoons behind and as the uproar faded Valerian heard another sound. He tilted his head, listening, then exclaimed a delighted "You found her!"

"Aye," said Herbert, his voice thready. "She was chasing . . . a mouse in the stable. I had . . . I had to put her in my pocket, but she's . . . quite all right."

"Which is more than one could say for you," muttered Valerian, narrowing his eyes as he searched for the road.

"I'll do," said Herbert. "You don't sound to be in—in prime trig, yourself. It was—truly splendid of you to—to come back for me."

"It was indeed. I cannot think why I go to so much trouble. But you'd best save your thanks. We're not out of the— Yes we are, by Jove! There's the Le Havre road! Hang on, Herbert! I'll be surprised has Marcel not ignored my instructions and slowed, waiting for us!"

At that same instant Elspeth was leaning from the carriage window calling an inquiry to Skye.

"No, I cannot see them," he responded tersely. "Yet. But 'tis too dark now to be able to distinguish clearly for any distance. I wish to God we'd another hack! I'd ride back and look for them! The next stable we come to I'm of a mind to do just that!"

"And leave my sister defenceless?" protested Vance. "My predatory relatives may yet be hunting us, and I'd be of scant use were they to—"

Skye interrupted with an excited demand that Marcel halt the team.

"What is it?" cried Elspeth, leaning from the window

again as the coach lurched to a stop. "Do you see them, Joel?"

"I see . . . someone . . ." he answered uncertainly. "But—I'm afraid there is but one horseman, so perhaps . . ."

"No! *It is!*" squealed Elspeth.

Her brother grabbed her skirt. "Have a care, Ellie! You'll fall out! Are you sure?"

"Yes, yes! 'Tis Gervaise! I'd know him anywhere! But—he's riding as if—"

Skye yelled, "Herbert's up on the mare behind him!"

"Praise God!" exclaimed Vance fervently. "Cheer up, Ellie! If that isn't just like a woman! Don't weep now, you ninny! They're safe!"

"I'm just—so grateful," she sniffed, dabbing a handkerchief at her eyes.

Her earlier remark still echoed in her brother's mind. "I'd know him anywhere . . ." His suspicions deepening, he frowned but said nothing.

Valerian and Herbert were greeted with an impromptu cheer when they rode up to the coach. Wan, bloodstained and exhausted, Herbert had to be all but carried inside and was hailed as a hero when he released an indignant Pixie from his pocket. The musket ball had struck him just above the knee and he had bled copiously. Valerian prepared to dress his wound, and Freda, recoiling from the sight of blood, hastily volunteered to sit on the box with Marcel so as to leave more room in the coach. Elspeth offered to help, but her brother said he hoped he was not completely useless and commanded that she avert her eyes while they cut away Herbert's breeches. Her vehement protest that she was a capable nurse with a deal of experience was ignored, Valerian pointing out that his unfortunate cousin was shy and would shrivel with embarrassment did a lady set eyes on his naked limb. "Until he grows up," he added, this deliberate provocation drawing an amused scold from Elspeth, a chuckle

271

from Vance and a predictable if faint objection from Herbert.

Skye mounted Valerian's mare, Marcel whipped up his team and they were off on the final leg of their journey.

It was not easy to tend Herbert's wound in the rocking carriage and Valerian's inability to use his right hand hampered his efforts, but between them, he and Clayton managed. Their patient endured bravely but fainted away when the final bandage was being tied.

"He did well," said Valerian. "Fortunately, it is a clean wound and the ball went on through. He's a healthy fellow and should heal nicely."

Elspeth, who had peeped several times, said, "You have all my admiration, gentlemen! But what now, Gervaise? Herbert and Vance, and you also—though I know you will not own it—need rest. Dare we stop at Madame Bossuet's pension?"

"I think we must, no?" said Clayton. "Herbert can't walk onto the quay wearing these shredded breeches."

Valerian nodded. "True. And he'll likely find it difficult to walk at all. We shall have to find him a cane. But our stay must be very brief. I've no doubt the dragoons are hard after us!"

Their stay was brief indeed. Initially welcoming Valerian with coy smiles, Madame Bossuet began to flutter when he tried to rent a room, and Herbert's gory appearance did little to reassure her. She was sorry, she twittered nervously, but after the last time . . . not that she held it against them, of course . . . but trouble followed them, and . . . perhaps an inn closer to the city would be more . . . Her protests faded when Skye started to count louis d'or onto her desk, and she reluctantly agreed that they might use the best bedchamber and parlour . . . "For one hour only!"

Valerian helped his cousin limp painfully into the pension, while Skye unloaded the Bath chair and wheeled "Mrs. Newell" inside. Madame Bossuet's parlour maid lost all her colour and fled before them, her horrified eyes saying clearly that she too remembered "the last time." Elspeth and Freda left the carriage gratefully and Madame drew "Nurse" aside and murmured that she was indeed sorry to see that the surgeon had been unable to help the old lady. "Poor Madame Newell! She looks thinner than when first you came," she remarked sympathetically. "And now two of the young gentleman have met with an accident! *Tiens* but you have a deal of misfortune on your hands, Nurse! I shall send medical supplies and hot water to you at once!"

She was as good as her word, and two steaming ewers, bandages, lint and salves were soon delivered, together with an offer of hot coffee or wine. They all chose the coffee, and Elspeth and Freda were banished to the parlour with one of the ewers while the men tended to Herbert and helped him change clothes in the bedchamber.

It was a luxury to be able to wash and repair wind-blown hair after what seemed interminable hours of travelling, but Elspeth and Freda had barely finished restoring themselves than Valerian was calling to them to make haste.

Elspeth hurried into the bedchamber and scanned the occupants searchingly. Herbert gave her a cheerful smile; he was pale but looking much improved now that he was clad in a clean coat and breeches. Vance's wig had been brushed and his skirts tidied so that with Pixie ensconced on her lap "Mrs. Newell" presented a neat and believable appearance.

Elspeth was troubled by the flush on Valerian's drawn face. "There surely is time for me to bathe your arm," she said firmly.

"Plenty of time," he agreed. "Once we're aboard the packet! No, don't accuse me of needless stoicism, Nurse Muslin. I promise you that under normal circumstances I'm a coward par excellence, but these are not normal circumstances and we risk arrest each moment we delay here. Those dragoons were much too close for my liking, and no less than your brother would I dislike being conveyed back to Monsieur le Comte's chateau!"

It was a telling point, and she bit her lip and looked to Vance questioningly.

He nodded in agreement. "It's truth, Ellie. Skye is galloping even now to arrange passage for us on the first vessel sailing for England."

"Which leaves you saddled with three cripples, I'm afraid," said Valerian. "We're a sorry rescue party, I own, but I promise you will very soon see the cliffs of Dover again. Meanwhile, Madame Bossuet has been good enough to sell us a sturdy cane for Herbert, and I'll lend him a hand. Can you manage to wheel Mrs. Newell to the coach? In view of our various impostures I hesitate to ask Beck to do so."

Bowing to this common sense, Elspeth said that she would have no difficulty in managing the Bath chair, but that the instant they were aboard ship she must tend his injured arm.

Valerian smiled and swung the door wide, and Madame Bossuet came to see them off and call her good wishes.

Supporting his cousin to the waiting carriage, Valerian murmured, "How relieved she looks, poor lady. I fear we will not be remembered as her favourite guests."

"Especially," said Herbert, "do those dragoons come thundering to her door the moment we've gone!"

Freda called, "I'll ride on the box, sir. You look ready to drop!"

Valerian thanked her but declined the offer and climbed up beside Marcel, where he imparted a breathless order that the coachman drive as fast as he dared on the dark roads.

Marcel sent his whip cracking out over the heads of his leaders and, leaning to Valerian's ear, said, "I see you've your pistol ready, monsieur. You expect perhaps that the soldiers they come after us?"

"If they do," answered Valerian grimly, "I'll attempt to dissuade them!"

"*Mon Dieu!*" groaned Marcel. "I have aided Milady Elmira Bottesdale many of the times, but never a time like this one! I think I must retire and grow cabbages!"

Valerian laughed. "You old fraud! What would you do for excitement?"

There were, the coachman advised, many avenues a man could take to find excitement, adding demurely, "As I am assured you know well, monsieur!"

Valerian was silent.

The moon was beginning to find a path through the clouds, and peering at his companion, Marcel saw an odd expression on the handsome features. He had seen this man preparing eagerly for violent action, overcome by mirth, sneeringly cynical or punctiliously polite. This was the first time he had glimpsed a look of wistful sadness. 'So-ho!' thought Marcel, and, like all Frenchmen wise in the ways of *l'amour,* he grinned as he cracked the whip again, urging his horses to greater speed. As a result of their reckless pace he was often unable to discern potholes in time to avoid them, causing the coach to lurch alarmingly, but his expertise enabled him to right the vehicle without overturning them.

Valerian's constant scanning of the road to Rouen revealed occasional gleams as of moonlight on breastplates. The relentless pursuit was unnerving, but as the miles slipped away and the dragoons did not gain ground his hopes rose that he could keep the promise he had made to bring Elspeth to Le Havre and thence safely back to England.

The moon was bright when they reached the outskirts of the city, and despite the lateness of the hour, the port was bustling. Joel Skye rode to meet them as they drove towards the docks, where countless torches, ships' lanterns and flambeaux blazed, reflecting on the dark water and wet roads.

He announced triumphantly that he'd managed to secure passage on a fishing vessel but was indignant at the exorbitant fee he'd been obliged to pay to persuade the captain to delay sailing until they arrived.

"Well done!" said Valerian.

"Which way?" called Marcel.

Skye led them to a less crowded quay where a large fishing boat rocked to the pull of the tide. It was a far cry from the packet that had carried them here. Climbing stiffly from the box, Valerian flung open the door and handed Elspeth from the coach. "I fear you will not enjoy luxurious accommodations on this vessel, ma'am," he said. "But we are lucky to—"

"Ah, but it is the friend of the Duc de Belle-Isle!"

Stiffening as the cheery hail rang out behind him, he saw Elspeth start. He turned lazily and beheld youth and a splendid and familiar uniform. " 'Pon m'soul," he drawled with a smile, "but you're a conscientious fellow, sir! Do you never rest?"

"Seldom, monsieur," answered the young officer lightly. "But what is this? You have an injury, I perceive!" His eyes flashed to Herbert. "And your friend also. Not an accident, I trust?"

"Better it had been," said Valerian. "We were attacked by thieves, sir."

"Disgraceful! In behalf of La Belle France, I make you my apologies, gentlemen!" The Frenchman's gaze drifted to Elspeth and he smiled warmly. Becoming aware that Valerian had not responded, he glanced at him, encountered ice and said hastily, "You reported the matter to the authorities, of course?"

"To the local agent, who assured us he would track down the criminals."

The officer gave a fatalistic shrug and remarked sadly that today's breed of rogues were of an impudence past believing. "And your lady," he said, "your aunt, as I recollect—she is unharmed, I trust?"

"Fortunately." Lowering his voice and stepping away from the coach, Velerian said, "Unhappily, the physician we consulted was able to do little for her."

"Alas! That, it is very sad." Peering into the coach, he said, "Ah, yes. I see that the poor lady does not look at all improved. But it is well that she still has her little cat with the white blaze on the tail! You are returning to England on this ship, monsieur? Scarcely a suitable craft for people of Quality. I most strongly advise that you wait for the packet which sails at eight o'clock in the morning. This I can arrange for you." He saw Valerian frown and his eyes sharpened. He said silkily, "Unless, of course, you have some reason for haste?"

Valerian sighed. "It is my aunt, monsieur." He added more or less truthfully, "It seems that it is only a matter of time. You will comprehend."

Repentant, the Frenchman said that he understood perfectly and, in an attempt to make amends for his insensitivity, asked, "May we offer assistance in lifting the unfortunate lady from the coach?"

Skye came up at this point, wheeling the Bath chair. Valerian thanked the now sympathetic young official for his kindness, was wished a pleasant journey and drew a relieved breath as Marcel led a porter to them, who piled their luggage onto his barrow and trundled off to the fishing boat.

Elspeth, able to breathe again, took the handles of the Bath chair and murmured that she pitied the lady who would become Mrs. Gervaise Valerian. "Her prospective husband is so expert at twisting the truth that she will never know when she is being gulled!"

"Really, Nurse!" he scolded, laughter glinting in his eyes. "Such naughty expressions you do use! You had best guard your tongue else you're not likely to become Mrs. Anybody!"

Following them while lending Herbert his arm, Joel Skye overheard the remark and said, bristling, "Miss Clayton has nothing to fear on that score, Valerian! I would be more than proud if she would consent to take my name! Nor am I the only one!"

Elspeth said with a trill of mirth, "Thank you, dear Joel, for coming to my defence! You are most gallant!"

Amused, Herbert asked innocently, "What did you say, Gervaise?"

Valerian grunted, "Nothing gallant, I promise you," and stamped off to say good-bye and reward their faithful coachman.

Elspeth hurried to join him and also express her thanks to Marcel, who snatched off his tricorne and blushed fierily when she pressed a grateful kiss on his cheek. He was clearly saddened to part with these new friends, but his sorrow was alleviated by the generous douceur Valerian slipped into his ready hand.

A sailor came up to urge that they make haste to board the *Belle of Sussex* and murmured a warning that it would not do were they to be subjected to a close inspection by the Le Havre Port authorities. Nothing would do, however, but that Valerian delay long enough to bid a fond farewell to the little mare who had borne him so devotedly. She seemed equally affected by their parting, and he was discussing with Marcel the possibility that he could buy the animal when an urgent hail and the flourishing of a rope gave notice that the fishing boat was about to set sail without him.

Completing his scrambling arrival on deck, he was indignant to be met by Freda Beck, who advised that Miss Elspeth was tending the "poor gentlemen" who most needed her care. "Then lead me to her at once," he demanded, clutching his arm. "For I am in far worse case then either my cousin or her brother!"

Freda knew him well enough by this time to comprehend

that he spoke in jest. She was inclined to suspect, however, that there was more truth than fiction to his words and she lost no time in conducting him to a cramped and stuffy cabin belowdecks. Inside, Clayton watched Joel Skye assist Elspeth in her efforts to make Herbert as comfortable as possible.

She looked up with a smile as Valerian entered. "Were you able to arrange for the mare to be shipped?" she asked, but before he could answer she exclaimed, "That is just right, Joel! Thank you! You would make a first-rate surgeon!"

Valerian sat on the opposite bunk beside Clayton and muttered that he wondered "Mrs. Newell" did not put a stop to Skye's constant attempts to ingratiate himself with Miss Elspeth.

"Why ever should I do so?" replied Clayton, regarding him with innocently upraised brows. "You are probably not aware of it, but they have been close friends since nursery days. For years he has nourished a *tendre* for her, as have several other gentlemen."

With a curl of the lip Valerian drawled rudely, "All of whom have asked your permission to pay their addresses?"

"Several have. Nicholas Drew, for one."

"A sterling candidate," sneered Valerian, who actually admired Drew.

"I agree," said Clayton, deliberately misinterpreting the sarcasm. "Did you suppose Skye to be her only suitor?"

"Of course not. I only thought—" Floundering, and quite aware he had no right to voice any criticisms, he continued, "I mean—That is—I'd not have, er, judged him—"

"To be worthy? Why? I consider Joel to be a thoroughly acceptable aspirant to my sister's hand, and I believe our mother shares my views."

"Oh, Skye's a good enough fellow, I grant you," said Valerian grudgingly. "But I'd fancied you would aim higher for your sister. She is, after all, a diamond of the first water!"

"I agree absolutely. Elspeth rates a fine gentleman of

rank and fortune. Have you such a fellow in mind?"

Valerian tightened his lips and was silent.

Gently applying the coup de grace, Clayton murmured, "Of course, the situation is now somewhat changed."

"How so?" asked Valerian.

"Why, it appears I may be the heir to a considerable fortune, and since whatever I possess will be shared with my family, it is unlikely that anyone of lesser prospects would court Elspeth. Fearing, you know, to be dubbed a fortune-hunter. Save in the case of a long-term attachment, of course."

"Of course," muttered Valerian hollowly.

Watching him from the corners of his eyes, Clayton said, "You are very flushed. I wonder if that wound is making you feverish."

Valerian jerked away from the enquiring hand placed on his brow and said irritably, "Oh, have done! Deuce take you, if you think to have put me in my—"

"Gad, but you're burning up!" exclaimed Clayton, genuinely concerned. "Elspeth, this silly fellow is not going along very—"

"Go to the devil!" snapped Valerian, and stalked from the cabin.

He was sitting on a coil of rope on the deck when Freda sought him out a little later.

"Whatever be you doing out here in the cold, sir?" she scolded mildly.

"Thinking. I've a lot to think on, and need peace and quiet to concentrate."

Refusing to take the hint, she argued, "Well, it bean't peaceful nor quiet out here with the wind coming up the way 'tis. And Miss Elspeth wants as you should come inside so she can tend to your arm."

"Convey her my thanks, but my arm does not require attention."

Freda continuing to peer at him through the darkness, he said, "Run along now, like a good girl."

She giggled and said she would never dare to run on the deck of a ship. "I'd likely slip and tumble overboard. And Miss Elspeth said to say as if you said no, but preferred to sit up here and sulk she would have to come out to you. Which she'd as soon not do, on account of the poor lady being tired, d'ye see, sir?"

Valerian scrambled to his feet, which hurt the arm he knew very well required attention. He swore under his breath all the way to the cabin and had difficulty restraining some more vehement oaths when Elspeth gently removed the last bandage.

"Oh, my," she murmured. "Surely you must have realised how inflamed this was becoming? Gervaise, why on earth did you not tell me?"

"You were busy," he muttered.

Touching his forehead, she said, "And so you are feverish and small wonder! Well, if you insist upon behaving like a foolish child, you must pay the consequence! More hot water, if you please, Freda. Thank you. Now, try to hold still, Gervaise."

He managed to hold still by concentrating on her lovely face, the gentle touch of her hands, the way she tilted her head slightly when she feared she was hurting him. "I wonder," he murmured breathlessly after an especially trying interval, "whatever your godmama will have to say when you return to London."

"I doubt she will be anything but pleased that my brother is safe," she answered, and reaching for the salve, she added: "I am far more concerned about what will happen to poor Joel."

"I'm sure you are," he said dryly, and it occurred to him that while he had previously judged the outward-bound journey to have been a catalogue of disasters, the journey home was going to be even less pleasant.

It was certainly not as eventful; the wind was strong but far from being a gale; the *Belle of Sussex,* guided by expert hands, rode the waves serenely; and several of the passengers were able to snatch a few hours of sleep, although one only slept fitfully, and another slept not at all.

When the sun brightened a cloudy sky the following morning, the fishing boat was tacking along England's south coast. The Captain, a wily individual, mindful of certain instructions given him by Lieutenant Skye, avoided Dover's tidal basin, anchoring his craft instead in a quiet cove a few miles southwest of the port. The matron lady and her kitten, the two young women, and the three gentlemen were rowed ashore and directed to a nearby hedge tavern where a coach could be hired to transport them on the final leg of their journey.

Huffing and puffing as he manoeuvred the Bath chair across the pebbly beach, Skye panted, " 'Twould seem we had no need to keep Clayton in his petticoats after all. I see no sign of any minions of the law."

"Thanks be for small mercies," muttered Valerian, finding the ground oddly unstable under his feet as he attempted to steady his cousin's wavering steps.

"Thanks be, indeed!" declared Elspeth. "We have restored my dearest brother to England and safety at last!"

"And here is the tavern," said Herbert breathlessly. "With luck and a halfway decent coach and four we'll be in London before evening!"

"I cannot see a coach," said Skye, as they trod the more even surface of a lane that ran along the edge of the beach.

"There's a barn," said Valerian. "And I think I see a coach and—Oh Jupiter!"

The coach he had glimpsed left the barn at speed and

drove towards them. It was a black coach with an all too familar crest on the panel.

"We are to be greeted by Whitehall," said Herbert glumly, as the carriage pulled up before them.

"And only look who is come to greet us," murmured Valerian, watching the sturdy, rather nondescript individual who climbed from the coach.

"Joshua Swift," groaned Skye. "Oh, egad!"

"Oh—no!" cried Elspeth.

"Dammitall," said Vance Clayton.

Striding to face them, a trooper on either side of him, Joshua Swift called triumphantly, "Ladies and gentlemen! Welcome home! You may all consider yourselves under arrest!"

19

Thin wisps of vapour were eddying around the city streets and the daylight was fading fast when the two carriages made their lumbering way through heavy traffic towards Whitehall. London could scarcely have been said to be at her best, but to Vance Clayton this city of his birth appeared lovelier than he had ever beheld her, and in spite of exhaustion and the discomfort of barely healed injuries he experienced a great surge of gratitude that he had been spared to reach home again. He was also grateful to Joshua Swift, who had, despite his gruff manner, unbent sufficiently to permit "Mrs. Newell" to go into the tavern before they set out and change into male garments.

At the moment there were four of them in the coach; Elspeth sat beside her brother, with Freda and Valerian opposite. Joel Skye and Herbert rode with Major Swift in the lead carriage, and both vehicles had a military escort. Elspeth had been alarmed by the Intelligence officer's grim demeanour, but Valerian had made light of her fears, insisting that Swift enjoyed "puffing off his consequence" and that they had broken no laws and could not be charged for having freed a British subject held hostage in a foreign land. "Pay the silly fellow no heed," he'd said carelessly. "He'll likely want to question us if only to convince himself of his importance, and then he'll send us off to our various homes."

It had been a tedious and lengthy drive, this last stage of their journey, and they all had dozed off and on. Now that they were only a short distance from the Horse Guards, Elspeth was plagued by misgivings and she murmured uneasily, "Major Swift said we all are under arrest. How long do you suppose we shall have to stay?"

"He may keep us unfortunate males for an hour or so," answered Valerian. "But I doubt he'll dare detain a lady of Quality."

With her hand securely tucked in her brother's arm, Elspeth said, "Perhaps not. But he will dare detain poor Joel!"

"Skye will know how to defend himself, dear," Vance assured her. "Never worry so. After all, he rescued this valuable British citizen!"

"Yes, for which I shall always be grateful," she said, squeezing his arm fondly. "But only think how flagrantly he disobeyed orders. He was told to arrest Sir Simon, instead of which he helped him escape."

"What a piece of work you make of it," drawled Valerian, bored. "Swift cannot prove my father was ever with us. All we have to do is claim we held Skye captive because he followed us and behaved strangely."

Elspeth nodded. "I suppose we could say that," she murmured dubiously.

"Not unless you want to risk being charged with interfering with an officer in pursuit of his duties," said Vance, with an irked glance at Valerian.

"I will re-word," said Valerian. "*You* can claim that *I* held Skye at gunpoint. You, Clayton, are obviously in no condition to have bested Skye, and Miss Elspeth will scarcely be judged responsible."

"As if we would throw you to the wolves only to protect ourselves," said Elspeth indignantly. "Besides, I doubt the scenario you sketch would help Joel's career."

"Help it! More like to end it!" exclaimed Vance.

"That's what worries me so," said Elspeth. "You never think they will charge poor Joel with something really dreadful? Like desertion?"

Valerian sighed. "Heigh-ho, but there's no satisfying you people! For a while it appeared none of us would survive at all! Here we are, home and alive, and you're still grumbling! Since you value your friend so highly, have some confidence in him. Skye may not be brilliant, but he seems to have an adequate head on his shoulders and will doubtless contrive. Certainly, worry is so much waste of time. My advice is to get some more sleep." Closing his eyes, he proceeded to do so.

But Elspeth did worry. Even were Joel able to satisfy the military on the grounds that Vance had been rescued, he had disobeyed his orders to arrest Sir Simon. She had gained the impression that Joshua Swift was a ruthless and inflexible officer whose pursuit of Sir Simon Valerian had indeed become an obsession. Further, she considered that he was quite aware of Gervaise's determination to spirit his father out of England. Because of his love for her, Joel Skye had played a part in frustrating the Major's ambitions, and Swift was Joel's superior officer. She scarcely dared contemplate what the result would be, and when she thought of Joel's irascible sire her fears were magnified.

At long last the carriage slowed and trundled between two sentry boxes, with their apparently frozen occupants, and into the yard of the Horse Guards. The carriage doors were flung open, Valerian and Vance Clayton stepped out, then Elspeth and Freda were handed down. At once surrounded by guardsmen who seemed as menacing as they were tall, they were hurried into the large and forbidding building. They entered a busy world populated almost entirely by uniformed officers of the Army and Navy, each of whom had some apparently vital opinion to voice. Spurs jingled, boots stamped, scabbards rapped against the walls as men drew aside to allow the ladies to pass. The target of a score of admiring stares, Elspeth tried to catch sight of Joel, but he had been whisked away almost immediately and her attempts were futile. She and her brother, Freda and Valerian were taken to a cheerless room by yet another very large sergeant of dragoon guards whose eyes rested always at some point above their heads as he barked a request that they "Be so good as to wait yurr."

Wait they did, while the clock on the wall ticked and the hands jerked their way around the dial, and from the corridor outside came the muted sounds of boots and spurs and voices.

Elspeth was seated at a long table, with Vance beside her. Valerian prowled about restlessly and at length pulled the door open to be confronted by the grim-faced sergeant, who said tonelessly that he was sorry, but no one was permitted to leave this room.

"Deuce take you," snarled Valerian. "We've been driving all day, the lady is tired and it's blasted cold in this charming little dungeon! Send in some hot tea at once or Lord Holland shall hear of the insensitive treatment you deal out to people of Quality!"

The sergeant clicked his booted heels together, offered a stiff bow and frightened Elspeth half out of her wits by suddenly roaring, "Corporal!"

The door was slammed shut. Valerian staggered to a nearby chair and sat down. "Jove," he muttered. "Battlefield lungs!"

"I wonder he didn't shatter the windows," said Clayton.

Valerian grinned. "Let's hope he woke up someone in authority."

"Tea sounds heavenly," sighed Elspeth.

"Of course it does, poor girl," said Valerian. "You must be worn to a shade."

"Oh, no." She forced a smile. "I'm just so worried for poor Joel."

Valerian's lip curled, but he said nothing. It was typical, he thought. What with one thing and another they had really contrived very well. Their most important accomplishment was that Sir Simon was safe away and by tomorrow would probably be reunited with Mama . . . Dear pretty Mama, who had waited so long and patiently for the return of the husband she adored . . . Then there was the business of Vance Clayton, who had been snatched from the very jaws of death (which the silly fellow had brought upon himself if one came right down to it). Herbert had taken some deuced hard knocks and acquitted himself splendidly, and he himself was feeling—well, never mind about that. But all the lady could think of was "Poor Joel." Confound "Poor Joel," anyway!

The door opened again and a young trooper carried in a tray with tea paraphernalia. "Compliments of Major Swift," he announced, and fled.

"My apologies to the galloping Major," murmured Valerian, as Elspeth manipulated teacups, milk jug and sugar bowl, "he has a heart, after all!"

Major Swift entered as they were finishing the tea and before he could say a word, Valerian waved his teacup at him and declared, "Miss Clayton has had a very trying journey, sir. I trust you will see your way clear to at once restoring her to Madame Colbert."

Eyeing him keenly, Swift said, "You look as if you stand in need of a physician, Mr. Valerian. Perhaps one of our Army doctors should look at you before—"

"I have my own physician, I thank you," said Valerian,

288

refusing to acknowledge that he would be most grateful to be allowed to lie down.

Elspeth glanced at him anxiously. "I expect Lieutenant Skye will have informed you of what happened, Major Swift. I must tell you that he behaved with the greatest gallantry and—"

"He has told me a lot of poppycock, ma'am," he interrupted, his heavy eyebrows bristling, "and will be held to face charges of dereliction of duty!"

Elspeth paled and gasped a distressed "Oh, surely not! If you would but listen to—"

"You will have your chance to make a statement, Miss Clayton. As Mr. Valerian has said, we must not detain you. I have already called up a coach and you will be conveyed home directly."

"Very good," said Valerian.

"Stuff and nonsense," said Elspeth. "I go nowhere, Major, until I am satisfied that Lieutenant Skye is being treated fairly!"

"Give me strength," muttered Valerian, irked. "Order your sister to go home, Clayton!"

His lips twitching, Clayton said mildly, "Go home, Elspeth."

"Do not imagine I'm unwilling," she answered. "We are all very tired, Major Swift. My brother has been handled cruelly and is still weakened; Mr. Valerian took a nasty wound and is in a deal of pain, though he'll not admit it; Lieutenant Skye was brutally beaten, and Mr. Turner—"

"Such a litany of disaster," said the Major, shaking his head sympathetically. "The more reason, ma'am, for you to obey your brother and allow us to take you to Madame Colbert's home." His voice rose. "Sergeant . . . !"

The large dragoon marched into the room, shook the floor as he sprang to attention and barked, "Sir!"

"Escort Miss Clayton to the home of Madame Colbert on South Audley Street!"

Elspeth drew back.

The sergeant stamped towards her.

"Take one more step," she warned, "and I shall scream at the top of my lungs all the way to the carriage!"

The big dragoon quailed and cast a terrified look at his Major.

Valerian gave a hoot of laughter. "She'll do it, too," he declared. "Never cross a lady in love, Swift! Only think of the picture you'll paint for the people in the street!"

Elspeth turned her head and stared at him.

Swift said in a near purr, "I was thinking more along the lines of having Miss Clayton confined to a cell, or gagged and—"

Valerian said as softly, "Do—not—dare . . ."

In years to come Elspeth would remember the two hours that followed as an unending nightmare. They were conducted to a bleak and dim room wherein a few candles cast light on their various faces so they seemed to loom against a spectrally dark background.

Major Swift commenced what he called an "interview," but which Elspeth considered to be a merciless inquisition. Lieutenant Skye was required to stand as questions were hurled at him in an endless stream. Time after time he offered his version of the train of events and time after time Swift would repeat his question in a slightly different way, then insist that the answer differed from that given previously. Occasionally, one or other of the rest of them was "interviewed," and although Elspeth was spared, Freda was reduced to tears when her replies were judged "contradictory."

Infuriated, Elspeth's protests were stilled when Valerian

bent to her ear and murmured, "You would have this, ma'am. Take care; Swift is an extreme dangerous man. The more you antagonize him the harder it will be for Skye!"

It was all too clear that Skye was tiring and that his defense was not impressing the Major or the two other officers who had entered and stood in the shadows behind them.

Elspeth was startled when a harsh voice from the back of the room exclaimed, "For the love of God, sir! You must have more sensible reasons than you have offered for disregarding your orders! If the woman entrapped you—say so!"

'Joel's horrid papa!' she thought, her heart sinking. It was an ominous development. She was well aware that Colonel Sir Walter Skye had always intimidated his son and his presence here could only add to Joel's misery.

Skye had jerked around at the sound of his father's voice. He looked strained and haggard, but he said firmly, "If by 'the woman' you refer to Miss Clayton, sir, there was no attempt at entrapment. Her brother, to whom she is devoted, was held by force at the chateau of—"

He was interrupted by a muffled groan, and Valerian sank to his knees and bowed forward, clutching his injured arm.

Dismayed, Elspeth exclaimed, "Oh, my heavens!" And bending over him, she said angrily, "Now see what you have done by forcing a wounded gentleman to endure this inquisition!"

Swift looked momentarily alarmed and motioned to the sergeant to pull up a chair, Herbert half-lifted his cousin into it and Valerian slumped weakly, murmuring apologies for being "such a Milquetoast."

"You are nothing of the sort," stormed Elspeth. "Your wound is badly inflamed and should have had treatment long since! Only look how pale he is become, Major Swift. You should be ashamed! I insist that you have Mr. Valerian con-

291

veyed to his flat, where his physician can attend him!"

Colonel Skye barked, "Certainly not! Valerian was the instigator of this conspiracy as well you know, Swift! *He* is the one whose scheming resulted in your quarry slipping through your fingers! You will be wise to have him clapped up at—"

Herbert threw his arm around his cousin as Valerian sagged in the chair clearly near complete collapse. "Fiend seize it," exclaimed Herbert in an unprecedented outburst of wrath. "Your pardon, ladies, but this is past permission! My cousin's wound is bleeding again! I demand—"

"What you demand pays no toll," roared Colonel Skye. "Valerian is as good as a traitor, and must be held accountable for—"

He had gone too far, and resenting this usurpation of his authority, Major Swift interrupted harshly, "I think, Colonel, that *I* am quite aware of Mr. Valerian's schemes, but I hope the British Army has not sunk to such a level of barbarism as to refuse aid to a wounded gentleman!" Ignoring the Colonel's purpling countenance and menacing glare, he said, "If Mr. Valerian will give me his word of honour to hold himself available for questioning and not leave the City . . ."

Valerian lifted his left hand in a weak gesture of acquiescence and said faintly, "You . . . have my word . . . Major."

"In that case," said Swift, "call up a coach, Sergeant. You are free to take him to his home, Mr. Turner."

Herbert helped his cousin to stand and Elspeth moved closer to peer into the stricken man's drawn face and asked anxiously, "Will you be all right, Gervaise? I'll call on you as soon as—"

Valerian lifted his drooping head and looked squarely at her. "Not at all the thing, ma'am," he muttered, with cutting sarcasm. "My debt to you is paid in full, I believe you will agree. I bid you farewell and wish you a happy future unencumbered by—Deplorable Dandies."

Pale and stunned, she stepped back. Herbert avoided her eyes and supported his cousin's uncertain progress from the room.

Colonel Skye snarled, "If I do not ask the impossible, perhaps we may *now* try to come at the truth of this farrago of nonsense!"

"If you care to take a seat, Colonel," said Swift icily, "I will pursue *my* investigation—without further interruption! By all means be seated, Miss Clayton. Now, if I understand you, Lieutenant Skye, you were attempting to apprehend Sir Simon Valerian aboard the packet—um," he consulted his notes, "the *Sea Lassie,* when you were attacked by his son and nephew. You claim you had not laid eyes on Sir Simon at this point . . ."

On and on it went. Elspeth thought wearily that they had already gone all over this, but she was no longer afraid of the "very dangerous" Major Joshua Swift. She was instead prey to an aching grief. Gervaise had spoken to her with such biting scorn—he had as well have struck her. He had looked terribly ill and worn, yet he'd made not the least attempt to persuade her to accompany him. Not that she could have done so, of course; not and abandon Joel to face this terrible ordeal alone. But Gervaise should have known how deeply she was indebted to this dear and faithful friend who had risked his career, his very life, to help save her beloved brother. She'd been so sure Gervaise *had* understood, and had sensed how much her feelings towards the Deplorable Dandy had changed. She'd even fancied that of late a tenderness had crept into those very expressive grey eyes when they rested on her. That he might even . . . But she'd been mistaken, quite mistaken. She could hear again the contempt in his voice when he'd said so softly, so acidly, "My debt to you is paid in full . . . I bid you farewell . . . and wish you a happy future unencumbered by Deplorable Dandies."

Suddenly unable to see clearly, she blinked away scalding tears. She had been a fool. He'd only used her to help his father escape. At least he hadn't deserted her then, but like an honourable man had kept his promise and rescued Vance. Whatever else, she must always be grateful for that. But a door she'd thought open had been slammed in her face. His cold "farewell" had clearly said that it was over now, and whatever *tendre* he might have felt towards her had been a transitory thing and was also over. It was his right, certainly, and—

Vance's hand closed over hers and he scanned her face anxiously.

Major Swift thundered, "I shall ask you again, Miss Clayton. I find it extraordinarily difficult to comprehend that, however clever the disguise, any woman would have failed to realise that the 'lady' she was hired to assist on the voyage was actually a man; probably Sir Simon Valerian, a traitorous fugitive! Exactly how long *did* it take you, ma'am?"

'What, again?' she thought wearily. "Major, I have answered that question at least three times before. I cannot think—"

"That is all too apparent, ma'am!" interrupted Colonel Skye explosively. " 'Pon my soul, but *I* cannot think why a lady of your birth and breeding should—"

"Be so good as to allow Miss Clayton to answer my question, sir," snapped Swift, reddening. "If you persist in interfering with my investigation—"

"D'ye call this an *investigation*?" roared the Colonel. "I'd rather describe it as a molly-coddling fiasco, not worthy of the name!"

"Whereas *I* would describe it as a well-intentioned but no longer necessary interrogation."

At that quiet voice all heads turned to the door, which had opened unnoticed by the occupants of the tense room.

Two gentlemen stood there.

The younger of them was tall and good-looking, with

reddish-brown hair and a pale face scarred by a sabre cut, at the sight of whom Elspeth's heart gave a leap and she whispered a joyous "Nicholas!"

The other man was older, frail-appearing and leaning on a cane, but with firm, thin lips, hard eyes and an undeniable air of authority, at the sight of whom Joel Skye's heart also gave a leap and he gasped disbelievingly, *"Uncle Clifford?"*

Swift and Colonel Skye both came to their feet.

Swift bowed. "Your lordship!"

The Colonel's bow was little more than a nod. "Thought you was confined to your bed, Hayes."

Lord Clifford Hayes, until recently a director of the mighty East India Company, answered Elspeth's curtsy with a graceful bow, shrugged and said mildly, "As you see, your brother-in-law is still ambulatory, Walter. Your servant, ma'am. Good day t'you, Swift. Hello, Joel. I gather you have offended. Are you still browbeating the boy because he chose Navy instead of Army, Walter?"

Colonel Skye's jaws champed. He practically spat out the words, "My son chose also to disobey orders. We've always been aware he is your favourite in the family, so perhaps you countenance such behaviour. I do not!"

His lordship gestured, and Nicholas Drew pulled over a chair for him. Sinking into it with a faint sigh of relief, Hayes said, "What you or I, or Swift here countenance has little to say to the matter."

Colonel Skye scowled, but before he could comment Lord Hayes added blandly, "Oh—forgive me, I believe you and your brother know this rascally fellow, Miss Clayton, but perhaps the gentlemen are not acquainted with Mr. Nicholas Drew."

"I certainly know the bounder," said Vance Clayton, crossing to exchange a warm handshake with Drew.

"How glad I am to see you home safe," said Drew, adding a rather stern "And you also, Miss Elspeth."

Sensing that the atmosphere in the room had changed markedly, Elspeth dropped a polite curtsy and Drew grinned and bowed an equally polite response.

Swift grunted, "We have met, my lord."

"Know of him," acknowledged the Colonel with obvious reluctance. "Though what the devil he has to do with this escapes me."

"No doubt," agreed his brother-in-law. "It escapes me, on the other hand, why your presence here is either needed or desired, my dear Walter."

Elspeth's tired eyes brightened.

Joel Skye grinned faintly.

Major Swift put a hand across his lips.

His face taking on a purple hue, the Colonel snarled, "I might say the same of you, sir! This is a military matter! And I—"

"Are retired, I believe." His lordship raised a thin hand and added sweetly, "I fancy you would say that I also am retired. You would, to an extent, be mistaken, Walter. Really, you must not write me off yet. In certain—ah, diplomatic matters His Majesty still relies on my—er, expertise."

Quick to adjust to the shift in the balance of power, Major Swift said, "I'm very sure his confidence is well placed, my lord. Was—er, that what you implied when you said what the Colonel or I countenanced had little to say to this matter?"

"You have a quick ear, Major," said his lordship with a faint smile.

"Well, I thought it a rude remark," blustered the Colonel, "and should like it explained, if y'please."

"But of course. I am only too happy to explain matters if it will help your understanding." Lord Hayes glanced around the room and, with an eye on the sergeant who stood at attention beside the door, murmured, "However, this is a sensitive matter, Swift."

The Major asked that the sergeant escort Miss Beck to

a waiting room where she could be comfortable, after which he should remain on guard outside this office.

As the door closed behind them, his lordship said, "I am not at liberty to go into detail. I presume you have already had a report from Mr. Vance Clayton, Major?"

Swift's colour was heightened. He said uneasily, "My first concern was with the failed apprehension of a traitor, sir. Sir Simon Valerian by name."

"What a pity." Lord Hayes tapped the handle of his cane against his pursed lips, then murmured, "Have you then obtained evidence of Sir Simon's treasonable activities? I had thought the gentleman was presently residing with his wife in Italy."

"To the contrary, my lord, I have personal knowledge that Sir Simon conspired to aid several Jacobite rebels to escape to France," rasped Major Swift defensively.

"And this, ah, 'personal knowledge' of yours can be substantiated and presented in a court of law?" murmured his lordship. Swift hesitated and Lord Hayes leaned forward and, in a voice of ice, snapped, "In other words, Major, have you absolute proof, or reliable witnesses who will swear to Sir Simon's involvement in treasonable activities? Or is it all so much inadmissable rumour and hearsay, which could be manufactured and spread about by a jealous relative with an axe to grind, or some employee who bears the gentleman a grudge?"

"The point is," growled Colonel Skye, "that instead of apprehending him, as ordered, your nephew assisted him to escape!"

"Walter, Walter, you mistake it, as usual, I fear," said his lordship, as cool as the Colonel was heated. "The point is that His Majesty was advised that Vance Clayton carried a letter from a certain—um, lady of the Court of Versailles. A letter of great interest in diplomatic circles. Unhappily, Mr. Clayton was wounded and held captive on the estate of an—

um, ambitious nobleman of France. It was feared that Mr. Clayton would be forced to reveal the location of this letter, which could then be used to create great mischief internationally. Thanks to Mr. Clayton's physical endurance and the efforts of Gervaise Valerian and an intrepid group of others, including my nephew, Mr. Clayton was rescued and can now safely divulge the location of this vital document." He paused and turned enquiringly to Vance Clayton.

Moving forward, Vance said, "When I realised I was being hunted down I was able to send it to my sister in Wales for safe keeping, not knowing Ellie had removed to London, sir. No doubt my mama is holding it for her. However, I swore an oath to—er, to the French lady who hired my services. I am still bound by that oath, you will understand. I must deliver it as instructed."

His lordship smiled. "I appreciate your sense of honour, Mr. Clayton. Have no fears. My agents have already been in touch with the lady, and she gives her full permission for you to give her letter into my hands." He chuckled as Clayton hesitated. "You are apprehensive I see. Very good. Here—" He held out a folded letter. "You recognize your employer's hand, I feel sure."

Clayton scanned the note swiftly, then looked up and said a clearly relieved "Thank you for your patience, my lord. Yes, I am absolved of any further responsibility."

Lord Hayes glanced to Major Swift. "I suggest a troop, Major. At the double!"

The Major nodded and started to the door.

"Also," said his lordship, "it is his Majesty's wish that in the absence of verifiable evidence to the contrary, the matter of Sir Simon Valerian's being judged a traitor be at once dismissed. Therefore, no charges are to be pressed 'gainst any of these good people. In truth, we owe them instead a great debt of gratitude!"

20

＊

*H*ow glad I am that you enjoyed such a delightful visit with your friend." Madame Colbert rustled into the parlour of her cosy London house and beamed at her god-child, who was sitting by the fire and rather listlessly scanning the *London Gazette*. "Do but listen to that wind! 'The Tides of March,' I think those winds are called, or some such thing. Why learned professors or philatelists or whatever they are should name winds 'tides' I cannot fathom. Perhaps 'tis because, like tides, winds can quite ruin one's coiffure, to say nothing of blowing smoke down the chimney, horrid things! Though tides do not come down chimneys, of course. I am only sorry I was from home when you arrived yesterday, my love. But how fortunate it is that you encountered your dear brother, for, to tell the truth I was afraid I may have been remiss in my duties to have allowed you to go off to those friends of yours when I really knew practically nothing of them! Still, one can always rely on Coachman Abraham, and your abigail, however pert, is clearly devoted to you, so I was confident nothing untoward would befall you."

Elspeth smiled and thought drearily, 'Nothing unto-ward . . .' But perhaps it was truth. Perhaps "nothing unto-ward" was exactly what she had almost succeeded in converting to "Something of Vast Import!" How incredible that dear Godmama had scarcely missed her, nor even sus-pected that she had behaved so improperly as to cross the channel in the company of four daring young gentlemen (and one in particular!); been pursued across leagues and leagues of France; ruthlessly attacked; kidnapped; acted the part of a gypsy dancing girl; and experienced numerous other shocking adventures (including the loss of her heart!). And had in the end been cast off and abandoned like . . . like an old shoe, as her reward!

"Like an old—what, dear?" asked Madame curiously, and peering at her godchild, she went on: "Are you sure you enjoyed yourself? You look quite cast into the dismals. Ah! I know what it is! You are worrying about Vance. In view of the fact that he had been so ill while in France, I really think he is going along very well. So kind of Mr. Drew to allow him to share his flat, though he'd have been welcome here, you know. But then of course they always were bosom-bows. Now you must not sit here and fret yourself to flinders, child. True, 'tis a windy morning, but the little finger of Mr. Sun is peeping through. Why don't you go for a drive in the park? I can call up the carriage and—"

She was interrupted by the advent of Geroux, who bowed and said with his customary measured poise that Mr. Drew had called to enquire if Miss Elspeth would care to go riding.

Within fifteen minutes Elspeth was mounted on her little mare and riding beside Nicholas Drew towards Hyde Park.

"Thank heaven you came, Nicky," she said gratefully. "I have been so eager to know what happened."

Nicholas Drew turned a surprised face. "But I told you

yesterday, Ellie. Lord Hayes was kind enough to accompany me to the Horse Guards, and—"

"Yes, I know that part," she interrupted. "But then Sir Mortimer Hallbridge called and you had to leave, and I still do not understand how you knew we had returned to England, or why you should have called upon Lord Hayes for assistance. It was exceeding good of him to help. I had thought the poor gentleman would be too ill to have stood up 'gainst that terrible Intelligence officer and poor Joel's horrid papa."

Drew concentrated upon a sheet of paper the wind was bustling along the street. "Swift is not really terrible, m'dear. He is passionate about the work he does, and especially passionate if he suspects someone may be disloyal to our island, but basically he is a fine officer."

"And do you judge Colonel Skye to have been a fine officer?"

"From what I've heard of him, he was. A finer officer than a father, I gather."

"Most definitely! And you have evaded my question with typical Intelligence Department skill, sir!"

He said hesitantly, "You know that I sometimes work at the Horse Guards, Ellie. Fortunately, I have friends there, and am able to access information that is not available to the general public. Only see how that paper is being—"

"You must have a remarkable source of information indeed," she again interrupted impatiently. "I'd have said that no one even suspected we had set foot in England!"

Striving for nonchalance, he shrugged and said lightly, "Well, you see, I had left word with various people that in the event any news was received about a certain young lady whom I most earnestly desire to make my wife someday, I was to be notified immediately."

She knew he was watching her, and as they turned into the park she managed to avoid his ardent gaze. "I see," she murmured, after a pause he thought interminable. "And I take it that I am not to ask questions of so secretive a government agent. But—you can tell me surely about—" The words froze in her throat. She finished lamely, "About—my dearest brother. How is Vance today, if you please?"

Drew sighed. "Speaking of evasions . . . Very well, your brother is coming along splendidly, eating like a horse, and means to pay you a visit this afternoon. Which is not what you really wished to ask me, I think."

They had slowed to a walk, and staring at her horse's ears, knowing she was blushing, Elspeth faltered, "You—you know very well how close we are, Vance and I. Surely it is but natural in me to be concerned. He—"

She stopped speaking as Drew put his gloved hand over hers and said with a trace of resignation, "I would betray a confidence if I told you that Gervaise Valerian came for me."

Her eyes shot to his face. Noting how those lovely eyes had brightened, his faithful heart sank.

She said breathlessly, "When? Do you mean—yesterday? Or—"

"You know what I mean, Ellie. He rode to my flat at the gallop. I'd have brought Lord Hayes to Whitehall sooner, had not the silly fellow tumbled out of the saddle on my doorstep, and—"

Paling, she tightened her grip on his hand. "Lord Hayes?"

"Valerian."

"He—he *galloped*? But—but he was near to collapse! He could not possibly have managed to come for you!"

"Should not have, perhaps. But as soon as I was able to bring him round he started screaming at me that Swift meant Joel Skye's execution for disobeying orders and giving aid to a known traitor, and that your heart would be broken if he succeeded, and—Would it, Ellie? Is your heart given to Joel Skye?"

At the moment her heart was thundering, but despite a delicious surge of joy she was touched by the wistfulness she saw in his fine eyes. Still clinging to his hand, she said gently, "My heart is given, dear Nicky. But not to Joel."

"And not to me, alas," he said wryly. "Oh well. I need not tell you he's a rogue and a rascal. That you already know. Still, I suppose he cannot be the irresponsible here-and-thereian he portrays, else he'd not count so many good men among his friends. And whatever else, clearly he is true to those he loves."

Her cheeks very hot, she said with an uncertain little laugh, "You are so generous, Nicky, but you go too fast. Mr. Valerian may affect frippery ways, but his behaviour was not at all offensive whilst we was in France. He never once uttered a word of—of endearment, and he most certainly has not declared himself."

Nicholas Drew nodded and, like the fine gentleman he was, asked, "Would you like to go and see him?"

⁕

Seated in the parlour of Gervaise Valerian's comfortable London flat, Vance Clayton frowned into his tankard of ale and said slowly, "The thing is, I simply cannot remember the gentleman, except as someone very tall with a great booming voice. Why he should have chose to name me his heir is beyond understanding."

Valerian asked curiously, "How does your cousin Beech come into the picture?"

"Sir Brian Beech is my mother's half-brother. My father detested him and held he was a proper Captain Sharp. I've no doubt he was right. I know Mama found it hard to defend him because he was always getting into some sort of scrape. I believe Papa had to pay his debts more than once to avoid a scandal, and was vastly relieved when he and his son left England."

"Still, had you not been in his way, young Conrad would stand to inherit? Jove, there must be a considerable fortune involved to warrant an attempt at murder!"

"Yes, I believe there is. And only think how cunning they were. Had it not been for you and my little sister, I'd have been done away with at that ghastly chateau and not a shadow of suspicion would have fallen upon the Beeches! I cannot—" He broke off as Valerian's man opened the door.

"I told you I was not to be disturbed," snapped Valerian, irked.

Despite the fact that he was a very large individual, Mr. Maltby's salary enabled him to patronize a good tailor, and he presented an elegant appearance. At the moment, every inch of his rotund person radiated disapproval and with disdainfully raised eyebrows he advised the ceiling, "As I informed her, sir. But the lady insisted—"

Clayton grinned.

Valerian lost all his colour and leaning forward in his chair demanded the name of the lady.

"She calls herself Nurse Brocade," Maltby informed a painting on the wall. "But she had no card, and—"

"Idiot!" growled Valerian. "Show the lady into my study at once, offer her refreshments and my apologies and say I will join her directly."

Startled, Clayton had sprung to his feet. "Wait!" he commanded, and turning to his host, he said, "If Elspeth has come to find me it must be of some urgency! She would never call at the home of a bachelor in this vulgar fashion!"

"Do as you're told, Maltby!" ordered Valerian, coming painfully to his feet and leaning on a cane for support.

His man, recognizing that dangerous tone of voice, abandoned stateliness and fled.

"And as for you, Clayton," said Valerian, frowning, "What convoluted reasoning leads you to suppose that she would call at *my* flat to see *you*? I give you good day!"

"What the devil d'you mean—'good day?'" argued Clayton indignantly. "Oh—I see. Very well, I'll collect my sister and—"

"Damn your ears!" exploded Valerian. "*Will* you take yourself off and leave your sister alone?"

Clayton stared at him. "Now, see here, Valerian. I comprehend that you're a very sick man still, but—"

"Not too sick to throw you through the window," snarled his rude host. *"Go—away!"*

Bemused, Clayton said feebly, "But—"

Valerian took a step towards him. Moving hurriedly to the door, Clayton rallied. "Look here, Valerian, she is *my* sister, and I've a right to guard her even if she were not also an—"

"Also—what? An heiress? Is that what you fear? I am *very* well aware of that fact, sir!" Valerian raised his cane. "Now are you going, or must I—"

Clayton beat an ignominious retreat.

Elspeth was standing by the bookcase, glancing at some well-worn volumes, when she heard the study door open and turned, smiling. Her smile died. She had expected him to look pale and ill, but the cane frightened her.

"Don't maudle," he said, reading her expression rightly.

"Well!" she exclaimed. "Is that all you have to say to me, sir? As a nurse, I have a right to maudle!"

He glanced around and said irritably, "I told them to offer you refreshments!" He reached for a small silver bell on the desk.

Elspeth said, "I did not come here for a glass of wine, Gervaise."

Ushering her to a wing chair, he occupied another. "I expect you will tell me why you did come. It had better not be to babble your thanks. Ours was a mutual collaboration, nothing more. I had as well start mouthing a lot of fustian about your invaluable assistance tossing boxes of . . ." His words trailed off as the flirtatious curl at her temple caught his eye. Recovering, he said hastily, "Er, where was I?"

"Mouthing a lot of fustian." Her voice softened. "And Nicholas told me how you rode to find him. It was—forgive me—most gallant."

"Well, of course it was. I am gallantry personified. 'Tis as well you realize that, ma'am." Her smile was very tender. Struggling, he asked, "And how is friend Joel? Gad, but the poor fellow has a scoundrelly sire! And why do I always say what I should not, I wonder? My apologies." He bit his lip, clenched his good hand hard and asked in a rush of words, "Shall—shall you mind having a scoundrel for a—er, papa-in-law?"

Elspeth folded her hands in her lap and, gazing at them, replied demurely, "Joel's mama is delightful, and would be pleased to have me for a daughter-in-law, so she says."

"Oh."

"And Joel has been reprieved, had you heard?"

"No."

Her lips twitched as she heard the despondency in his tone. "Then you will be glad to know he was congratulated by Admiral Lord Branscombe, who is apparently very much Somebody, because that wretched letter my brother carried has put them all in high gig. Lord Hayes was delighted. Colonel Skye went off grinding his teeth with frustration—though I think he became alarmed when he realised his son stood in real danger and wanted only to see Joel leave the Navy. Anyway, Joel is promised command of a new frigate! What d'you think of that?"

"Jolly good," said Valerian in a voice of doom. "So he'll be promoted to captain or some such high rank, and will be able to afford a wife, eh?"

"Oh, I should think so. At least, that's what he told me." He was silent, and glancing up under her lashes, she saw his scowl and said innocently, "When he offered for my hand, you know."

"Did he! And I suppose you twittered and fluttered and piped, 'Yes, poor dear Joel,' or something romantically asinine."

"Well, I probably should have. I expect you think I am at my last prayers."

A gleam crept into his grey eyes. He said, "Decidedly. An ancient crone. But then, you're an heiress now and will likely have lots of offers from—"

"From gazetted fortune-hunters, is what what you mean, Gervaise?"

"Yes." Desperate, he drew in his breath and took the plunge, saying in a strained and shaking voice, "Like—like me, for instance. I have always w-wanted to marry an heiress!"

"Really?" Elspeth stood. "I shall add your name to my list, Gervaise. Now I expect my brother is waiting for me on your doorstep. I caught a glimpse of him through the window and he appeared to be most agitated for some reason."

Standing at once, he moved too fast, flinched and had to resort to his cane. "And would be more so if he guessed you were to be annoyed by—by another gazetted fortune-hunter."

Elspeth regarded him gravely.

He threw the cane down, reached blindly for her arm and toppled to his knees.

"Great heavens!" she exclaimed in alarm. "There is not the need to—"

He said with a gasping laugh, "I should allow you to misinterpret my rare humility, darling Elspeth. Truth is— this ridiculous pose is—was involuntary!"

"Oh, my poor—"

"No! For God's sake—do not pity me! I'm just a trifle unsteady—all the brandy I've been . . . Oh, to hell with it!

Jupiter! What a cake I'm making of myself! Forgive, and do give me a hand up, Nurse Brocade! This is dashed hard on the knees . . ."

"Impossible creature!" With a broken little laugh, Elspeth bent and put her arm around him. In some peculiar fashion that she could not comprehend, both his arms were around her and she was on her knees also and being ruthlessly kissed.

"Gervaise!" she gasped, when she could say anything at all. "Is that all I get in the way of an offer? No! Gervaise!"

"I am . . . a Deplorable Dandy . . . and a gazetted fortune-hunter . . ." he said between kisses. "But, oh, my gallant little love, my heroic tosser of pussycat commodes . . . lady I worship, and will for as long as I live . . . Will you take this most unworthy Dandy to . . . to be your deplorable husband . . . ?"

There was a shout from outside.

The door burst open.

Rushing in, Vance Clayton cried, "How *dare* you! Unhand my sister, you—you dastardly villain!"

"You got my titles wrong, Vance," said Valerian, still clasping Elspeth shamelessly in his embrace and smiling up into Clayton's outraged face. "No, you cannot shoot me until I have my answer." His grey eyes, brighter than Vance had ever seen them, gazed adoringly into Elspeth's blue ones. "Well, little love of my life? Will you take my name? It is—I dare to think—an honourable name, and I swear will never disgrace you."

Elspeth smiled and touched his cheek.

Vance did not hear what she said, but he saw the glory in her eyes and there could be no doubt of her answer. Awed, he closed the door softly and left them to their happiness.

In the hall, Mr. Maltby waited anxiously. "Please, sir," he stammered, wringing his hands. "I am most fond of my master! Is—is everything all right?"

Vance wandered past, shaking his head numbly. "Be

dashed," he murmured, and then, with a broad grin, he snatched up the tricorne he had left on the hall table and tossed it into the air. "Be jolly well *dashed*!" he exclaimed, catching it again. "Oh—yes, Maltby. Everything is just about perfect! In fact, I think you and I are entitled to partake of a glass of Mr. Valerian's finest cognac in honour of my future nieces and nephews!"

Mr. Maltby readily agreeing with this excellent plan, they sat together and enjoyed not one but several glasses, after which Mr. Vance Clayton walked jauntily into the rain.